Silk or Gritstone

John Lea

Best Wishes

J R Lea

Sep 06

Published by Oaklea Books,

The Oaks, Shellow Lane, North Rode, Congleton, Cheshire.

CW12 2NX. Tel. 01260 223255

Printed by Biddles Ltd, King's Lynn, Norfolk

Although this story was inspired by a visit to the picturesque Wildboarclough Valley lying on the Peak District side of Cheshire, the town, village and people in this book are completely fictional and any resemblance to anyone living or dead is completely coincidental.

Acknowledgements

My sincere thanks to the knowledgeable and helpful staff in the different sections of the Macclesfield Silk Museum.

Particular thanks to John Eardley and John Bowler, two extremely knowledgeable countrymen.

A special thanks to Harry Owen for proof reading/copy editing.

By the same author but published by Churnet Valley Books, 43 Bath Street, Leek, Staffordshire. 01538 399033

Down The Cobblestones

My Countryside

Time To Change

The Peover Eye (limited edition).

Chapter One

"Take care girl," said the driver, lifting two baskets of groceries from the back of his open-topped wagon and placing them on the gravel beside her.

While Helen paused to watch him climb back into the cab a few big spots of rain fell. Then, as she bent down vainly trying to cover her groceries, there was a frightening crack of thunder and the rain really came down.

"Here, let me help you with those."

Helen looked up to find a tall man with a moustache bending to reach for her baskets. The sound of his motorcar must have been masked by the storm. "Come on," he called, "jump in. You're already soaked and I soon will be."

As he hurried round to the driver's side she scrambled up onto the running board and into the front seat. Even though the car hood was up and there were flaps hanging over each half-door rain still blew in around them. Reaching across to place a waterproofed cape over her lower limbs and pulling a second one over his own, the tall gruff man said, "I'm Joshua Mainthorpe – and you are?"

With her head shyly bowed she replied, "Helen Brindley, Sir."

"Well, Miss Helen Brindley, I presume you're taking those groceries home, but where is home?"

"I live with my Grandpa in a cottage near the bottom of Leckon Lane, which is just off the road to Gritstencrag village, Sir."

"Well now, that's handy because I was on my way up to Leckon Grange Farm. I'm thinking of buying it."

"Are you a farmer, Sir?"

"Good heavens, no. I own a silk mill in Fletchfield but I'd love to live out here overlooking this valley. But tell me, why is a girl of your age doing the shopping?"

"I'm eleven, Sir," she said indignantly, "and since Grandpa's been ill I've been selling our eggs each week at Fletchfield market, then bringing the shopping back home."

"And whose was that old wagon?"

"Oh, that's Bob Fairclough's, Sir. He'll give us a lift into town for sixpence on market day."

The driving rain blew in both round and under canvas door flaps so that it ran down the capes wrapped around each of them. They had only travelled a short distance when Mainthorpe turned the car into a gateway and manoeuvred it so that the back was towards the wind, which gave them some shelter. Switching off the engine, he said, "I think we'll sit this out for a while. Now tell me how come you speak so well with hardly a trace of the local dialect?"

"My mother wasn't from these parts, Sir, and she made me speak proper."

"And where's your mother now?"

As the wind and rain battered and rocked the car, the severe-looking mill owner persuaded the slightly tubby young girl to tell her short life story.

Although her Dad had worked on the farm as a boy, when he left school he refused to do farm work even though he had been offered a job on Leckon Grange farm. Instead he walked over the hill each day to work in the office at the small coal mine there. Head still shyly bowed, Helen went on to explain: "My mother was the mine owner's niece and stayed with her uncle for the summer. His house was by the coalmine and she got to know my Dad. When the owner found out he threatened to send her back home but she wouldn't have that."

"So what happened?"

"They ran away together. Dad got a job in Matlock and they lived there until after the war started in 1914."

When the girl stopped Mainthorpe asked, "What did they do in the war?"

"Dad decided to join the Army and, thinking that the war would only last a few months, he brought Mum and me here to live with Grandma and Grandpa, but other than those few months at the coalmine Mum had never lived in the country and hated it."

"When did she leave you?"

"About three years ago; it was just a few weeks before the war ended. She got a telegram telling her my Dad was dead – two days later Mum just up and left. She promised to send for me but I've never heard from her since."

Catching the heartbreak in her voice, Mainthorpe changed the subject. "So if I'm to buy the Grange what can you tell me about it?"

"They get lovely sunsets, Sir."

"But don't you see the sunset too?"

"No, we are in the shadow of that hill, but up at the Grange you can see through a fold between the hills right across the Cheshire plain."

"Anything else I should know about?"

"The curlews, Sir. They come back each spring to nest up on Leckon Moor. I could spend all day up there listening to them."

"I must tell my wife about the sunsets and the curlews; it might make her a bit keener to move up here."

"Grandpa says that with farming prices falling so much the landlord will have a job to find a tenant. Is that why you are buying it, Sir?"

"You're a very astute young lady. Maybe that's why they want to sell it to me."

The rain stopped as suddenly as it had started so Mainthorpe jumped out to give a few hefty swings on the starting handle. When he climbed back in Helen said, "Grandpa says the rain comes across the Cheshire Plain in a bucket and when the bottom catches the top of these hills it tips it out. If it tips right over, the rain soon stops but if it only splashes out it can keep on all day"

Manoeuvring the car back onto the road, Mainthorpe said, "Your Grandpa sounds to be an interesting man. If I'm going to be his neighbour I'd like to meet him. What about Grandma?"

"She died just over a month ago. Grandpa's not been well since."

The Ragil stream ran between the gravelled road and the rugged steep hillside Helen had pointed towards earlier. With dark clouds overhead the surrounding ash trees cast a gloomy shadow over the lane. Raindrops falling from the overhanging boughs pattered noisily on the canvas hood as they turned off the bottom road to climb up Leckon lane. In places this downpour, or a previous one, had washed the surface gravel away exposing the upward edge of solid rocks, causing the Mill owner to drive carefully.

Suddenly Helen screamed, "Stop!"

The girl was out of the car like a little squirrel. Mainthorpe followed her to where an old man lay under a low overgrown thorn bush.

"Is this your Grandpa?" he asked, bending to feel for a pulse.

Helen fell onto her knees beside the old man and his eyes opened. "I came to meet thee with a coat – but th'storm beat me down."

Mainthorpe took a firm grip on the old man's shoulders and hoisted him up. "Let's get you into the car and take you home."

When the girl had scrambled over the front seat into the back, Mainthorpe lifted her Grandpa onto the front seat and within minutes they were parking the car by two small, semi-detached stone cottages.

Striding across the little yard, Mainthorpe was well aware that if the deal went through both these farm workers' cottages would be part of his new country estate. In fact he had already told the agent that, although there was a worker in the other cottage, it was ridiculous to allow a retired farm worker to remain in this one and play with a few acres as though it was a little farm. He made it clear that he was only going to buy Leckon Grange if this cottage was made vacant so he could house an active farm worker.

The Grange had come on the market following the death of the tenant. Not believing in farming partnerships Bolesworth, the estate agent, told the deceased tenant's five working sons to decide which of them would be the new tenant. He left them to it for several months during which he heard rumours of fistfights and arguments. When he returned to the farm he gathered the five stalwart lads around him only to find that they were still arguing. Raising his riding-crop in anger Bolesworth announced, "If you lads are not men enough to decide which of you should farm then none of you are man enough to take it on, so you must all be out by September."

It was mid August after the grouse-shooting season had started when Bolesworth met the landlord taking a walk across his estate and admitted that he had failed to find a suitable new tenant, making as his excuse that produce prices had fallen considerably since the war. "Excuses – that's all I hear from you," the estate owner said, thrashing the top off a thistle with his thumb stick. "When the war was on you used it as an excuse for not raising rents and now three years later you're using it again."

"It's the government's decision to repeal the corn price guarantee, my Lord," Bolesworth blustered. "It's sucked in cheap grain from the new Commonwealth countries. And it's been a very dry year. They got the harvest in quickly but the yields were poor. I'm afraid, my Lord, that confidence among the farmers is very low."

"This is grassland country, man." Not used to hearing excuses, His Lordship vented his anger on another thistle. "They make their living from dairy cows and sheep. What cereals they grow here are mostly used to feed their animals."

"Yes, my Lord, but there's a general fall in all prices including milk. I think we'll have to give some encouragement to find a good tenant to take on the farm."

"Encouragement! Grief, man, you've already got three of my tenants behind with the rent; how do you expect me to live if there's no money coming in?"

"There are two good farmers who have made an offer, but they want it rent free for two years."

"Rent free! What do they think I am – a charity?"

When the agent kept a discreet silence and there were no more thistles in striking distance, His Lordship proclaimed, "I'll sell it first. Yes, that's what I'll do. Put it on the market, but not the grouse moor. I need some fun in this miserable world."

Then with an afterthought he added, "You can rent the grazing on the moor to whoever buys it – that is, if they want it."

Mainthorpe heard this story when Bolesworth, having invited him to enjoy a day's shooting on that very grouse moor, was complaining over lunch about his boss's expensive tastes. "Damned horses and women will be the end of this estate."

"Was there no son to take on the farm?" Mainthorpe asked.

"The youngest one, Joseph, would have done but some of the older ones wouldn't agree."

Having had thoughts about a country property for some time, and in spite of his wife's reservations, Mainthorpe moved quickly. Now, with a price already agreed, the Grange was his subject to his final confirmation.

Opening the cottage door he was surprised by how tidy everywhere looked; there was even a kettle boiling on the hob. Out in the yard Helen was helping her Grandpa down so Mainthorpe turned back to the car and, hooking the old man's arm over his shoulder, half carried him to a solid wooden armchair standing near the fire. He turned to the girl: "Before you do anything else go and get out of those wet clothes and dry off."

Her gaze met his for the first time and for a moment it held him transfixed. Under the mousy hair there was still the rounded face of a child, but the large turquoise eyes held his with a worldly maturity that was so startling he was still holding his breath when she turned and scampered through the doorway and out of the room.

Seeing the tea caddy on the mantelpiece next to the old man's tobacco pouch, he brewed the tea then found a jug of milk keeping cool on a stone slab out in the scullery. Pouring out a cup, he added in a generous tot from his hip flask before holding it gently up to the old man's lips.

Helen came back with her mousy hair obviously towelled but not brushed and a clean if somewhat frayed dress hugging her young growing figure. Mainthorpe gave the old man another sip. "I think we should get him up to bed and then I'll go for a doctor."

"Grandpa says we can't afford to have the doctor, Sir."

"Well, I can afford so I'll get him."

With the young girl scampering ahead he almost carried the old man up the steep stairs. Surprisingly, he wasn't too wet and he commented on it to the girl. As Mainthorpe helped to slip the old man's clothes off, she said, "Grandpa has always said that a thick old thorn bush gives the best shelter in a storm and, not standing as tall as other trees, it's unlikely to be struck by lightning."

After asking Helen for the Doctor's directions, Mainthorpe stepped through a gap in the dividing fence to the next-door cottage. He had already met the occupant, Harry Aimsley, the farm waggoner, when he first looked over the Grange, so Mainthorpe wasn't surprised at the reaction when he gave his name to the young girl who answered the door. After much whispering and rustling, a careworn woman finally appeared. Trying to smooth down a crumpled and less-than-clean apron she said, "I'm sorry, Sir, but my Harry's not back from th'farm yet."

Mainthorpe explained what had happened next door and received assurances that the Waggoner's wife would go round and wait with Helen until he returned with the Doctor. He strode across the small yard towards his car intending to set off down the valley towards the Gritstencrag village.

Pausing to look up, Mainthorpe noticed how the clouds had parted in the West allowing the evening sun to send beams of golden sunshine on the higher ground behind him. It also lent a golden halo to the clouds overhead and, sure enough, the steep hill did shade the cottages just as the girl had said.

Chapter Two

Looking out of the bedroom window, Helen noticed the tall, gruff man's limp. It wasn't too obvious but it was enough for her to recall the conversation she had overheard just the night before when she had been washing the eggs ready for market. Grandpa was puffing on his pipe by the fire when Mr Aimsley came in grumbling "Have yer heard – th'estate's selling th'farm to a townie."

Grandpa's reply was too quiet to hear and anyway Helen was concentrating on the eggs. Mr Aimsley continued, "Arr, he does limp but th'keeper says he's all right on level ground but it bothers him right enough when he's out on th'grouse moor." There was more talk but she could remember one thing clearly: "It wer' falling off that horse as kept him out of th'army. He volunteered all right but they wouldn't have him so he stayed on in Fletchfield; arr, and he made his fortune doing it."

There had been more grumbles from Mr Aimsley about how he might soon be taking orders from a townie. "And if talk's owt go by he's a hard 'B' of a townie at that. He'll want to drop our wages."

Mr Aimsley muttered on but Helen only caught the last part: "Now they've done away with th'wages board there's nowt to stop him."

Helen suddenly realised it was that same hard 'B' who was out in the yard. Watching his stern profile as he glanced up at the sky before climbing into his car, and still young enough to believe that grown-ups know best, she was puzzled.

Mainthorpe reflected on the girl as he drove bumpily back down Leckon Lane and turned left towards the village. Being recently married to a very attractive woman, he was sure that it wasn't a sexual attraction but there was something about that girl. Coming to the hump-backed bridge he carefully turned sharp right to cross over and then went left as the lane followed along the other side of Ragil brook. It was remarkable how, having risen some two feet or more in such a short time, the once placid stream was now rippling and frothing over its stony bed. On his right a flat meadow curved away from the road but because it nestled in shadow of Helen's hill it lay flat and featureless in its darkening shade.

Even from the bottom of the valley he could see the fold in the hills that allowed young Helen's sunsets to be visible from Leckon Grange.

Stopping for a moment to step out and look across the brook to his left, he could see the roofs of the Grange glowing in the late evening sun. Although it stood among the more gentle grassy slopes some four or five hundred foot above the brook, the Grange was dwarfed by the heather-clad top of Leckon Moor which, lying above and beyond it, looked dark and sombre in the shadow of passing clouds. Nearer to him crows were cawing in a clump of trees, no doubt arguing over which of the trees were the best to spend the night in. Nine mallard ducks flew overhead with wings whistling as they circled a small pool of floodwater before dropping down to feed on the grubs forced up by the temporary flood. Mainthorpe was aware of these things without really thinking about them. His latter schooldays had been spent helping on farms and it was then that he learned to take part in country sports and in turn become more aware of nature. Many were the times in his youth he had waited by such a pool to pot a brace of ducks for his parents' table. He would have liked to stop longer but instead pushed on towards the doctor's. "Anyway," he told his motor as it bumped through more pot-holes, "you're going to see a lot of these hills because I'm going to live up there."

At a jumble of large boulders, the road switched back again to cross the brook over another small humped stone bridge then followed the other bank. Nearer the village he had to negotiate an even narrower bridge as the road again changed banks.

Helen had said the doctor lived in the nearest house to the outcrop of rock jutting out of the hill behind the village. It was from this gritstone outcrop that Gritstencrag village got its abbreviated name. Not that there was much to the village. On this bank besides the doctor's house, a blacksmith's forge and a few other cottages stood haphazardly between the lane and the steep hillside. On the other bank a woollen mill made use of the stream to wash and dye the wool produced on the hills around. A stone bridge took a side lane up towards the Mill Manager's house where, with the Church, school, village shop and in between them a few more up market cottages, it still caught the late evening sun's rays.

The doctor's cottage was in the shade and when Mainthorpe explained why he had come the doctor's face looked equally dark. "I was just sitting down for my tea but if it is as serious as you say I suppose I had better come," he grumbled and reluctantly drew on a topcoat. "It will take me a few moments to harness my pony."

"There is no need to do that. I've got a car and it will get you there much quicker, so come on, jump in."

"I'll need my pony to get home again."

Mainthorpe reassured him that he would drive him home after the visit. He had a second motive for seeking the doctor's company: there was no one better to fill him in on the local characters and gossip. So, generously passing over his hip flask, Mainthorpe waited until the doctor had slaked his thirst before getting him to chat as they drove along in the evening shadows.

Back at Leckon Cottages, Harry Aimsley had returned from attending his horses and was waiting with Helen when Mainthorpe arrived with the doctor. Seemingly convinced that the deal on the Grange and the farm had already been done, Harry grovelled around until Mainthorpe became so irritated he suggested he went back to his cottage. Leaving the doctor upstairs with Grandpa,

Helen came into the room. "I milked the cow while Mr Aimsley stayed with Grandpa but I need to go out and shut in the hens and geese before the fox gets them."

Mainthorpe had another pot of tea ready for when the doctor came down to give his report. "It's his heart." There was a shake of his grey head. "It's not good! Someone else needs to stay with the lass tonight."

Hearing him as she stepped in through the back door, Helen said, "I can manage on my own."

But when the doctor shook his head, Mainthorpe over-ruled her protests and went next door to arrange for Mrs Aimsley to stay the night. Helen had served the doctor a large piece of current loaf by the time Mainthorpe returned. Before driving the doctor back to the village, he had him promise Helen that he would return to visit again in the morning.

Arriving back home in the late evening, Mainthorpe knew as he unlocked the house door that his cook would by now be in bed. He got the expected complaints from his wife, Jessica, at his lateness. The resulting cold cheese and pickled onion supper lay heavy in his stomach when he finally slid under the sheets. The image of those unusual turquoise eyes didn't help either.

Jessica was not one to let one late night come between her and her chosen man, for she had indeed chosen him and it was not just because he was tall and handsome. Jessica came from a family who had never quite made it in life but were greedy for advancement. It was her ambitious mother who had literally pushed her towards this tall, stern mill owner by engineering a fake accident. Not that Jessica needed too much pushing towards one of the wealthiest men in Fletchfield, and she was quite prepared to take the gruffness along with the wealth.

They made a very handsome couple, him tall with slightly curly black hair contrasting with her blonde hair and shapely figure. Their wedding was one of the town's highlights of the year, mainly because Jessica had made it into a lavish occasion;

but she had not been prepared for what came next. Behind that brusque exterior she found the most considerate of lovers; one who did not expect too much from her around the house but knew how to please and arouse in the bedroom. Oh, she still kept her eyes wide open where the money was concerned but it was more enjoyable than expected to please and respond to him, if and when she was in the mood. Therefore, seeing him late home and hearing him mentioning something about a girl as he restlessly thrashed about in bed, she answered the threat in the best way she knew by snuggling her shapely figure up to him.

The next morning Mainthorpe left his wife asleep and came down to find that his cook was making up for his frugal supper by preparing a more appetising breakfast. He took time to enjoy it before setting off to check that all was well at the Mill.

The silk mill was not large because most of the weaving was done elsewhere by highly skilled self-employed craftsmen. When the industry was depressed just before the war Mainthorpe had bought a block of specially designed three-storey houses that had been built for just for this purpose. Each two semi-detached cottages had a full width top floor or garret running across both homes, fitted with large clear windows for maximum light. Some housed two handlooms and others four plus the winding gear that went with them. Although self-employed, the tenants were carefully chosen by Mainthorpe, and because many of them had been taken on since the war ended he had been fairly ruthless with his terms. More than one was heard to say behind his back, "The mean bastard made a fortune while we were crawling about in muddy trenches and now we're back home he's making another fortune out of us."

And Mainthorpe was. He charged them a rent for the cottage, another rent for the use of his loom and of course by providing the silk they could not sell the finished article; it was always his. Though to be fair his piecework rates were reasonably generous. On the other hand, no one stayed on in one of his cottages once their active weaving days were over.

With his business concluded at the Mill, Mainthorpe drove towards the hills into the gleam of the rising sun. The sky had cleared before dawn to allow a sharp early October frost, which glittered on the trees and hillsides along Gritstencrag valley. As the morning sun warmed them, ash leaves previously yellowed by the autumn chill lost their grip on life to float gently downwards towards nature's compost.

Seeing the doctor's trap almost filling the small yard, Mainthorpe parked out on the lane before walking to the cottage. The doctor met him at the back door. "There was nothing I could do; he'd gone when I got here. Anyway, he's lived on borrowed time for the last five years. I'll send you the bill."

And with that parting remark the elderly doctor undid his pony's reins, climbed into the trap and clucked the horse into motion. Looking back over his shoulder he said, "Be kind to that girl."

Inside the cottage Mrs Aimsley met him with, "I've sent our Harry, my eldest lad, for th'undertaker."

"That's very good Mrs Aimsley. Now will you leave us while I talk to Miss Helen?"

Mrs Aimsley obviously didn't like it but the mill owner's steely gaze left no room for argument. When Helen's large eyes met his they were dry but a red rim told of earlier weeping. "Well, Miss Helen, what's going to become of you on this sad day?"

"I know you want the cottage for a workman, Sir."

Used to more subservient, grovelling responses, Mainthorpe was momentarily flustered by the girl's direct response. "I didn't mean . . . What I mean is . . . Well, at eleven you're too young to live here on your own."

"I can manage, Sir. I've got a cow and my hens. There's a pig to kill for winter and I've got some geese to sell for Christmas. There's still the rushes to mow for cow bedding. When they're properly dead perhaps Mr Aimsley will scythe them off for me."

"You should be in school, not looking after all those animals."

"I've looked after them for weeks now, Sir, and other than market day I've never missed school before today."

At a time when the Silk industry was in decline, Mainthorpe's success in bucking that trend was mainly from his insistence on quality and his ruthlessness with any employees who fell short in any way. He had earned his reputation as a hard man and was proud of it – but now he had difficulty in meeting those steady turquoise eyes. Fortunately, the sound of the undertaker's pony and trap saved him further discomfort. Deciding to respect Helen's independence and leave her to deal with the undertaker, Mainthorpe strode outside to have a word with him before driving on up to the Grange.

Outside a few minutes later, he felt surprised how a few chance remarks by an eleven-year-old girl could cause him to look at it from an even more appreciative perspective.

To satisfy his less enthusiastic wife, Mainthorpe asked Mrs Bolton, the last tenant's widow, if she would mind him looking round the house again. He liked it even more and when he looked out of the large stone mullioned front window he could visualise the girl's lovely sunsets.

He was back out in the farmyard when the estate agent's tall hunter clattered onto the cobbled stones. As the two men shook hands the agent said, "Well?"

Mainthorpe said, "Yes! I'll have it."

"Right then. I've heard the old man has died so I'll just get that girl out of your cottage and it will be all yours to take over after the tenant's sale next month."

"No, wait a minute. The girl has just lost her Grandfather; perhaps we should give her time."

Bolesworth said, "When these five sons leave this farm next month there'll only be the waggoner working here, so you'll need that cottage pretty quick."

When Mainthorpe still looked hesitant, Bolesworth added, "Either I turn her out now or she's your responsibility."

Chapter Three

Still unsure whether Mr Aimsley was right about that tall, gruff man, Helen was grateful that at least he had let her stay on in the cottage. But she was under no illusions; it was just for a trial period and Mr Aimsley's eldest, Amy, had to sleep in the cottage with her.

Amy was delighted to get the chance to be out of her crowded home, if it was only overnight. She was determined that when her fourteenth birthday came in November she would both leave school and escape from the horror of sharing a two-bedroom cottage with her parents and five siblings. Until then, on Mr Mainthorpe's instructions, Amy could help her mother after school with the younger children's tea, help put the youngest two to bed and only then go to Helen's for peace and quiet.

It was Amy who later told Helen how she had hidden behind the dividing fence when the Vicar and Mr Mainthorpe stood out in the yard discussing Helen's future. "The Vicar said that if there wasn't a relative to take yer then yer'd have to go to an orphanage."

"I'm not going to an orphanage," Helen said. "If they try to make me I'll run away and hide in the hills."

"Mr Mainthorpe said he wouldn't let that happen, that yer mun stay here to look after yer stock while he tries to find a relative. The Vicar got very angry but in the end agreed – as long as I slept here with yer each night."

Helen gave Amy an appreciative smile and kept quiet about her Aunty Emily and Uncle Horace who lived further across the hills in Derbyshire. Not that Helen could remember much about them because she had only been four when last she saw them.

The funeral was heartbreaking for Helen. If Mr and Mrs Aimsley hadn't walked on either side of her it was doubtful if she could have got through it. As it was, she bravely followed the coffin up the aisle to the front of the church and then out into the graveyard. The fact that each of the Aimsleys tucked a hand under each arm gave her the strength to stand by the grave as Grandpa was lowered down. "Goodbye Grandpa," Helen whispered and turned to walk away but was surprised by the throng of people; it seemed as if the entire village was there. She tried to smile through her tears to those who offered a word of comfort. Then the tall, gruff man stepped forward and said, "Come on, you've had enough today. I'll take you and the Aimsleys home now."

On the journey back Mainthorpe asked Harry, "Is there a will, do you know?"

Harry said, "Yes, I witnessed one and it left everything to Helen."

She said, "Yes, I've found it."

"Then it needs dealing with officially. Would you like me to see to it for you?" Mainthorpe asked.

Each morning before school Amy left Helen and went home to help her mother get her young brood ready for the day. Helen was left on her own to milk the cow and feed the pig but because it wasn't properly daylight she had to wait to let the hens and geese out. This was the very last job before setting out to walk over a mile to school. Somewhere in the middle of that she got her own breakfast and made a small packed lunch consisting of a chunk of buttered bread and a raw egg.

The small schoolroom was heated through the winter term by a cast iron stove on which the teacher would boil a pan of water each dinnertime. Those children who brought an egg could have a hot lunch, if a boiled egg counted as a hot lunch.

After school Helen ran most of the way home to feed the hens, geese and pig while it was still light enough for them to eat outside, for as the sun went behind the hill it cast a gloomy shadow over the two cottages. She ran down the field for the cow and, with no light in the little shippen, she had to milk, feed and bed it down for the night in the darkening gloom. After that the eggs needed collecting and if it wasn't completely dark there could be time to get her tea while waiting for the hens and geese to go inside their cotes. Helen had learned through her short life that the last few birds would only go in when it was almost black dark, which was about the time a fox might be on the prowl.

Helen was disappointed that with the shorter days of autumn her hens were following nature's pattern by not laying many eggs. This in turn meant that there would not be enough to take into Fletchfield to pay for her shopping. Helen remained determined, though, not to spend any of the money Grandpa had kept hidden under his mattress, because she remembered him saying how much it had cost to bury Grandma and how he had added with a laugh, 'Look, there's just enough left to bury me.'

Helen was mulling over her money problem when the undertaker came with the funeral bill. Asking him to sit by the kitchen table, Helen went upstairs to fetch Grandpa's money.

"You don't need all that lass, it's only this much – look," he said, showing her the bill.

"But Grandpa told me it took a lot more than that for Grandma's."

"No lass, you've got it wrong."

The undertaker didn't look her in the eye as he counted out a few pounds and handing the rest back saying, "Go and hide that again and don't tell anyone about it."

When Helen came back down again he asked, "Well lass, what would you like on your grandparents' grave stone?"

"But Grandpa told me that we couldn't afford a stone."

"No, you've misunderstood him. It's already paid for. It's just a matter of carving the words and I'll erect it."

"But it can't be . . ."

"It is lass, it's paid for. Now about the words -- I suggest . . ."

And so young Helen, clear minded enough to know that there was something strange about this transaction, found that her bills were paid up with a handsome surplus left over.

The following day was not one of her best. Usually alert to the mischief of older boys, she allowed one to catch her daydreaming and slap the pocket with the egg in, which left a messy pocket and just a chunk of bread for dinner. When school finally ended, it was raining as though the bucket had tipped over again. The shade from the hill added to the evening's gloom to such an extent that Helen had to drive the reluctant hens out from their cote to peck the grain she scattered outside.

Not being waterproofed, Helen's overcoat soaked up so much rain that it felt as though there was a sack of corn on her back when she walked up from the field with the cow. The only ones enjoying the cold autumn rain were the geese, who gaggled about in the flooded gateway while she milked and fed hay to the cow. The sole bright part of the afternoon was that Mrs Aimsley had come in to light the fire before Helen returned from school. It was a weary and hungry young girl who finally flopped into Grandpa's chair with a chunk of bread, a slice of cheese and a homegrown apple.

Curlews called overhead, grouse chuckled among the heather and the smell of new spring growth, enriched by the warm sunshine, made Leckon Moor seem magical. She was brought back to reality by Amy shaking her shoulder. "It's dark, have yer' shut th'hens in?"

Fortunately it had stopped raining as Helen, still confused by her dream, ran out of the house. Running towards the hen cote, she heard the cackles of panic. As she threw open the door there was a glimpse of a brown streak racing out through the small inlet slide, but in the near darkness she could only see feathers, and they seemed everywhere. Gradually her eyes focused. Beneath the feathers were mutilated bodies.

All the Aimsley family gathered round. Mrs Aimsley crouched down to give comfort while her husband went to bring a faggot from the fire to provide some light inside the dark cote. Helen, though, saw none of it – her little body finally gave out and her heart broke.

Someone must have carried her upstairs because, although she had been aware of Amy sitting by her bedside and of Mrs Aimsley making her drink, something with a bitter taste, she had no other recollections until daylight streamed in through the threadbare curtains.

"Mum says yer' mun stay in bed today."

"But what about the hens? I must do something with them."

"Dad plucked six last night but we didn't find any more. He told our Harry to look for th'rest and milk yer cow before he went t'school. Harry could only see five live hens and th'old cockerel and he moaned like heck at doing th'milking."

When Helen pushed the bedclothes back Amy said, "No, yer've got to stay there. We've got a good fire going so I can make some toast if yer' like?"

It wasn't long before Amy came back with two pieces of toast and a cup of milk. "Mum's put one of th'hens on yer' fire to boil. She says it'll be done by when yer' get up at dinner time."

The Aimsleys and Helen's grandparents had enjoyed a good neighbourly relationship. Although both cottages had an outbuilding, a pigsty and a small paddock, Mr Aimsley, still working long hours on the farm, only had time to look after a pig and grow some vegetables. Whereas Grandpa, since retiring, relied on his milk, butter and eggs to supplement his small income. Mr Aimsley, who was allowed a daily pint of milk from the farm, let Grandpa mow his paddock to make hay for the winter and in return Grandpa had let him have eggs and butter for a nominal rate.

Thinking over all this, Helen dreamily drifted off to sleep. She was woken again by Amy's rough shoulder shake. "Come on, Mum's lifted that old hen out of th'pot an she says I can stay an eat with yer if yer'll have me?"

Flecks of grey in his black hair and moustache made Joshua Mainthorpe seem much older than his thirty-odd years. His no nonsense manner added to the impression of a man who wasn't to be trifled with. The facts were that he was filled with ambition and in a smallish market town ambitions are best kept hidden. His gruff manner helped protect him from inquisitive people. In decline before 1914, the Silk industry had enjoyed a minor boom through and just after the war but now again it faced stiff competition from cheaper imports. Mainthorpe succeeded while others failed because he specialised in quality; exclusive fabrics that could justify his traditional labour-intensive methods. But he was not satisfied. His ambition was to do away with the garreted houses and get his weavers into one large mill on more modern looms. If the whole process was under one roof, from preparing the skeins of imported raw silk through the design stage to the finished fabric, he could keep an iron control over quality.

Mainthorpe knew the very mill. Built a few years before the war it stood five storeys high near to his garreted houses. The cost of building and equipping it with the latest Jacquard looms had driven the owner into financial trouble. Although the uplift in the price of silk through the war had helped, it was not enough to stave off the inevitable disaster now prices were falling again. Although the owner had already offered it to him at a fair price Mainthorpe was sure that, in the present depressed state of the industry, if he waited he would in the end buy it for considerably less. All he had to do was to watch and be ready to pounce when the receivers eventually moved in. For that reason he couldn't afford to spend too much time sorting out the Grange farm business.

Exercising their right as retiring tenants to hold a sale of all the farm assets, the Bolton family had planned to have it in two weeks time. Then the family would move out and he would start to farm, but without either a complete staff or the necessary stock and equipment. He was country wise enough to know there would be no chance of any bargains at the sale because Mrs Bolton would arrange for a friend or relative or both to bid against him. At the same time he couldn't risk being away from town – perhaps out in the country on a cattle or machinery buying trip – in case the receivers moved into his dream mill.

Mainthorpe appraised the old farmhouse standing near to the Grange. It was the original farmhouse that had been left standing to house a farm manager when the much more grand Grange house had been built for a member of the landlord's family. Boasting four large bedrooms and a smaller one, which could be made into a bathroom, the old farmhouse was far from small and far from derelict. The 15th Century stone walls were over two feet thick making it difficult to do any major alterations but fortunately it was structurally reasonably sound. The problem was that it had received little attention since the last farm manager moved out when the Grange had been let to Mr Bolton, whose five stalwart sons would provide cheap labour making it unnecessary to house a worker in the old farmhouse. Although now grown up, two of those sons slept in it, claiming thus to give the family more space in the Grange. Their mother understood how grown men need a bit of privacy. "Mind you," she was heard to remark, "it doesn't seem to include meal times."

Mainthorpe went into the Grange to talk to Mrs Bolton. "Have you got anywhere to live when you leave here Mrs Bolton?"

Wearing the traditional widow's long black dress with white frills on the end of each sleeve that flapped as she hesitantly patted her hair bun while she thought, Mrs Bolton finally said, "No, I'm waiting to see what the sale raises and for all the lads to decide what they want to do."

"Do they want to stay in farming?"

"Not the oldest two; they say there isn't enough money in the job. Caleb hasn't settled since he came back from the war and Nehemiah's never had his heart in farming."

"Nehemiah. It's unusual, even for a Bible name."

"We call him Ned now," Mrs Bolton chuckled proudly. "When he was young he wanted to know where the name came from so I read him the story from the Old Testament. You remember it, don't you? How when Nehemiah was re-building the walls of Jerusalem he organised his men to work in pairs, one working the trowel while the other held both swords? Anyway, when Ned heard it he said, 'I'm going to be a builder when I grow up' and that's what he's doing now."

"An interesting story, Mrs Bolton, but what about the others?"

"Joel's keen but he's going to work for his future father-in-law just across the brook. That leaves my daughter Anna, who needs a position, and the two youngest, Isaac and Joseph, wanting farm work but most farmers are laying staff off."

This was what Mainthorpe wanted to hear but he thought he would change the subject. "All Bible names; is there any significance?"

"Mr Bolton was a Methodist local preacher. He named both them and the four girls from the Bible. When it got to the ninth I'd had enough so I called him Joseph and said, 'That's it - we're stopping there'."

It was Joseph that Mainthorpe was really interested in. The village doctor had said he was the brightest of the lot and Bolesworth had confirmed that saying, "I would have been happy to set the tenancy to Joseph had the other brothers agreed and been prepared to work for him. They didn't like the idea of their nineteen-year-old brother becoming the boss."

"Would you be interested in staying on in the old farm house if I offered jobs to your two youngest?"

Mrs Bolton went all flustered, completely thrown out of her usual farmer's wife confidence.

"I'll tell you what. I'll go and have a talk to the boys while you think it over."

He found Joseph with two of his brothers tidying up some old machines ready for the sale. "Joseph, if you don't mind I'd like to talk to you on your own."

He could hear Joseph's clogs clattering on the cobblestones behind him as he walked across the yard to lean against a rugged stone wall. Without preamble Mainthorpe said, "I need a farm bailiff. You know the farm. If we can come to an arrangement would you be interested?"

"Yes, sir, I would."

And so the two men fell into deep discussion. Mainthorpe was surprised how tough a negotiator young Joseph was; he wanted to know exactly what would be within his responsibility over cropping and stocking the farm. When Mainthorpe told him he was also thinking about offering his brother Isaac a job, Joseph said, "No, if I'm the Bailiff then that's up to me. I'll ask for your agreement but it's for me to offer him a job, because I only take on the farm if I have the right to hire and fire."

"All right, I'll agree to that, but I set the limit to the wage you pay any man."

"I would expect that but I hope you'll agree that if you want to good man you have to pay a fair wage."

"Yes, but prices are falling and farm wages are following. What wage are you men on at the moment?"

"We lads just take pocket money but Mr Aimsley's on 38 shillings a week."

"Good grief, man, I doubt if there's a farm worker in the valley getting more than 32 shillings and that's the top I intend to pay."

"Dad wouldn't drop his wage; he said he was a married man with children. I agree, though, that things have got worse since then so I suggest a fair wage to start the men off on would be thirty-three shillings."

Mainthorpe realised this was no subservient yes-man and liked him for it. When he agreed and suggested they go into the house to see what his mother had decided, Joseph said, "Wait a minute, Master. We've not discussed my pay."

Knowing that the term Master was the traditional way farm-workers addressed their employer, Mainthorpe thought he'd got the lad and suggested forty shillings. Joseph said, "No. If you want to make this a farm to be proud of, then I want double that – but I'll earn it."

Mainthorpe locked his steely stare onto the sandy-haired youth's blue eyes and saw no hint of brashness, just an unusually calm confidence. Joseph broke the silence, "And if Mum wants to housekeep for me then I want the old farm house done up. Some of the rooms need re-plastering, some windows need replacing and we want it with a bathroom fitted before we move in."

Realising that he was taking on more of a man than he had first thought, the mill owner said, "Right, then let's go and talk to your mother."

With the best china laid out on the long dining table and twenty-one year old daughter Anna serving out tea and cakes, Mainthorpe observed the family as he discussed terms. It would seem Anna and Joseph had inherited their sandy hair from their mother whereas the older boys outside seemed to be much darker and Anna, whilst far from fragile, had the same lean athlete's figure as her brother. He admired the tidy way they were all dressed, particularly the girl whose smart dress, hanging to just below her knees, was covered by a clean white apron. What became obvious to him during the discussions was how Mrs Bolton deferred to Joseph and seemed to presume that his older brothers would accept whatever he said.

Before the afternoon was over not only had Mrs Bolton agreed to housekeep for her son but Joseph asked Mainthorpe to agree that his sister could help his mother in the house and do part time work on the farm. Turning to her Mainthorpe said, "Well, all right for now, but later we will need help in the Grange. Perhaps you could consider a position there."

When the three Boltons were all relaxed, happy that their immediate future was secure, Mainthorpe casually said, "About your farm sale. You have forty dairy cows, I need about forty dairy cows; you have five horses, I need at least that number and you've got all the implements to go with them. I'll have to buy your hefted ewes on a valuation price if I'm to graze the open moor so why not let me appoint a valuer and buy everything, lock, stock and barrel?"

Seeing glances being exchanged he added, "It would save you the Auctioneer's commission and all the hassle of getting it all ready for the sale."

Joseph, beginning to realise that his townie boss might know more about farming than they had first thought, looked towards his mother and when she gave a nod he said, "If we agree then we'll also appoint a valuer. That way any disagreement will between them and not us, and if we are keeping the cows we'll have to value the unthrashed oats in the shed. Although we've booked the thrashing machine for next week expecting that the cows would be gone and the shed would need emptying before we leave."

"What would you have done with it if you weren't leaving?"

"We'd thrash one bay now for cattle feed and the other would be thrashed February time. By then we'd know how much we needed for our own cattle and the rest would be sold."

"Then have it all valued and we'll do it just as you would have."

When Mainthorpe rose to leave, Joseph mentioned that long term they would need at least two more men and asked about Helen's cottage. Mainthorpe was explaining how he was giving the girl a little more time when Mrs Bolton told him about the fox, adding, "With a fright like that hens just stop laying and they won't lay again until spring."

"Can I buy a dozen eggs of you?"

"You mean for the girl, Master?" Mrs Bolton asked. "Well, if you're going to call on her then you'll take a dozen eggs and a slab of cake but you'll not pay us."

Chapter Four

The aroma of cooking hen and the thought of boiled potatoes and turnip enticed Helen down to the kitchen. When Mrs Aimsley came round to check if the old hen was cooked Helen persuaded her to take a leg for her own dinner and to cook another hen for when Mr Aimsley came home that night. The two girls, lacking in carving skills, soon discovered that after more than three hours of boiling it was easier to pull the carcass to pieces by hand. The fact that meat was not an everyday part of their diet made it a feast to remember.

That afternoon, insisting Helen went back to bed, Mrs Aimsley made complaining young Harry milk and feed the cow as well as shutting up the geese for the night. The seven hens and the cockerel chose to roost high up in a clump of alder trees, which to their little minds was much safer than getting trapped in the hen cote with a fox.

Out early on the following morning Helen milked and cleaned out the cow and the pig before feeding the geese and her few hens. It was a struggle to get the fire going and when it eventually burned up it took another half hour for the kettle to boil. By that time Amy had set off for school without her. Not that Helen intended to go to school; for she wanted to be on her own with time to think and there was only one place to do that. Packing the last scraps of the hen along with a chunk of bread and a bottle of cold tea she climbed the steep path behind the cottages and walked out onto the moor.

Quarry Moor was separated from Leckon Moor by sloping pasture fields running down to the fast running Bullerstone stream and a steep tree-covered bank called Leckon Wood on the other. Only a couple of yards wide in normal weather, the brook gurgled and rippled down the hillside to Ragil brook. Bullerstone was the local name for a large boulder lying in a stream. This boulder that gave the stream its name was larger than a loaded cart and, lying in the brook bottom, it had once acted as a natural dam but through a few thousand years the stream had gouged a narrow channel round it. Sometimes, though, when the brook flooded, branches and other rubbish would wash down and block that narrow channel, forcing the stream to race over the boulder and recreating the dramatic waterfall from long ago. On those occasions water flowed over the boulder with such force that it had gouged out a small pool below. About four foot at the deepest and much wider than the rest of the brook, it was a safe pool for children to splash about it on a hot summer day. All the farm children had learned to swim in it, including Helen under the watchful eye of Joseph.

On the near stream bank a wide sloping pasture approached close to the boundary wall of Quarry Moor, named after the now disused quarry whose walls stood high above the small croft where Helen had just put her cow. The two cottages and most of the field walls were built with stone quarried there.

Helen climbed on up a steep winding path to reach the Moor beyond the quarry lip. There wasn't much heather here, mainly tussock grass and rushes. It had felt relatively mild when Helen was doing her chores round the animals but up here in the breeze she was glad of her topcoat, which had dried out hanging on Grandpa's old chair by the fire. To many the autumn colours would have seemed drab but not to young Helen. She loved the mixture of browns ranging from the sandy coloured tussock grass through the different shades of the dying rushes to the hint of purple in the deep bronze heather. It took a few hundred yards of uphill walking before she came to the real heather moorland. Quarry Moor was far from level and as she walked further she could see over the boundary wall across the sloping pasture and over the Bullerstone Valley towards the higher Leckon Moor beyond.

It was quiet. Helen knew that at this time of year the curlews and pewits were probably paddling in some distant estuary. Just a dozen snipe took off from a boggy spot with startling zigzagging speed. The sun came out changing the browns of autumn heather and dead grasses into a brighter mixture of russet and fawn. Eventually, coming to a flat slab of stone that felt slightly warm to her bottom, Helen sat deep in thought. The sheep must have been gathered off the Moor so apart from a pair of carrion crows flying lazily past and the call of grouse in the distance there was little movement to distract her thoughts.

It wasn't by accident she had chosen this stone; her dad had carried her here on his shoulders and lowered her onto this very stone to tell her he was going away. "Will you be away for long, Dad?"

"I don't know my pet. I've got to wear a uniform and maybe go to a foreign country."

"But you will come back, won't you?"

Her dad clasped her to his chest and shed a tear before saying, "How can I miss your next birthday?"

But Helen remembered how he had never promised that he would come back. Now she gazed across the Moor to where the chimney pots on the roof of the Grange stood like sentries between her and the distant church steeple that marked where the village stood. Standing solemnly facing the church tower she said, "Dad you didn't promise but I promise – I will be back. I don't know when and I don't know how but some day I will come back to my Valley."

Eventually she munched the left over chicken in the quiet solitude that she had grown to love.

It was three hours before Helen returned home. The sound of a motor engine drew her to the cottage door. Opening it she found the tall gruff man, this time with a hint of a smile. "Mrs Bolton has sent you these. May I talk to you, Miss Helen?"

Helen placed the cake on the cold stone slab in the pantry before turning to where he stood with his back to the fire. He already knew the answer but gently asked, "Have you no relatives?"

"I do have an Uncle and Aunt at Flacton near Matlock."

Holding up the letter she had just written she added, "My Aunt usually writes on my birthday so I've written to ask if they will have me but I haven't got a stamp."

Mainthorpe was so surprised by her calm statement that he stood speechless.

"I realised after the fox had been that I couldn't manage on my own so I went up on the moor to think it over. I'm not going into an orphanage and they're the only relatives I know of."

Mainthorpe wandered over to the window before asking, "How are you for money? Have you managed to settle the funeral bill?"

"Oh yes, but I don't understand it because it was a lot less than Grandma's – even with a stone – and I'm sure Grandpa said we couldn't afford one." She reached the receipt from off the mantelpiece.

He examined it in front of the window to hide from the girl any hint of satisfaction that the undertaker had only charged the difference between what he paid him and the total. Turning back to the girl he continued, "I'm sure it's all in order. The undertaker would know what he was charging for, so I shouldn't worry about it. Would you like me to post your letter and then come to see you again when you get a reply?"

Mainthorpe not only posted the letter but he also urged the Matlock acquaintance, who was checking out the Uncle and Aunt, to redouble his efforts.

Making sure that none of the older boys broke her precious dinner egg again, Helen got on with the daily grind of school and livestock. It was two weeks before her aunt's welcoming letter arrived by which time Mainthorpe had also learned that the uncle and aunt were seemingly respectable and hardworking people. So he called to see her.

Helen said, "My aunt will have me but I can't go until I've sold my livestock."

"I've bought the Boltons' livestock at a valuation price; would you like their valuer to do yours as well? You can't really take your furniture with you so if you agree I will also buy that."

Not knowing anything about such dealing she asked a few questions before agreeing to have both livestock and furniture valued. Intrigued by the adult way she spoke, he said, "I've taken Joseph on as my bailiff. Do you think he'll be all right?"

"Oh yes, Sir, I spent a lot of time with him when I used to go to the farm with my Grandpa. Grandpa used to say that he was the best farmer among all the boys and I like him."

"Good! It's nice to know that I'm starting off right."

"Aren't you going to live at the farm then, Sir?"

"Well yes, but not straightaway and not all the time, although I'd like to. I think it's better that we keep the townhouse so that I'm close to the mill through the week, and for now just come up here each weekend."

"But you'll miss so much not being here all the time. You won't really be the farmer, will you, Sir?"

"You are too observant, Miss Helen. I think I ought to go before you scold me more."

When the valuer came he could see that the pig was ready for slaughter so he suggested that he could arrange for her to sell it to the local butcher. He valued the cow and the geese but the few hens she decided to leave for Mr Aimsley – if he could catch them!

The Butcher came on a motorbike with a craftily built sidecar which, with a little ramp for a back door and a strong net over the top, was large enough to carry a couple of lambs or pigs. When he parked it by the sty door Helen's pig took one look at it and fled to the back of the sty. There was a lot of squealing and not all it from the pig before they managed to push the loudly protesting animal up the ramp into the sidecar.

The butcher paid Helen the price set by the valuer.

A few days later Helen ushered the reluctant geese along the drive while Harry Aimsley drove her cow up towards the Grange. Harry was not a happy man; he blamed Joseph for his wage reduction. "He should have stood up to him but what can you expect having a bit of lad in charge? He'll let this bl**** townie ruin all our lives. How am I going to manage with five shillings less?"

"If my hens lay you a few eggs next year, Mr Aimsley, maybe that will help."

Fortunately she didn't hear Mr Aimsley's muttered reply.

Mainthorpe was waiting with his cheque and some advice. "You now have a nice little sum. I wouldn't tell your aunt and uncle just how much, so why not open a bank account and just take a small amount with you?"

The village had a Bank sub-branch that opened just for one short day each week. As it was that day, Mainthorpe drove her down to the village and made sure that the bank gave her the best terms possible.

Bob Fairclough sent a message that he was going over to Matlock the next day. Would she like a lift? The fact that he was only going because Mainthorpe was paying him was not mentioned. And so the slightly tubby eleven-year-old girl took a last tearful look along the picturesque Ragil valley before climbing up into Fairclough's old lorry.

Chapter Five

Helen had only travelled as far as the Black Grouse Pub in one direction or Fletchfield in the other since moving to Grandpa's some six years before. Standing on nearly the highest part of the moor was the field by this Pub where local farmers held their sheep fair each autumn. The fair was little more than a day when each could bring back sheep that had strayed onto the wrong part of the moor. Mr Bolton had brought Helen and Joseph a couple of times and she remembered being surprised how many people were there. Some farmers brought tups to sell and these were lined up and judged as to which was the best. Once that was over those farmers needing a new bloodline in their flock called the judge useless, pouring scorn on the prize tups before haggling over the price. Mainly, though, it was a day for gossip and relaxation.

Those nostalgic memories reminded Helen that she had failed to say goodbye to Joseph. The other brothers had either teased or ignored her whereas Joseph had been like an older brother whenever she was at the farm.

Regrets were soon forgotten when Helen became enthralled with the changing scenery. After the Black Grouse they gradually dropped down off the moor. When grey granite rocks gave way to white limestone Helen thought she had never seen anything so pretty. The fact that there were no brooks in most valley bottoms fascinated her because, although learning about underground rivers at school, it was hard to visualise in reality where the water ran and where it would emerge.

Whatever Helen's thoughts were about moving she held them in a worried silence. As one of the few children at Gritstencrag School to speak without the local dialect, she had not developed a close friend. The other two posh speaking children belonged to the mill manager and it was not likely they would be allowed to play with a retired farm worker's granddaughter. Would a Derbyshire dialect contrast with her King's English and create more taunts from the next village's children? There were no memories of Uncle Horace or her Aunt other than he was a lead miner. The occasional letters her Aunt wrote never told much about their life. She had no idea of what was to come.

Helen was surprised to discover that Flacton was even smaller than Gritstencrag but there were more small farms and cottages dotted about the countryside. Bob Fairclough pulled up by a row of four stone terraced cottages. "This is it, girl."

A woman came hurrying down the garden path as he lifted her battered case and tied bundle down and, just as he did on market days, said, "Take care, girl."

There were no hugs or kisses but Aunt Emily's welcome seemed warm. "I'm sorry that I haven't seen much of you in recent years. I know I should have come to both funerals. It must have been hard for you on your own, but travelling across the hills is so difficult. You do understand, don't you?"

Helen just smiled but no, she didn't understand. If she could only know where her own brave father was buried it would be worth walking across England just to touch his grave. As for her mother, although Helen had long believed her to be buried in an unmarked grave somewhere far away, the fact that she had deserted her only child had left a scar deep inside.

"This is your room," Aunt Emily said placing Helen's case on the bed. "There's a bathroom next door but the privy's down the garden. I'll go and get you something to eat while you unpack."

Helen looked at the stained dirty wallpaper and the chest of drawers balancing on a brick where a front leg was missing and sat on the bed. She was near to tears. The immensity of the dramatic changes in her life overwhelmed her. Her Aunty seemed nice but she longed for the comfort of her Grandpa and Leckon cottage.

When Aunt Emily came to look for her she was still sitting there. Suddenly she was engulfed in her Aunt's arms and the tears finally flowed.

Later, after helping Helen to put her few belongings away, her Aunt explained that Uncle Horace was still working but he usually came home early on a Saturday. Over a cold dinner Helen learned that he was one of the last independent lead miners. Most of the other miners had left their small mines to work for a large mining company digging for lead deep underground. Uncle Horace and one other scraped a living by working out the many small abandoned mines.

Trying to hide her nervous feelings, Helen asked many questions. Her Aunty explained how she used to help her husband but found that the work was too heavy for her. "So when the old man who supplied the village with milk died," she explained, "we rented his croft. Now I look after three cows and deliver milk to some of the other cottages."

"Do the cows have calves?"

"No, we buy them from a dealer just after they've calved. He buys them from cheesemakers, because as cows get older their milk's not so rich. That's why the cheesemakers sell them but they're ideal for us."

"Grandpa kept just one cow and milked it until it was dry, then he sold it and bought another. We made butter; do you?"

"Yes, when we have a surplus of milk. We also keep a pig to peat up any waste."

Helen heard a cockerel crow and began to feel at home. If there were hens, a pig and three cows there would be jobs that she could help with. Going outside to explore she discovered that since this was the end house on the terrace the garden was quite large. Sloping upwards towards a steep limestone hill, the garden consisted of a well-tended vegetable plot with the hen pen behind and the stone pigsty with the privy attached standing along one side. From what her Aunt had said the croft where the cows lived was about four hundred yards down the road. Helen was soon to find out because Aunt Emily called her to say she was going to milk the cows now.

Her Aunt balanced a yoke across her shoulders, hooked a three-gallon tankard-shaped can on each end and strode off down the lane. The lane ran along the valley bottom and the croft Aunt Emily turned into lay in a field on the other side, which sloped upwards towards a more rugged limestone cliff. The three cows were waiting by a small stone building standing on an outcrop of rock about halfway up the field. Out of a pipe in the rocky outcrop a trickle of clear spring water splashed into a natural stone trough, which in turn overflowed to vanish among broken limestone rocks. All this Helen took in with the understanding of an experienced country girl.

Aunt Emily drove the cows inside the shippen and tied each one by a neck-rope in a stall. Taking two buckets down from a hook in the loft ceiling of the small loosebox next door she said, "In a morning Uncle Horace cleans out and milks one cow while I milk another, then while that milk's cooling he goes off to his work and I milk the other cow. By then the first milk is cool enough to deliver. When I've delivered that I take the other cow's milk home for ourselves and the other three cottages in our row."

While she was talking she dipped the two buckets into the water trough to rinse them. Taking a bucket and a three-legged stool from behind the door, Helen went to the nearest cow and sat down. Aunt Emily seemed surprised. "Are you sure? Can you milk?"

With her dress pulled up above her knees and the bucket firmly held between her crossed legs, Helen's strong young arms were already rhythmically pumping milk into the bucket.

Her Aunt was not very talkative and so Helen just watched as she poured the milk from the first two cows into the cans and left them floating in the cool spring water while she milked the third cow. Then, with that milk also cooling in the floating bucket, her Aunt walked up the hill to the back of the building. The ground here was so much higher that they just walked into the loft and pushed a feed of sweet-smelling hay down through a hole in the floor to the head of each cow. "Do the cows stay in all night?"

"Of course, it's November. We try to keep them out in the day so they can get a drink and graze a bit of grass."

Only a few of the larger village families had milk delivered in an evening as well as morning. Even so, Helen enjoyed the friendly greetings as her Aunt introduced her to each customer in turn. Soon they were back at the water trough scrubbing out the two milking buckets before Helen carried the remaining milk home carefully balanced in the two small tankards that hung from the yoke across her shoulders.

A pair of clogs behind the back kitchen door testified that Uncle Horace had returned home. Aunt Emily said, "He'll be having his bath. He always comes home early on a Saturday, has a bath before tea and then goes off for a pint later."

Tea consisted of brawn, which Helen had helped her Grandma make from the pickled neck muscles and cheeks when they slaughtered their own pig. Helen said, "I like this. It has more vegetables mixed in than Grandma's had."

Aunt Emily smiled but Uncle Horace just kept on eating. Topping up with bread and jam, Helen was surprised at the lack of conversation. Grandpa and Grandma had always chatted away throughout every meal but her Aunt and Uncle hardly spoke. Nor did they ask her any questions or encourage her to speak.

After washing up, her Aunt got out her sewing box and began working under a lamp hanging from the ceiling. Helen went through to the small lounge and discovered a bookcase containing several books, both children's and adults'. "Where have they all come from? Can I read them?"

"They were my wedding present from the big house where I worked. Not that I get much time to read now, so you enjoy them. I'll light the other lamp then you can sit one side of it and I'll sit the other."

The weeks became very pleasant. Although Uncle Horace exchanged little more than a few short sentences, Helen set out with him each morning after an early breakfast, Helen to milk two of the cows while he milked the other and shovelled the overnight accumulation of dung into a barrow and pushed it out to the midden. She then skipped along with her Aunt helping to deliver milk until school time. After school she came home for a jam butty and then helped her Aunt with the evening milking. Perhaps because she was mixing with the parents as well as the children, she escaped most of the expected teasing over her posh accent.

Some of the boys tried to tease her but when the ringleader asked if she was a toff, Helen said, "My Grandpa was just a farm worker like your Dad."

"My Granddad owns our farm and my Dad will be the farmer some day."

Helen smiled, "Then you're the toff because I will never own a farm."

When she went to do the milking one evening the lad followed her to the shippen, which he insisted in calling a cowhouse. When he saw the stream of milk generated by Helen's strong arms he defended her from then on against any hint of teasing.

January brought some very cold weather and with it came painful chilblains. Uncle Horace bought her some clogs that were a good size too large. He told her to stuff them with hay and to change it each week like he did. At first they seemed clumsy but after a few weeks Helen enjoyed the noisy clatter and by choosing the softest of hay they were extremely comfortable, much warmer than any shoes she had ever worn.

Of lead mining Helen had learned very little. That Uncle Horace worked with another man and that they searched among old abandoned mines for traces of lead, which they then dug out, was all that she had been told. Becoming bolder with her grumpy and uncommunicative uncle allowed Helen to question him one frosty morning as their clogs clattered along the gravelled lane towards the cowhouse. He said, "We never go down a mine without having someone up top. Not that we do any deep mining.

Lead's funny stuff, it lies in fissures in limestone or in fluorspar (which is a type of limestone). It might run in veins as thin as silk and suddenly widen out as thick as your arm. In other places there is nothing more than the line of a fissure to lead us to a ball of lead. We often find it right near the surface where others have given up."

That was the longest statement she had heard from him on anything. It prompted her to ask, "How did the lead get there? Where did it come from?"

"It's there and that's what matters, so get a bucket under that cow and stop nattering."

On the milk round later when Helen asked aunt Emily about it she was told that there was a book on lead and mineral deposits back at the house. After school and evening milking Helen got it down.

From that book she learned how a great upheaval, probably a massive earthquake, many millions of years ago had so shaken the district that it had cracked and split up the layers of limestone rock. What the book could not say was how the lead and other minerals had formed in those cracks and fissures. It just posed the questions: was it forced up from the bowels of the earth or formed by slow deposit left from the passage of water through those millions of years? Parts of the book were a bit too technical but what did surprise her was that lead had been mined in that area since Roman times. Fascinated, she read how in 1777 a Roman pig of lead was found near Cromford with a Latin inscription on top, which read – IMP CAES HADRIANI AVG MET LVT. Although the author could not understand its full meaning, he said it was obvious that the lead had belonged to Emperor Caesar Hadrian Augustus (A.D. 117-138).

After several nights of study Helen learned more of how there were strict rules on lead mining, with a Barmote Court that settled everything from disputes between miners to the royalty each mine or miner paid to the Duke of Devonshire, who owned all the land in the area. It appeared that Uncle Horace and his partner had the right to claim any unused mine and (after applying to the Barmote Court) to rework it. Later, when she tried to discuss it with him he just grunted uncommunicatively.

Chapter Six

The Boltons were surprised by how quickly Mainthorpe acted. Within days of finalising the purchase of the farm he had builders working in the old farmhouse. Hot water, a new kitchen sink and a bathroom were among many of the improvements installed, which also included plastering the worst rooms and completely decorating it through. For Mrs Bolton it was a luxury that she had never experienced and she couldn't help smiling even though there were still three hefty sons to feed and look after. Her eldest had left the area to find work in Manchester, Joel had gone to live with its future in-laws and Ned, who developed his skill on the many stone walls around the farm, now worked for a local builder, but he still chose to live at home.

The builders helped Joseph and Isaac carry the furniture from the Grange to the old farmhouse.

Some of the restoration work needed at the Grange was obvious so they went to work on that under Mainthorpe's careful eye while he persuaded Jessica to come and decide what further alterations she would like at the Grange.

As for Joseph in his role as farm bailiff, he was in his element. Although it was a surprise to most people in the village that he had been given so much responsibility at such a youthful age, he just took it in his stride. It was as though he was fulfilling what he had been born to do. Perhaps walking round the farm as a boy watching his father supervise the men working in different fields had prepared him for the role. As they walked Joseph's father would share his thoughts, why each man was doing what and why it had to be done that day and not the next. He listened to his father grumble about one worker's carelessness or give praise to another for his skill and effort. That some of those workers were Joseph's older brothers did not spare them from his father's judgement.

The result was that he learned to think like a farmer – to carry the whole picture of the farm in his mind with its pressures of seasonality and weather. What he had not enjoyed was the few months after his father died when no one had been in charge of the farm. It had not taken him long to realise that you can't farm with a committee and that's what his family were without the authority of his father. Even a simple decision about when to mow the grass for hay had nearly ended in a fistfight. When he thought the weather was good and they should cut, another had said that it would rain within a day or two and they should wait, while another thought that there was not sufficient grass to mow for another fortnight. And that was only on one field. There had been similar disagreements over the next four fields and the arguments had gone on when the hay was dry: was it really dry enough to stack into cocks today or should they wait till tomorrow? Joseph had had enough of that. He concluded that it needed one man to walk across the cobbled stone yard and say, 'Right, we mow; we stack; we cart'.

Now he did just that. He walked out of the farmhouse in the morning, looked up at the sky, tested where the wind came from and made his decisions. What was more, he enjoyed it, particularly the need to think ahead. While Harry Aimsley was ploughing a field for winter wheat he made sure that the corn drill was oiled and greased days before Harry had finished and the ground was cultivated and ready to sow. The new binder, (that had now replaced the simple reaper with its need to hand tie each sheaf) would have every complex moving part meticulously examined long before the corn was ripe for harvest. It was more than just machinery though. Crop rotation was an important part of this mixed farm, which meant that he knew what crops had been grown in which field for the last ten years and what crop he planned there next year. All that was in his head as it had been in his father's without a written record, though now he was learning to keep records so that he could satisfy the overview of his new boss.

There was a bit of trouble with the men over the reduced wage. The Waggoner did a lot of grumbling, particularly to Isaac who in turn grumbled to Joseph. When they came into the shippen for afternoon milking Joseph said, "You're doing a lot of grumbling about your wages; it stops now. I checked the neighbouring farms and there isn't one paying as much, so either work and be grateful or leave."

They knew better than to leave. Farm men were often laid off in the autumn but this year many of the so-called regular men were also being laid off. There weren't many weeks when one or more desperate men wouldn't knock on the farmhouse door looking to work. Isaac and Harry knew that Joseph had already engaged one new man and was in discussion with another over Helen's former cottage. In response to Joseph's tough ultimatum they each reached for a milking stool and bucket and hid their faces behind the flank of a cow.

Mainthorpe gave Joseph a surprising amount of responsibility. He came in to inspect the new cows when the dealer delivered them but referred to Joseph to accept or reject any. He took Joseph with him in the car to select and buy an extra heavy working horse but again allowed Joseph to make the final decision and to negotiate the price. It was Joseph, though, who had a four-mile walk leading the horse back to the farm. After that, although he came to the farm most weeks and discussed all aspects of its business, he allowed the lad to get on with the decisions of his day-to-day work without interference.

Where Joseph failed was that he could not relax over his work in the way that his father had managed to do. Maybe it was because he was working for someone else or maybe it was just lack of experience but the fact was he was trying too hard to be both a farmer and a worker. It came to a head when Mainthorpe made one of his rare midweek visits. He had bought a handy cob for his use on these occasions. A tall, spirited hunter would have been a dangerous animal on those boulder strewn hilly fields whereas the steady cob could be trusted to walk between the rocky outcrops on the high ground but, with a few digs with his spurs, could be persuaded to break into a canter on the more level pastures if need be.

Joseph had engaged a new man, Tom Smith, to work as Shepherd and general farm worker and installed him and his wife in what had been Helen's cottage. He was an agreeable sort of fellow but Joseph had suspicions that he was a bit of a slacker when he wasn't there to supervise and because of that he had set him on a job with his brother Isaac. They were laying a drain across a pasture field. Digging with a spade may have been monotonous but it was not heavy work; the skill was in getting the right fall on the drain. He stayed with them for an hour to make sure they understood exactly what they were to do and then left them to get on with it.

Stone walls were a feature of this hilly countryside and through the years Joseph, with his sharp brain and quick hands, had become an expert at building them. One of the shire horses had had an itchy bottom and soothed it on a convenient stone in the field boundary wall. Now a length of that wall needed rebuilding. Joseph knew that now Ned had left he was the best builder on the farm so he went to put his skill to use. As he worked steadily on, selecting each stone carefully before he picked it up, he chuckled about the sermon he had heard in chapel last Sunday. Perhaps the Methodist minister had been watching someone building a wall because he based his message on the fact that a good wall builder never puts a stone down but uses each stone he picks up, saying, 'Christ will make use of every man that responds to his call'. After the service on the way out, when Joseph shook hands with the Minister, he told him, 'You've got it wrong, preacher. A good stonewaller only picks up stones that are the right size and shape to fit'.

Joseph smiled at the memory as he worked on through the morning carefully selecting by no more than the judgement of his eye the right stone each time. He needed to keep busy because there was a strong East wind whistling over the Pennines and swirling through the gap in the wall. It froze his hands until they became numbed and clumsy. His thick tweed trousers were tied below the knee so that they didn't pull when he bent down but, warm as they were, tied like that they left a little gap above the top of his clogs and the cold wind found it. Perhaps it also muffled the sound because he didn't hear Mainthorpe's cob approaching. "Good morning, Joseph."

"Good morning, Master." Straightening up and rubbing his hands to get some warmth into them Joseph looked up to where his boss towered above him on the horse's back. "I didn't expect to see you today, Master, but it's a bracing day for a ride."

Mainthorpe slid down off the horse and stepped over the loose stone to Joseph's side. Testing the firmness of some of the stones with his hand he said, "You're good at this, aren't you Joseph, and because you are good at it you enjoy doing it, don't you?"

"Well, I suppose so Master, but the fact is none of my men are good wall builders so I may as well do the job myself."

"But that's where you are wrong. While you are working hard here, your two men who should be digging that drain are in fact sitting out of the wind behind a stone wall having a quiet smoke."

Joseph tried to apologise but Mainthorpe cut in, "I don't employ you to build walls up, I employ you to get the job done. The farm won't prosper on how hard you work but on how hard and how well you make sure others work. I don't know much about farming but I know a bit about employing men. There's a saying, Joseph, that the best fertiliser is the farmer's boot and you're the farmer, not me." He patted Joseph on the shoulder and swung back up into the saddle and rode on his way.

Joseph took a last appraising look at the wall and strode across the fields towards the drain, determined that from now on he would be the Boss and he would make sure his staff knew it.

He was aware that taking on the job had created a rift between him and his brother Isaac. Now if Isaac was going to let the new man Tom Smith lead him astray he was going to be just as firm with his brother as he would with any other man.

Thinking about Tom Smith and the fact that he was in what had been Helen's cottage reminded him of the girl. Through the last few years her grandfather had been alive, although too old to do active farm work he had still come to the farm for a few hours each day to do some light jobs around the yard or garden. During those visits when Helen came with him she had often attached herself to Joseph. He wondered whether it was perhaps because he was the youngest or maybe it was because he was just thoughtful and liked to explain things to her. Laughing at the memory of how she wanted to know about everything and how quick her mind was, he wondered how she was going on far away in Derbyshire. A couple of times he had been tempted to ask the Master for her address but thought that he might think it silly for his bailiff to want to write to a young girl.

Smiling to himself as he rode away, Mainthorpe was not in any way cross with his farm bailiff. He was young, he was a bright lad and it was all part of learning. He had gone over the farm books with him only the week before. Although they were both disappointed how the price of grain continued to fall, Mainthorpe was not too concerned because Joseph explained that most of the oats were fed to the cows so the price of milk was more important. Listening to his bailiff's plans he remained pleased with his farming venture.

Not only was Mainthorpe sure that he had a good farm bailiff, he also had a reasonably good manager at the mill. He was not up to running the business like Joseph but he could supervise the day-to-day activities, which meant that Mainthorpe could take time away from either business without too much worry. What was concerning him was that he still had not acquired that larger mill in Fletchfield. The present owner was taking too long to go bankrupt. Maybe it was time that he looked at who bought what from the man and put a bit of pressure on to hurry to process along.

Mainthorpe was in a good mood mainly because, to his surprise, he found immense satisfaction just riding across his own farm. Business had been the driving force in his life; it had come before pleasure and marriage, but now he was both married and learning the pleasure of relaxation. Crossing one of the more level pasture fields, he kicked the reluctant horse into a canter and laughed out loud at the thought of what some of his wealthy friends with their blue-blooded hunters would think of this rough-legged cob. Yet strangely it had an easy gait, which made it much more pleasant than trying to walk with his dodgy ankle. Thinking about it made him think of his early teenage rashness when he had believed that he could ride any horse. Now a permanent ache if not a more intense pain reminded him that caution has its part to play in the most active of lives.

He needed this relaxation. Since buying a motorcar and dispensing with his pony and trap he had been in too much of a hurry. His car got him everywhere too quickly and because of that he had lost the art of making time for contemplation. It had taken a while for him to realise how important it was in business to step back, to let your mind drift. He had done that for years jogging along in the trap behind his pony, sometimes even frustrated by the lost time, but with hindsight it had been time well spent. Now the fresh air, the sight of his own herd of cows grazing the last of the autumn grass over the wall on the next field, crows cawing in an ash tree, all intruded into his consciousness and yet they seemed to stimulate his thoughts about other things. Yes, he was sure that he needed this time away from his office when his thoughts could range over the wider picture. He reined the cob round to take a longer route back along the banks of the Ragil brook.

Water hens, quarrelling noisily as he approached, now splashed on clumsy wings across the water. The occasional pair of duck took to the air, startled by his passing, but his thoughts turned to his marriage. Although Jessica was a very attractive woman he had come to realise that she was also quite a selfish one and it was beginning to irritate him how much influence her mother had in her life. Now with the restrictions of pregnancy and morning sickness Jessica seemed to have a permanently petulant look that he found very unattractive. He was convinced if his marriage was to succeed he needed to hasten this move to the Grange and away from her mother.

His real reason for coming to the farm in the mid week was to urge the builders to get one wing completed so that he could move his wife up here as soon as possible.

It was therefore with some satisfaction when he returned home in the evening that he told Jessica, "They've finished the main wing and it looks good. All it needs, Jessica, is for you to come over with me this weekend and choose the decorations."

"I'm not sure if I'll feel up to it this week end, and mummy says it's not good for me to ride out in the car too much."

"But Jessica it's much smoother than any trap and it's such a lovely ride – and the fresh air will do you more good than just sitting in the house here." When he saw her looking more petulant he added, "Anyway, I thought you would be interested to see what it looks like now it's finished. The views from the front windows are stunning."

"You might find the views stunning but all I see are boring fields and hills. I'd rather see houses and people and shops and mummy says – "

"I don't want to hear what your mother says. You're married to me. I thought you'd want to live where I want to live."

When a pouting lip seemed to be her only answer he walked out of the room.

During the next few days Mainthorpe kept thinking about the conversation, reluctant to admit just how much it had irritated him. As an outlet for his energy he switched his mind back to the mill he had his eye on; he wanted it settled within months rather the years. There was one way to hurry it along – the mill owner would soon be bankrupt if he couldn't sell his products.

In the Silk Industry just about everyone knew everyone and Mainthorpe's success gave him some influence: enough to persuade one buyer not to pay for the last delivery of silk and a second buyer to refuse the next batch he was due to buy on the grounds that it was not up to standard. As a result, within a couple of weeks the receivers were in at the five-storey mill. Mainthorpe did not rush to make an offer but kept his ear open for any whisper of someone else's approach. When he finally made his offer the receivers dismissed it as derisory. He was sure though that he was the only one interested in buying the complete mill lock, stock and barrel. It took a little time and he had to increases the price just a little but towards the end of the winter he got his mill.

Chapter Seven

In Derbyshire the cold, frosty weather continued into late January, then it snowed. It was a dry kind of snow and falling onto dry, frozen ground every flake stayed where it settled. There was about nine inches covering everything when Helen set out with her Uncle the next morning. Their clogs were soon blocked up because the snow just built up between the irons. Uncle Horace showed her how to clear them by kicking the heel of one clog against the toe of the other, but each step collected more making it very tiring to walk.

When they got to the cow house he said, "It's too cold to let the cows outside so you carry in some water from the spring and give each a drink while I clean out the muck."

The bucket was heavy and awkward and when Helen went back for a second bucket the water that had splashed had already turned to ice. "Don't fill your bucket so full girl, you'll have me with a broken leg if you're not more careful."

"I'm sorry Uncle, I was just trying to be quick."

He grunted and took the other bucket and a three-leg stool to the nearest cow.

Snow lay in an attractive mantle over the rocky higher ground. Behind the cowhouse Bole Hill was covered but what before had looked like white limestone outcrops now looked a dirty cream against the brilliance of the snow. Even so there was not the contrast in colours that the rocks and rushes around Gritstencrag gave to her old home. Helen longed to be back on the boggy moors at Leckon and see those dark grey rocks and winter-browned rushes giving a real beauty against the whiteness of snow.

When the last cow's thirst was satisfied Helen rinsed out her bucket, took the other stool and milked the next cow into the same bucket.

There was time to think while milking a cow and her thoughts turned to what she had learned from her book studying. The name Bole came from a term used in ancient lead smelting when stone hearths, built on the western side of a hill, were called boles. With wood laid on them the westerly winds raised the fire to the heat required to smelt the lead. Helen resolved that when the snow cleared away she would climb up Bole Hill and look for the remnants of such a hearth.

On the way home from school in the afternoon she saw a lady sitting with an easel and paints just inside their croft. Walking over to her, Helen asked, "Can I look what you're painting, Miss?"

"Of course, look, I'm trying to capture that small cow house. See how the heat from the midden has melted some snow. I used it to give colour to that side of the picture while that trickle of water running into that trough makes a feature on the other. And look," the lady said pointing with finger-free mittens, "see how the icicles have formed along the roof edge where the warmth from the cows inside melts the snow; in fact it melts so slowly that it freezes again as it runs over the edge. Aren't they spectacular?"

In her eleven years Helen had never met anyone with such a vivid, lively personality nor had she quite appreciated the beauty lying before her. She saw how the icicles had grown while she had been in school, how the one she had broken off from the spring outlet had reformed and when she looked at the lady's painting she was enthralled. It was all there, the gleam of the evening sun and the hazy steam rising from the midden looked so real in the picture. Helen watched fascinated as the artist mixed colours to get the right shade for the foreground.

"Do you paint?"

"No, Miss, I've never had paints but I can draw with a pencil."

"Oh good, I'm ready for a break. You come and sit on my seat. Now here's a clean sheet and a pencil; you draw while I stretch my legs."

That invitation was to change the young girls life. For what appeared on that paper in black and white, with seemingly very little effort, captured the same scene in a more distant perspective with startlingly clarity. By that time the lady was looking over her shoulder with surprised admiration.

"I think you had better use my paints and colour that picture just as you see it."

"I'm supposed to go home for a butty and then come back to help my Aunt milk the cows, Miss."

"You can have one of my butties and if you tell me where you live I'll go to tell your aunt where you are. Just get painting before the light goes altogether."

And so Helen sat engrossed. She got jam on her fingers and paint on her dress, and although the sun went down behind the hill she painted the memory of its colour. By the time the lady returned, walking alongside Aunt Emily with her yoke and two milk cans, dusk had descended. Introducing herself as Mrs Belthropp, she said to Helen, "Its Saturday tomorrow. If I come back will you pose for me with your aunt's yoke and then I'll help you re-do this picture?"

"Can I, Aunt Emily?"

"Of course you can, Helen. What time would you like her here for?"

Mrs Belthropp set a time, which Helen shyly agreed to.

It was a fascinating few hours. After Helen had posed with the yoke and milk buckets in front of the cow house, Mrs Belthropp showed how she had imposed her onto the original picture then rewarded her with a large tin containing an incredible range of watercolours with brushes, pencils and sketchpad. When Helen recovered from the surprise, Mrs Belthropp sat alongside, guiding her as to which colours could be used to capture the scene.

They met again on the following Saturday when Mrs Belthropp took her into a neighbouring village to sketch and paint there. There was just one more half day together before the artist's stay in the area was over, but for Helen it was just the beginning. From then on, whenever there was time, she roamed among the limestone hills to find a suitable scene and, once found, sat with sketchpad across her knees.

Spring came with its many different colours as the varying shades of new green leaves emerged and wild flowers decked the meadows with a greater variety of colour. Uncle Horace replaced two of his cows with newly calved ones and as the new grass grew they responded with a lot of milk. Although her aunt had made butter occasionally throughout the winter, now with the flush of spring milk Helen's Saturday work increased dramatically. Surplus milk, which had been allowed to go sour through the week, now had the risen cream skimmed off and the cream was poured into the barrel of a large wooden butter churn. Standing on four legs with the axle of the churn barrel slightly off centre, which meant that as Helen turned it the heavy wooden barrel rocked unevenly. It could take thirty or occasionally even forty-five backbreaking minutes continuously turning the handle to fully separate the butter. When it eventually separated it floated on the top of the remaining liquid buttermilk.

Even when the butter had been skimmed off it still needed a lot of hand squeezing and pummelling to remove all the remnants of liquid before it could be squashed into attractive butter-moulds. There were several half-pound butter-moulds each with a different carving of ferns or flowers on the lid. The one of a cow caught Helen's eye, but it took all her strength and skill to press the lid down in a way that left the finest details of the carving on the finished pat of butter.

Nothing went to waste. The original liquid left after the cream had been skimmed off was fed to the pig through the following week and the buttermilk left after the butter had been extracted was a highly valued drink. Helen loved it while it was still fresh for the two or three days after churning, but Uncle Horace and some of the other villagers drank it days later when it had become what they called 'ripe'. With both butter and buttermilk to carry, Aunt Emily was glad of Helen's help on the Sunday morning milk round.

Spring moved into summer with its longer days and warm sunshine. Whenever Helen had time she headed out into the countryside with her sketchpad. Sometimes she took her paints but usually the colour was added in the evening at home where she developed her eye for detail by taking a few wild flowers or foliage home.

Mrs Belthropp came back in late June for a two-week stay to again paint and sketch. Of course she wanted to look through Helen's work. She made a few helpful comments about several of the pictures until one in particular took her attention. Helen was embarrassed and excused it by saying, "I couldn't get it right, Miss; the cows were partly hidden behind the wild flowers, which swayed back and to in the breeze and the cows kept flicking their ears because of flies."

"When did you do this?"

"I was late for tea so when I saw those cows had escaped and were lying in that field of hay," Helen indicated the painting, "I just put my book on the wall and sketched but the cows were lying behind a hump so I could only see them through the waving grass and flower heads. When I tried to paint it in that night in my mind I could just see a mixture of colour and movement. I'm sorry; it just ended up a jumble of grass and cow's ears and eyes and things."

"Don't apologise; I like it. How you've twirled the reddy brown cows in with the deep blue of the meadow crane's-bill, you've got the colours right. There's lilac scabious contrasting with white yarrow and yellow hawkweed all mixed in amongst the grass seed heads – it's great. You must do more like this. It's fun to catch shapes, light and colours in an abstract way and it gives a feeling of action."

Her two weeks came to an end just as Helen's school broke for the summer holidays. Not that Helen would have had time for art because from then on she was kept busy helping Uncle Horace with the hay harvest. He and his mining partner, who also had a croft, worked at the mine in the mornings and when the weather looked fair each mowed his own grass with a scythe through the afternoon. After it had lain for two days Helen helped her aunt turn it over to let the sun and breeze dry the other side – not just once but each day until it was dry enough to build into small haycocks. And each day Uncle Horace mowed another patch of grass so that the two women were continually turning the drying grass over. When misty rain fell it wet the partially dried hay, which then lay for several days untouched but Aunt Emily was undaunted. "When the sun comes out we'll just start again, turning and turning until it's dry."

In that break, although it was too wet either to work or take out her sketchbook, she did walk across the hay field where she saw a flock of small birds. They were not a bird that she had seen before; either they did not come along the Ragil Valley or it was just that she had never seen them. It took her some time to realise they were landing on the tall sorrel seed heads to feed on the seeds. Realising they must be goldfinches by the beautiful mixture of red, gold and black, Helen was fascinated at the contrasting colours as the russet brown sorrel seed heads bent and swayed with the weight of the brightly coloured birds. She was also reminded of her Grandpa saying, 'It's the strong sorrel stalks that holds the hay open and lets th'wind blow through it to dry it, so yer must'ner mow before its seeds'll shed in July. Yer want some t'grow and the rest to feed the birds. '

Helen developed blisters until her fingers were raw but Uncle Horace still made her work. It was a continuous grind because as one patch was getting dry enough to stack into small haycocks they were already turning the next one.

The rocky outcrop under the cow house and from which the spring gurgled throughout the year was, with a few added stones, a natural division across the croft. Below it the cows grazed contentedly and drank from the spring through those early summer months but on the higher hay meadow they never set foot until autumn. By then the hay would be safely in the loft above the cow-house and the hay meadow covered in tasty young grass, while the lower pasture grass would be stale and brown.

As a result of that rocky division one could walk into the ground floor shippen from the front pasture or walk into the first floor loft from the hay meadow behind and of course carry the hay in when it was ready. That was when Uncle Horace and his mining partner, Ben Johnson, worked together. They carried the hay in on a simple homemade stretcher similar to a human stretcher with two ash poles for shafts and a few thinner ones fixed across the middle. It was placed on the ground by a haycock and the two men, one at each side with a pikel, half lifted, half slid the haycock onto the stretcher and carried it into the loft. Helen's job was to rake up any loose hay left behind and place it on the next haycock. Aunt Emily had the worst job, stacking the hay pikel-full by pikel-full in the hot loft.

With her twelfth birthday behind her, Helen's once tubby figure was changing quite dramatically, becoming both tall and slim. The old dress she wore in the hay field no longer reached her brown knees and with the top few buttons undone the growing shape of firm young breasts were very obvious. Helen became aware of her uncle's stare particularly when she was bent forward with the rake but dismissed it as one of those things a girl has to put up with. The range of books in Aunt Emily's bookcase had helped to educate her to the facts of life and the ways of men. She was well aware of what the knocking noise meant when it sounded through the small house on a Saturday night after Uncle Horace came home from the pub.

In recent weeks he had not been in a good mood. There was a coalition Government but the predictions for the coming election were that the Conservatives might gain power, and Uncle Horace hated the Conservatives.

Although self-employed, from the snatches of conversation Helen overheard during the early part of the hay harvest both men shared a hatred of all employers and verbally supported the lead miners when they flexed their muscles and went on strike. As a result of the strike there wasn't much money in the village and because of it Aunt Emily was struggling to collect her milk money. Helen listened when she tried to explain to Uncle Horace what was happening. He got a really angry. "You deliver the milk so you collect the money. All of it. If there's no money there's no milk."

"There are families with young children and no money coming in. I thought you supported the miners so surely we can wait a week or two?"

Uncle Horace slapped her across the face shouting, "I'm no charity, you stupid woman. I had to pay for those cows and the rent's due."

Thinking that he was going to slap her aunt again, Helen stepped forward to intervene but he pushed her roughly away. "You stay out of this, you useless wench."

The next morning Aunt Emily sent Helen to the homes behind with payment instructing her to say, "I'm sorry, but we can only deliver half your milk until you clear the bill."

Uncle Horace asked that night, "Have you given any more milk away?"

Aunt Emily said, "I've not been to any of the houses that owe us money."

The answer satisfied her uncle and made Helen smile.

The hay was almost all in when the accident happened. At the front of the stretcher uncle Horace could see where he was walking but at the back Ben could only follow along without sight of the ground and he put his foot on a loose stone. It should have no more than a sprained ankle but somehow he managed to drop with the ash stretcher shaft across his calf. Horace could not believe it. "All the rocks we handle every day down the mine and you break a leg walking across a hay field."

By the time they persuaded a neighbouring farmer to loan a horse and cart to transport Ben to the nearest cottage hospital, and also walk across the fields to tell his wife, it was too late to carry in any more hay that day.

There was only a good half-day's carrying to be done but the mid August dew did not dry off until late morning. After an early dinner Aunt Emily bravely took Ben's place at the back of the stretcher but it was too heavy for her. Uncle Horace kept looking up at the sky and, impatiently hopping about, repeatedly shouted, "It's going to rain. If we don't get it tonight we'll never get it in."

To console him Helen carried one shaft handle while her aunt held the other. Even then with one full haycock on the stretcher it was a struggle for the two women.

By seven all was safely in and the two women were trudging their weary way home but Uncle Horace strode ahead and was splashing in the bath when they reached the house. Tea was hardly on the table before he sat down grumpily demanding food.

It was later when Ellen was in bed asleep that she woke to hear raised voices. Her Aunt was protesting and crying, "I'm to tired, please not tonight."

When she heard what sounded like a blow followed by a frightened sob Helen jumped out of bed in consternation just as her bedroom door flew open. Walking unsteadily towards her came Uncle Horace, his voice slurred. "Then you'll have to do instead. Take your nightdress off, girl, let's have a look at you."

So used to obeying him, Helen slipped it over her shoulders and stood uncertain but conscious of being trapped between the bed and the wall. The light from the landing candle, flickering onto her tall, naked body, highlighted the youthful curves. "Aye, you'll do all right."

Helen tried to turn but he caught her arm and swung her round to face him. She could smell the beer in his breath as he pulled her hips tight to his and thrust hard against them. There was enough in Aunt Emily's books to know what was the hardness she could feel through his coarse tweed trousers, but she had read nothing to prepare her for the look in his eyes. She had seen anger on the face of boys at school, even hatred sometimes when they were falling out, and in Aunt Emily's books she had read words like 'leering' and 'lecherous' but none of them described the look on her Uncle's face. When he started to fumble with the buttons on his trousers his intentions were obvious but his look mesmerised her like a rabbit before a stoat. As his trousers dropped, he grabbed her shoulders, pushing her backwards onto the bed, then suddenly he was tumbling backwards away from her. His shoulders hit the bedroom wall with a thud and in the dim light Helen could see her Aunt on the floor grappling with his legs. "Run now – run – run!" she cried between sobs.

Clutching her nightdress, Helen scrambled across the bed and fled through the door. Revolted by what had happened, she paused on the landing to look back. The two of them were still fighting on the floor but her Uncle, now half sitting, was lashing out unmercifully. "Run! — Run!" her aunt cried.

Slipping on her nightdress, Helen ran next door and banged hard on the door. When it opened she cried, "He's killing Aunt Emily, he's killing her!"

The Jessops next door had a grown son living at home with them and he and his father ran into the house and up the stairs. Helen followed in time to see her Uncle kicking Aunt Emily's inert body. When the two men shouted he stared at them for a moment and turned to push past them and walk out of the house. Responding to Aunt Emily's groans, the neighbours lifted her gently onto the bed and Mrs Jessop rushed in to comfort her.

Aunt Emily must have whispered what had happened because Mrs Jessop took command, instructing Helen to collect her clothes and move into their house. When that was done she said, "There'll be no more trouble if I stay here overnight."

The following morning Mrs Jessop returned muttering, "Emily says she'll have to milk the cows but I doubt if she can even walk there."

Of her uncle there was no sign so Mr Jessop walked to the cowhouse with Helen and hung around while she milked but left her to do the milk round on her own. The striking miners' children didn't go short of milk that day. For the afternoon milking Aunt Emily walked with Helen but one hand was too stiff to squeeze the cow's teat so she just watched Helen do the milking.

After the work was over they both went back to the Jessops' for a cup of tea and a conference. The outcome was that Mrs Jessop would contact a sister in Fletchfield who, because her husband was a self-employed silk weaver, would possible give Helen a home in return for some help in his weaving garret.

Aunt Emily took little part in the discussion; Helen wasn't sure if she really understood what was happening because all she could say was, "I know what he'll be like when he comes home. I wish he wasn't coming home – but how will I manage if he doesn't?"

Uncle Horace eventually returned home. He just walked in and demanded his tea on the Monday night just as though nothing had happened. He neither spoke about nor asked about Helen. For that matter he said very little to his wife either.

Although she had been yearning to get back to Cheshire, Helen now felt regretful about leaving those dry limestone hills and especially about leaving her only known relative.

During the wait for a reply her aunt would not let her stay in their home but still expected her to help with the milking. As it was still August and the cows were sleeping outside both night and day there was no cleaning out to do so Uncle Horace did not go near the cows. The two women did the milking and when there was time to spare Helen took her sketchpad out into the countryside.

The telegram came on Saturday morning saying, "Pleased to give Helen a home. Expect her tomorrow or Monday."

Chapter Eight

Compared to the clean limestone hills, Fletchfield looked dull and dirty. Realising that perhaps it was more likely she had forgotten what a smoke-grimed industrial town looked like, Helen smiled that at least she could remember what a garret house was. Years before, when they were in the town one market day, she asked what those strange houses were and her Grandpa explained that the large third-floor windows were designed to let the maximum light into the silk looms. Now, with the curiosity of youth Helen looked forward to seeing inside one; there was something fascinating about weaving silk in your bedroom.

This time she was more confident and excited about the move. Although it wasn't to the Ragil Valley, at least it was nearer. One day she would keep her promise to a walk again through that Valley and onto the moors. Though less than a year had gone by Helen knew that she had changed, had become more adult; there was none of the fear and heartbreak experienced when going to Flacton. Or maybe it was just that anywhere would be better than staying with her lecherous Uncle.

When Mrs Buxton greeted her pleasantly and took her up the flight of stairs, Helen was surprised by how large the garret room was. Running across two houses, it held two looms and several other pieces of equipment and both looms were clattering in a bewildering way. Pointing to the nearest, Mrs Buxton said, "This is Mr Buxton."

He just glanced at her for a fraction of the second and nodded a smile but his eyes were back on the loom before she could speak. Helen was fascinated by how clumsy the handloom looked with seemingly innumerable upright and horizontal beams and a multitude of coloured silk threads passing in and out to form what looked like a giant cobweb. As Mr Buxton's leg beat out a tempo on the foot trestle, his arm, with fantastic coordination, reached out to catch the shuttle, which in turn passed back and to with astonishing speed. As she watched, Helen became aware of a boy standing at the other side of the loom pulling on a series of cords, his arms jerking up and down in coordination with Mr Buxton's. Mrs Buxton nodded towards him. "That's the draw boy, Jim. He pulls on the tail cords."

Helen had no idea what she was talking about but found it fascinating just listening to and watching the rhythm of movement, particularly the way the many different fine silk colours jinked and bounced as they were drawn into the weave. "We do the most complicated of finest silks for the Master. There are 600 warp threads per inch in this one," Mrs Buxton said proudly.

Before Helen could ask what a tail cord or a warp thread was Mrs Buxton stepped smartly to the other end of the machine where a bewildering number of silk bobbins unwound to the machine's tempo. She grasped the two broken ends of fine thread and joined them with no more than a twist of her thumb and finger. Within seconds she joined another and then another; in between she nodded towards the other loom. "That's our neighbour, Mr Grindley."

Through the floating haze of dust and fluff Mr Grindley gave her the same fleeting smile without taking his eyes off his loom. Helen saw his draw boy, Hector, but hadn't realised until then that there was another woman at the far end of that loom, twirling the broken ends of threads together. She looked up and smiled, "Hello, Helen."

Helen wandered back to watch Mrs Buxton work. She was confused by the speed of the woman's movements but Mrs Buxton pointed to where a thread was broken and when Helen's sharp eyes began to see the breaks Mrs Buxton did the twirling join more slowly so that she could see how it was done. Helen made several attempts, one bungled so much that it caused Mr Buxton to stop work. Surprisingly, he didn't seem cross but said as he stretched his aching muscles, "I was ready for a break and I need a glass of water".

The work was so absorbing that the afternoon went quickly but Helen was far from confident she'd got the knack of it when Mrs Buxton caught her eye and called above the clatter, "Take over while I go and get tea ready".

The feeling of panic soon passed and she settled to watch the hundreds of silk threads for any sign of a break. It was only when they knocked off for the night that Helen realised another schoolgirl had taken over from Mrs Gridley on the other loom, presumably while she had also gone down to get her family's meal ready. Not being part of the family when work was finally over, Jim the draw boy went home for his tea, leaving Helen on her own with the Buxtons.

To Helen's surprise tea was a pleasant occasion. The Buxtons chatted to each other and brought Helen into the conversation, asking her about life in Derbyshire and about her friends there. It was so different from the few grunts of conversation between Aunty Emily and Uncle Horace that in this happy atmosphere Helen began to chatter away like a parrot, which brought a smile to Mr Buxton's face.

They discussed Helen's future with her, explaining how they wanted her to go to school until she was fourteen but that they would expect her to help for an hour each morning on the loom and again after school for about two hours while Mrs Buxton did some house work and prepared tea.

It was strange not having to milk the cows or walk round the village delivering milk. Although she missed the people and the clean countryside of Flacton, Helen felt surprisingly happy despite Fletchfield's dirt and grime.

Hector, the draw boy who helped Mr Gridley on the other loom, turned out to be his nephew and it was his younger sister Lizzie who had come to help after school. Living just around the corner in the next street, Lizzie called for Helen the next morning on her way to school, chattering all the way there and, after school, all the way home. Most of it was nonsense but Helen did ask how the men were paid. "They work on piecework rates for the silk they produce. Up to last year we wound the silk on the bobbins ourselves. Now it's provided by the Master but we still have to wind it onto the pirns."

"What are they?"

"They're small long bobbins used in the shuttle and we have to do it while the men are entering the warp into the loom. They set the colours out for us and we wind them on – it's boring."

Such was Helen's enjoyment with the silk looms that the weeks passed quickly. The other children had accepted her more readily that she expected but even so she couldn't wait to run home from school and up the stairs to the weaver's garret. To her it was never boring. It did not matter if it was joining the broken threads or winding it onto a pirn, she loved the feel of the silk in her fingers and was fascinated by the range of colours. Whenever Helen stopped to watch the many threads of silk being drawn into the chattering machine under Mr Buxton's skilled hands, she longed to hold that finished length of cloth. And she was indeed soon holding each finished length because each in turn was spread on a shiny table to be 'picked', which meant literally picking off all the little bits of loose thread and fluff. With her sharp eye and nimble fingers Helen became the expert and while picking off the bits she marvelled how such an ugly, clattering machine could produce the most beautiful of fabrics.

The only thing that interfered with the smooth running of Mr Buxton's loom was the health of the draw boy. No one seemed to know what his problem was but it caused him to tire easily. Some nights after school Helen took over his job while he rested for a while. At first she made a few mistakes but Mr Buxton was always patient and after a few nights he told her she was better than Jim. It was hard work though, so after a half an hour Helen was glad to let him have his job back.

Over tea one night Mrs Buxton asked, "Helen, have you not got any friends in Fletchfield?"

"Only at the market, Mrs Buxton. I used to come with Grandpa and after he was ill I came on my own to sell the eggs and shop for the week. I got to know a few people on the stalls then."

Mr Buxton said, "There's a school holiday next week. Perhaps you'd like to go and have a walk round the market?"

"Oh yes, I would love to. Can you manage without my help for a few hours?"

With the reassurance that they managed without her when she was at school, Helen went off to the market. To her surprise, most people remembered and asked where had she been. Even Bob Fairclough asked in his usual taciturn manner, "How have you bin, girl?"

The disappointment was that there was no one there from Ragil Valley and no one could tell her if Joseph and Mrs Bolton were still at the farm or how the Aimsleys were. From the marketplace she could see the range of small hills standing between the town and the Valley. Even the higher peak that cast the evening shadows over her old cottage was clear in the afternoon sunshine, as was the fold next to it that gave the view from the Grange across the Cheshire plane. The range of the Pennines behind them, which of course included both Quarry and Leckon Moors, dwarfed those nearer hills. Seeing them in the distance triggered in Helen a nostalgic longing to walk through her lovely valley again.

The sketchbook had little use. She attempted a few sketches and paintings but the town and buildings failed to stimulate her. After that visit to the market, however, Helen returned there to sit on a low garden wall to sketch that scene with the hills towering behind the houses and the church tower. Somehow her beloved hills grew out of proportion, dominating the picture to the point of distorting it.

The fun side of living in town was that there were plenty of other children to talk to or to play with. Not that Helen played much. Perhaps because she had grown up with older people, many of the childish games seemed silly. Christmas was fun though; the

Buxton's really made her feel that she was one of the family and Lisa and Hector next door were equally good company.

Heavy rain in January caused flooding in the lower part of the town with many houses damaged by the water. When it drained away a flood remained on a derelict area and after several nights of keen frost it froze over and remained frozen for several weeks. Local children congregated there after school and again after tea. Rooting out a pair of old skates that could be screwed on to the bottom of Helen's clogs, Mrs Buxton said, "These were mine but I never had much confidence and I don't fancy the bumps and bruises at my age."

"I never had a pair of skates," Helen said. "I don't know how to use them."

Mr Buxton laughed, "We'll soon cure that."

He held up his own skates, which were already fastened on the bottom of a pair of clogs. "I wanted an excuse to have a go again. It will be fun to teach you."

Although Mr Buxton still insisted Helen came back to work in the Garret after school, he knocked off from weaving half an hour earlier so that they both could go and join in the fun.

He proved to be really good at skating. Taking one of her hands in each of his he skated slowly backwards. At first Helen just held her feet in line to glide after him. After a few minutes Mr Buxton demonstrated how to take a step and then, holding her hands again, encouraged her to do the same. After several uncoordinated attempts it suddenly clicked and Helen swept forward, crashing into him. He clasped her firmly in his arms intending to steady her while she found her balance but Helen, feeling his coarse tweed overcoat pressing against her chest and face, panicked. It was as though Uncle Horace was thrusting against her and this time she was determined to fight him off. Not understanding what it was about, Mr Buxton held her more firmly trying to reassure her but it was only when she fought free and collapsed onto the ice that her panic subsided.

After that he just held her hand and skated alongside and within a short time she was away. Once Helen became steady on her skates, he went off to skate on his own, leaving her to enjoy the company of the other younger people.

It was an exhilarating evening out in the frosty evening air. Back in the warmth of her bedroom sleep came quickly – and then the nightmare came. It had been a couple of months since the last time but it was still as terrifyingly real. Clamped in the arms of Uncle Horace, she struggled but couldn't move and his leering eyes were within inches of her own and his coarse tweed trousers thrust hard against her naked hips. As always, her struggles woke her. Though sweating and panting with fear Helen knew that she had not screamed because no one came to give comfort. It was her nightmare and too personal to share with anyone else.

The work in the Garret carried on as usual. Helen heard the Buxtons discussing the Master but as he only came occasionally, and that when she was a school, she no idea who he was. She became aware from those conversations that they both respected and feared him. Not just their jobs but also the tenancy of their home depended on his satisfaction with their work.

When summer holidays came Helen was pleasantly surprised that the Buxtons didn't make her work all the time. They gave her a few hours during the day to herself. On market day she walked round the many stalls and, although there were a few villagers, there was no one from the farm. Much as any news from the Valley was of some comfort, her longed-for chance to visit never arose. The Sunday school Helen had to attend each Sunday morning did organise two day-trips but, as neither went into the hills, her picturesque valley and the people in it were becoming a nostalgic memory.

To try to retain the scenic pictures in her mind, Helen often walked to where there was a view of the hills between the house roofs and smoke-grimed factories. There, in her imagination, she was again tickling trout with Grandpa or up on Quarry Moor listening to the curlews among the heather.

Saying something about her nostalgia for her green homeland valley over tea one night got an unexpected response from Mr Buxton. "It might be too far to walk back there but we could go for a walk along the canal towpath. It's not far away and we'd soon be out among the fields."

Helen remembered seeing it years before from the back of Bob Fairclough's wagon. It lay above the town and on the outskirts as they dropped down from the hills on market day. "Oh, could we, Mr Buxton? Can we go this Sunday?"

Sunday was a bright late summer day. "Just the weather for an afternoon stroll," Mr Buxton said as they leaned over the stone bridge watching the boat traffic for a few moments before setting out along the towpath.

"Is it always this busy on a Sunday?"

"The 'Bargies' don't work for a wage, they work for themselves and a barge standing still is earning nothing. Anyway, you can hardly call it work just sitting watching the scenery while the horse takes the strain."

They had not walked far along the towpath before Helen realised just what an assortment of horsepower there was to do that work. They ranged from heavy horses down to light ponies. A couple of mules and even one donkey could be seen in the distance. Some of these motley mixture were tethered along a wider verge near the first lock and close to where several barges were moored; the rest were dotted along the towpath between this lock and the next one and even further on. Mr Buxton pointed to the lock. "This is the first for many miles coming from the North but, as you can see, it is the first of a run of locks going south."

There was one elderly lady sitting in a rickety-looking chair on the towpath with about half a dozen scrawny hens scratching in the longer grass between her and the hedge. With her four knitting needles clicking away faster than the eye could see, she looked up and gave Helen a long stare. "Are yer having a Sunday afternoon stroll then, duck?"

Mr Buxton laughed, "You come from Biddulph, then?"

"Yer can guess by my accent then, duck. Arr, we did once."

With a bit of encouragement she explained, "We had a small rented farm up on Biddulph Moor only we wer scratting about like them hens trying to make a living."

Pausing to change to the next needle, she continued, "Then one night he wer in'pub when a bargie got drunk an sold him his barge."

There was another pause while she changed needles again and then, with a deep-throated chuckle, she pointed to an old chap leaning against the lock gates puffing at his pipe. "He came home an sold our two cows an a few bits an pieces to th'neighbour to pay for the barge an by daybreak th'following day we'd hitched th'old horse to the boat an wer on our way."

There was another deep-throated chuckle and a change of needles. "Rent wer due so we had to go in a bit of a rush, like. Any road, that's how I come to have a few old hens; I just put em in a sack and brought em along. Mind yer, these aren't em - we ate em years ago."

Tearing her eyes away from the clicking needles and the fast-lengthening sock, Helen looked at the barge tied alongside. It was beautifully painted a pale-green with long curving red streamlines and golden castles and red roses on the cabin sides. It was a completely new experience for her; there had been no canals at Flacton and the few times she had crossed the bridge over this one she had perhaps been too young to really notice it. Now the colour and the movement of horses, dogs and people filled her with excitement. Oh, how she wished she had brought her sketchbook.

When Helen was walking away she heard the old lady say something about being held up because a gate had jammed a few locks further down. But it did not matter to Helen; the scene was perfect. She stood by the lock looking down the canal. Four boats were tied up between her and the next lock and four more between the next two. They all looked to be decorated with the same symbols. It seemed that each one must have had at least two dogs because, perhaps excited at being let free from the barge, there seemed towards a dozen chasing each other in and around the tethered horses and mules. Most of the men had walked down to where the gate was jammed but there were women working on some of the barges. Some just nodded but one paused from draping her washing over the cab. "Hello, duck, yer fancy being a bargie then?"

Helen said, "It looks a colourful way of life."

"I reckon it is but if yer going to do it yer mun choose a man yer get on with because yer too damn close together in this little boat if yer don't. I'm glad to see the back of my b***** for an hour."

It was two weeks later when the sunshine encouraged Helen back to the canal. Mr Buxton had told her not to go on her own so she asked Lisa to go with her. They were leaning on the canal bridge parapet when Lisa realised how far it was to the nearest boat. "I'm not walking all that way; if you want to go to those locks you can go on your own."

Helen watched her departing back for a few moments before turning to stride down onto the towpath.

By a strange coincidence the same old lady was again sitting out on the towpath. The socks must have been finished because two large needles were clicking halfway down what looked to be the front of a jumper. The same hens scratched round the old horse, which stood sleepily on three legs. "Have you been here all the time?"

"No, duck, we're on our way back but he likes th'beer in yon pub."

There was another barge moored below the locks so Helen walked down to look at it, realising how good the scene looked. Smoke curled up from the chimneys of both barges, with hens, horses and a dog alongside the giant lock gates and the second boat in the foreground. Walking a few yards further down the canal she sat on the warm, dry grass and began to sketch.

A youth jumped out on to the towpath and walked over to her. Looking at the sketch he said, "You have to pay if you want to draw my boat."

"I'm just sketching the scene, it's fascinating. I'm interested in everything about the barges."

"Would you like to come on board to have a look around?"

Wanting to see inside a barge, Helen was just hesitating whether to or not when the old lady waddled breathlessly down the path. "No, duck! Yer wer going to have a cup of tea on my boat when yer'd done yer sketch weren't yer?" Then she said to the youth, "Yer get back on yer barge and leave her alone."

The youth swore at her but went back on board. She said to Helen, "He's a wrong un, duck. If he'd got yer on board he'd have cast off and gone with yer, and yer wouldn't have been the first one."

Not having time to really paint, Helen just dabbed in some of the colours hoping to finish it at home that night. There was a cup of tea waiting for her at the old lady's barge and over it she was told about some of the worst characters that made a living on the barges. It destroyed most of the romance that had built up in her young mind.

Chapter Nine

The months seemed to fly and before Helen realised it the school had broken up for Easter. By summer it would be two years since haymaking at Flacton and the memory of Uncle Horace. Though the nightmares came less often they could still be triggered. It only needed the smell of beer and in the early hours of morning that smell of beer would be on his breath in her dream as she silently fought him off. The strange thing was that a couple of times after a nightmare Helen checked with Mrs Buxton if she had heard anything in the night and she hadn't. It was obvious that, terrifying as they were, she still remained silent and because of that never told anyone about them.

It was on the last day of that school holiday when she overheard a conversation while she was quietly winding silk. It being a two-man job to enter the warp into the loom, the two weavers worked together to help set up each other's looms. Considering that it took four or five days just to enter the warp threads on one loom, it gave them a chance to talk. Mr Gridley said, "I wonder how much longer we'll be doing this together? They reckon he's closing all the other Garrets so I reckon that he'll move us as well."

"Well, he's said nothing yet and we're supposed to be his best weavers," Mr Buxton argued. "Perhaps we can persuade him we'll do a better job here than in his new mill, but he's been more difficult for a couple of years now."

"Ah, well it's since his wife lost that baby and moved back into town."

"She didn't like the farm life but he must because he still goes up there without her each week end."

"Eh – an he still visits that widow in the next street one or two nights a week so I reckon it's not just living on the farm that she's said no to," Mr Gridley chuckled.

Hearing that conversation, Helen realised the Master could be the same tall, gruff man who had helped her some years before but, try as she might, she couldn't remember his name. She knew that Lisa was not just a gossip but also an avid listener to other people's conversations so Helen asked her if she knew anything about the Master. Lisa said, "Not much. I just heard that he moved his wife onto a farm in the hills when she was expecting a baby. Something went wrong and he drove off to get a doctor, but it took too long and she lost the baby."

"How terrible! But what happened next?"

"When she got better she moved back into town and people say she has never been back there again."

"But what's this about a widow?"

"Oh, I thought everyone knew about that. When one of his weavers died a few years ago old Mainthorpe moved his young widow into a small house further down our street."

"Well, what's wrong with that because he would want the Garret for another weaver?"

"Yes, but he visits her a couple of times a week and you must know that's not just to collect the rent?"

The Buxtons allowed Helen to continue with her reading, which meant that she was worldly wise enough to know what was implied but she found it hard to believe. Deciding to find out if the Master was in fact her tall, gruff man before admitting to anyone that she might know him, Helen said, "If you know what night he comes, I'd like to hide and watch."

The following Thursday night the two girls stood in a dark doorway near to the widow's house. It was a cold night with the east wind funnelled down the street chilling the two girls but it was worth the wait because, sure enough, a car pulled up. There was just enough light from the two gas lamps at each end of the short street for Helen to believe she recognised the limp and the dark moustache but of his features she could see so little that she was still unsure.

Lisa said, "There he goes again cheating on his wife. Mum says that all men would cheat on their wives if they could afford to. And he can afford it. You should see how many new dresses she has."

Helen protested, "But if his wife won't live with him at the Grange perhaps it's understandable."

"He's not at the Grange now, he's here in Fletchfield and his wife's in a big house just a few streets away."

Helen stayed quiet.

Jim's health didn't improve and his doctor finally advised him to take an open-air job, which left Mr Buxton short of a draw boy. Helen was now fourteen and as children were legally allowed to work part-time from the age of twelve it was suggested that she took time off from school to help out. Mr Buxton said, "You can have the job full-time when summer holidays come. I'll pay you the going rate."

"If I am going to earn a wage then I want to pay for my board. How much will it be, Mrs Buxton?"

"You don't have to pay me yet, child, not until you leave school properly."

"I know what the going rate is for board and lodging so if you are going to argue I'll just pay you that."

"But there won't be much left from what Mr Buxton pays you."

Helen smiled to both of them. "I know, but you've both been so good to me that I'm determined to at least pay my way from now on."

Mrs Buxton hugged her. "Oh Helen, Helen, the pleasure's been ours. You've more than paid us both with the work and the fun you've given us."

It was soon after this that she again overheard the two weavers talking. "They say the Master's closed all the other Garrets now; he'll close ours too."

"Maybe not. We've always done his specials; perhaps he'll let us be."

"No, this Garret isn't high enough to take his new looms and he reckons the work's too uneven with our old looms using a draw boy. I reckon he'll make us move to his mill or we'll not work at all – and it's his house we live in."

They were each just finishing a new and intricate pattern. Mr Buxton's was still on the loom but Mrs Buxton was spreading Mr Gridley's on the shiny picking table for Helen to pick over when she glanced out of the window. "Well, you'll soon find out because the Master's here."

Within a minute or two Helen heard heavy footsteps on the wooden stairs and then he was striding across the room. "Let's have a look how you've got on with the new pattern, Buxton."

Recognising the limp, Helen moved away to the end of the room to where she had left her sketchbook. Except for that night in the dark, she had never seen Mainthorpe since moving away from Leckon cottages and other than a few more grey hairs he looked just how she remembered him. Watching him bending over the silk, closely examining the weave, she instinctively reached for her sketchbook. Suddenly he straightened up and pointed down. "This isn't right. Look here, you've got this wrong." Both Mr Gridley and Mr Buxton crowded close to look down. Before they could say anything Mainthorpe said, "That's it then. I can't afford these mistakes; you're both coming into the mill. Once the cards are punched out on those new jacquard looms you can't get it wrong."

Mr Buxton protested, "We've always done you a good job, Master, and we're our own bosses in here. We prefer it this way."

"What you prefer doesn't matter. I need the silk up to my standard and in my mill everything is under my control. Anyway, you'll still be on piecework so you'll still be free to come and go and you won't nccd to pay a draw boy."

Helen sketched away as the argument went back and to but Mainthorpe was the boss and the weavers finally had to accept his decisions. Mr Buxton said, "All right, I agree, but what about my draw boy? She leaves school this summer and I've promised her a full-time job."

Mainthorpe looked up and, seeing Helen for the first time, froze. Not that he would have recognised her tall and now shapely figure but those eyes – they were unforgettable. He walked uncertainly towards her. "It's Miss Helen, isn't it? What . . . er . . . how do you come to be here?"

"I been here nearly two years. I live here now and help Mr Buxton."

Regaining his composure, Mainthorpe turned to Mr Buxton. "Do you want to explain?"

"There was some trouble with the uncle. We don't talk about it but it was decided that she should live elsewhere and we were the lucky people. Do you know her then, Master?"

Mainthorpe was not going to explain himself to a mere employee so he picked up Helen's sketchbook and again was silent for a few moments. The top sketch was the detailed scene that had just happened, where he was leaning over the loom while Mr Buxton worriedly stood by. "Did I look this angry?" When Helen smiled he looked at Mr Buxton and said, "And you looked this worried?" Mr Buxton still looked worried.

"I suppose you've every right to look worried because you have to buy that length of silk now it has a fault, and it will cost you more than a week's earnings. Though it might not be a bad idea to make your wife a new blouse because in the mill you'll be working on ties."

"I would like to buy it, Sir, if I may," said Helen. "It's such beautiful material."

Mainthorpe, who was still looking through the sketchbook, smiled. "And I know you can afford it but that doesn't settle your future. Have you any thoughts about just what you would like to do when you leave school?" When she shook her head without replying he continued, "There's a three year course starting at the Art and Design College later this summer. Looking through your book, I think it might suit you. Would you like to go?"

"I would but if I'm not working I can't afford to pay for the college. Anyway, if I'm not working for Mr Buxton I'll have to get a full-time job so that I can pay for my board and lodgings."

"I've been looking for a suitable art student to sponsor on condition that at the end of the three years they work in my design department. Would that interest you?"

Helen asked a few questions about the course and Mainthorpe explained that it was particularly designed to prepare students for the silk industry but it also covered cotton, and students were taught general subjects as well as art and design. He would pay for the course and give her an allowance that would cover her living expenses.

When he had gone Mr and Mrs Buxton asked a whole string of questions as to how she knew the Master. Helen just said, "He helped when my Grandpa collapsed. He brought the doctor and after Grandpa died he bought my things and gave me some advice."

When she would not add to that explanation, Mrs Buxton said, "I can't believe that he's going to pay for you right through college."

Mr Buxton said, "And you a girl too."

"And why not?" Mrs Buxton said. "It's time girls were allowed into that college. Anyway, they took a girl on last year but she dropped out before the end of the year so Helen won't be the first. But I don't understand why he is doing it."

"What I don't understand," Mr Buxton said thoughtfully, "is why a full-time student? He's never done that before. He's had apprentices but they've had to study at night and work hard for him through the day. So why has he chosen you?"

Mrs Buxton picked up Helen's sketchbook. "Perhaps this is why. I've been telling you how good she is."

"There's more to it than that. What aren't you telling us?"

Helen smiled and shook her head. "There is no more to tell."

It was obvious that they thought there was and were disappointed when she wouldn't say more about her meetings with the Master. But they readily agreed to Helen becoming a paying lodger.

What none of them knew was that Mainthorpe had recently become a Governor and was well aware that with the decline of the silk industry student numbers were falling and would fall more. By widening the course into more general art and design and admitting girls, he believed the college could attract more students. He was determined to set an example by bringing in a girl and one who he was confident would stick the tough course through the full three years.

Chapter Ten

Students came from a wide area. Five or six who were from the industrial towns on the other side of Manchester found lodgings in the town while many others from the nearside of Manchester commuted by train each day.

The full-time students studied English language, business and general economics. Nature and the natural designs within it featured strongly in the art course work.

The college courses were still based around the silk industry. Not that all the students were going to work with silk, but silk in its different forms was the basis of the town's wealth and it was the owners of the silk mills who, when the industry was far more powerful than now, had put the money up to start this college in the first place. They had needed men to come into the industry who understood both cloth construction and the weaving process in order to design suitable patterns. It was very much based on a fundamental principle of the arts and crafts movement, which was to strengthen the link between artist and craftsman.

The college had attracted students from the cotton industry for a good many years because, of course, there was much in common. Mainthorpe still wove his designes but others used prints and methods of printing cotton were basically the same as for silk. Now the wider curriculum attracted general art students but Mainthorpe's fellow governors still insisted that the work be mainly based on silk. Not that he argued against that too much.

And so Helen learned to be familiar with the mechanics of the loom in order to understand both its limitations and its possibilities. She was taught how weaving in different ways would change the texture, lustre, weight and pattern of each fabric. Working in the garret had given her a head start over many of the students but she was fascinated to find the effect produced through using a different weaving process.

Some of the students were local with family traditions going back several generations of working in silk. They spoke very much with a Fletchfield accent, while a few other locals were mill owners' sons with a private education that had erased their local accent.

From a small child either Helen's accent or just the fact of moving from school to school left her with a feeling of being an outsider. Now she felt part of this group more than at any of her schools. Even so, having mixed with older people throughout her life, she did not seem to have a lot in common with the more immature and frivolous of the youths.

The fact that Helen was one of only two girls among so many boys caused her few problems although a couple of the boys resented the presence of both girls and spoke derisorily to them. Perhaps the fact of being one of only two girls found Helen standing on the outside of the main group of students.

The other girl, Elizabeth, had been to a finishing school. She was older and gave the impression of being superior to Helen. Was it because she was older or maybe that she'd been to an all-girls school that Elizabeth seemed to need the approval of the boys? Whatever the reason, it took her into the main body of students where she revelled in their attention.

The feeling of being one of them but standing on the outside of the main group didn't worry Helen. Anyway, boys are boys and with her good looks some were soon hanging around. More than one tried to get serious but Helen, with the memory of Uncle Horace's coarse trousers pressing against her naked thighs, could not bear to feel any man standing against her. To save embarrassment, if any become over familiar Helen simply put them down with a smile. But there was one, Simon, who, because of a slight stammer and thick-lens glasses, had through school suffered his share of teasing and because of it didn't mix as freely as he might. It seemed natural that he and Helen should become friends.

With no silk industry background, Simon (whose father had recently bought a cotton mill) found it hard to learn the many different phrases. Although some phrases were the same in the manufacturing of both cotton and silk, others were confusingly different and Simon, embarrassed by his stutter, was reluctant to ask when he didn't understand. At those times Helen was able to help him. They had to learn a vast range of different names used for different printing techniques. And some of the earlier techniques had strange names like: 'tie-die', 'madder' and 'batik' confused her as much as the silk industry's names did Simon.

Visits to a real mill were an important part of the curriculum and of course Mainthorpe's mill was the nearest. Not that he was very pleased to have crowds of students interfering with the smooth running of his operation but, being a Governor, how could he refuse? To reduce the disruption the students were split into three groups, each of which went on a different day so as not to overcrowd the mill.

When Helen's group visited, Mainthorpe met them in the downstairs area where the designers worked. He greeted them in his usual gruff manner, made a little speech about the running of the mill and the importance of training, then with no more than a stern glance Helen's way handed them back to their tutor to guide them through the visit.

It was left to the tutor to explain how the imported skeins of silk were delivered dyed ready for the next process of 'throwing', which took place on the second and third floors. Throwing was the name given to the various processes from winding, cleaning, spinning and doubling as well as throwing. Helen was fascinated to watch one lady working a machine that wound 140 bobbins of silk at the same time, and at incredible speed. In the garret they had a little foot pedal machine to slowly wind just five. No wonder the Buxtons gave up using it and instead relied on the silk wound on this machine. She resolved to ask why a similar machine had not been developed to wind silk onto the pirns.

The machines for all this work were electrically powered but Mainthorpe believed the looms on the top floor created a better quality material when driven by hand or, more correctly, by foot.

Helen had been longing to see the weaving room on the top floor. Although Mr Buxton had described what it was like, when she entered it came as a shock to her. After the relative quiet of Buxton's garret the clatter of noise seemed unbearable. With about forty men and their looms in the one room and as many young girls and women watching for the broken threads, every bit of floor space was occupied. As well as the noise there was no fresh air. Mainthorpe wouldn't risk an open window in case it might let in soot from nearby chimneys, and with the looms packed so close to each other the air was stifling. While the students squashed in round one loom to watch it working Helen stepped back to observe the room as a whole. There were particles of fluff floating in the air in the garret but nothing like this. Here the view down the room was obscured by the density of the larger bits of fluff hovering and drifting in the air. Millions of smaller particles could be seen dancing where the sun's beams shone in through the large windows. Workers continually coughing and clearing their throats added to what was, for Helen, almost unbearable noise.

Although many women had in the past worked looms in the garrets above their own homes, Mainthorpe believed that in the mill they were better employed where they could use their nimble fingers. Older women worked on the picking tables on the fourth floor where the finished silk was then sorted by the most experienced into batches suitable for each customer.

It was only when they got back to the ground floor that Helen saw both Mr Buxton and Mr Gridley working with two others in a small room at the back of the mill. They had worked on the top floor at first but when Mainthorpe updated their looms he offered them the chance to work their own looms. As the last to be moved into the mill, though, they ended up in this small back room. Over tea one night Mr Buxton had told Helen how "the light's not good but it's quiet and peaceful compared to the bedlam on the top floor."

Leaning over his shoulder as he worked, Helen said, "I now understand what you meant about the bedlam up there and the peace down here."

In the design department Helen was fascinated. She watched four men all sitting side-by-side on high stools, each meticulously painting onto what looked like large sheets of graph paper. All the students were bubbling with interest but the tutor held up his hands to quieten them by saying, "You've already learned about point paper and that they are an enlarged scale drawing of the weave. Now you can see the designers meticulously hand painting in a design they previously created."

One student asked, "How long does it take?"

One of the men held up a much smaller, intricate design in one hand and the larger point paper in the other hand. "It will take me about two weeks to paint this in."

Just then Mainthorpe stepped in through the doorway, cleared his throat and looked at his watch. The tutor, jumping as though he had been stung, said, "We're not going to dwell here today because it will be next term when we cover this section in depth," and with that hurried them back to the classroom.

"Mother nature is the most artistic designer," the tutor repeated on numerous occasions and to prove it the college arranged an early summer field trip. The sun shone into the open-topped bus slowly grinding up the winding road towards the moors. They paused part way up to let the engine cool off.

"Look at the curving uniformity in ash tree leaves," the tutor said, stripping some from an overhanging branch and laying them to overlap on the road. This created a twirling pattern. As they all crowded round he pointed to the grey granite stonewall. "Now look at that wall. See how it's built in layers to create a completely different pattern of irregular straight lines. Although each layer is a different thickness, by the builder's skill they are all horizontal."

The engine suitably cooled, they drove on, passing the Black Grouse and dropping down the winding road to where the limestone began. It reminded Helen of that journey four years earlier when Bob Fairclough's open-topped lorry took her towards a new life. And it had been a good life despite what Uncle Horace had tried, because it was there she had been given her first sketchbook and that sketchbook had brought her here.

Her nostalgic thoughts continued when the bus stopped and they all climbed out to walk among the crumbling limestone rocks. Tramping across the firm green grass where wild flowers and the occasional butterfly reminded Helen of her wanderings through the fields in Flacton, the tutor tried to get everyone to study the completely different and very knobbly limestone walls.

The midday meal at the Black Grouse was basic bread, cheese and pickled onions followed by apple dumpling. After the meal the tutor told them, "You can have a couple of hours. Walk through the heather and along the walls. Sketch whatever takes your imagination. If it's a possible design so much the better. But stay in sight."

Simon followed Helen out onto the moor where she stood looking longingly towards Quarry Moor. "Wh-wh-what are you l-looking at?"

"That's where I was brought up. The cottage my Grandparents lived in is just beyond that moor."

Walking a little further, Helen said, "I could walk there and back in an hour."

"B-B-But w-we mustn't go f-far."

"I'm not asking you to come. I don't want to get you into trouble but I'm going to go," and with that Helen started to walk. Simon looked back hesitantly for a few moments and then ran to catch her up.

The footpath Helen set out on crossed Quarry Moor and went onto the field leading down to the bridge over Bullerstone

Brook. It would eventually join the path from the Grange down to Gritstencrag Church and of course the village. Not that Helen intended to follow it anything like that far. Once on Quarry Moor she turned off the path and headed across the open moor towards the top of the old Quarry behind what had been Grandpa's cottage.

"Eh, s-s-slow d-down. I'm n-not used to walking."

"I'm sorry, Simon. I didn't think. It's just that I want to see my old home again and if we are not back in an hour I'll get you into trouble."

When Simon caught up with her she set off again. They walked on the sheep paths through the heather where breeding lapwings rose high in the air and swooped down, noisily protesting. The haunting call of the curlews from nearby Leckon Moor brought nostalgic tears to Helen's eyes. Even a skylark hovered overhead to add his shrill voice to what seemed like a welcoming choir. Coming to the boulder where so long ago she sat to eat the remains of her fox-killed hen, Helen sat down to wipe a tear away. Simon flopped down beside her. "Wh-Why the tears?"

Telling him the story she added, "When we get to the edge of the moor over there we will be looking down at the two cottages. Then, mill owner's son, you will see what a humble background I come from."

"It's n-n-not wh-wh-where you come from that counts, it's wh-wh-where you're going that m-matters."

"Simon, that's kind of you, but where am I going to?"

"O-O-Over there," Simon smiled and pointed towards the edge of the moor.

They looked over the Quarry lip down at the cottages. Mrs Aimsley's washing hung out on the line and when Simon saw it he started to laugh. Helen asked him why but he was laughing so much he could only point. She said, "Oh those. She always made the children's undies and her drawers out of old cotton flour sacks. Her husband gets them from the farm and they've all got writing on. Grandpa used to say to Grandma, 'It's coarse-ground this week' because that was written on one pair and 'fine-ground' on the other. I used to think it funny but Amy, her daughter, was embarrassed when she saw them hanging on the line."

Simon was still laughing too much to speak and he was still chuckling when they knocked on the door and found no one in at either cottage. Having been out of touch for so long, Helen had not realised that with all her children now going to school Mrs Aimsley had taken a job cleaning at the Shooting Lodge and her daughter Amy had left the area. The Smith family in Helen's old cottage had no children and so Mrs Smith worked full-time in the mill in the village.

Walking out onto the lane Helen saw new limestone gravel glinting white in the sun. "When I left there were deep ruts where heavy rain had washed the gravel away. And, look, these walls were falling down and now they've been rebuilt."

"W-W-We ought to g-go back."

Looking past him up the lane, Helen exclaimed, "Oh no! Here's the Master coming. He would just have to drive out this way today."

Mainthorpe jumped out of the car looking more angry than usual. "What are you to doing here? You should be in college."

"We're on a field trip, Sir," Helen said.

"What, here at Leckon?"

"No. We were at the Black Grouse and I took the chance to walk across the moor to show Simon my old home."

"Well, it isn't your home now nor should you be here. If you're on a field trip at the Black Grouse then that's where you should be. I'm not financing you through college for you to go scrounging off whenever you get the chance."

Simon tried to speak but Mainthorpe cut him off. "I'm not speaking to you so you stay out of it." Then, indicating the car, he said, "Get in the back of here and I'll take you back. I'm going to have a word with that tutor."

Helen started towards the car but Simon, placing his hand on her arm, said, "You can have a word with whomever you like but we walked here and we're walking back, so good day to you, Sir."

Still holding Helen's arm he led her back past the cottage and up the path on to the moor. They reached the top of the Quarry before either spoke, then Helen said, "Simon you didn't stutter once Do you realise that you just told my boss off but you did it without stuttering."

A slow smile spread across Simon's face, "I did, but he asked for it."

Chapter Eleven

College life was so enjoyable that the months slipped by almost too quickly. There was a dramatic change in Helen's relationship with the Master after that confrontation on the field trip. Presumably he said nothing to the tutor because he made no comment about her and Simon's absence but what the tutor did say was that Mainthorpe seemed to be taking a greater interest in her studies and was asking questions about her activities out of college.

It was well into the autumn term when the tutor passed Helen a written note from the Master. 'Please come to my office on Thursday next after college.'

In his office Mainthorpe said, "Your three years in college is costing me a lot of money. Now I know from your tutor that your work is good but I don't want you spoiling it by having a silly romance."

"There is no romance! Simon and I are good friends. He wants to learn just as much as I do and with only one other girl there I have to mix with boys."

"You could choose that girl as a friend rather than hanging around with him all the time."

"I could not. I neither like her nor does she like me."

"Well, there are half a dozen girls on this year's course so you shouldn't feel so alone."

When Helen didn't reply Mainthorpe gave her a long, searching look before continuing. "All right, but I'm going to demand a little more from you here. College finishes an hour earlier than my workers in the mill so I want you to spend that hour watching how the various departments work. When the workers knock off on Thursday evenings you report to me in my office. I'll expect you to give a report on your week's college work. You start from tomorrow night in the mill and report to me next Thursday."

Each Thursday's session was quite an intensive interview lasting up to an hour. During it Mainthorpe expected Helen to relate the college work to what was going on in the mill. If he thought she was wrong he corrected her to the point of disagreeing with some of her tutor's ideas. Gruff and factual as Mainthorpe was, Helen never felt intimidated by him and he usually ended the session with a smile and a thank you.

Afterwards Helen went back to the Buxtons' for a late tea while Mainthorpe drove to the King's Head for a not too leisurely dinner, because Thursday night was one of the nights he visited the widow in the next street to where Helen lived. The surprising thing was that Mainthorpe never hid his visits but boldly drove up to the door and parked his car where all could see and, because most were his workers, they made sure they both saw and had a giggle behind his back.

Mixing on an equal basis with young people from different backgrounds helped Helen too grow in confidence and eloquence. In fact her speech, lacking the local dialect of many of her contemporaries, coupled with her now tall and graceful figure gave her an air of mature sophistication. It would have kept her outside the main student group if it were not for Simon. Since that confrontation with the Master on the field trip Simon had never stuttered. Occasionally there was a little hesitancy at the start of a sentence but somehow he managed to speak precisely in a way that bypassed it. Helen marvelled at the transformation in him. The shy boy who had hung back from mixing and seldom saying a word in class was now an assertive, natural leader. It was not clear whether Simon, who was a couple of years older than Helen, had joined the main group of students or that they had naturally collected around him but whichever it was it brought Helen into the group with him. Elizabeth, though, after several flirtatious affairs with different boys, had lost that sophisticated shine and without it she seemed a rather dumpy and plain girl. Attracting boys was easy when there were so many vying for her attention and perhaps this had gone to her head and yet, with the boys milling around her, Elizabeth still resented Helen. Mentioning it to Simon he said, "She's just jealous of you."

"Don't be silly. With her background and her schooling why should she be jealous of me?"

"Perhaps you should look in a mirror," Simon smiled. "You are everything that she's not and she hates you for it."

Used to admiring glances and lustful looks from many of the boys, Helen just took them as part of life. Even the Master, when she reported to him in his office, sometimes revealed his inner thoughts as she walked towards him but he quickly switched to business and never once made an improper suggestion.

The students were encouraged to take an interest in politics and there was political turmoil in parliament at the time. With the balance of power shifting between the three parties, the result had created three general elections in three years. In the first of those elections the Conservatives had gained power but without an overall majority. They were soon ousted and in the next election Labour gained so many seats that King George V asked their leader, Ramsay Macdonald, to form a government. The leaders of capitalism did not trust Labour and gave them an uneasy time. Eventually, after a series of scandals, in 1924 they were driven out of office. Though that happened prior to Helen entering college, the implications were discussed in depth and the policies of the new Conservative government led by Baldwin, with Churchill as Chancellor, were kept under observation.

The Conservative policies were creating an artificially high exchange rate, which drove the mine owners to reduce the miners' wages. When the miners went on strike, the TUC backed them and on May 5 the strike became general. There was not talk of a revolution, just solidarity with their fellow workers, but it took four million out on strike in support of the miners.

Although the unrest among the lead-miners had been obvious a few years earlier back in Flacton, then it had been a local thing; now this was nationwide. Just as agricultural wages had fallen, so had other wages. Although prices fell in line, leaving workers with much the same buying power, the effect created a feeling of unrest throughout the country.

Mainthorpe thought he was protected by having most of his weavers paid on piecework rates slightly above those negotiated with the Hand Loom Weavers' Association. Perhaps, too, because he had originally paid a slightly lower wage than some for those workers who were not on piecework and as a result he still maintained that rate. There was no real unrest among his employees and yet they walked out with the other mill workers.

The students were neither part of it nor fully understood the reasoning behind the strike. Mainthorpe was furious. His mill stood almost silent; almost but not entirely, for a few of his weavers braved the picket lines. Mr Buxton was one who was prepared to, saying to Helen, "We're self-employed and the Master's always been straight with us, so why try to bankrupt him?"

"If you go to work than I go in with you," his wife said.

The following morning Helen walked with them through the picket line. There was no violence just a bit of heckling. Perhaps the one that hurt Helen most was, 'With the boss's darling living with yer yer've got to crawl to him, haven't yer?'

There was an incredible atmosphere throughout the town. The students who travelled by train just didn't come because no trains ran; everywhere people stood about in little groups talking, and yet the mood was not nasty. Street sellers moved among them offering toffee apples and other goodies to the idle workers. Outside the mill an impromptu football match broke out in the street between the police and the strikers.

Surprisingly, within days more workers followed the Buxtons' example and returned to Mainthorpe's mill. Although the general strike lasted for nine days the mill was back to normal well before that.

From her meeting with the Master Helen learned of how the strike had damaged the country. Business throughout the industry had been flat for some time, increasing reliance on the Banks. Mainthorpe was sure that some mills would not reopen or would be so financially damaged that bankruptcies would follow.

What changed during those last few months before the strike was the way the interviews went during those Thursday night sessions. The Master began to discuss the more general running of the mill, showing Helen samples of his latest patterns and discussing market outlets and how he could improve his range of products. At first Helen had felt hesitant about making comments but gradually her confidence grew until she was making suggestions on an almost equal basis to him. Sometimes the discussions were so interesting that they continued on well over the original hour.

At one session just after the strike Mainthorpe said, "Two companies who buy from me are forcing the price down. Yet since the government slapped a duty on imports last year prices should really be going up. Both companies make scarves and ties and from what I can see are making a good profit. I'm thinking of having my own Making-up Department. Why don't I sell the finished article, my own range of ties and ornate silk scarves?"

"It sounds interesting but you're working to full capacity already."

"Yes, but that small cotton mill across the street has stood empty for a while. There's a good chance I can buy the building and the site behind it. I need to broaden my range and go into power looms. Those derelict buildings could be cleared to build a new factory to hold them."

"You've obviously thought it through so the sums must add up."

"I believe they do. Yes, but remember I don't want anyone to know what I'm planning. It's more than just clinching a deal on the building; I'll be going into competition with some of these companies I supply. If any get wind of what I'm planning they could cancel their orders before I'm ready."

Helen became completely involved in the discussion to the extent that it was well after seven o'clock when she arrived back at the Buxtons' for tea.

"Where have you been?" Mrs Buxton asked as she looked at Helen rather strangely.

"I . . . well . . ." Not able to say what the discussion had been about Helen flustered round for an answer. "He . . . he had some new patterns he wanted to show me and we got so involved that I didn't realise what time it was."

"Helen, you're not getting involved with him, are you? He's already got one mistress in the next street, I don't want him ruining your life as well."

Mr Buxton butted in. " What do you mean ruining her life? That woman dresses better than anyone else in either street and she's always got money when she goes into the shops. I reckon she knows a thing or two."

Mrs Buxton snorted, "You men . . . you would think that. Maybe you fancy doing the same thing, do you?"

"No love, you know I don't mean that," he laughed. Trying to break the tension, he added, "Anyway, he's going to be late tonight or go without his meal before he collects the rent."

The following day most of the students knew that Helen had stayed late in the mill and more than one made a bawdy suggestion as to why. Looking at her a bit strangely, Simon asked, "Do you want to tell me about last night?"

"I can't really say anything but it was nothing like they're suggesting. It was just that he wanted to discuss business."

"C-C-Come off it, Helen. He's not going to tell you his confidential business, so what were you doing?"

Helen didn't want Simon to think the wrong thing and, slightly flustered with embarrassment, said, "There's an empty building across the street. It might have given him ideas."

Simon gave a thoughtful look out of the college window. "What, that old mill? What could he want that for?"

The three years had sped by so quickly that the end came as a surprise. "What are we going to do?" Helen asked Simon. "I have a week off before I start in the mill and I want to do something interesting because I'm not sure that I'm looking forward to it."

"B-But it's what you've always wanted to do."

"Yes, but it's old Grimshaw who's head of the design department. I just don't get on with him and he makes it plain that he doesn't like me. I suspect he thinks that I'll tell tales to the Master."

Simon said, "I know one thing we can do. Father's loaned me his car as a reward, so how would you like to have a day out with me? You choose where we go."

"I've never been back to my grandparents' grave. Would you take me to Gritstencrag?"

"Of course I will. Afterwards we'll have a ride in the hills, p-perhaps into Staffordshire. I have always wanted to go there."

"Shall I make a picnic?" Helen asked.

"N-no I'll get cook to make one up; we may as well do it in style."

"You never say much about your home, Simon. Are your parents very well off with lots of servants?"

"Y-Yes I suppose they are. Although not always. It's just that Father did well out of some property deals. It was before he bought his cotton mill. I'd be about twelve when he bought a larger house, and I think I've just taken the servants for granted."

The mid morning sun was shining into their faces when Simon turned his father's open-topped car into Gritstencrag Lane. He pulled into a wide gateway while they both put on sun hats. "W.-Who lives here?" Simon pointed to the high stone wall and wrought iron gates.

"It's Lord Clayburn's shooting lodge. That's where Mrs Aimsley works. He doesn't live here all the time but comes for the grouse season and occasionally in the summer to fish for trout. Not that he fishes the brook –his father dammed a small stream to form a five acre lake," Helen laughed.

"Why are you laughing?"

"Because in those days Grandpa worked for the family and had to help, and from what he told me it took them most of the summer working with just spades and wheelbarrows."

Helen was still smiling. "It was backbreaking work so the men moved no more soil than they absolutely had to. Grandpa thought it would be washed away in the first winter's flood but it still there seventy years later."

"It's a shame all those trees block the view; I'd like to see it."

"It's a lovely stone house with lots of chimneys and large mullioned windows. You can see it clearly from off Quarry Moor. He owns both Quarry Moor and Leckon Moor. When he sold the Grange to the Master he kept the moors but allows the Master to graze his sheep on them."

"I'd like to have a look at it. Is there a path up without going through your old cottage garden?"

"Yes, it goes across the next field before we get to Leckon Lane. f you then go through Quarry Wood you climb up onto the moor where you can look down on to the shooting lodge. But if you want to do that I'd like to go to the graveyard first."

They drove into the village and parked by the Church. Simon walked with Helen to the grave then left her to shed a few tears in memory. It was a good half hour before she came back to where Simon waited by the car. "Let's have a walk through the village; there are so many people I'd love to see."

To Helen's surprise the bank was open and she went inside to inquire about her account. It had never been touched since Mainthorpe opened it for her all those years before and it was surprising just how much it had grown to. When she told Simon, he said, "Gosh, you could buy a terraced cottage with that. My father's just bought a row that have cost less than that each."

"Is he going to sell them again?"

"He hasn't said. Though I think he'll rent them out because he seems to be building up a rented property portfolio."

They wandered further down the street to the village shop. There were lots of people hanging about and few of them were faces Helen could remember. She didn't know the woman behind the counter but she bought a bag of sweets and asked, "Why are there were so many people standing about in the village?"

"Have you not heard, luv? The mill's closed, it's gone broke."

"Oh, no! Half the village worked there. How will they manage?"

"How will any of us manage?" the shopkeeper said. "I rely on what money they spend but they were daft enough to go on strike to support the miners and now we're all in trouble."

The two young people walked onto the bridge and leaned over the wall to watch the stream rippling on its way. "It's happening all over the country," Simon said. They went on strike for some noble ideal and now they're left with nothing. There'll be so many people out of work that wages will come down more yet, and more strikes won't get them anywhere."

Helen just watched the brook rippling on with a mixture of emotions – the joy of returning to the village she loved and the sadness of what she had learned.

Simon became excited when a kingfisher flew under the bridge. Helen said, "Aren't they lovely? They should still be feeding young but in a couple of weeks they drive the young away. It used to be fun just sitting on the bank watching them."

"Are those mayfly?" Asked Simon, pointing down towards the water.

"No. Mayfly are much larger. Those are Olives. Anyway, the mayfly season's over now."

"How do you know so much about wildlife?"

"Because this was my home and Grandpa loved it is much as I do. He used to take me for walks, but his old legs were so tired we spent most of the time just sitting and watching. I learned a lot just being with him."

They eventually walked to where the blacksmith was hammering at a horseshoe on the anvil. When the glowing red metal faded to black he thrust it back into the forge and looked up. Staring at them for a few moments, he said, "It's not Helen Brindley is it? Grief, girl, you've altered, but I'd know those eyes anywhere. Eh, and now you've got everything else that goes with em."

When they left the village Simon was still keen to go up onto the moor to get a view of the shooting lodge, so at his suggestion they carried their picnic up the field and through the wood onto Quarry Moor. Helen pointed to how the bluebell seed heads were dry and opening, tipping some of the seeds out onto her hand to show Simon.

Helen couldn't help remembering the last time she had picnicked up among the heather. Then she had held the carcass of that old hen in her fingers while she chewed the meat off the bones and thought through her future. Now out of Simon's basket came knives, forks, plates, exquisite sandwiches and dainty cakes. There was even a small bottle of wine and two glasses. She looked at it all and said, "Good gracious!"

"P-Papa says that it's no good working hard and making money if you don't use it, and our cook can certainly use it."

"But you haven't made it Simon. This is your father's money that's bought all this."

"Yes, but I am his only son and did I tell you? He's offered me a job as his assistant and he expects me to take a keen interest in the mill."

They were sitting on a mound of turf by a small round pond. Thinking that Simon would share her interest in nature, Helen pointed to both small tortoiseshell and large white butterflies when they flew past. When a small blue landed on the birdsfoot trefoil flowers just by them, Helen got excited and jumped up to take a closer look. Later, gasping at thc bcauty of a dragonfly that settled on rushes at the edge of the pond, Helen said, "Look at that incredible colouring on its body. Its wings are so transparent that they are almost impossible to paint."

Simon had shown little interest in anything but when he saw the disappointment on Helen's face he managed to ask, "It seems unusual – a pond up here?"

"It was a bell mine. Grandpa used to get his coal out of here when he was first married. It was already opened when he came to the cottage so he worked it for a few years, but when the landlord opened the coalmine on the other side of the moor he made the estate tenants buy their coal from his mine."

"What do you mean by a bell mine? I've never heard of one."

"Grandpa explained it to me. The coal seam was only about 18 inches deep but it lay about nine feet down below this black shale." Helen touched a patch of the shale where it was exposed on the edge of the bank.

"H-How did they get to it, then?"

"They a dug a central shaft down and when they reached the coal they just dug outwards leaving the walls sloping up like the sides of a bell. We're sitting on some of the black shale that they dug out to get at the coal."

"Why couldn't they just buy the coal?"

"They were hard times. Though Grandpa wasn't too worried when the estate stopped him because his was already filling up with water. He told me that he must have dug close to an underground spring because it soon filled right up. Then gradually through the years the sides fell in taking with them quite a bit of the rubble they'd dug out and thrown on the bank. There are a few more dotted about on this side of the moor. They've all fallen in but most of them are just dry holes."

"What happened to the landlord's coalmine?"

"It was where my dad worked. I don't know much about it because it closed two or three years before I left but I seem to remember that as they tunnelled further this way the seam became too shallow to be worth working."

Detecting a look of boredom on Simon's face, Helen lay back on the bank, closed her eyes and was drifting off in the warmth of the sun. Without warning Simon rolled against her and kissed her. Relaxed and enjoying the day so much, she let him kiss her again. Suddenly his hands were searching her body and his knee was pushing between hers. The horror of Uncle Horace panicked Helen so much that she pushed him away and angrily jumping to her feet. Striding to where there was a view of the shooting lodge, she pointed. "Look, that's what you came to see. Take a good look at it and take a good look at me because when you get me back to Fletchfield you go your way and I go mine."

Simon tried apologising but Helen was so angry she refused to speak to him. There was no way for her to explain that attempted rape, how if any man pressed his body against hers it would trigger memories that inevitably ended with a nightmare of being vulnerable, naked and mesmerised by Uncle Horace's evil eyes.

They had travelled a few miles down the road before Helen realised that it was all a bit silly. That the nightmare would come there was no doubt, but it wasn't Simon's fault. Why shouldn't he want to kiss her – and, after all, did she not kiss him back? "Simon, I'm sorry. I have enjoyed today. It's just that I had a bad experience once, and anyway I value your friendship but I don't want it to go further."

Simon drove on in silence.

Chapter Twelve

Much as this was her dream job, the months did not fly. In fact, thanks to old Grimshaw after the first few weeks of excited anticipation they began to drag.

There was a calendar hanging on the wall in the design room. Helen looked at it and thought, "Grief! I've been here eight months! I'm eighteen and for eight tedious months I've done the mundane fetching and carrying for old Grimshaw and I've yet to submit even a sketch for his approval."

The fact that the mill workers were always so nice made work acceptable, though Helen modestly thought it was more that they felt grateful to Mr Buxton for leading them back to work, which in turn created a feeling of goodwill towards all in the Buxton household. The legacy of the strike in many local industries was redundancies and reduced wages whereas Mainthorpe still held their rates of pay steady. Mr Buxton was better educated than most of his fellow workers and, without him wishing it, they looked up to him and saw him as a leader. Helen was convinced, and had told Mainthorpe so, that the Buxtons' walking openly to work that morning had done more to break the strike than anything he had done.

Grimshaw's inability to get along with women was not a new thing. He was without doubt an exceptional senior designer but he seldom had to deal with women. In fact, Helen was the first woman he had actually worked alongside, and he made it clear he hated it. Some said he had been jilted as a young man and if that was the case, Helen decided, it had turned him into a woman-hating bachelor. On top of that it seemed that he thought she was the Master's pet and seemed determined to grind her out of his life. "And he's doing a good job," Helen said running up the stairs to the top floor for the third time in an hour. "At least it's keeping me fit."

On the way down she met the Master. "You seem to run up and down the stairs a lot," he observed. "What are you doing this time?"

When Helen explained he grunted derisorily. Turning to go on his way, he stopped. "How's your art coming on? When am I going to see one of your creative designs on my desk?"

"Mr Grimshaw wants me to get a sound grounding in the department before I touch a paintbrush."

"Does he now?"

It was then that Helen realised just how often the Master had been around in the last few days, sometimes just looking in through the door of the design room, at other times standing watchfully about the mill, but each time she was aware that he had seen her. There had been no Thursday night meetings since college finished; she presumed that the Master valued Mr Grimshaw's work so much that he wasn't going to interfere in the smooth running of the design division in his mill.

It came as a complete surprise on the following Thursday when the Master stepped into the design room and said, "Mr Grimshaw, I'd like Miss Helen to stay behind tonight. I've something I wish to discuss with her."

Grimshaw didn't like it. He scowled, he growled and found even dirtier tidying up jobs for her to do, but at knocking off time he had to go home, leaving her in the design room.

It seemed strange to Helen to be sitting there when everyone had gone. Used to the hum, the noise and the vitality of the building, now as the last workers left on their way home it seemed as cold and lifeless as a corpse.

When Mainthorpe strode in Helen noticed as she jumped to her feet how his limp seemed to become more pronounced towards the end of each day. When he perched on one of the high stools and indicated another, she tentatively sat down again. "This isn't working, is it?" Mainthorpe said, looking at her appraisingly. "I can understand Grimshaw being a bit suspicious about your relationship with me but I haven't invested in your education to have you running about with messages."

Unsure of what to say, Helen remained quiet. Mainthorpe reciprocated and there was a strange, almost smouldering silence hanging between them while he studied her. Helen met his gaze but it was hard to read his expression behind that bushy moustache. She noticed there were now more grey hairs, and Helen wondered if it was the moustache that added to his reputation of being gruff. Fidgeting on his stool, Mainthorpe said, "I've missed our Thursday night meetings. It may seem strange to you but I need to be able to talk through my plans with someone sensible. It doesn't do to share my thoughts with my manager until I'm clear as to what I am going to do, and as regards the bank manager –" He dropped into another reflective silence.

Helen said, "Surely you can discuss things with your bank manager?"

"You might think that, yet he was the only person with whom I discussed my ideas for the building across the street. I thought I ought to warn him about my plan to expand into both power looms and a making-up department and would you believe it – just when I got the price down to where I wanted it someone jumped in and not only bought the building but they've now had the cheek to offer me a lease on it."

Helen had a horrible thought about Simon's father and his investments in property. "Who bought it?"

"The offer's from a Stockport property company. Mind you, they've agreed to clear the site behind the mill to build the factory and do the alterations I want. Although the rent they are asking is high I think it's manageable. Still, I suppose I might get it down a bit before I sign up but I can tell you I'm really angry. It's not just that I prefer to be my own landlord; property is a good investment."

He chuckled for a moment. "Anyway, the bank manager hasn't told them everything because, though they know about the power looms, they've presumed I'm just putting in more hand looms on the top floor of the old mill."

When Helen remained quiet Mainthorpe slapped the desk. "Oh, forget it. I can't accuse him of it or I'll get nowhere with him in future. Look, I'm going up to the Grange tomorrow afternoon to meet the builders. I should be back by early evening. How about coming with me? We could talk on the way and you'll enjoy it because, as you well know, spring at Leckon Grange is beautiful and Master Joseph tells me the first lambs have arrived."

"Aren't they early? They didn't used to lamb until well into April."

Mainthorpe laughed. "Yes, well, Master Joseph bought two young tups and like most things Master Joseph does it was a month ahead of tupping time. Anyway, he shut them in the building overnight and the next morning they were gone. They found them up on Leckon Moor with the ewes and, seeing that it was midday before they caught them, Joseph reckons there could be 50 or 60 ewes in lamb. Anyway, I don't think we need to worry because the weather is very mild for mid-March."

"I was old enough when I left the valley to know it can change overnight."

At the end of the Friday morning shift Helen returned home to have a snack and change out of her working clothes. She was still buttoning up her dress when the car horn sounded outside. Within a minute Helen was in the car and Mainthorpe was heading out of town. "I don't suppose Mr Grimshaw liked you having a half day off?"

Helen mimicked Grimshaw's voice. " 'No one has a half day off without a good reason.' Then when I wouldn't tell him why he was furious, so I just walked out."

"I'm sorry, I should have told him. I'll have a word with him tomorrow."

Realising that it was a different car, Helen said, "This is luxury. Aren't these seats comfortable?"

"Yes, it's a Riley. Seeing that I travel back and to a couple of times each week I thought I'd have a bit more comfort – and it doesn't rain in."

They both had a good laugh at the memory until Helen remembered Grandpa and went quiet. Not being warm enough to have the hood down Helen settled back to enjoy the scenery through the window. It was too early in the year for there to be leaves on the trees but buds were swelling with the promise of spring. Here and there on the sloping meadows and in some places along the roadside the leaves of wild primroses showed green among the winter-yellowed short grass. Helen remembered riding in the back of Bob Fairclough's open-top lorry a little later in spring and seeing how in places the bank sides were draped a creamy white. In a sheltered hollow a large thicket of blackthorn, just coming into full flower, caught Mainthorpe's eye. He pointed. "Those white flowers herald snow according to Joseph. Have you heard the saying?"

"Grandpa used to say that you could never rely on spring until the blackthorn flowers were over. Do you believe in these old sayings, Master?"

"There has to be something in them but discussing them isn't why I asked you to come with me. I'm meeting a builder about the Grange. I've discussed it with Joseph, in fact it's more his idea that mine. He's convinced our farm is too high above sea level to grow cereals successfully so we're thinking of extending the buildings to house more dairy cows. It will be a lot of expense just when I am going to develop the manufacturing side of my business. By the way, I've signed the lease on that mill this morning but I had to pay a year's rent in advance to clinch it."

"You won't be able to keep it a secret much longer."

"No, but we'll just let people think I'm extending my weaving capacity. Anyway, that rumour's already out in the trade. I don't know how it's got around so quickly; I've already had some second-hand looms offered. In fact I think I might go and look at them, if only to keep the rumour going. "

"Perhaps it is a good idea to show an interest. But about the farm Master – you mentioned not growing cereals. Don't you need both grain and straw for the cattle?"

"Well yes, that's how we've always farmed but Joseph's convinced me that with modern motor lorries we can easily transport in what we need from arable farms down on the Cheshire plain."

Helen thought about her visits to the market and how it was noticeable that there were more farmers with cheese for sale than there had been when she visited it with her Grandpa. Among them was Joseph's brother Joel, now engaged and on that occasion selling his future father-in-law's cheeses. When Helen asked him why they still made cheese he said, "Phoebe's people used to make cheese. They stopped for a few years but about the time I joined them the dairy they supplied got a bit difficult so we started up again."

"How do you mean, difficult?"

"I think they were over-supplied because not only did they drop the price but occasionally they found some excuse to reject the milk and send it back."

Pointing to his cheeses he added, "Between you and me, these thin cheeses are not the best but that's what we're set up for and the locals seem to like them."

Quoting that conversation to Mainthorpe, Helen asked, "Are you sure you can sell your extra milk, Master?"

"Yes, things have moved on since you left. Bob Fairclough has a larger wagon now and he takes milk from most of the valley farms into Manchester each day, and I know the dairy owner we supply."

"But can you trust him?"

Mainthorpe laughed. "I'll have to take you with me next time I go to see him, then you can tell me if you think he's sincere. What he wants is for me to supply him with more milk through the winter months. He claims it's because many of the local farmers still keep the traditional spring calving herds and, as you well know, their cows are usually dry by Christmas."

The discussion died as Mainthorpe turned into Ragil Valley where Helen gazed wistfully out of the window. Not having been back since that visit with Simon she felt a childish urge to leap out of the car and run across the meadows in the spring sunshine.

A large sheepdog sat behind Joseph, who stood waiting in the farmyard. Greeting Mainthorpe respectfully, Joseph stared uncertainly at Helen. If Mainthorpe had not previously said that Helen was now working for him Joseph doubted whether he would have recognised her. As it was, when she stepped out of the car, he caught a glimpse of shapely legs between the top of her calf-length boots and her warm topcoat and didn't know where to look. The sheepdog, equally uncertain, slunk round the car and came behind Helen to sniff at her heels. Joseph was completely unprepared for the attractively mature young lady smiling happily at him. Seeing his embarrassment, Helen stepped forward to shake his hand with a smiling greeting. "Joseph, it's good to see you again."

Finding the large turquoise eyes of the once tubby young girl now almost level with his disconcerted Joseph even more, until Mainthorpe saved his embarrassment. "It's all right, Joseph. She has that effect on most men. You and I need to get down to business and discuss these plans again before the builder arrives. "

Joseph finally let go of her hand when Helen said, "If you don't want me, Master, I'd like to have a chat with Mrs Bolton and then walk down to the church to see my Grandparents' grave?"

"No, you go ahead but be back by about five o'clock; that should give us time to get home for dinner."

Mrs Bolton was so pleased to see Helen that she gave her a big hug and a big hug in Mrs Bolton's muscular arms was a bit breathtaking. With the kettle boiling on the hob it was hard to refuse a cup of tea. They chatted away like two teenagers, which amused Helen because the last time she saw the farmer's widow was when, as an 11-year-old, she drove the geese to the farm before leaving the valley. Then Mrs Bolton had come out to give her a gentler hug and wish her well.

To Helen's questions, Mrs Bolton told her how all the members of the family were, adding, "Joel's getting married this summer and lives with her folks now but I've still got four at home. Even Ned's still at home, though he's a builder now. It's his boss who's coming to see the Master today."

"What about the other three?"

"Anna still helps me in the house but she works in the Grange when the Master's staying here. Isaac works for Joseph. I think he's got a girlfriend, not that I've met her yet. Now Joseph, well Joseph just lives for his work."

"I expected Anna would have been married by now. She was always so thoughtful to me."

"Yes, well, she was engaged but the young man was killed. It was a runaway horse - it's rather sad because she hasn't found anyone else."

There was the obligatory tour of the newly refurbished house before Helen took leave and set off down the track towards the church. Where the field sloped more steeply the track reduced the slope by curving in an S shape, which created a steep bank on the upper side of those curves. On them, where the banks were shaded from the midday sun, wild primroses grew profusely, heralding spring by showing a touch of colour on the swelling flower bud tips. Helen gently stroked the silky leaves, knowing that within a few weeks they would hang down to the path like a creamy white curtain. She could hear the tutor saying, 'Patterns of nature', and he was right; there was nothing more beautiful. Seeing one clump on the lip of the bank, Helen looked for a tool of some sort. Finding a short length of branch, she used it to loosen its roots and carried it with her to the grave.

There was just a headstone inscribed to her Grandparents with the dates of their births and deaths but underneath, at Helen's insistence, the undertaker had carved 'and in memory of their son George who died July 1918 on active service in France'. She rooted with her stick by the headstone to make a small hole and, planting the clump of primroses in it, said, "You always loved them Grandma, and I always loved both you and Grandpa. I'm sorry I don't bring flowers like I should but these will be with you always."

Resting her hands on the cold headstone, Helen said, "This is my only memory of you, Dad. I wish I could have known you or just remember your face."

She took a different route back to climb more steeply up onto Leckon Moor. Helen met the chill as she walked into a stiff breeze that had developed while she was in the churchyard. Pausing on a high spot to enjoy the view of the valley, Helen heard the call of a curlew overhead and then another answered from further away; she almost danced with the pleasure of hearing their haunting spring call. She knew that they had probably only just returned from their wintering grounds and that it was still too early in the year for them to nest but Helen turned to follow their hovering flight. That was when she saw the dark clouds billowing up in the east. Though they were still some distance away they looked to be moving threateningly fast.

Such a strange sky would fascinate any artist. Dark, billowing clouds rolled across the hills from the East whilst from the West, shining brightly between scattered light grey clouds out of a blue sky, the sun cast her shadow on the hillside. Helen marvelled how it would make an incredible picture but doubted whether anyone would believe the sky could have such contrast.

Looking down towards the farm, Helen saw men working on a sheepfold next to the farm buildings and walked down off the moor towards them. The path took her across a pasture field where a small flock of sheep grazed. Their bodies were round and full, their udders tight and it was obvious they were heavy in-lamb. Then, to her surprise, in a sheltered spot by the wall one ewe was mothering two baby lambs and no doubt there would be more hiding in sheltered hollows elsewhere. One of these was so newly born that it was wobbling about too much to find his mother's milkbar. Helen stopped to watch for a few minutes before turning towards the farm.

Recognising Isaac and presuming that the other man was the shepherd, Tom Smith, Helen walk towards them. They had already made a row of small pens out of sheep hurdles to form one side of the sheepfold. Now they were busy covering them up by laying a hurdle across the top of each pen with the intention of tying straw battens over those hurdles. Greeting Isaac, she said, "This is a fancy sheep pen. I thought you used to lamb them in the fields?"

"Arr, we did but have you seen that?" Isaac pointed towards the billowing dark clouds. "Joseph predicted that this morning and set us to work because these sheep are due now."

"What, all of them now? You mean tonight?"

Tom Smith said, "Arr, all fifty-three of em. How about that in one night, lass? Just two tups, by that 'ud be a night to remember, eh?"

Not liking the way he had looked at her as she walked up, now Helen liked him even less when he finished the sentence with a lecherous wink.

Embarrassed, Isaac quickly explained, "The shippen wall should shelter the other side of the fold, then as the ewes lamb we can pop each ewe and lamb into these pens along this side. But we haven't much time because we must get them in here before dark."

Helen said to Tom Smith, "You throw some more battens on top and I'll tie them along this side while Isaac ties the other."

Handing his ball of string and penknife over to her, Tom Smith began to place the straw battens while Helen and Isaac worked along each side of the pens quickly tying them to the wooden hurdles. It wasn't easy though because if Tom let go of the battens before they had hold of them the gusty cold wind, driven ahead of the advancing low clouds, would sweep them away. Within minutes Helen could barely feel the string between her numb fingers. They were both engrossed with their work when Tom Smith said, "Eh, Isaac, you'd better look up at yon sky."

They both looked round to see the black clouds that had been billowing low over the hill was now almost above them. "Let's have them in quick," Isaac said setting off at a run. "You go that way and I'll go this." Then, looking back towards Helen, he shouted, "Maybe you can help turn them in when they come."

Knowing that they had no dog because ewes with new born lambs would turn and fight one off, Helen smiled at the men's noisy attempts to get the sheep moving when from behind Joseph's quiet voice startled her. "It's coming quicker than I thought. I reckon there's a couple of foot of snow coming our way and it's sure to drift so these shelters aren't going to save all our lambs."

"Why didn't you build this earlier? Anyway, I heard you had taken on another man; where is he?"

"The hurdles were only delivered yesterday and as to the other man, well, when the agricultural wages committee came in we were paying more than they recommended so last year the Master said I either drop the men's wages or stop a man."

The flock was getting closer so both Helen and Joseph spread out on the muddy field trying to guide the sheep into the fold. The wild hill ewes had other ideas and Helen found herself leaping one way and then the other with arms outstretched and voice screaming against the wind. Slowly the ewes accepted the inevitable but not without one or two last ditch attempts to escape past the outstretched arms.

Snowflakes were swirling past their faces as the sheep crowded into the fold. It took a lot of hand waving and shouting to get the last one or two wild hill sheep inside. Leaving Helen to close the entrance by tying two hurdles together, the three men ran back across the field in different directions to gather up newborn lambs. Within minutes they were coming through the swirling and thickening snowflakes, each carrying lambs with their mothers rushing round the men's legs bleating madly. This time it was Mainthorpe who walked up behind her. "Grief, girl, what have you been doing? Look at your clothes!"

Helen looked at her nice new winter coat. It was covered with bits of straw and the drifting snow in turn was covering that. And then she saw her boots. "No!" she exclaimed, lifting her calf-length dress and looking at the thick mud daubed right up her legs, even above the boots. "They were new! I can wash my legs but these will be ruined."

Looking appreciatively as her exposed knees, Mainthorpe said, "Well, you'll certainly have time to have a bath because we're not likely to be going anywhere tonight."

They left the men to pen the young lambs in with their mothers and walked towards the house.

"I thought you told me you already have some newborn lambs, but I haven't seen them."

"Joseph's got them in a loose box where they are snug and warm; there's enough in there though so I am not sure what he'll do when the pens in that fold get full."

Helen said, "He'll have some plan but it's going to be an awful night."

"I'll tell Mrs Worsley to run you a hot bath."

Helen had heard about his housekeeper and didn't expect her to be thrilled when told to run a bath for a mere mill girl. And Mrs Worsley wasn't. She glared at the muddy boots, at the snow and straw falling from Helen's coat and almost snarled behind the Master's back when he gave her the order. Not that Mainthorpe noticed because he was walking through the lounge towards the sideboard to pour himself a whisky.

Mrs Worsley vanished, leaving Helen to take off her soiled boots and coat in the outer kitchen before walking barefoot through to the lounge. Seeing the Master was preoccupied with the whisky decanter Helen took the opportunity to look round the room. Flames were leaping up from the logs in the fireplace, which was surrounded by an unusual pink stone that had an almost wood-like grain. On the deeply grained oak mantelpiece, expensive-looking ornaments reflected the light from two oil lamps suspended over the armchairs standing on either side of the fire. A matching settee stood with its back to Helen and dotted around were more comfortable chairs. Several landscapes adorning the walls caught her eye. Stepping closer to the larger one she read aloud the name, 'Gainsborough', and turned to find Mainthorpe standing by her shoulder. "Yes it is. Unfortunately it doesn't show up too well in lamplight but I hope by next year we should have electricity up here."

"I don't think I should be here with all this mud. Perhaps you should direct me to the bathroom."

Looking down as her muddy legs and bare feet, Mainthorpe said, "I'll get Mrs Worsley to look out a pair of Jessica's slippers. In the meantime – upstairs, turn left and it's the first on the right."

At the top of the stairs Helen met a frozen-faced Mrs Worsley pointing to the bathroom. "There's a towel and dressing gown in there."

An indoor flush toilet was almost a novelty; at the Buxtons they still had to run down the garden path and in this sort of weather it wasn't fun. The bath, long enough almost to stretch fully out, was luxuriously hot. After the cold wind outside it would be easy to go to sleep but eventually, drying off in front of a full-length mirror, Helen looked at the curves reflected back and decided it would be better to wipe the mud smear from her own dress rather than wear the seductive low-necked dressing gown Mrs Worsley had hung behind the door.

Chapter Thirteen

There were just two dining places set at the large oak dining table. The armchair on the end was obviously the Master's so Helen instinctively walked towards the other placed alongside the table. She was about to sit down when she realised that Joseph's sister Anna, in black dress and frilly white apron, was discreetly standing behind the chair waiting to push it forward. Helen said, "Anna, how nice to see you."

Anna smiled affectionately in response and looked disconcertedly towards Mainthorpe, who was respectfully waiting for Helen to sit down. He said, "I'll open a bottle of wine while you girls pop into the kitchen. You can then chat away freely."

About two years older than Joseph and of course much older than Helen, Anna had always been a kind person. Before her Grandpa died, Helen had often gone with him when he worked in the Grange garden and on those occasions when Anna brought out a mug of tea for Grandpa she would always include a cream cake or something equally tempting for Helen. Not only was this a treat but she also made time to chat and Helen, like most children, remembered affectionately those grownups that acknowledged her.

Mrs Worsley hovered disapprovingly nearby while the two girls gave each other a hug, but soon interrupted their conversation. "If you've quite finished you will now serve the soup."

"But you usually serve at table, Mrs Worsley," Anna said.

Mrs Worsley scowled, "I serve my betters. I'm not going to serve a mill girl and I'm not going to explain myself to a maid so get on with it."

Back at the dining table Helen looked at the place setting disconcertedly. A knife, fork and spoon were the only cutlery used on the Buxtons' table; here there was a full table setting. Noticing her embarrassment, Anna discreetly touched the soupspoon after she ladled the soup into her dish and Helen took the hint. After that Helen watched Mainthorpe in order to decide which knife or fork to use and when. As to the wine, Simon had introduced her to it on one or two occasions but this was the first time she had sat at a formal table with a glass of wine. When Anna brought in the main course Mainthorpe raised an eyebrow. "No Mrs Worsley tonight then?"

"She's just helping cook in the kitchen, Sir."

"When she's got a minute ask her to step in, will you, please, Anna?"

Helen began to talk about the farm but within a few moments the housekeeper came in. "Ah, Mrs Worsley, there's nothing wrong is there?"

There must have been a silent headshake behind Helen's back because he continued. "Good. I've had a word with my wife on the telephone and it's snowing hard down in Fletchfield. I think we can presume we are here for the night so please prepare a guest room for Miss Helen."

When the kitchen door banged a little hard there was a hint of a smile under the moustache. "I think we can presume that Mrs Worsley's not too pleased."

Helen decided to try again to steer the conversation back to the farm. "Joseph seems to think that he may lose a lot of lambs tonight. Will it be that bad?"

"He tells me it could be and he's the expert. I'm afraid it's partly my fault."

"Your fault? Why?"

"Well a couple of weeks back he wanted to buy those hurdles to make that fold but I told him it was a waste of money, that these ewes lambing early is a one-off thing, and anyway, in mid-March the weather should be all right."

"You told me how you believe in letting your managers get on with it."

There was definitely a smile behind the moustache this time. "You're right as usual but I'm going to be a bit stretched. What with the advanced rent on the new mill, the cost of thirty sewing machines and the wages of the women to work them all, it adds up to enough without these extra farm buildings."

"But if you lose lambs now you'll have that many fewer to sell later."

Mainthorpe laughed. "That's why I invited you along; you just say how it is with no smarmy phrases."

While Anna was serving the pudding, Helen said, "If there's a pair of Wellington boots I could borrow I'd love to go and see how the men are getting on with the sheep."

"Mine are in the back kitchen," Anna said, then realised she was speaking out of turn. "I'm sorry, Sir, I was tr – "

"That's all right, Anna, and may I say how well you've served the meal tonight."

Leaving Mainthorpe to linger over his brandy, Helen went in search of the boots only to find Anna waiting with both them and a waterproof coat and hat.

The snow had eased off a little and the wind didn't seem too bad until Helen walked round the corner of the building. Where the snow had drifted it was above the top of her boots. Hearing voices inside, she stepped in through the door to the warmth of the shippen fodderbing. The hot breath from twenty cows chained by their necks in ten double stalls created considerable warmth. In front of the cows, this wide fodderbing was where hay was dropped down from the loft above to be fed to the cows each morning and night. It was in here that the men were working; they had moved all the hay to the far end and were tying hurdles across the fodderbing. Each hurdle just reached crossways and there were already several fixed in place with the ewe and two lambs between each. "We are just bringing the twins into the warmth here; the singles should manage in the pens outside," Joseph said with no more than a glance in her direction.

"Can I help?"

"Go and hold the fold gate while Tom carries the next two through."

Helen was amazed how much she could see against the white background, particularly considering the sky was still fairly black overhead and there were snow flakes falling. A couple of hayracks had been added since she left and where the sheep were milling around them the snow was trampled flat. The rows of pens Helen had helped to cover were now closed in along the backs and, because the wind came from that direction, were surprisingly free of snow inside. Before she could look further, Tom Smith was walking towards her with a lamb dangling by its front legs from each hand. Holding the hurdle gate open, Helen was almost knocked over by the enraged mother. The ewe didn't stop but set off across the field bleating madly. The Shepherd did an amazingly good imitation of a lamb's bleat and the ewe responded by turning back to stare agitatedly towards them. He carried the two lambs towards her and, still imitating their call, put them on the snow and backed away. "Her's a wild un is this un."

"Will she come back?"

"Aye, I reckon. When her does you get behind her while I carry em in."

Helen walked out on the seemingly flat field only to plunge knee deep where the drifting snow had filled a hollow. While she was extracting herself, the ewe ran bleating to her lambs and, with Helen walking behind, within a few minutes the ewe and her twin lambs were secured behind a hurdle. Tom Smith said, "That's the last of em now, Boss, an it's a good job we've only had a few twins."

Joseph said, "Good. You go back to the sheep while we get the milking finished."

"I'll give you a hand," Helen offered, "but I have to get the snow out of my boots first."

Joseph held the lantern while Helen balanced on one foot, emptying the other boot before lining it with some of the soft, dry hay lying about the floor. Conscious of his stare riveted on her leg as she lifted her skirt and raised her foot to push it into the top of the wellington boot, Helen tried to break his trance by saying, "They were a couple of sizes too big anyway so perhaps they won't feel so wet and cold now."

When he still seemed hypnotised by the sight of her other leg as she did the same with the other boots, Helen asked, "Isn't it a bit late to be milking the cows now?"

"What else could we do? We had to get the sheep in before dark. If the Master hadn't argued I'd have had those hurdles in place days ago."

Joseph gallantly held the door against the wind whilst Helen stepped out into the cold and followed him round the end of the building to the shippen. Again Joseph held the double doors while she stepped in onto the walk behind the cows. Isaac and Harry Aimsley were each sitting on a three-legged stool with a bucket clamped between their legs, milking away. It was the first time Helen had seen Harry since leaving and so they went through the ritual of greetings but Harry didn't pause from the squirt, squirt, squirt of milk into his bucket.

When he had finished milking that cow, Harry said to Joseph, "That's the last of the new-calved uns, Boss, and my hands have about had it for tonight."

"That's all right, Harry. You go home and get some tea."

"Right, Boss; I'll just check th'horses before I go."

Anna came into the shippen carrying a milking bucket. "I've finished in the house so I thought I would give you a hand here."

Joseph said, "Good, but we need another bucket for Helen."

Helen took one of the buckets, reached a three-legged stool from where they hung on the wall and walked to the nearest cow. She had to hitch up her skirt to get a tight grip on the milking bucket between her elegant legs while sitting on the low stool. Joseph seemed to watch the manoeuvre with interest.

Milking was always a time for banter. After a hard day out in the fields it was relaxing to sit and just pump away with practised hands. Helen soon found, though, that her hands were out of practice. The cow she had chosen was fortunately in calf again for May and as a result didn't give much milk. The second one was the same, so when that one was finished Helen just sat on the stool and rested whilst listening to the banter between the two brothers and sister as they each milked away. Anna said, "You're not going to see that girlfriend tonight, are you Isaac?"

"If we finish up quickly I've got time to walk over there now it's stopped snowing."

"You can hold hands with me in the sheep pen," Joseph said with a laugh, "and if you're feeling romantic maybe an old ewe will give you a kiss."

Anna said, "I thought Tom Smith would be staying with them overnight?"

"Yes, Boss, why isn't he?" Isaac asked.

The farm staff had changed the bailiff's traditional title of Master to Boss so that they could differentiate between Mainthorpe and Joseph. Even his family now called Joseph 'The Boss' and now he reminded them that he was.

"When we've finished here, Isaac, you take over from Tom. He'll go home and have a few hours sleep and be back here again by four o'clock."

"That's not fair," Isaac protested. "What are you going to do – go to bed?"

"I'll have a bit of supper, put on a dry pair of trousers and take over from you so that you can go to bed. But mind you, be up early for milking."

"Aw, poor Isaac. Can't love wait for another night?" Anna teased.

Helen found it amusing just to listen to them. When last she had been in their company they were all grownups whilst she had been but a child, so now it was strange to feel equal to them. It was even stranger to see Joseph treat her with such deference when years ago he had often teased and called her 'Big Eyes'.

The milking over, Helen chatted to Anna whilst she worked in the dairy sieving and cooling the milk. She felt a reluctance to go back into the Grange, not just because of Mrs Worsley's antagonism but because she felt out of her depth in the house alone with the Master.

Unable to put it off any longer, Helen went in, took off her borrowed clothes and walked through to the lounge. Mrs Worsley jumped to her feet. "The Master's already retired. I'll show you to your room. Please follow me."

Helen followed up the lovely polished oak stairway, admiringly running her fingers on the silky smooth handrail, when the housekeeper, looking over her shoulder, announced, "I've put you in the Mistress's room next to the Master's. I presume he wants you close." Then she turned and stumped noisily up the stairs, muttering, "What goes on in this house is none of my business but I'm not going to run . . ." The last was lost when she rounded the corner of the landing.

Since Helen had left the area a reservoir had been created further back in the hills. Mains water had been laid on to the village and also to the less isolated farms. Although there was still no electricity, an ingenious plumber had created two hot water systems in the Grange. The first worked from a Scandinavian kitchen stove. Mainthorpe had imported this all-night burner not just for its cooking potential but also because of its capacity to heat lots of water. By the simple process that heat rises it supplied the two upstairs bathrooms. The second worked on the same principle from a back boiler in the lounge to heat the main bedrooms.

In the dairy earlier, to Helen's amusement, Anna had asked, "When the mistress stays I had to come in early each morning to light the lounge fire so that the bedrooms were heated for when she got dressed. Will I have to do that for you?"

"If the Master can get dressed in the cold then I'm sure that I can."

Chapter Fourteen

Among Mainthorpe's many improvements to the old farmhouse, the one that Mrs Bolton really enjoyed was the hot water system. The black-leaded kitchen range included a back boiler, which heated enough water for the working farmhouse kitchen and the upstairs bathroom.

When Joseph came in for a late tea and to change out of his damp clothes his mother had already run him a hot bath. He didn't need much persuading to make use of it.

There had proved to be quite a few benefits to becoming the farm bailiff. Among them was the pleasure that this refurbished house gave his mother. That she missed her husband there was no doubt but her loss was offset by the pleasure of seeing Joseph in charge of the farm. Now, as he lay back in the bath and let the hot water soak away the cold of the blizzard, Joseph ran these thoughts through his mind. Then the vision of Helen took over. He couldn't get over the transformation between the rather tubby girl who had followed him about the farm and the tall, elegant young woman who stepped out of that car. It was those long, shapely legs that troubled him most. Joseph remembered how two or three times he had had to retrieve a small boot out of the mud when a small girl had lost one. Had he really held her leg while he slipped the boot back on? He imagined doing that earlier tonight in the fodderbing.

The thought stayed with him. Even after a hearty supper and clean clothes, that dreamy thought was still with him out in the sheepfold.

Although there was still some heavy clouds overhead, between those fast-moving clouds stars twinkled and where the moon shone through, strange, eerie shadows floated across the snow-covered fields and mountainsides. Joseph heard the hoot of an owl as he gazed at the beauty of it all and rejoiced that he was a farmer. He revelled in the challenge that each season brought. Now it was these ewes, next month it might be an illness among the dairy cows, later there could be a drought and a very poor hay crop or there could be plenty of rain to grow great crops of grass but no sunshine to make it into hay. What would it be like to have a woman with whom to share it? Laughing at the way his thoughts had drifted, Joseph turned back to his sheep.

Not used to being confined in a small fold, the restless hill ewes trampled the snow down across most of the pen to the extent that it was no longer a danger to newly born lambs. Though it would be cold to lie on, it wouldn't soak into their wool like fresh snow. There was one ewe pottering restlessly away from the others, and eventually it lay down and began to strain. Joseph watched for a while. When there seemed to be no progress he caught it and helped a single tup lamb into the world. Shutting it into a side pen with its mother, Joseph watched the other sheep for a few minutes, but when all seemed quiet and content he walked to the farmhouse.

After the cold night air, an armchair in front of a hot fire proved to be dangerous. Three hours later Joseph woke up and with a feeling of guilt dashed to the window to look out. There had been more snow; just an inch, but seeing it his heart sank. It would be enough to chill newborn lambs and when he got out to the sheep it had done just that. Two ewes had given birth to twins and one of each was dead. Joseph knew from experience how the firstborn lamb, still wet and hungry and desperately needing its mother's full attention, could easily be neglected while the ewe gave birth to the second. Cold, fresh snow would soon chill it and bring death. The two surviving single lambs also looked to be suffering so Joseph carried them into the fodderbing hoping they would recover in the warmth.

It seemed the only moments later when Tom Smith's voice startled him. "How's it going, Boss?"

Furnished with a lovely mahogany suite, the large bedroom intrigued Helen. Perhaps the frilly curtains and the ornate chaise longue at the foot of the bed told her something about the Master's wife. Even the pictures, though it was hard to really see them in lamplight, were modern and garish. Then Helen saw a second door. It couldn't be to the bathroom because she had just come from there. Could it be a connecting door with the Master on the other side? There was no key in the lock and, not daring to try the handle, Helen stared at it for some time but the handle didn't move and there was no noise from the other side, and her bed was inviting.

In the morning's post there had been a letter, which she presumed was from her Aunt but she had not found time to read it. Undressing and slipping into a lovely, soft, if somewhat revealing nightdress placed there by the housekeeper, she moved the brass oil-lamp to the bedside table and in the luxury of a heated bedroom re-arranged her pillows so that she could sit in bed to read it.

Dear Helen, I hope this letter finds you well. We buried Uncle Horace today. It was a small rock fall, nothing really but one hit his head. I didn't write earlier because I knew you couldn't get to the funeral. I don't suppose you would have wanted to come anyway. I'm not sure that I wanted to be there because after you left he became awful to live with.

Things were going wrong with mining, the price of lead fell and it was getting harder to find workable mines. What money he did make he spent in the pub and he wasn't nice to me when he got home. I know it sounds awful to speak like this about someone I once loved but I just have to get it off my chest. What's worse is that he's left no money. I've got the cows and they're milking well but they're going to be hard work on my own and I'll be struggling to pay the rent from just the milk sales.

I'm sorry to go on about my troubles but I'm glad that in your Christmas letter you sounded so happy. To have been through college and get a job in the design department sounds wonderful; it would have made your Grandparents very proud.

Anyway, I'm proud of you. I loved having you here and was heartbroken at what happened, but that's all in the past now.

As your only relative I feel I should give you advice but the only thing I can think of is for you to be careful as to what sort of man you marry. Don't make my mistake. There was always something cruel in his character but I pretended it wasn't there. If you have any doubts about a man then don't marry him.

Helen re-read the letter several times, and each time she felt sadder for Aunt Emily. In spite of Uncle Horace, living with them had been a pleasant experience and just being there had changed her life.

When she eventually put the light out, the contrast between the warmth of the bedroom and the cold wind she had been in earlier made her feel sleepy but sleep would not come. The letter reminded her of that night with Uncle Horace and the memory triggered other thoughts in her drowsy mind. Why had the housekeeper laid out a nightdress with such a plunging neck and put her next to the Master's bedroom? Why no lock on the door? When Mainthorpe invited her here, had he planned to stay the night? But surely he couldn't have known it was going to snow? Helen tried to console herself with the thought that between a wife and a mistress any man ought to be satisfied, so what could he want with me? Though why does he spend so much time alone out at this farm?

Used to getting up early, Mainthorpe was out in the farmyard just after six o'clock. His first call was to the sheepfold where he listened to a report from Tom Smith. "We've not done too badly Master, just seven lambs dead and one as is a bit dodgy looking."

"That's not too bad Tom; I feared it would be much worse. You've done very well."

"It's Boss who's been up most of th'night."

Deciding it would be polite to have a talk to his bailiff, Mainthorpe stepped inside the warm shippen where the two brothers and their sister were each on a stool, milking away. After the usual greetings and comments on the weather he said, "You've done very well with the lambs, Joseph. When I saw that storm I feared a greater loss."

"Thank you, Master, it could have been much worse. We've now got a problem with the milk. I had a talk to Bob Fairclough on the phone and he tells me that the main road's closed, so there's no chance of sending it into Manchester today."

In the stable Harry Aimsley was using a shovel to mix rolled oats, bran and chaff in a large wooden bin. There were two empty stalls because, with eight stalls and a loose box for a foaling mare, it was larger than most farm stables. Having been used to horses all his life, Mainthorpe felt more at home in the stable than the shippen. He never felt confident to make an intelligent observation on the condition of the cows but in here he could judge just how well each horse looked and, patting his own cob, he complimented the Waggoner on them. The conversation soon turned to the weather and Aimsley told him about the depth of some of the snowdrifts he had seen on his walk to work.

On hearing that, Mainthorpe took a walk down the lane to see conditions for himself but after misjudging the depth of one drift turned back to empty his boots in the warmth of the Grange.

The solid sleep of a tired, healthy body eventually came and as a result Helen was late down for breakfast. Mrs Worsley made her disapproval very plain. "The Master's gone for a walk outside and made me hold breakfast up until you're ready. Although who you think you are lazing about until this time of morning I don't know."

"She's my guest and I expect you to treat her as such," Mainthorpe said as he stepped through the kitchen doorway behind her. Mrs Worsley fled past him into the kitchen where there was a clatter of pots and pans and muttered conversation with the cook.

Standing with his back to the dining-room fire, Mainthorpe said, "There was more snow in the night and it's blown quite a bit. Aimsley walked down to the bottom lane before he came to work and he says there are deep drifts in places. He's certain there's no chance of getting a car through until it's dug out."

"How long will that take?"

"With the mill closed there's enough men out of work in the village but it's getting the council to pay them; and if you're out of work you'd like to be paid for shovelling snow. No, I think it could be Sunday or even Monday before we're out."

The porridge was as stodgy as the look on Mrs Worsley's face when she plonked it down in front of Helen. Noticing Helen's reaction and misunderstanding it, Mainthorpe said, "I'm afraid breakfast here is a very masculine affair. Realising that I'm usually on my own I gave instructions to just serve a dish of porridge followed by bacon, egg and black pudding – if we have any. I presume Mrs Worsley didn't think to ask if you would like anything different?"

"No, but it's all right and I'm enjoying it."

"That's more than Mrs Worsley seems to be doing."

Trying to cover up her embarrassment, Helen told him about Uncle Horace's death. Mainthorpe asked a few questions including why she left there but didn't pursue it when, instead of answering, Helen told him about her aunt's financial difficulties.

They were lingering over a cup of tea when Mainthorpe ran his eyes over Helen. "You are still wearing the same dress I see. Perhaps because I keep my outdoor clothes up here I didn't think about you. If you want to go outside then take a look in the wardrobe in your bedroom. I'm sure you'll find something suitable."

"I couldn't, they are Mrs Mainthorpe's . . ."

"Don't let that bother you. Jessica bought a wardrobe for the great outdoors but seldom wore them, and hasn't been near them for two years or more." He wandered across the room and stood looking out of the window for several moments before continuing.

"Jessica's not likely to come back here and if she was here she would want you to dress for the weather, so please help yourself."

Chapter Fifteen

Snow played a serious part in the life of those hardy folks who dared to live in the hills, sometimes with devastating results. But there is a bright side because on the steep banks it creates great sledging runs. Tramping through it now in fur lined leather boots, sheepskin coat and cord breeches, Helen smiled at the memories of her childhood, and wondered what the sophisticated Mrs Mainthorpe had intended to do in such unfeminine attire. But what did it matter? The fur boots, long enough to cover the breeches' buttoned legs, had obviously been bought to go with them. This outfit would have been great in those early years when Helen joined the village children skimming down that field towards the church on shiny-bottomed sledges. She remembered one moonlit night in particular when the wife of the mill manager brought out hot chocolate and Christmas cake for everyone. Helen had been much too young to be out that late but Grandpa let her stay because Joseph was there to keep an eye on her. But isn't that the fun of being part of a village, she thought, knowing everyone is looking out for each other? That thought reminded her again of just how much she had missed being away from the valley.

Looking inside the open-fronted cart house Helen saw how, by standing with its back to the East, it was almost clear of snow. The free-range hens were crowded inside; it did not need a very big brain to know it was much warmer under there than tramping around the cold snow. Some were perched on the reaper-binder, others on the corn drill and more on various pieces of haymaking machinery. What surprise her most was seeing the very same sledge hanging on wall that they had used years ago. Reaching up to touch it, Helen was surprised when from out of the yard Joseph's voice said, "Do you fancy having a go this afternoon?"

Spinning round and more than a little flustered she said, "I was just remembering – they were happy times, but I think I'm too old for careering down a hillside on a small sledge."

"Nonsense. We knock off at 12 o'clock on Saturdays so I've got a couple of hours between lunch and when I've to be back for milking. Anyway, Mum suggested I ask you to have lunch with us today, so how about it? Then afterwards we'll have a run on that sledge."

Letting him convince her about the sledge, Helen said, "I'd love to have lunch with you all, though I'd better go and warn cook that I'll not be joining the Master for lunch."

"Hadn't you better ask the Master if he doesn't mind?" Joseph asked.

"Why?"

"I thought perhaps . . . that maybe . . . well . . ."

"Whatever you thought, you thought wrong. I'll go and tell cook."

The cook smiled agreeably but just as Helen turned to leave the housekeeper came into the kitchen. "What are you doing in the mistress's clothes? You've no rights to wear them."

Before she could reply, the Master, looking more serious than usual, strode through from the lounge. "I think they are a very good fit, don't you, Mrs Worsley? Though perhaps they are a bit loose round the waist."

Not waiting to hear any more, Helen turned and fled from room.

Studying both the cook and his housekeeper for a few moments, Mainthorpe said, "I'll be in my study. Perhaps, Mrs Worsley, when you have a moment to spare you'll join me. I think it's time we had a little chat."

He was getting tired of his housekeeper's sour disposition. It wasn't just about Helen; she seemed to be a dissatisfied sort of person. The pleasure of talking to Helen this weekend filled a need in his life that previously he had not admitted was there. His wife no longer shared a substantial part of his time. Jessica blamed losing her baby on being isolated here when it was due. Although the doctor had tried to assure her it was not the case, that there would have been no way of saving the baby had he been on hand or had she been in town, his arguments were of no avail. Jessica now refused to even to visit the Grange. There was more to it than that. Mainthorpe had realised for sometime that Jessica was only happy in town where there were theatres to visit or dinners to attend, in fact anything where she could dress in her finery and have him parading alongside in an evening suit like a trophy husband.

Mainthorpe stared out of the window, marvelling at the beauty outside, how the snow, clinging on branches and smaller shrubs, created unusual shapes in the garden. Further away on the hillsides the drifting snow left walls and rocky outcrops exposed, creating contrasting patterns in the pure, white, fresh snow. Yet that beauty failed to lift the sadness from his mind. If only the baby had lived, if only they could have another child, but the doctors had told them firmly that Jessica must never conceive again. Now they were in separate bedrooms there was little left to share. His two-nights-a-week town arrangement went some way towards resolving his physical needs but a man should never discuss business with his mistress nor could Jessica take part in a serious conversation about anything other than social events and fashion. Grief, he remembered when Jessica used to come here, how she always dressed in the evening and wanted him to change for dinner even when they were here on their own. Mainthorpe hated the thought of it. Part of the attraction of coming to the Grange was being able to relax in his old tweeds.

Mrs Worsley's knock on the door broke into his musings. "You wanted to see me, Master?"

"Yes, I do Mrs Worsley. I'm unhappy with your attitude to Miss Helen. It's not of choice that she's staying here, but the fact is that she is here and I expect you to treat her with the respect that you would use with any of my guests." Mrs Worsley started to protest but he cut in, "No argument. Miss Helen was part of this valley before you or I came near it and I suspect she'll be here long after we've gone."

The housekeeper made a silent retreat.

The morning seemed to go very slowly for Joseph. He had to concentrate on the work because as usual there were decisions to be made. The sun came out with just enough warmth to cause a slight thaw, only a little but enough to melt small patches of high open ground where the blizzard had swept most of the snow away. As with all blizzards, three-foot drifts lingered behind the walls and in hollows while in between small areas of green grass began to appear. The ewes and lambs were too concentrated in the fold so Joseph helped the Shepherd sort out those with strong single lambs and put them out onto the exposed areas of grass.

Joseph was thankful that there was water laid on to the shippens, with a bowl for each cow to drink when it wanted to. Only a couple of years before, the dairy cows would have been turned out each morning to drink at Bullerstone Brook and on a morning like this would have returned to their stalls shivering from the effects of the stomach full of icy cold water. There was still snow to clear from strategic places round the farmyard so that the cows could be fed and cleaned out, but Joseph's mind kept switching to the little girl who used to sit securely between his legs as they sledged down that long slope years ago. He blushed at the thought of doing that now.

Avoiding the deeper snowdrifts by staying on the higher part of the fields, Helen walked right down to Gritstencrag Lane. It was a picture-book setting; in places the road was almost clear and then within a few yards a drift of three feet or more both filled and blocked it. Arms of some of the deeper snowdrifts reached out over the water to create picturesque shapes over the bubbling, gurgling brook. Occasionally one reached right across to form a snow bridge, which footprint evidence revealed, had already been used by both rabbits and water-hens. She soon moved away from the overhanging trees when a slight breeze disturbed the snow-covered branches to send it showering down.

Lunch with the Bolton family was a very pleasant occasion, although when Helen thanked Mrs Bolton for inviting her the reply was, "Lunch? You should know this is dinner, or it was until the Master came to the Grange. Now I don't know what it is. We have dinner at 12 o'clock then Anna goes to help serve dinner at the Grange at seven o'clock when we're having tea. Now even Joseph's calling my dinner lunch so I don't know where I am."

Isaac said, "Don't worry, Mum, it looks good, it tastes good and after the last couple of days I could eat a horse."

There was a happy family atmosphere. Both Ned and Anna teased Isaac about missing his date the night before but Joseph didn't join in. Not having seen him in this family setting before Helen wondered if he was always this quiet. It became obvious that he wasn't when the others also noticed and began teasing him.

Of course, they were interested in Helen's experiences during the last few years but no one asked a question about why she had left Flacton. Helen presumed that village gossip had informed them long ago.

After the meal the rest of the family had other things to do so Helen walked alongside Joseph to the top of the bank overlooking the church. Village children were already there, squealing and shrieking as they hurtled down the slope at breathtaking speeds. Helen had forgotten just how steep and long the sledge run was. "We didn't go down that, did we?" She asked.

"We did and you used to enjoy it," Joseph said, pointing towards one girl whizzing down. "And you used to squeal even more than she is."

Joseph lined the sledge up but Helen was distracted when two older girls, pulling their sledge back to the top, recognised her. They were soon engrossed in conversation exchanging memories and asking each other questions about the last few years. Helen turned to signal to Joseph that he should make the run, and then all three girls watched him go flying down the hill. Helen was surprised when one of them said. "I'd like to take a tumble in the snow with him."

The other said, "It would be more fun in the hay but I doubt if you'd get the chance."

When several children came puffing and panting up to the top with their sledges Helen chatted and laughed with them and in turn gave each a push off down the hill.

Wearing a farm bailiff's traditional cord-breeches and leggings, Joseph was striding back up the steep bank, and from his red face and wide grin he had obviously enjoyed it. "That was great. I'd forgotten how fast you go on that steep stretch."

"How do mean that you've forgotten?"

"I haven't had a go for a few years. I didn't think that a farm bailiff should be playing with the children but hey – it's fun. Come on, it's your turn."

With the sledge run lying away from the East, the snow had settled right down the slope and now after a few hours of use by the villagers it was packed and hard. In fact when Joseph lined the sledge up he had to hold it while Helen sat down and then he sent her away with a hefty push. Helen had wrapped a scarf round her neck and tucked the ends under her sheepskin but obviously not firmly enough because it was soon streaming behind as she shot over the brow of the steep bit with exhilarating speed. There was a rope tied to each front corner of the sledge that in theory enabled her to steer but Helen had forgotten the skill and pulled too hard. The sledge responded and veered down an even steeper incline. Somewhere on the way she lost the scarf altogether and near the bottom hit a bump that threw the sledge sideways to send her rolling into a deep drift. Unhurt but winded, she staggered to her feet only to feel cold snow slipping down her neck and more in her boots. Running down to her rescue, Joseph lost his footing on the slope and, after a couple of spectacular somersaults, came to rest just a couple of yards away. They both grinned happily but Joseph had the last laugh when Helen wriggled and squirmed as the melting snow slid further down inside her clothes.

After another tumble later in the afternoon and a few well-aimed snowballs, they left the village youngsters to enjoy their fun. On the walk back Joseph looked in at the sheepfold to find that one ewe was having difficulty lambing. Helen leaned against a hurdle while he eased another tup lamb into the world. By then the sun was sinking behind the hills leaving a real nip in the air. This, coupled with the melted snow, which had now reached various parts of her body where snow was not meant to go, gave her a sudden chilly feeling.

Again the hot bath was a real luxury. Refreshed and back in her bedroom Helen couldn't resist taking a look in the wardrobe. There were several calf-length day dresses, all too fancy for her taste, and four with a very expensive look for evening wear. Two of them, in the mid-1920s fashion that Helen had only seen in fashion magazines, had what Helen had heard called a handkerchief hemline. Holding one in front of the mirror it was obvious that, though it might reach to her upper calf at its lowest it would give a provocative glimpse of a knee elsewhere and the neck-line was hardly one to wear in a blizzard.

Not bothering to even take the others out, Helen examined her own dress to find, with some relief, that after her careful sponging it had dried without a stain. That pleased her because to buy both it and the new coat had needed a dip into her savings.

Slipping it on, Helen remembered those troubled thoughts from the night before, and was pleased the shop assistant failed in her attempt to persuade her into buying the latest mid-knee fashion. This was just a high-necked plain green woollen dress with a brown front panel and brown trimmings but, though it hung modestly below the knee, when she looked in the mirror the straight waist still showed her curves a bit provocatively. The natural wave in her short, mousy hair needed no more than a good brush to bring out a healthy sheen but, sitting in front of the dressing table mirror, she decided to make use of the range of cosmetics presumably left by Jessica.

Downstairs in the lounge Mainthorpe was fiddling with the wireless controls when Helen walked in. "I'm trying to tune in for the news. Do you have a wireless at the Buxtons'? Arr, there we are – just in time for the six o'clock."

Mainthorpe moved back to his armchair and indicated for Helen to sit on the other. "Do you mind if we listen?"

"Of course not. The Buxtons bought a wireless this Christmas and we listen to it most evenings."

"Would you believe that since John Reith became manager last year the news reader has to wear a dinner jacket to read the news? Think of it," Mainthorpe laughed. "Sitting behind a microphone, though no one can see him, he still has to look like a stuffed penguin." He chuckled a few moments then added, "I think he must be related to Jessica."

They sat quietly listening to the newscaster's cultured voice describing the events of the day including how many roads were still closed by the unseasonably late snow. The programme following was a live interview with an economist on the relative economics of Britain and America. In very cultured English the Economist said, "Despite the continuing effects of the national strike and the depression in agriculture this country is relatively wealthy and America is booming." When the presenter challenged him with the counterargument, the economist was adamant. "I tell you America is booming and it will carry us with it in the coming years." Mainthorpe began to argue as though he was in the room. "Nonsense, man! Too many businesses are borrowing too much money and each year they're borrowing more. As regards America, you don't know what you're talking about; it's even worse out there."

He turned to Helen and pointed to the wireless. "I'm sorry but he's wrong. There are lots of small town banks in America competing against each other to lend more and more money. There's sure to come a day of reckoning."

"We looked at the comparative banking systems in college," Helen said. "The tutor thought that because their banks were small they were better placed to make decisions about local businesses."

"Yes, maybe there's something in that but they're lending too much in relation to their assets. The trouble with small banks is if one catches a cold they all get jittery and pass it on."

"If you're so troubled, are you sure you are doing right expanding?"

Mrs Worsley broke into the conversation to announce that dinner was ready. They were both still deep in the discussion when Anna came in to serve the soup. Smiling her thanks, Helen was very conscious of her strange situation; over lunch she and Anna had shared at the family table as equals but now Anna waited on her with deference. It disturbed her to the point that she missed what Mainthorpe was saying other than the end, which was something about wages. Waiting until Anna left the room, Helen said, "I know that as an employer you must think now we are down to a fifty-hour week that wages are too high, particularly now food prices are falling. If I remember correctly, that economist said that wages are now 11% higher in real terms than in 1914, but if you talk to your married man with small children he'll soon tell you how much he's struggling to make ends meet."

Mainthorpe protested, "You've misunderstood me. I'm talking about the cost of dole for over one million unemployed. If they were in work, even on a lower wage, they'd be contributing to the nation's wealth. Now they're just draining it."

It was only when Anna came in to ask if she could she serve the main course that Mainthorpe's mind switched to other things. "Ah, you are gracing our table again, Anna?"

"Yes, Master. Mrs Worsley thinks it would be good experience for me."

"I think I know what Mrs Worsley thinks, but I suppose it will be good experience for you. Anyway you've already served Helen one meal today."

Anna gave an uninhibited giggle. "Yes, but she had to help wash up after that one."

Mainthorpe joined in the laughter.

Chapter Sixteen

With the fickleness of spring, the snow was already melting by the time they finished breakfast on the Sunday morning. In the garden those shrubs that stood in the shadow of the house were still weighed down by the snow but further away the snow had released its grip, allowing the leafy branches to regain their shape. Helen pointed across the valley. "Look how the melt water is streaming down on the far hill side. Where the morning sun is directly on it the snow's nearly gone."

"Yes, but it will be mid-day before the sun shines on this side of the hill and the road is mainly on this side. I think it's still a bit risky to try and drive out before lunch. I might walk down to the church for morning service. Would you like to come?"

Helen thought for a few moments about the implications. "I'm not sure, Master. It might be misunderstood."

"Nonsense, you're my guest. Anyway, I think Mrs Bolton will probably be going, so if you feel it more suitable, why not sit with her?"

When they arrived at the church Helen was surprised to find that the Master had not got a personal pew. In her schooldays everyone of any importance had their own pew and some would ask strangers to move if they accidentally sat at the wrong place. Whispering this when the two of them paused at the back of the church, Mrs Bolton explained, "He doesn't come very often and when he does he just sits anywhere near the back. Anyway, I'm not sure whose pew is whose. I've only started coming because it's too much trouble to get the trap out to go to the chapel."

While they were talking, Mainthorpe was striding up the aisle to an empty pew where he turned and indicated to the two ladies to join him and go in first. Helen went first and was thankful that Mrs Bolton followed. Even so, she was aware of some strange looks.

Back at the mill on the Monday morning everyone seemed to know about the weekend and there was more than one suggestive remark. Even the new outfit had been noted and one woman said, "You have'ner bought them clothes out'er your wage, eh? There's another woman in th'next street wears good clothes like them."

Helen decided to admit to having a small legacy, which she had dipped into for the first time. At the same time she wondered what would have been said had the thaw not set in. Hearing the suggestive remarks from her fellow mill workers, she was glad there had been the formidable presence of Mrs Bolton between her and the Master in Church, and even more glad that he had managed to drive out of the valley immediately after lunch on Sunday afternoon.

The accidental early lambing was not as disastrous as Joseph had feared. There were more deaths than normal but some of those were one of twins, which meant that the ewes still had one lamb and one lamb was all he could expect a ewe to provide milk for this early in the year. In fact, that was the reason why he didn't lamb the ewes before late April. In a cold spring there would be insufficient grass earlier and without grass a ewe wouldn't produce enough milk.

A few days after the snow cleared, the ground dried out enough to start Harry Aimsley ploughing last year's stubbles. Now that the Master had agreed to build the shippen extension and buy in extra cows Joseph knew it meant harvesting more hay to feed them through the following winter. To do that he had to seed these fields down to grass this spring. His trouble was that, despite having so much to plan, his mind kept wandering away from the business of farming, distracted by a tall, attractive girl who had come back into his life.

Striding across the fields to where Harry was ploughing, Joseph reflected on his problem. He knew that at twenty-seven he was leaving it late to be thinking about marriage but, since taking over it had been so satisfying just to be running the farm, perhaps he hadn't mixed enough with other young people. Now those large turquoise eyes were disturbing him so much that just the night before he put a calving cow into a loose box and forgot about her. Had he been there, more than likely that calf would have been born alive. Not that he could know that for sure, but it was obvious that puzzling over Helen's relationship with the Master was distracting him from his work.

The weekend had been an enjoyable one for Mainthorpe. Reflecting on it afterwards he tried to analyse just what it was about Helen he enjoyed most. Though well aware how disturbingly attractive she had looked in what was no more than a plain dress, Mainthorpe tried to convince himself that her looks had nothing to do with it. "Grief," he muttered to himself, "I'm almost old enough to be her father." No, it wasn't that, it was the way the girl seemed to fit in at the Grange, how she immediately joined in the work and mixed so easily with the Bolton family. Then, remembering Joseph's obvious interest, he paused to think.

Mainthorpe well knew how dangerous it was but he couldn't help comparing the two women. Jessica wouldn't have gone near a sheep pen and, as regards milking, Mainthorpe smiled at the thought. Yet there was more to the girl than that. He remembered how enjoyable the conversation over dinner had been, how on the journey home they had been discussing business one moment and the beauty of the snow-clad hills the next. Mainthorpe had never before experienced that sort of a relationship with a woman. Jessica would never share his thoughts like that; it was doubtful if she would even notice the beautiful effects left by the drifting snow.

Behind the new rented mill the site was being cleared so that the building work could start on his new factory and the alterations inside were going apace. Mainthorpe was surprised how quickly the owner, who still thought he was doing it to house more handlooms, had responded to his ideas. In his mind Mainthorpe visualised rows of sewing machines in front of the large top floor windows and gave more thought to what exactly they would make.

He was convinced that first he must design and produce material of high quality and so distinctive in design that it differed from the material he supplied to other manufacturers. He hoped that then they would accept he was aiming for a different market and not see him as a competitor. Though Mainthorpe was under no illusions; he knew he must work on the assumption that once the sewing machines were installed the secret would be out and one or both of his main customers might leave him. Therefore, to maintain a cash flow there must be material ready to go to the makeup department before the sewing machines were installed. To do that it was time to get a design team working, but what on? Should they work under Mr Grimshaw or would it be better to have a separate team? Then Mainthorpe wondered who among his designers would have that sort of innovative flair. In the end he decided to ask Helen to stay back on Thursday so that they could talk it through.

When the Thursday night came they were both so engrossed with the issues that time flew. It was well past Helen's normal teatime when Mainthorpe checked his watch. "I hadn't realised it was that time. Have the Buxton's prepared a meal for you?"

"No, I told them I'd make myself something when I came in."

"Then let's continue this discussion over a meal. I have a table reserved for one; it can easily seat two."

"But I'm not dressed for dinner I'm only in an old working dress."

"You look fine to me. We're going for a meal and a chat, not a fashion show."

The table was in a discreet recess and the waiter took his time between courses, which allowed plenty of time for discussion.

To Mainthorpe's request for innovative designs Helen responded with ideas that had been formulating in her mind during the frustrating months since leaving college. Mainthorpe was interested but he wanted to see them on paper and in his obsession with secrecy about the project said, "If I involve my present design team the secret will soon out and you can't work in the design department without working under Grimshaw. Anyway, I don't believe he has the necessary flair and I doubt whether he'll let you use yours. Could you work from home?"

"It's going to take a couple of weeks to do two or three basic designs and much longer to put any patterns you choose onto point-paper, so it will be difficult without the Buxtons knowing what I'm doing."

"Then there's only one place and that's the Grange. Could you work there?"

"I could, but it might be misunderstood."

"Misunderstood? How?"

Helen hesitated, trying to find the right words. "I got quite a few suggestive remarks when I came back from that weekend in the snow. If I go for a fortnight I'm not sure what people will think and I doubt if Grimshaw would have me back in the design department."

"It's not what other people think that counts but what you think about yourself. Life's like a ladder; every time you step up a rung there will be someone who, either out of envy or spite, will try to knock you off. They are the ones who spread the tittle-tattle. I've given up worrying about them and so should you. As for Grimshaw, he'll do what I tell him. Anyway, you may not have to go back there because I intend to have a separate design department and by then it should be finished."

"Do you mean that the builders are nearly finished?"

"No, they've not even started on the factory but they're well on with the renovations in the new mill. The design department should be finished first and I've planned it so that it can be kept strictly private."

"You must know that I've not had enough experience to take this on."

"Maybe not, but you have that artistic flair, and don't forget I've seen the work you did in college. I can put an experienced designer alongside you; it's just a matter of choosing who."

After the frustration of being just a department dogsbody, Helen knew this challenge was too good to turn down, but . . . but . . .?

Seeing the excited interest mixed with doubts on Helen's face, Mainthorpe said, "I'll tell Grimshaw that you're having a few weeks off to help Joseph with the lambing."

By the time they finished discussing the different aspects of the project the evening was well gone. Mainthorpe gave Helen a lift to the end of her street and drove home, completely forgetting it was his usual night to collect the rent.

Simon came back into her life soon after. Helen was helping Mrs Buxton prepare Sunday lunch when the hoot of a car horn sounded in the street and she looked out to see Simon, grinning from ear to ear, standing proudly by a small car. He missed out the usual courtesy greetings when Helen stepped outside. "Look at this! It's mine. How do you like it?"

Recognising it, and having just heard on the wireless how Henry Ford had now built his 15-millionth Model T Ford, Helen tactfully said, "What a lovely car; what sort is it?"

"It's the latest 1927 T Ford Tourer; it's got a quad-coil ignition with a flywheel magneto for extra power and it's got two gears." By then Simon was back in the car twiddling with levers. "Look – you let the handbrake half off and push down the left pedal to engage bottom gear and then accelerate away before letting the handbrake fully off and the pedal right up to engage top."

Helen smiled encouragingly as he went on to describe how the super-strong alloy steel used in the chassis was the same as that used for battleship armour plating. When finally ending his enthusiastic description Simon said, "An-anyway, to celebrate I've booked a table for lunch, hoping that you'll join me?"

"That's sweet of you. I'd love to; that is, if Mrs Buxton doesn't mind."

Mrs Buxton not only didn't mind but invited Simon in while Helen ran upstairs to change. Now working full-time at the mill Mrs Buxton was well aware of the gossip surrounding the Master and Helen, which had been fuelled not only by the Master keeping Helen back again on Thursday night but by the rumour that they had gone out for a meal together. A young man calling may not be enough to quell the gossip but it reassured Mrs Buxton that the girl's relationship with the Master was still an innocent one.

Simon's invitation came on the Sunday before Helen was due to go to the Grange. Over the meal he brought the conversation round to Mainthorpe and his plans for the new mill. When it appeared that Simon seemed to know a lot about it Helen became suspicious and changed the subject. Simon was not put off and, pouring her another glass of wine, turned the conversation back to Mainthorpe. Helen said, "I can't tell you what he's doing in the mill. I'm taking a couple of weeks off to stay at the farm and help with the lambing."

Chapter Seventeen

Explaining to the Buxtons why she was going to the Grange was difficult. It was not just that they had given her a home; it was a house full of happiness, in which they cared for her as they would have had she been their daughter. After the grumpy misery associated with Uncle Horace, this lovely couple were just the opposite. Helen never heard them really quarrel. The occasional disagreement was just that; each stated their case and that was the end to it. Helen had read in books how when married couples work together they often become so bored with each other that love turns to hatred. But in this house, even working so closely together in the garrett, love had grown into a deep respect. Respecting them in return, Helen said, "I'm not going to lie to you but I can't tell you the whole truth. The Master wants me to do some artwork for him and because he doesn't want any of the design team to know about it he has asked me to work at the Grange. In fact, he's so obsessed with secrecy that he's telling people that I'm going to help with the lambing."

"You've never lied to us, it's just that we're worried about his intentions," Mrs Buxton said. "He has a bit of a reputation."

Helen gave her a hug. "He's never made an improper suggestion and I really will be working, but please don't tell anyone what at. Let them think what they want."

Mr Buxton turned to his wife. "I think, Missus, you might have got it wrong. Since that weekend away we've heard quite a bit about this farm bailiff chap. What's his name, is it Joseph?"

Helen said, "Oh, you two, you see dangerous men behind every tree."

Mr Buxton laughed, "For you, girl, there are dangerous men behind every tree."

There was a strained atmosphere in the design department on the Monday. Early in the morning Mainthorpe sent for Mr Grimshaw and from the moment he returned to the design room he never spoke to Helen. She had no idea what had been said but it was obvious that even if the Master wanted her to return Grimshaw would never have her back to work under him. One of the youngest designers, Peter Grandburn, being the most friendly, whispered, "What have you done to old Grimside?"

"Get on with your work, Grandburn," called Grimshaw from the other end of the room. Helen just gave Peter a knowing smile and continued with her tidying up.

On Mainthorpe's instruction Helen finished early and hurried home with a feeling of excitement. Home? But, Helen thought, this isn't home. Wonderful as the Buxtons have been, home is in those hills where her father had left her years before, where she and her Grandpa had wandered in spring looking at wildflowers or searching for birds' nests. Home was where she had picked wild flowers for Grandma or kept watch in case the gamekeeper caught Grandpa reaching into the stream to tickle a trout. Home was sitting on her favourite rock out on the lonely moor, trying to recapture a mental picture of her father – not that one ever came, but there were some vague memories of when they came to the valley as a family. Her father had stayed a few days before he left to join up and Helen could remember riding on his shoulders while he walked across the moor showing her where he had played as a boy. The clearest memory she had was when she slid off his shoulders on to that rock. Oh, I know it's a boulder, she thought, but to me it is the rock in my life because it was there my dad told me he was going away. Yet, as clear as that memory was, it never included her father's features.

There was a letter waiting when she got back to the house. It was from Aunt Emily and it was a long tale of woe. The gist of it was that Uncle Horace had owed more money than Aunt Emily had realised. On top of that, the depression in farm prices had driven some farmers to sell their surplus milk in competition with

her. As a result, the milk-round sales had decreased and her aunt
had to churn more of her milk into less profitable butter. It was
physically too much for her but there was no alternative other than
to get a job, and there wasn't much chance of that because the
unemployment in that area was serious.

Worrying about it while packing, Helen wondered if she
should send some money to her Aunt but decided it wouldn't be a
solution.

Her goodbyes to the Buxtons had been said when they were
leaving for work early in the morning. By the way Mrs Buxton
acted, Helen had the impression they thought she was leaving for
good. She tried to reassure them. "It's only for a couple of weeks
then I'll be back."

There were tears in Mrs Buxton's eyes. "You're grown up,
you have to live your own life, but we are here for you if you need
us."

"Come on, Missus, let's get off to work before we are all in
tears," said Mr Buxton heading for the door.

This time her own clothes were on the back seat of
Mainthorpe's Riley as he headed towards the hills. The feeling of
going home was poignant. If only it could be back to Grandpa's
little cottage rather than the Grange and Mrs Worsley.

Spring was unfurling her magic. In the town gardens both
plum and cherry trees were celebrating it with a mantle of white
blossom but a typical heavy April shower emptied the streets.
Then, as they left the town, the rain stopped and within minutes a
beam of sunshine was creeping across the distant hillside. Nearer
to the road the low-lying fields had responded to the longer days
by producing a fresh green mantle. In one, young lambs
gambolled energetically, unconstrained by age or care. When a
rolling cloud curtained off the sunshine, Mainthorpe said, "It won't
be this green up at the Grange. Eh, I wonder if it will snow
again?"

Laughing at the thought, Helen said, "You might think you're joking, Master, but look – the blackthorn flowers are still white. If it does snow at least I'm prepared this time, and I don't have to get back."

"No, but I do. I'm planning to take my horse out for a canter before lunch and drive home immediately after."

As they drew closer to the Ragil Valley, a mixture of memories and excitement was triggered in Helen's mind. Mainthorpe broke the silence. "By the way, like you asked, I told Mrs Worsley to prepare a guest room instead of Jessica's." He chuckled for a few moments before adding, "But I didn't tell her who was coming."

Helen wondered if that was because he dare not. Whatever the reason, it would be Mrs Worsley every day for the next fortnight. Though she dreaded the thought Helen was determined to try to get on with her.

But Mainthorpe had other thoughts. He had had enough of his housekeeper's sour disposition and unless she treated Helen with respect he was ready to make a change.

There were a lot of other things on his mind besides Helen and his unconventional decision to ask her to create new designs. Not that that had worried him. He knew from the start that if, by chance, Helen didn't come up with anything good there would only be the two of them who would know about it, and he would only have lost a couple of weeks.

It was the commitment of money troubling him most. Advance rental on the new mill had now to be followed by everything to equip the making-up department. For that he had already negotiated a deal committing the supplier to absolute secrecy but had no intention of taking delivery until Helen's patterns were coming off the looms – if, indeed, she came up with anything good. Later there would be the new factory to equip with power looms and everything that goes with them. Although he had done a budget, it depended on his present cash flow. If he were to lose customers, it worried him just how much backing he would need from his bank manager. The more he thought about it the more he felt he'd been a bit rash deciding to expand the farm buildings and increase his dairy herd in the coming winter.

Needless to say, with both of them deep in their own thoughts there was little conversation even when the rain hit them again on the way up the Grange Lane. Swinging the car round so that Helen was nearest to the house door, Mainthorpe said, "You make a dash for it and I'll bring your case."

Needing no encouragement, Helen took three quick steps into the porch; the door opened in front of her and there was Mrs Worsley's scowling face and critical eyes. "Oh, it's you, is it? To think I have been scurrying round getting everywhere tidying for the likes of you. Well, I'll not stand for it."

Stepping into the porch, Mainthorpe slipped his coat from over his shoulders. Giving it a shake, he said, "Is there something you don't like, Mrs Worsley?"

"Yes, I came here to keep house for a respectable family not some floozy out for a good time."

"I'm not sure what a floozy is, but Miss Helen is my guest in my house."

"Then I've no wish to be your housekeeper."

After studying her for a few moments, Mainthorpe said, "I'm driving back to town after lunch so if you're sure that's what you want to do I'll happily give you a lift to the station."

"I'll go and pack my things straight away."

Helen watched her stamp away in stunned silence then turned to Mainthorpe but he held up his hand to silence her, saying, "It's not just about you, it's been brewing for some time. We can talk over lunch but first I'll take your things up and then have a word with Cook before going for my ride."

Her room was on the other side of the bathroom this time and, though smaller than the mistress's, had an equally large stone mullioned window looking out over the garden and across the valley. The view held her enthralled. The remnants of the clouds that had brought the April showers still scuttled overhead whilst to the West, where she could see between the hills, the sun shone down on the distant Cheshire Plain. Helen was still enjoying the view when the Master rode out on his sturdy cob. Just then the sun broke between the clouds to light up the valley, sparkling on the water droplets splashing up from the cantering hooves.

Watching his handsome profile, Helen wondered what sort of man Mainthorpe really was behind that gruff, unreadable countenance? What did he want from her? She was wise enough to know that it was more than just designs on paper, but what? Could he really be trusted? Had he manoeuvred the housekeeper into getting the sack so that they would be alone here next weekend?

These thoughts were still running through her mind as she hung her clothes in the wardrobe. On the previous Saturday afternoon Helen had dipped a little further into her savings to buy some suitable clothes. Stopping to admire a new pair of cord trousers Helen remembered how distasteful it had been to wear Jessica's clothes on her last visit, particularly those cord breeches. Presuming they had been bought to make an impression and probably because there was no one here to impress, it was doubtful if they had ever been worn. Anyway, Helen, not wanting to be reminded of the Master's wife by buying a similar pair but knowing that there was a need for something warm when a cold easterly blew over the hill, solved the problem by deciding to buy this pair of cord trousers. The Fletchfield ladies' shops stocked very few slacks and seemed appalled at the thought of ladies' cord trousers. The third shop had both a ladies' and a men's section so Helen just asked to try some from the other section. The fashion-conscious shop assistant was horrified but Helen just smiled. "Where I'm going warmth is more important than fashion."

The shop assistant had been more enthusiastic about helping to choose coordinating jumpers and was almost exuberant when Helen said, "Now, about a dress suitable for a casual evening?"

"Look at our new spring range; they're the latest fashion, barely covering the knee."

Most of them were in a lightweight summer material but one looked promising, just a pale grey with two large floral designs embroidered across the left breast and the right skirt. It was an unusual contrast in colours that complemented both her hair and face. The price worried Helen. It was more that she had ever spent on a dress and how would her knees look when sitting down with that length of skirt? In the end, the persuasive shop assistant won.

Between enjoying the view and daydreaming over clothes it was nearing lunchtime when Helen finally went downstairs. A blazing log fire made the lounge feel cosy and, walking through to the dining room, Helen found Anna stoking up that fire. After they warmly greeted each other, Anna said, "You've got rid of the dragon, then?"

When Helen looked puzzled, Anna continued, "None of us liked her. She treated Mum as though she was a servant. I just hope the Master doesn't persuade her to change her mind."

Reassuring her that there wasn't much chance of that, Helen went on to ask how everyone was. "Everyone's well bar Joseph," Anna replied. "He just seems to be very quiet these last few weeks. But I can't stand talking – I have to lay the table for when the Master comes back."

"Come on, let's do it together."

The two girls finished the table and were in the kitchen with Cook when the Mainthorpe came in. He paused to take a deep breath. "A man should always come in through the kitchen. Not only is it the most important room in the house but you learn a lot without having to ask too many questions and something always smells good."

Wondering if he was developing a sense of humour, Helen said, "You sound as though you've enjoyed the ride Master, so when would you like to eat?"

"Are you ready cook? Good, then we'll go through."

Helen had learned from her previous stay that Mainthorpe liked a simple two-course lunch, no wine or other frills, just a jug of good, clear water.

When the main course had been served and Anna had left the room, Mainthorpe pointed with his knife to a large cardboard box. "I've raided the mill storeroom for everything I think you might need. There's paper, paints, brushes, you name it, if I've seen it in use in the design room then it's in that box. And if it's not then use the telephone and I'll bring it out on Friday evening."

Not sure what to say, Helen just murmured, "Thank you."

Mainthorpe concentrated on his food in silence. When his plate was empty he looked at her and said, "Now about the house. There's no housekeeper so you're in charge until I find someone else." Helen started to protest but Mainthorpe cut her off. "Every house needs a mistress. Not that you'll have any trouble with the cook or Anna but now the mill's closed in the village Tom Smith's wife was out of work so I've taken her on to do the washing and cleaning. I'm not too sure about her, though."

"I haven't seen her about."

"She's gone home today, supposedly not feeling too well. I suspect, though, that it happens fairly often, so be firm with her."

Helen was on the point screaming a protest when Anna came in to clear the dishes away. Mainthorpe jumped to his feet, saying, "I'll go and explain to cook and Anna," and followed Anna into the kitchen.

Within a couple of minutes he was back. "Well that's all settled then. I'll just have my pudding and then I'll be off."

Feeling completely out of her depth, Helen said, "Look, Master, I can't do this. You are expecting too much. I'm just a . . ."

"Nonsense, you're a very capable young woman. Ah, here's Anna with my favourite pudding, the first spring shoots of rhubarb, courtesy of Mrs Bolton, in a pie topped with hot custard."

Anna hovered around, topping up their water glasses and asking if the Master would like a whisky or a brandy. "No, I'm going to get straight off today but I'm sure Miss Helen would like something, perhaps a coffee? But first would you mind going up to see if Mrs Worsley's ready?"

And that was it. Within a few minutes both he and Mrs Worsley were gone, leaving Helen nursing a cup of coffee and a whirl of confused thoughts.

Chapter Eighteen

What troubled Helen most was that there was no one to take into her confidence, or to share her worries. It was obvious that Mainthorpe's insistence on secrecy was not about the actual designs but more likely because he was taking a gamble by involving a young girl. Helen had no doubt that if she failed to produce anything good Mainthorpe would pretend it had never happened and that she really had been here to help with the lambing. That thought took her to Joseph. He was the only person in Mainthorpe's confidence so it followed that he was the only one with whom she could discuss her fears. But first there was a letter to write to Aunt Emily.

Writing released some of her feelings. After expressing her sympathies with her aunt's financial predicament, it seemed easy to spell out her own predicament. How on the one hand there was the excitement of the challenge Mainthorpe had set, and on the other the niggling doubts as to why he had dismissed his housekeeper.

Strangely, the act of writing out her doubts seemed to reduce them. The fact that the Master had always been completely straight and had never once made an improper suggestion grew in her mind. Eventually Helen decided that it was best not to discuss them with Joseph; he might think she was being silly. Instead, a brisk walk down to the village post office would be both enjoyable and allow her to try out the cord trousers and warm topcoat.

Walking out of the house into the garden Helen was surprised how neglected it had become. The shrubs that Grandpa used to keep carefully pruned were now overgrown and straggly and the herbaceous borders were covered with last year's dead trash. The overgrown shrubs, though, provided ideal nesting places for garden birds and now, despite the chill in the air, they seemed to sing just for her. Pausing to listen, Helen recognised both a blackbird and a song thrush and then, just a she was leaving, a robin hopping about in the trash added his more gentle call.

Once out in the field and away from the shelter of the house and buildings, the cold east breeze tested her new clothes. Following the winding path down the sloping field, almost parallel to the sledge run, Helen was disappointed that her new wellington boots felt a bit clumsy. The memory of that enjoyable afternoon lifted her spirits: the speed of the sledge, the laughter of the young people and Joseph . . . what about Joseph? Could she share her thoughts with him? Dare she tell him that she was having doubting thoughts about the Master?

Now, less than a week from lambing, the ewes were mostly in small groups scattered across the field, but there seemed little for them to eat. Compared to the green pastures near to Fletchfield, here on these hilly fields the grass was brown and shrivelled. Helen noticed how in the hollows most sheltered from the east wind there was some green grass and it was in these areas that many of the sheep grazed.

The cold wind may have checked the grass but had not stopped nature. Helen stopped to look at how the primroses, which were now coming into bloom, would soon provide a swathe of creamy white here and there along the steep banks above the path. With a skylark hovering in full song overhead the scene was magical. Among the sheep on the lower part of the field the occasional lapwing searched for a nesting site while high above her mate soared and swooped in a noisy display of courtship.

What really thrilled her was the haunting call of the curlews. How many times in the past months had she dreamt of that call only to wake up and find she was still in a grimy back street in town. Although the curlews were mostly hovering in the distance over Leckon Moor, the occasional one flew overhead calling as though saluting her homecoming. Helen couldn't resist throwing up her arms and calling back, "Yes, I'm back in my valley."

Saying the same again at the graveside, Helen touched the headstone, running her fingers over her father's name.

The village was much quieter than on her last visit. Chatting to Miss Hunter in the village shop, Helen learned how many of the locals, who lost their jobs when the mill went bankrupt, were still out of work while others had found work away from the village. In the mood to have a good moan, Miss Hunter continued, "I only moved to the village because Dad got a foreman's job in the mill and with it the chance to rent this house and shop. It was ideal because I always wanted my own business, but now the mill's closed things are not so good. Those who are working outside the village are buying provisions near their work, and the villagers who are still out of work aren't spending much."

Helen made polite noises and was leaving the shop when Miss Hunter said, "Even my dad can't get a job. No one wants a 65-year-old, though he'd settle for a bit of part-time gardening."

Having noticed on her walk that those ewes that had been lambing on her last visit were now over the brook on Bottoms Field, Helen decided that work could wait. Saying hello to the blacksmith and smiling a greeting to anyone else out and about, she walked on through the village and down the lane towards the Bottoms Field.

When Mainthorpe told Joseph that Helen was coming to the Grange for a couple of weeks, he said it in such a possessive way that Joseph became sure there was more than a working relationship between them, particularly when Mainthorpe's explanation about the confidentiality needed with the new making-up department didn't ring true. Telling people that Helen was coming to help with the lambing wouldn't be believed either. As regards Helen, Joseph was confused; in his mind one moment she was a young girl in need of his protection and the next she was a tall, elegant young woman who made him feel like a blushing schoolboy.

Finding that he did his best thinking when walking through the fields, Joseph set out to check both the sheep and the grazing. Between the trees and bushes along the brook banks and the woodland covering the lower slopes of the westerly hills, Bottoms Field nestled like a suntrap hidden from the cold spring winds. Joseph leaned on the gate, smiling at the antics of the playful lambs. Seeing how well they were doing and feeling the satisfaction of knowing there was enough grass on this sheltered field for the ewes made him more than content with his farming lot. If only women were as easy to understand, he thought.

A group of lambs held his attention as they gambolled along the brook bank side. When they gathered round a tree stump, one jumped on and another tried to follow but was knocked back with a head butt, while a third came from behind and tipped the first head over heels and off the tree stump.

"Do all lambs play King of the Castle?"

Startled and embarrassed, Joseph spun round at the sound of Helen's voice. "You . . . what . . .? I didn't hear you coming."

Helen laughed, "It's my new wellies. They're a softer rubber so I'll be able to creep up on you. Oh, look how those lambs run."

The lambs, tired of playing king of the castle, were now racing along the steep bit of bank right above the water. Helen said, "They are incredibly surefooted, you'd expect them to knock one another in."

"But they don't," Joseph said, recovering some of his composure, "they just grow up to be boring old sheep."

They walked back up to the Grange together. Joseph wanted to say something about Helen's relationship with the Master. Instead he mentioned how well the lambs were doing, pointed to the lapwings and together they paused to listen to the lark's music from the sky but he could not find the words to say anything about the Master. Helen broached the subject. "I often wondered how difficult it was to change from working with your own family to working for the Master, and on the same farm where you grew up."

"Well, I suppose it would be nice if it was my own but this is the nearest thing to it. I love this farm, this valley, these hills and the Master's great to work for. He leaves me alone to get on with it, as long as I can tell him what I intend to do and why."

"You mean he never interferes with how you run the farm."

"He has his say, particularly when he drives me off to buy some cattle or more machinery but I enjoy those talks and usually they're more wide ranging than just the farm."

"You obviously respect him."

"Grief, yes, more than any man I've ever met."

"Will you take afternoon tea in the lounge now Miss Helen?" Cook's question startled Helen while she was balancing on one leg to remove her boots. "To start with I'm not Miss Helen, I just work for him like you, so please just call me Helen. As regards tea, yes I'd love a cup."

The tea came on an ornate tray loaded with teapots, hot water, milk, sugar and a selection of cakes. Placing it on the coffee table near to the fire Cook said, "There you are Miss Helen, now about dinner . . ."

Helen cut in, "I'm just Helen, and please come and sit down while we talk about meals."

Cook took a bit of persuading that Helen was not to be treated as though she was an honoured guest but she eventually agreed that Helen could join her at the kitchen table for breakfast. That Cook enjoyed preparing a gastronomic dinner for the Master at seven o'clock was obvious by her reluctance to agree to Helen's request for a simple meal for both of them at six. Helen wasn't sure whether it would hurt Cook's professional pride too much to mention lunch but in the end took the plunge. "About lunch, I don't want to break off at a set time and as I don't eat much. Would you mind if I made my own?"

"Do you want to get rid of me as well as the housekeeper?"

"Good heavens, no. I just want to make it easier for you while there is no housekeeper. For instance, while I'm here on my own there's no need to light the dining-room fire because I intend to work in my bedroom. That is if you will give me a hand to carry in that small table from off the landing?"

Realising there were opportunities in a reduced workload, Cook said, "When the Master doesn't need me here I usually go home for two days in the middle of the week. Would you mind, Miss Helen, if I did that tomorrow? I'll be back on Thursday night to prepare for the Master on Friday."

Feeling very uncomfortable with the way Cook kept calling her Miss and liking the idea of just being herself, Helen said, "Of course, yes, but how will you travel?"

"My nephew delivers papers to the village shop each morning. If I'm at the end of the lane by half-past eight he'll give me a lift."

Chapter Nineteen

By the time that Mainthorpe was due for his evening meal on Friday evening Helen had fallen into a routine: breakfast on the scrubbed wooden kitchen table followed by a brisk walk down to the village shop for a daily paper and perhaps a few sweets, then back up to her bedroom to work.

Or at least that was the theory. There were so many interesting things to see, from the curlews up on Leckon Moor to a happy half an hour watching the frolicking lambs. Then the temptation to relive childhood days by looking for the nests of lapwings and skylarks on her walk across the fields was irresistible. Even when Helen finally sat down to work, the view for the bedroom window was as distracting as it was inspirational.

Anna was a treasure, keeping the kitchen stove running in Cook's absence and the lounge fire well fuelled to provide for a comfortable evening and to send its warmth up into her bedroom. The only disappointment was the approach Mary Smith had to her work now there was no longer a housekeeper in charge. By Friday morning Helen had seen enough and pointed to the accumulating dust in the dining room. "The Master won't expect to see any of that when he arrives this evening."

The cleaner said a few strong words but Helen stood her ground and by the time she came down for a late lunch the grime and dust were gone.

She changed into her new grey casual evening dress. When she had bought it Helen had thought the dress would not look too seductive but now, giving a twirl in front of the full-length mirror, she wasn't too sure. The square neck met that criterion but the skirt length revealed more than expected. Through the Twenties fashion hemlines had risen, first to mid-calf and then to upper calf and it now barely covered the knee. When Helen placed a chair in front of the mirror to see what it was like when sitting, it looked disconcertingly revealing. "Oh, well I've bought it so I'm going to wear it regardless."

When Helen entered the lounge Mainthorpe was reading 'Farmer and Stockbreeder' while listening to the six o'clock news. He looked up. "My, that's a pretty dress. It makes you look more mature. You are an exceptionally attractive woman, you know."

Embarrassed and disconcerted by the unexpected compliment, Helen blushed and went to sit on the other armchair opposite but, suddenly conscious of her dress and that Mainthorpe was still watching, changed her mind and walked over to the bookcase.

Watching Helen take down a book and sit partially hidden behind the other armchair, Mainthorpe realised he had embarrassed the girl. After all, with two women in his life he had learned what sorts of things a woman likes to hear and after such a compliment either of them would have puffed up with pleasure. They were mature in womanly guile whilst this girl, with a mind that provided companionship far beyond anything they had to offer, was obviously put out by what he thought was just a polite remark. It made him question his motives; what did he want from this girl? He was fairly confident Helen would eventually come up with designs that would be creative and different but it could have been achieved in some other way. No doubt if he'd discussed it fully with Grimshaw, instead of keeping his plans secret, Grimshaw would have relished the task. So why had he brought the girl here?

Perhaps it was because that one weekend in her company had been so enjoyable he wanted more of it, though suggesting that Helen should come had been a spur-of-the-moment idea. Mainthorpe still marvelled that a woman should match his feelings for both the countryside around this valley and the workings of the farm. And in the evening that this same woman could linger over dinner to discuss the politics of the day or astutely challenge his business ideas gave him an incredible feeling of satisfaction.

Mainthorpe was wise enough to know he had a reputation and because of it there would be talk. It was perhaps seeing how attractive she looked that set him to musing over his inner motives. He was troubled to realise that those turquoise eyes, which had haunted his dreams through the years, were now even more disturbing because behind them was an incredible young woman with a figure to match. He was still mulling over the situation when Anna announced dinner.

The fact that Helen treated Anna as an equal no longer embarrassed her and Mainthorpe seemed to welcome Anna's chatty service style. When she left the room he said, "I prefer these country girls; they know how to be respectful without being smarmy. Are you surprised that Anna's become a really good maid?"

"She is not my maid, she is my friend. I don't wish to talk about her like this. You've put me in a very difficult position, leaving me here and expecting me to run the house."

Mainthorpe chuckled. "Yes, I know, but I've noticed that this dining room's cleaner than it was last weekend, so maybe you're not doing too badly."

Helen stayed quiet.

Eventually Mainthorpe broke the silence. "I'm only staying one night. I'll ride out in the morning, then after an early lunch I'll drive back to Fletchfield. There's a charity dinner in town and as it was my birthday this week Jessica's persuaded me to go and celebrate."

"Did you have anything else for your birthday, Master?"

"Yes, Jessica gave me the latest Sherlock Holmes by Arthur Conan Doyle. It's called *Shoscombe Old Place*. Have you heard of him?"

"I've heard of him but I've never read any. I didn't take you for a book reader, Master."

"I usually read for a half hour each night; it helps me relax. I'll let you have it when I've finished it."

The period of quiet while Anna served the main course was broken when Mainthorpe said, "Did you see in today's paper where next month Charles Lindbergh's planning to fly solo across the Atlantic Ocean? It will be incredible if he does."

Helen listened to him describing the aeroplane and wondered what it was about men and machines that got them so carried away. When Mainthorpe finally exhausted the subject she said, "I've been having a look round the garden. Grandpa used to keep it tidy. Don't you have anyone to do it?"

"It's something I've been meaning to sort out. Perhaps I should put a notice in the village shop?"

When Helen told him about the shopkeeper's father, Jack Hunter, Mainthorpe said, "He sounds ideal but I've no time to see him this week. But we don't want to miss him so how about you asking him to come and look at the garden? If he wants the job take him on for, say, about two days each week."

"I don't think that I should hire your staff for you, Master."

"No, perhaps not. I'll have a talk with Joseph then perhaps the two of you can decide if he's suitable, and if he is put him to work. Right, now you've sorted that out for me, how about a housekeeper? You mentioned this aunt of yours. Would she be suitable?"

Helen told him more about Aunt Emily, how she had been in service here and always spoke fondly of the village and the Grange. Mainthorpe said, "She sounds ideal. Write and tell her that there's a job here and that if she's interested to send me her details. Then if I like the sound of her we'll go and interview her the week after next."

Chapter Twenty

Joseph was so troubled about Helen's relationship with the Master that not only was it distracting him in the daytime but it also disrupted his sleep. Eventually, and trying his best to make it sound casual, he asked Anna what was going on. "There's nothing going on as far as I know," Anna said with a shrug. "They seem to talk about everyday things over dinner and I've been into the lounge later on to make the fire up, and nothing."

"How do you mean – nothing?"

"Well, the Master was reading the paper and Helen was reading a book and soon after she went up to bed."

None of it made sense to Joseph so he persisted. "What about her bedroom? What's she doing in there most of the day?"

"Helen keeps the door locked when she's not in there – eh, you're getting very curious about Helen, aren't you?"

Joseph blushed and walked off across the farmyard.

Having deliberately avoided Helen through the week Joseph realised he couldn't avoid her any longer when the Master told him to see her about engaging a gardener. Helen met him with a smile. "Joseph, you seem to have had a busy week. Has the Master mentioned hiring a gardener?"

"Yes, but he just said for me to talk to you."

Both of them were a bit embarrassed by the situation. In the end it was agreed Helen would talk to Jack Hunter when she went for the Saturday morning paper and, if he was interested, arrange for him to come and see the garden and meet Joseph.

In the event, Mr Hunter was so keen that he arranged to come to the Grange for one o'clock that afternoon. By arranging it so quickly, Helen thought – and suggested it to Mainthorpe over lunch – that he could talk to Jack Hunter before setting off back for

Fletchfield but Mainthorpe said, "No, I've complete confidence in you and Joseph."

By 12.45 Mainthorpe was striding across the yard to his car and, with a parting "Good luck with the gardener", drove away. There was no alternative left for Helen but to explain to Joseph that there were just the two of them to meet the gardener. Joseph smiled. "You should know the Master by now; when he tells you to do something he expects it done. Anyway, he seems to think you know more about the garden than anyone so you have to do the talking."

Helen groaned. "Oh, no, I just said it was getting a bit rough, that it needed tidying up."

"Well, here's the man to do it so you tell him what you have in mind."

Mr Hunter seemed keen and enthusiastic when he saw the garden and was asking what needed to be done when Simon walked in. Helen introduced him to both Joseph and Mr Hunter before asking, "What are you doing here, Simon?"

"I heard that your boss was going to this fancy dinner so I thought that if you were on your own you might enjoy a night out?"

Though he was obviously a friend of Helen's, Joseph took an instant dislike to Simon; his approach was too brash and the way he withdrew but stayed in listening range while they talked to the gardener offended Joseph. He was already feeling uncomfortable with the way the Master had given the responsibility to Helen. Not that Joseph was really interested in the garden. It was just what he walked through sometimes on the way to his real work in the fields, though he loved to hear the birdsong and used to enjoy seeing it tidy. Before the Master reduced his workforce he even had one of his men work in it occasionally but none of them were really interested. Now he left Helen to lead the discussion with Jack Hunter. It was Helen who suggested which shrubs could be pruned and which should wait until autumn, and it was Helen who decided that Jack would need a couple of extra days to get it tidy and after that two days each week would be enough. Joseph only joined in the discussion when it came to hours and pay.

Agreeing to start the following week, Jack Hunter left for home and Joseph walked back to the old farmhouse, but he was still a troubled man. For a start, he just couldn't comprehend the transformation of the tubby schoolgirl into this tall, attractive young woman. Now he was surprised at her confidence and disturbed about what the relationship could be between her and the Master to give her that confidence.

There was a Laurel and Hardy film showing at the Fletchfield cinema so Simon suggested they see the first house and have fish and chips afterwards. Originally looking forward to an evening on her own, Helen decided it might be fun to spend an evening with him and invited him in. Leaving him in the lounge, she went through to the kitchen to make them both a cup of tea and tell Cook that she would not be back for an evening meal. It was a few minutes before Helen returned to the lounge with a tray of tea and cakes and when she did Simon wasn't there. Walking in from the hall he said, "I thought I'd have a look round while you were busy."

Helen said, "It's not my house or I'd show you around."

"Ouch, am I being reprimanded?"

The night was a complete change from the serious discussions with Mainthorpe. Simon's persistent questions about Mainthorpe's plans irritated Helen but the hilarious antics of the two film stars put her in a happy mood. Though the fish and chips smelled tempting they resisted opening them, instead keeping them wrapped and warm while Simon drove out into the country to park in a quiet gateway.

The fish and chips over and still chuckling over the film, Helen let Simon kiss her. He tasted of vinegar and chips. It wasn't her first kiss and it wasn't the most exciting. After three kisses the taste of chips receded but the excitement didn't increase. Perhaps it did for Simon because his hands started to wander. Glad that she was wearing an out-of-fashion longer dress, Helen decided it was home time when Simon reached for the hem.

On the drive back to the Grange Simon wondered about this girl. He liked her more than anyone else and yet she was so elusive, both in the information she parted with and when he wanted more in the car. He was even more disappointed when, pulling up outside the Grange, Helen just gave him a quick peck on the cheek, said, "Thank you for a lovely evening", and vanished inside. Having had at least expected an invitation in, Simon struck the steering wheel in frustration and drove thoughtfully away.

The Boltons again invited Helen to join them for lunch after morning service. When the washing-up was finished Helen said to Anna, "Let's go for a long walk. I'd love to see the curlews on Leckon Moor and perhaps we could go through the wood onto Quarry Moor."

Under a cloudy sky the views were terrific. From the high point on the moor they could see across the Cheshire Plain to the west as far as Frodsham, southerly across the rolling hills of North Staffordshire, and on the other sides the higher, rugged Derbyshire Peaks seemed to go on forever. They spent a happy thirty minutes pointing out different features of the distant landscape before wandering over to the edge of the wood to sit on a log, watching. Indicating the curlews Helen said, "Aren't they great? But listen to the woodland birds behind us."

"It's the threat of rain. Joseph says it always brings them on to sing," Anna replied.

"He loves this valley, doesn't he? Do you think he could ever settle anywhere else?"

"I don't know what he'd do if he had to leave here," said Anna, touching Helen's arm. "But then you had to leave and you coped."

"There is something I wanted to ask you," Helen said. "It's about Ned. He seems to work strange hours and I heard Isaac pulling his leg about something."

"He's got a girlfriend; but she is not a girl, she's a married woman. I think her husband's some sort of salesman. Whatever he is he stays away from home a couple of nights each week and Ned must keep her company."

"But surely your Mother doesn't approve?"

"He's good at making excuses," Anna said with a grin. "In summer he tells her he's working late and when the evenings get dark he claims to be helping the keeper look for poachers, but I think Mum knows. Mothers always know. Oh, I'm sorry, I didn't think about you."

"Come on, let's get across Quarry Moor before it rains," said Helen, catching hold of Anna's hand.

When collecting the daily paper on Monday morning Helen posted the letter to her Aunt and within a short time was upstairs in her room. Concentration was not a problem and ideas, which had eluded her the previous week, now began to take shape.

Joseph was kept busy helping his shepherd now that the sheep were lambing. They had moved the in-lamb ewes onto the smaller field; lying below Quarry Moor it was more sheltered from any easterly winds. Even though the weather was fairly mild the two men took turns to walk through the flock. Tom Smith looked after the sheep most of the time but Joseph took a turn when the shepherd went for his lunch and again after tea in the evening. Needless to say, with all the other farm work demanding his attention there wasn't much time to rest and he was glad. Consumed with a sort of restlessness that he didn't understand Joseph found that keeping busy seemed to hold it at bay.

After a busy day spent working in her bedroom, a warm mid-week evening tempted Helen to take a walk across the lambing field. Seeing Joseph leaning against the wall at the far side of the field she walked over to him. "I was watching this ewe with twins," said Joseph. "One had got away from her and she didn't know whether to have it back again. She's letting it suckle now so I think it should be all right."

They chatted about sheep and the farm and all the time Joseph's eyes were roving across the field. Helen thought it was understandable when the sheep were lambing but in fact Joseph had another reason. With Helen wearing just an unbuttoned cardigan over her dress and low shoes with ankle socks, Joseph had caught a glimpse of curves where curves were meant to be and he was too shy to look. Until Helen walked away – then Joseph took his eyes away from the sheep for a while.

Jack Hunter proved not to be as competent in the garden as Helen had thought, and a couple of times each day he asked Cook to ask Miss Helen to have a word. When Helen went out it was always something elementary like should he prune this shrub or divide those herbaceous plants? Having learned a bit about gardening from both her Grandpa and Aunt Emily, she knew enough to know that she didn't know much but when Jack needed a decision she made one. The trouble was that her bedroom window looked out over the garden and Jack's indecision distracted her.

Nevertheless, Helen made progress with a design. Starting from a sketch, each design had to be developed in full colour onto small graph paper. Even at this stage it was necessary to understand cloth construction because the design was not just about colours but also the pattern of colours, which had to be mixed in the right way to produce the correct strength in the finished cloth. Each square on the paper represented an intersection of the warp and weft. To get the correct material strength the size of repeat and the number of colours available all came into her calculations.

Once the design emerged in her mind it was completely absorbing. With a rough sketch of a second waiting on the table suddenly there was urgency, even though each would need Mainthorpe's approval before the final working design was begun.

Normally that was when Mr Grimshaw gave his approval to his junior designers. Such was his experience that he could tell at a glance if a design would produce a stable fabric. There was no way that Mr Grimshaw would let a member of his team spend ten or fourteen days meticulously hand-painting a design onto large point paper unless he was sure it was suitable.

On the Friday night Mainthorpe, arriving just in time for dinner, was wearing boldly striped plus-four tweeds and equally colourful stockings with matching jumper. Compared to his usual well-worn tweeds and baggy jumper this new version of her Master made Helen smile. Mainthorpe noticed. "What? Don't you like them? They're the latest country wear. Jessica insisted I did something about my appearance. She said I looked like an old tramp. I thought perhaps you were thinking the same."

"Good heavens, no. You'll frighten the sheep in those." Helen tried to hide a giggle. "Anyway, you look more relaxed in your old tweeds."

That brought a smile and a promise that he would be back in them by the morning. After dinner Helen brought down the two designs. Although one wasn't finished there was enough for Mainthorpe to see and he took a long time over his examination. By the movements of his head and hands it was obvious to Helen that he was calculating the material strength in the design. Eventually he said, "Ohm, yes. They're certainly different but I think I like them."

Helen said, "Nothing would ever go past this stage without Mr Grimshaw's approval."

"And these won't go past this stage without my approval – but you've got it, so don't worry."

The discussion moved back to the renovation progress. Explaining that it would be another week before they could move into the design department, Mainthorpe said, "I've been giving some thought as to who should work with you. Young Peter Gradburn came through his apprenticeship with flying colours and I like what he's done since. Could you work with him?"

When Helen nodded enthusiastically, Mainthorpe continued, "I've got the chance of a contract to make collars and bows for ladies' dresses. It's one of the firms I already supply material to; they guessed what we're up to."

"That's good news. It's a lot better than losing a customer and if you get the costs right it should increase the cash flow in the making-up department."

Next morning they were just finishing breakfast when the post was delivered. The letter for Helen was from Aunt Emily who was really enthusiastic about the housekeeper's position. Making it plain how she had enjoyed working at the Grange as a school leaver and had been reluctant to move to Matlock with her mistress, the letter went on to say, *'I long to get back to Gritstencrag. Life is becoming impossible here, people seem to blame me for Uncle Horace's debts.'* The letter included a list of positions Aunt Emily had held with her mistress but it did not include being the housekeeper. Helen showed the letter to Mainthorpe who read it carefully before saying, "Well, she's had quite a bit of experience and from what you've told me your Aunt's a hard worker with it, so why don't we go and see her?"

"My Aunt's given the local doctor's number. Apparently he's one of her customers and if we ring him he should pass the message on."

"Right, then you arrange for us to go over there next Tuesday afternoon. The Waggoner's saddled my horse so I'm off for a ride."

Deciding it would be enjoyable to ride through the village, Mainthorpe set off down Leckon Lane. The lambing field rose towards the moor on his right where he could see both Joseph and Tom Smith working among the sheep. In the field on his left some of the newly lambed ewes were grazing and mothering their young lambs.

When Mainthorpe reined the horse round to follow the lane running alongside the brook into Gritstencrag, he turned that way satisfied with his day. Not just because good men were working in his fields among healthy-looking livestock but also because he had found a way to keep that girl visiting the Grange. Recalling making this journey in his car years before when he went to fetch the doctor to Helen's grandfather, Mainthorpe had no idea then just what an important part that young girl would play in his life. Oh, he was well aware that having her with him at the Grange was risking both his reputation and hers, but he had now found the solution, and chuckled at its simplicity. If Aunt Emily was anything like suitable he resolved to have her installed in the Grange, then Helen would have a legitimate reason for visiting.

Casting his eye across the bottom field and the older lambs, Mainthorpe was even more pleased to see how well they looked. Although the grass was grazed bare Joseph had already told him that these sheep would be moved up onto the moor in the next few days.

All seemed well with the village. Several people greeting him and even the blacksmith laid down his hammer to say, "Good morning, Sir."

Mainthorpe always made this circular ride this way round because of how steep the track was from the Grange. To ride down it threw his weight onto his stirrups and his dodgy ankle could ache for days afterwards but riding up bank was much more comfortable. There was just one gate to open by the Church and to his surprise the vicar was waiting by it. "Good morning, Vicar; it's good of you to open the gate for me."

The vicar started to open the gate then stopped. "I wanted to have a word with you, Sir. It's come to my notice that you're entertaining a young lady un-chaperoned. I feel some responsibility for young Helen Brindley and – "

Pointing his riding crop towards the vicar, Mainthorpe interrupted him. "Don't you tell me about responsibility. If you'd had your way she'd have been in an orphanage. Now she has a responsible position working for me and, anyway, it's none of your business."

"I only want what's best for the child."

"Child? Grief, man, she's not a child but a very sophisticated young woman. Now if you'll open the gate I'll bid you good day."

Still feeling irritated by the vicar, Mainthorpe refused to go with Mrs Bolton and Helen to morning service, instead riding out across the moor. Again Mrs Bolton asked Helen to join her family for Sunday lunch. They were such a happy family that the afternoon was well gone when Helen got back to the Grange. Mainthorpe had left a note saying, *'I'll pick you up on Tuesday at 10.30. We'll have lunch on the way and be with your Aunt about two o'clock'.*

Having already arranged for the cook to have the afternoon off, Helen was again alone in the large house. Yet strangely it didn't feel lonely; in fact it simply felt like home.

Taking a pot of tea and a few sandwiches on a tray to the lounge window, she sat where she could gaze across the valley and contemplate. Simon had guessed that she would be alone and had telephoned earlier to see whether he could visit. When she refused him he said, 'But you'll be lost on your own.' With a view like this how can anyone be lost, Helen thought, and why can't Simon, who's been my best friend, understand how much this valley means to me? Why was Joseph so quiet over lunch? He used to have lots to say but now he was so quiet that Anna and her brothers were teasing him. Then Helen remembered how, when she tried to draw Joseph into the conversation, not only did he not respond but there were some strange looks from Mrs Bolton to both her and him.

A buzzard glided into view with outstretched wings, riding the breeze with such skill that his only movements were a tilting of his tail and a rippling in the feathers on his wing tips. Rising higher to circle over the garden, his mottled colours became lost against the grey sky. The effect made him look almost as dark as a crow. It's funny, Helen thought, when I'm here I feel as free as that bird but in Fletchfield I feel hemmed in by buildings and people.

Those thoughts took her on to the Master. What does he want? When he wanted approval for his new clothes it had touched her that he should care what she thought, and over dinner, though the discussions ranged far and wide, he was always considerate of her points of view. No, it wasn't just that he was considerate; he actually wanted to hear her opinion and watched intently while she gave it. Then Helen remembered how Mainthorpe not only looked intently into her eyes when she was speaking but was also covertly watching her more than he used to. She dismissed the thought because all men did that; particularly now hemlines had risen dramatically in just a few years.

Gazing across the valley with a feeling of gratitude to Mainthorpe, for the very fact that she was here and for the influence he had played in her life, it made her aware of just how much she had grown to like and respect him. He was a man who seemed to be entwined in her future, but to what end?

Chapter Twenty-One

After an enjoyable three weeks' stay at the Grange Helen found the industrial grime of Fletchfield depressing. It was offset, though, by the genuine pleasure expressed by the Buxtons on her return. The exciting challenge at work and a substantial increase in salary also helped.

Peter Gradburn joined Helen in the new design department after Mainthorpe had taken Mr Grimshaw into his confidence. To Helen's dismay, he admitted that he had not only shown Grimshaw the first of her two designs but also told him to come across to discuss them with her. Helen waited for Grimshaw's visit with a feeling of dread. Carrying the suitably covered design, Grimshaw walked into her design room and with a deadpan face suggested an adjustment that strengthened the weave without disrupting her basic colour pattern. As to the second one, which Helen was still working on, he studied it for some time and, again to her surprise, approved it. This time, to her amusement, he primly addressed her as Miss Helen.

From then on, although Grimshaw didn't work alongside them in the new department, his was the final authority over which design was submitted to the Master.

Knowing that there was no one working for him with the right experience, Mainthorpe gave some thought to who should oversee the making-up department. By chance he was having lunch with one of his South Manchester customers when the old man, a product of a rags-to-riches life, complained, "I've just sacked one of me best workers."

"Oh, why?"

"Because her wer arguing with me overseer about how th'job should be done. The trouble was her wer right but when I put a man in charge I expect him to be obeyed."

"Sounds like you sacked the wrong person."

"No, yer canna have a woman in charge of fifty chattering women; there'd be nowt done."

On the pretext of knowing someone who wanted a good seamstress, Mainthorpe obtained her details and drove out to her home that afternoon. The product of a working-class background, Ruth Douglas, a tall, broad shouldered forty year old, nevertheless impressed Mainthorpe sufficiently for him to invite her to the new mill the next day. In fact, he told her to go to the new mill and ask for Miss Helen, later telling Helen to give him a ring when she came and in the meantime to show her around.

When the two of them met it was Helen who was less at ease. Mrs Douglas had a natural confidence that at first Helen found disconcerting. From her questions, the woman had obviously been taken into Mainthorpe's confidence, which meant that they were able to discuss the project openly. It wasn't long before Helen realised that Mrs Douglas's assured demeanour came from a remarkable grasp of the industry.

Mainthorpe joined them on the top floor where the many tall windows lit up the newly decorated room. He and Mrs Douglas were soon discussing where best to site the sewing machines and other working arrangements. Helen turned to go back to work but Mainthorpe called her back and from then on drew her into the discussions. Suddenly, in his abrupt way, Mainthorpe settled terms of employment and said, "You'll have to excuse me. Miss Helen will tell you anything else you want to know. Good day."

Mrs Douglas watched him walk noisily down the empty room. The limp was more noticeable. Was it, Helen wondered, because he had hurried up these stairs twice today? Mrs Douglas was too discreet to mention the limp but bold enough to say, "Tell me, Miss Helen, is he your father?"

"No."

"Uncle perhaps?"

"No. We are not related. I just work for him."

"You mean that I've met a man who promotes women?"

Helen laughed, "I think it's a new experience for him."

It took a month for Aunt Emily to settle her affairs back in Flacton and make the move to the Grange. It didn't take that long for Mainthorpe to suggest to Helen that her Aunt would be pleased to see her during the coming weekend.

Bob Fairclough now employed a driver for his milk lorry and had bought a bus. He carried workers from Fletchfield out to a quarry and then circled round the lanes past the end of Gritstencrag Lane, collecting passengers on the way back into town. In the evening he did the reverse journey. When Mainthorpe suggested, "Helen, about visiting your aunt this weekend – you can have a ride out to the Grange with me if you'd like," Helen explained about the bus and declined. Mainthorpe said, "But you'll have to walk from the main road."

"Yes, but I love that walk along the brook; it's part of the pleasure of going back."

Considering his offer, Helen was surprised to find that Mainthorpe wasn't at the Grange on that Friday evening. Helen and Aunt Emily had one of Cook's high teas in the kitchen and afterwards relaxed together in the lounge. Relaxed was not quite the right word, though, because her Aunt was so full of being back in the village she was bubbling over with the thrill of being reunited with old friends.

To Helen's dismay Aunt Emily had, on Mainthorpe's instruction, prepared the same bedroom. Helen argued, "I'm visiting you. I should sleep in the servant's section with you."

Aunt Emily said, "Then if you are a servant you sleep where you're told."

After Saturday morning breakfast Helen strode out across the fields to look at the young lambs. Walking over the bank towards where a bridge crossed Bullerstone Brook she was surprised to see Joseph. With his faithful sheepdog sitting by his legs Joseph stood with his hands resting on the bridge parapet. Whatever he was watching was hidden from her along the back of Leckon Wood so she stood watching him. Looking directly into the sun with the peak of his deerstalker shading his eyes, the profile of Joseph's clean-shaven face and his intense stillness touched her heart. It wasn't just that he was handsome but more that he typified these hills. To wrest a living up here it took rugged determination and this was written on his face and on the way he stood. He also looked more lithe and handsome in a pair of trousers and boots than in his usual cord breeches and wellingtons. Just one movement of her foot caused Bob to turn with a growl. The spell was broken and Joseph spun round, slightly embarrassed. "What were you watching?" Helen asked.

"There was a fox slinking along the edge of the wood. If it's hunting at this time of day it'll be a vixen with cubs."

"Is that a problem now you've finished lambing?"

"Tom reckons we've already lost about fifteen lambs and now she's started in them she'll carry on until they grow too big."

"When will that be?"

"It's hard to say. Maybe when they're about six weeks old, but she could take a lot be then."

This wood had fascinated Helen when Grandpa took her through it years before. Like many of the old estates this one had existed for generations to give pleasure to the landlord's family. It was not just that they enjoyed shooting and hunting but, like most landlords, they took pleasure in the aesthetic value of their property. These trees were an example, planted perhaps three generations before to create a mixture of colours that could be seen from both the Grange and the high part of the shooting lodge garden. Not that guests would be there many times in the year but if they were there now they could see a spring show of hazel catkins along the lower side near the brook. Although they were beginning to fall, interspersed among them the new pale green leaves of hazel and hawthorn were emerging and soon hawthorn, the mayflower of the hills, would be dressed as a young bride shrouded in white lace.

The trees were not in view from her Grandpa's cottage but as a girl she had climbed the steep bank to the top of the quarry just to see the changing colours of spring and early summer. One of the pleasures of living there had been to see those changes as the naked branches of winter slowly clothed themselves in different shades of green. Even the sombre evergreen scotch-fir broke its winter mourning by sprouting a bright new dress of fragrant green.

Memories of those happy days were flashing through Helen's mind as she joined Joseph on the bridge. "Joseph, look, soon the mayflower will be out, and see over there . . . further back in the wood . . . horse chestnut candles. Sometimes a red glow in the early morning sky behind them could make them look like fairy candles."

"You think a lot about this valley, don't you? I never realised before just what it means to you."

"Of course I do. And Grandpa taught me to understand it. He used to bring me through here and make me name each tree."

"My father did the same and each spring he'd take some larch branches, just as the flowers were emerging, back for mother. I'll get some on the way back because mother says the fragrance of larch in spring fulfils God's promise of new life."

They walked further along the edge of the brook, looking across into the wood until Joseph pointed to fresh soil on the far bank amongst the trees. "They're in there all right. Look, there's even some lamb's feet near the fox earth. Come here, Rob. Stay!"

"What will you do?"

"I'll get the keeper to deal with them. In the meantime I don't want the dog disturbing them or the vixen'll move elsewhere, though now she's got the taste it won't be out of range of my lambs."

Helen walked with him through the sheep and up onto Quarry Moor where he wanted to check how soon he could move the sheep on to it. It was marvellous to see the change in him. The tongue-tied young man who had sat opposite her at Mrs Bolton's dinner table was now talking freely about heather growth and sheep numbers. Noticing that the bilberry flowers were just opening, Helen mentioned coming here with her Grandpa to pick the berries each July. Joseph asked, "Have you ever picked bearberries up on Leckon Moor?"

"I've never even heard of them. Grandpa never said anything about them."

"It's easy to miss them because they're only about six inches high. There's even a small area on this moor."

Joseph led her through the heather and bilberries to where a few prostrate bearberries grew. "Not that there's much to see yet. They won't be in flower until late June or July."

Realising her interest, Joseph dropped onto one knee to point out other species just emerging among the leggy heather, which was also tipped with fresh green shoots. "That's why I've come; I wanted to check there's enough growth before I move the sheep on."

"I've heard it said that by eating the new shoots the sheep are killing both heather and bilberries; is that right?"

"No. Not if there's not too many sheep on the moor. You know the squire's agreed that we can divide the moors so that each farm has its own section? Yes, well, we started last year but it'll take a lot of stone and a few more years of hard work. Anyway, he made us start by fencing the sheep out of one section to see what will happen."

"Will the bilberries grow taller?"

"I doubt it. I think between the grouse and the hares they'll still be kept trimmed."

Realising the implication of dividing walls across the moor, she asked, "Does that mean the end of having to heft sheep and sort out those who wander?"

Joseph laughed, "It'll have to be a good wall to stop these hill sheep from wandering."

The day went all too quickly and, as there was no bus on the Sunday, Helen had to leave to catch the Saturday afternoon one. As she walked along the brook-side lane, the sound of birdsong left her feeling deprived to have spent only one day there.

The following Tuesday Mainthorpe asked, "Why didn't you stay another day?"

"There are no buses on Sunday, Master."

"But you didn't need to catch the bus. You could have returned with me on Sunday afternoon." Seeing that she was at a loss as to how to explain, he continued, "Next weekend I've got a couple of guests coming to fish on both Saturday and Sunday. The father runs a distribution business and I hope they will handle my goods. Now the son's more your age so I wondered if you'd help to entertain him?"

"How do you mean, help to entertain him?"

"I've arranged an early lunch for when they arrive and after that I expect they'll fish the brook through the afternoon. If they're enjoying it perhaps we can have a late dinner. They don't know the brook so I thought if I took them down and left them perhaps you might wander down there and see if they're at ease?"

Helen smiled mischievously. "Is that all? I can do that on the way to the bus."

"No, it's not all. Join us over dinner and brighten up the conversation. Anyway, I can look after them on Sunday morning because I've arranged with Bolesworth to fish Lord Danesbury's trout pond."

On the day, Mr Stoddard and his son Edward arrived on time and were soon seated at the dining table. Finding it strange to be waited on by people whom she had always thought were her betters, Helen became more embarrassed when both Aunt Emily and Anna mischievously addressed her as Miss Helen. In return she pulled faces at them when the guests were not looking. The conversation was mainly between the two older men. Sitting between Helen and Mainthorpe, Edward said very little and neither Mainthorpe nor his father tried to bring him into the conversation.

Lunch over, the guests hurried out to prepare their tackle. Mainthorpe lingered and cleared his throat couple of times. Eventually he said, "My ankle's playing up today. Will you take them along the brook and I'll look after them tomorrow? It's not so undulating round the lake."

Why protest? The sun was shining, it was a lovely afternoon for a walk and the brook was always interesting.

Not having had much to do with fly-fishing, Helen was intrigued to watch the preparation. From the colourful fly-festooned tweed hats and the ritualistic greasing of the silk line it seemed more like religion than sport. When she said as much, Mr Stoddard smiled. "That's just what my wife says but I love these little brooks. Even though the fish are not very big it takes a rare bit of skill to hook one."

Leading them down to the stream below the Grange, Helen was surprised when Mr Stoddard suggested that the two men split up. Edward was told to fish upstream and his father, after leaning over the bridge parapet for a few minutes to watch the water, decided to walk down to the village and fish on the way back upstream. Helen walked alongside, encouraging him to talk. In a soft Lancashire accent he talked about his life, though his interest in the countryside was such that he talked more about that. Where the road crossed back over the brook Stoddard again leaned over that parapet, just watching the water. Eventually he broke the silence. "It's too early for May fly but there's an olive hatch on and, look, there's a trout just taken one. I'll have a try for him with a dry fly on the way back."

Not wanting to show her ignorance and as it was obvious that the sport completely absorbed him, Helen left him and walked through the village towards the graveyard.

The afternoon sun had brought people outside, either to work in their garden or to chat with neighbours. Although Helen didn't know all the villagers they all seem to know her and most of them wanted to talk. It was well over an hour before she returned to the brook. Completely unaware of being watched, the fisherman was crouched down and creeping towards the edge of the brook. Some five yards away from the lip of the bank he rested on one knee to cast upstream. On the third cast there was a splash and his rod bent with a jerk. Helen walked forward to stand just behind him when the fish came into the net. "What a lovely fish. Is it your first?"

"Oh, hello," Mr Stoddard said turning around, "I didn't realise you were watching and, no, this is my fifth. None of them would weigh a pound but I've kept the two largest."

Helen watched him fish for a while before walking on along the lane to look for Edward. He wasn't hard to find. Fishing a more open length of water, his clumsy approach was upright and, with his back to the sun, it was casting a shadow on the water. Helen might not know much about fly-fishing but she knew quite a bit about tickling trout and Edward would not get near them. Walking along the opposite bank she called, "Have you had any luck?"

"No, I've hooked a couple and lost them. I expect father's caught a bagful by now. If I don't catch a couple he'll be lecturing me all night about what I'm doing wrong."

Encouraging him to keep on trying, Helen watched him for a few minutes and then walked back to the bridge. Where the water rushed out from between its walls a pool had formed, which surprisingly had changed little since Grandpa's day. This had been one of his favourite spots. Lying face down and hidden between the bridge and a thorn bush (with her acting as lookout on the bridge) Grandpa had tickled a few dinners out of here. Glancing round to see if anyone was watching, and lifting her dress so that the grass wouldn't stain it, she dropped onto her knees, then lay flat to reach into the icy cold water. Discovering that her arms were a little longer than when she had done this under Grandpa's directions, she moved her hands slowly through the water and within seconds touched a fish. It was as though Grandpa was standing behind saying, 'Gently stroke its tummy. Now slowly close your hand round it.'

Within a few minutes her fingers closed round a second fish. Wriggling backwards to toss it onto the bank, she found Edward leaning over the parapet with eyes transfixed on her legs. Embarrassed, Helen jumped to her feet and pointed. "There's a couple you can show your father tonight."

Although Edward expressed his thanks he continued to look at her in such a disconcerting way that she took her leave.

Dinner was both pleasant and amusing. Stoddard senior recounted his fishing exploits but his inquiries as to how Edward had caught his two fish were answered by what seemed to be a modest shrug. Sitting round the fire after dinner, things became more uncomfortable because Helen repeatedly caught Edward's gaze riveted on her body and legs.

There were just two bathrooms in the main part of the Grange and neither of them was en suite. As Mr Stoddard's bedroom was opposite the Master's he would share what was normally Mainthorpe's bathroom and Edward was to share Helen's. The facilities being far more luxurious than anything in her previous experience, Helen thought little about them until bedtime, then, remembering Edward's bold stare, she bolted the bathroom door. Finishing in there, Helen loosely tied her dressing gown and unbolted the door. It burst in to send her staggering backwards into the washbasin, and within a second Edward was trying to kiss her. It took the strength of both hands to hold his face away and while she did he pulled on her dressing gown belt then gripped both wrists, forcing her arms down backwards to her waist. It was then Helen realised that both dressing gowns were open and beneath them both of them were naked. Still a virgin and not having seen a man's arousal before, Helen was momentarily transfixed. Seeing her look, Edward said, "Take a good look because now you're going to feel it."

When he pushed forward Helen brought her knee up, and she did feel it – painfully hard even against a bony knee. Edward slumped moaning onto the toilet seat.

Chapter Twenty-Two

As the months flew by, each week became a routine, five nights in Fletchfield and two at the Grange. The Buxtons were not offended, perhaps because out of her now substantial salary Helen paid them a generous allowance for her board.

The making-up department was nearing full capacity under the eagle eye of Ruth Douglas. When it had come to hiring women to work in that department, Mainthorpe left Helen and Ruth to conduct interviews and hire or not as they saw fit. To make it convenient for those applicants in regular work, many of those interviews were done in the evening and through that experience the two women developed a really good working relationship.

Although she did not hold any official position in management, the new staff accepted Helen's authority and surprisingly the others, knowing that she was close to the Master, treated her with respect.

The Master kept any business handled by the Stoddards within his office. Helen often wondered if he was aware of what had happened, or perhaps he sensed by her coldness towards them on the Sunday morning that something had upset her. Helen had surprised herself as to how controlled she had been over breakfast. The nightmare that night had been the worst ever. Edward didn't come into it; it was Uncle Horace's evil eyes leering into hers as he crushed both wrists in his powerful grip, forcing them behind her waist, and it was to the horror of his coarse trousers that she woke.

Edward did write to apologise, making his excuse how he found her so attractive that he was overcome by desire. There was half a page of compliments ranging from her skill in catching fish to her beautiful hair. Helen noticed, however, that it did not mention the thing that he seemed most fascinated with – her legs.

He finally ran out of compliments and finished by begging to be allowed to see her again.

Helen wrote a very terse letter back that would, she believed, curb any further aspirations Edward might have in her direction.

Work on the new factory had taken longer than anticipated but at last it was nearing completion and would soon be ready to install the power looms. Just what would be produced in it was the source of several dinner discussions. Friday evening dinner at the Grange now replaced the Thursday evening after-work discussions, presumably (and Helen smiled at the thought) because they interfered with his rent collection.

During those relaxed evenings Mainthorpe voiced his ideas in the expectation that Helen would challenge them. On the other hand, Helen's confidence and her grasp of the business had grown to the point that she was putting forward her own ideas. When Mainthorpe repeated his intention to weave both silk and rayon fabrics, Helen said, "But it will mean competing with existing producers. If they have contracts with manufacturers it won't be easy unless we undercut on prices. Ruth gave me an idea today: why don't we increase the range by including knitted ties?"

"But we'll still have to compete somewhere along the line."

"Yes, but it will be nearer the customer. It will be our design and our quality competing on the shop's tie rack."

"It's worth thinking about," Mainthorpe agreed. "Let's do a little work on it and talk again next week."

Although knitting ties had been Ruth's idea it was obvious that she was fully occupied in overseeing the making-up department. When Helen mentioned that it was time to appoint an overseer for the power looms, to her surprise Mainthorpe suggested Mr Buxton. "He's the best weaver I have and he's as straight as a die. If he agrees I can arrange for him to get experience of both rayon and the knitting process in a friend's Lancashire factory."

Mr Buxton did agree and the following week journeyed into Lancashire to begin a month's working experience. It was a fortnight before Helen and he met again. He had come home for the weekend and she had returned from the Grange early, so over Sunday afternoon tea he related his experiences. His description of the different working practices over there – some good, some bad – interested Helen so much that she described some to Mainthorpe. After listening thoughtfully he said, "Then perhaps you should go over there for a week or two. There's a daughter, perhaps a bit older than you, but you should get on."

And they did get on. Jade was a dynamic 23-year-old who, in answer to Helen's question, said, "Position? I haven't got a position. I float somewhere between office boy and general manager depending on what mood father's in that day."

It was a fascinating week both watching Jade at work and staying in her family's imposing home. Helen was persuaded to stay for a second week. "Not that you'll see anything very different next week but we can have a great weekend in between."

"Why, what have you got in mind?"

"I have a boyfriend, Philip, with a 22-year-old younger brother who's home from university, and both are great dancers – so stay. We'll take you out and dance your feet off. Have you done the Charleston yet?"

"No, what is it?"

"It's a new dance from America. It's crazy fast. After a few cocktails your head will be spinning faster than your feet. Don't tell me – you don't know what a cocktail is either?"

"Anyway, I've only brought everyday dresses with me."

Jade wasn't going to let a little thing like the wrong dress prevent her from introducing Helen to exciting nightlife. The two girls spent a happy hour exploring Jade's extensive wardrobe without much success. Long evening dresses were out; Jade did a little demonstration Charleston to prove why. There were only a couple of fashionable short dresses and, although Jade was almost as tall as Helen, the fact that she was slightly broader with a fuller bust ruled those two out. The difference between them was so much that the only solution Helen could think of was a last minute shopping trip. Laughing happily, Jade said, "The answer lies behind the door," and reached a dress down from behind her bedroom door.

Helen protested, "I can't wear that. It's new, it's still covered in tissue paper."

"Nonsense! It's made for you; plunging necklines are all the rage. Look, we can adjust the halter neck and there's a loose sash to pull the waist in. Let's try it on."

The fact that it looked far more expensive than anything Helen had ever bought made her protest more. And when Jade refused to listen, Helen said, "Anyway, it doesn't cover my breasts."

"We can soon cure that." Jade promptly untied the halter strap and, doing a simple left-over-right knot just below her chin, re-tied it. Doing a twirl in front of the mirror, Helen was horrified to see so much naked flesh but Jade read her thoughts. "It's perfect. That tantalising open window will have the men tripping over and if you're worried about the low back here's a silk shawl to put round your shoulders." Then, craftily changing tack, Jade said, "You've got fantastic knees. Mine are all knobbly compared to yours."

Younger brother Mark was indeed a great dancer and with the music played at a frantic beat Helen soon forgot about modesty. The shawl hung on the back of her chair and Mark proved it was possible to watch the movement of her breasts through that tantalising window without tripping up or embarrassing her. Perhaps it was that crazy dance or that she drank too many fancy cocktails that melted Helen's inhibitions.

Mark proved to be equally adept at seduction, as Helen discovered in the back seat of Philip's car in the early hours of Sunday morning. Or perhaps it was just the feeling of being safe with Jade chatting away to Philip in the front of the car. Whatever the reason, Helen let his hands wander where no hands had been before and found it dangerously exciting.

The following day the two boys offered to take them into the hills for a Sunday afternoon picnic. The late summer sun did its best to warm the day and a couple of thick travelling rugs insulated them from the damp ground. The meal was hardly finished when Jade and Philip gathered up one rug and discreetly vanished behind a small hill, leaving Helen to cope with Mark's wandering hands.

In cold analysis, Mark was not her type. His range of conversation was cricket, nightlife and girls. On the journey he hardly noticed the grimy but quaint stone cottages or the lovely countryside, other than looking for a suitable picnic spot, which had to be secluded and have some long grass for obvious reasons.

No, Helen thought, he's not the man for me but by then she was lying back on the rug hidden in the long grass while Mark went to work. This was not Edward's crude bathroom technique or Simon's immature fumbling. Helen had read enough to know that, despite his immature conversation, Mark was experienced in the technique of seduction; he knew just how to kiss and where to touch. Her earlier resolve to resist melted as his caressing fingers released those inhibitions locked in long ago by Uncle Horace. When Mark rolled onto his knees, the urge to pull him down was overpowering, or it was until a sudden thundery squall sent him scrambling for his coat.

Thinking about it the following week in drizzly Fletchfield, Helen marvelled how the natural elements seemed to affect her life. Years before, a thunderstorm had produced a tall, gruff man who through the years had helped to shape her young life in a dramatic way, and on that Sunday afternoon a similar storm saved her from giving away her most precious asset. But the experience released feelings that lingered, sensations Helen had never known before, and they were not for Mark.

What those experiences taught was how to recognise a certain look in a man's eyes. That look had been in Uncle Horace's eyes when he cornered her by the bed back in Flacton, as it had in Edward's that night in the bathroom. That same look was in Mark's eyes when he knelt over her in the long grass – and to her surprise it was in Joseph's the next Saturday afternoon in the hayfield.

Not that haymaking at the Grange needed the hard-working drudgery demanded by Uncle Horace. Here there was a horse-drawn mower, swath-turner and hay-rake but the hay still needed stacking into haycocks to season out for a week or two and that needed hard work with a pikel. Seeing dark thunderclouds billowing across the Cheshire Plain, the farm staff were desperately trying to stack the whole field into small haycocks before the crop got soaked. Working harder than anyone, Joseph urged them on, saying, "It's been soaked three times already. If it gets rained on again it will be worthless."

Even Ned came in the field to help, although Helen wondered whether he might have regretted it when the others began to tease him. Isaac asked, "Not building today then, Ned?"

Tom Smith put it more crudely: "No, he can't get his leg over when her husband's hanging about. Doesn't it bother you to think of him having a poke at the weekend?"

"Less of that crude talk," Joseph said. "There are ladies in this field."

With top neck buttons loose, Helen's short, sleeveless dress covered all the essentials while working in the sultry Saturday afternoon heat. It was when they had nearly finished that Helen looked up and caught Joseph's eyes glued on her shapely figure, and in them was that same look. A look that was terrifying in Uncle Horace, repulsive with Edward and intriguing in Mark's seductive eyes now, in Joseph's clear blue eyes, triggered a shiver of excitement. So much so that, when he looked up guiltily, Helen smiled to him with a new self-assurance.

It had been a difficult year for Joseph. Not only had the Master dithered over his decision to extend the buildings until it was near hay-harvest time, but when the builders finally started it was made worse because he had agreed that they could have the help of one of the farm men with a horse and cart. That always seemed to be on one of the few fine days when Joseph was desperately trying to get on with farm work.

The wet weather that had delayed the reseeding in spring had continued to interfere with haymaking to the point that it had stretched out through the summer. Not only was it difficult to make hay in showery weather, having to turn the hay time and time again created a lot of extra work and produced only poor quality hay. To Joseph's relief, this was the last field. Throughout the summer Helen had come to the Grange most weekends, always pleasant and full of life, particularly when joining his family for Sunday lunch. But the fact that she was alone with the Master most weekends weighed on his mind.

Not being the sort to discuss his personal problems with anyone, Joseph had sunk into a morose state. In that hayfield, while he was covering his embarrassment by fiddling with the last haycock and the rest were running for shelter, Helen stayed with him. "Come on, Joseph, quick! The rain's coming across the valley."

When he hesitated she caught his hand, saying, "Come on – run!" And they did, hand-in-hand across the field, laughing at the flash of lightning and the heavy rain soaking through their thin clothing. Diving in through the farmhouse back door, Joseph finally let go of Helen's hand and shyly turned and was transfixed. Unaware of the water dribbling down his face or his shirt clinging to his wiry frame, all Joseph could see was the laughter in those large turquoise eyes and a now almost transparent dress hugging that sensual young body.

Resting his foot up on a stool, Mainthorpe reached for his whisky. He had run back and to between the two mills too often and was suffering the results. It was one of his rare restful nights at home, or at the least that was his intention. After dinner, tired of hearing about dress shops and fashion, he tried to explain to Jessica how the workings of the new mill and making-up department were progressing. Jessica said, "New mill, old mill, making up, I don't know what you're talking about."!

"We call my original mill the old mill, the making-up department is in the new mill and the factory is behind it. Anyway, I've installed Helen in the office there. It was demanding too much of my time so I'm going to let her get on with it. She has _ "

"Helen, Helen, is she all you think about?"

Mainthorpe sipped his whisky and reflected how it was impossible to have a reasonable conversation. When they were courting, Jessica had feigned an interest in his business but once married any interest had faded quickly away. Now there seemed nothing left between them. Occasionally they had an interesting night out together but it was only when they were with company and he could leave her to get on with women's talk while he talked with the men. After one such enjoyable night Jessica seemed in such happy mood he was tempted into her bedroom. The screams of protests that drove him out still reverberated in his mind.

Mainthorpe sipped again and almost smiled in anticipation of his next weekend at the Grange. As though reading his mind, Jessica's hectoring voice cut through that vision of peace: "I suppose she'll be there?"

Helen was soon interviewing staff again, this time alongside Mr Buxton in her new office. And there was a difference in that Mainthorpe would have the final say on each selection. They were partway through the interviews when Mainthorpe realised there were more women than men being selected and voiced his disapproval. He still maintained his all-male policy on the handlooms but the power looms, being much less physically demanding, were ideal for nimble female fingers. When Helen told him so they had one of their very few arguments. It ended when, in his gruffest manner, he said, "All right, but I don't want any troublemakers so I'll second interview the men and you have another look at the women."

"I'm not sure that I can recognise a troublemaker."

"Well, look in the mirror when you get home."

During a break in the interviews Mr Buxton told Helen how he had been saving for years to buy a small cottage. Helen knew that now, with his promotion and his wife promoted to quality supervisor in the old mill, they were taking home more in a week than they previously earned in a month. "We want to get to the edge of town where I can have a garden. I want to grow marrows."

"Why marrows? They're tasteless things."

"Yes, but I want just to sit there and watch them grow."

Hoping to benefit from Mainthorpe's reputation as a good employer, they held some of the interview sessions at the weekend. Although there was a lot of unemployment in the town it was hoped that they could entice quality workers from other mills. They had reasonable success but, because knitting had never been a part of the Fletchfield silk industry, no one with that skill responded.

Mainthorpe heard that a Manchester manufacturer had just gone into liquidation and so suggested Helen went over there and try to recruit suitable staff.

Adverts in the local paper and an interview room in a hotel were easily organised but housing for future workers was the problem. When there was none on offer some of the most suitable applicants were not prepared to move. It took two weekends before Helen found the right people. One 22-year-old girl, with a brighter brain than most, convinced Helen that both rayon and silk ties could be knitted to a higher quality on old-fashioned hand frame machines. Helen telephoned Mainthorpe at the Grange and heard, "Helen, I miss you. This place seems empty without you."

Flustered, she said, "Don't be silly. Saddle up your horse and go for a long ride."

"I did that this morning. Now I've just had a lonely lunch. Anyway, how's recruitment going?"

When Helen explained what she had learned about quality knitting, Mainthorpe said, "I've heard it said. If we're going to compete we've got to compete on quality but I've never seen any hand-frame machines for sale second hand."

"There are several in this factory that's just closed."

"Stay over and try to do a deal with the receiver on Monday. If you can, then buy ten."

Having kept in touch with Jade, and now feeling a little bored and lonely, Helen telephoned her. After the greetings, Jade suggested, "Why not come here for the night? I'll drive over there and get you. It's less than twenty miles so even if I stay within the speed limit it will only take about an hour."

Helen had never ridden with a woman driver and it stimulated ideas, particularly when Jade let her drive for a short way.

With guidance from the college tutors Mainthorpe chose the best two non-sponsored art students and offered them a job. In Helen's opinion both were brilliant. Of course, the boy went to work under Grimshaw and the girl came to Helen. During a break from interviewing she was supervising Mary, the new girl, in the design department when Jessica came in and just stood looking at her. Dressed for a chilly day in a beautiful fur-trimmed coat, short enough to show a glimpse of her shapely legs above high-heeled fashion boots, Jessica posed in fashion model style just inside the door. Then, elegantly raising a slim cigarette holder to her lips, she drew in deeply. Smiling uncertainly, Helen said, "Hello, Mrs Mainthorpe. How can I help?"

"I've come to see what sort of woman my husband's off with each weekend."

Other than the smoke ring curling gently upwards, and both Peter and the young designer fleeing from the room, everything stopped. Finally letting out a long, deep breath, and suddenly aware of her heart thumping as though it was about to burst, Helen said, "It's not like that. He has never even made a suggestion to me."

"Oh, come off it. He used to want it every night. He may have slowed down a bit but you can't tell me that with a young slut like you there he doesn't use that connecting door."

Pausing to look Helen up and down, Jessica continued, "He tells me he goes up there to ride his horse but I bet that's not all he rides."

What shocked Helen was not just the crudeness but how in saying it Jessica drifted into a harsh, back-street Fletchfield accent. Contrasting that with the outward veneer of elegance made Helen feel physically sick. Suddenly anger took over and she rushed at Jessica, screaming, "He's not like that! Get out of here, you hateful woman!" and would have hit her if Jessica hadn't fled from the room.

A second later there was a screech of tyres and a bump. Then the room started to spin. Helen tried to catch hold of it but it was going too fast.

Chapter Twenty-Three

Someone was patting her face and there was a voice – it was Ruth saying, "Wake up . . . come on, Helen, wake up."

Realising she was now in her own office chair, Helen sipped the proffered glass of water and asked, "What happened?"

"There was an accident and you fainted."

That wasn't all and Helen knew it. Mr Buxton responded to her searching look. "It's the Master's wife; she was knocked over by a car."

"Is she . . . is she . . .?"

It was the Master, limping across the room, who answered, "No, she isn't dead but still unconscious. They've just taken her to hospital. What happened here?"

The staff did a vanishing act again, leaving Helen to answer. "She was awful. She accused us of . . . of . . . I got angry and chased her out and she must have run straight in . . . into . . . oh, God, I killed her, didn't I?"

"No, she's not dead. I'm going over to the hospital now but it's not your fault." Mainthorpe patted her arm and fussed about trying to reassure, then left.

Helen was still trying to compose herself when Ruth came back. "There's a policeman wanting to talk to you. Do you feel up to seeing him?"

The sergeant, who seemed to believe in the direct approach and had obviously asked a few questions elsewhere, said, "Now then, Miss, what was the row about? Mrs Mainthorpe had been to see you, hadn't she? And she rushed out after the argument, so what was it about?"

Hesitating in an attempt to martial her thoughts, Helen replied, "She accused me of having an affair with her husband."

"And were you?"

"No! No, we've never ever done anything like that."

"But you do spend each weekend with him? Did you push her?"

Ruth burst in. "That's enough. This girl's been out cold for quarter of an hour. If you're going to ask those sorts of daft questions come back tomorrow when she's feeling better."

And he did, with his inspector. They kept asking the same sorts of daft questions and challenging each answer until Helen's mind was in a whirl.

After they left, Ruth brought in a cup of tea loaded with sugar. "I've just heard from the hospital. The Master's wife is still unconscious and he's still there with her. What you need is a quiet weekend."

"I can't, not with the Master away, and I need to be here in case . . . in case . . ."

"In case she dies. Well, if she does there's nothing you can do."

Helen tried to sort out some papers but her mind didn't seem to be taking in the meaning. The telephone held her attention. She willed it to ring and for Mainthorpe to say, "It's all right, Jessica's come round."

When it did ring Helen was trembling so much she hardly dared pick it up. When she did, it was Jade. "This weekend at the Grange – is it still all right for me to come?"

There had never been a close girlfriend in Helen's life. Her posh accent and moving first to Flacton and then back again to Fletchfield had created the barrier of being an outsider. At first Lisa had befriended her but Lisa's head was just full of gossip and boys. Anyway, now that Helen was close to the Master Lisa kept a respectful distance, as did most other members of staff. But Jade was like her, not old enough to mix with other employers and yet holding a position that automatically isolated them from the people they worked with – and the two girls really liked each other. Helen poured out the horror of Jessica's accident and her feeling of guilt. Jade said, "This Ruth sounds like a sensible woman. You do need to get away. Get your things ready; I'm coming over right away. I've got my clothes with me in the office so I should be with you within a couple of hours."

Helen did a walking tour of both the factory and the new mill and was dismayed when, other than Ruth, none of the senior employees would make eye contact. Even Mr Buxton averted his gaze. Finally she blurted out to Ruth, "They think I'm guilty! What am I going to do?"

Taking hold of Helen's shoulders and looking straight into her eyes, Ruth said, "You're not guilty of anything but you must get away from here. If you don't, every time you come into the office you'll relive what she said, what you said, how you might have said it different. Go on – go. I'm working in the morning so I can ring with any news."

That experience in the hayfield shook Joseph but he was under no illusions. He believed it was just a spontaneous gesture on Helen's part to catch hold of his hand and run with him before the storm. It was the sort of thing she would have done years before and to him she was still the same infectiously happy girl. Then he remembered how she looked with that wet dress provocatively revealing the nipples on those firm young breasts and he knew she was the woman he wanted, but what about the Master? There had to be some sort of relationship between them. If he was right and there was, and he declared his feelings to Helen, there was a chance that she might tell the Master. Then where would that leave him? Joseph realised that this farm was everything to him. It wasn't just a job and his family's home, it was a way of life, a life that he could picture Helen sharing – but there was still the Master.

The village annual sheepdog trials took place just a couple of weeks after finally carting in the last field of hay, which meant that, being a member of the committee, Joseph spent the weekend helping to prepare the trial ground. A few local farmers toiled away to build temporary fences, holding pens, release pens and the various gates needed to create the course. It had grown into a sort of village fete made more colourful by the assortment of shepherds and dogs that gathered together from a wide area.

On the day, there were dogs trailing after their masters on bits of string, others tied to fence posts and one, tied outside the refreshment tent, managed to crawl under the tent side to steal a large meat pie. Joseph saw that incident when dashing in for a well-earned cup of tea during a break from releasing sheep.

The trials were not going well. Some days the sheep trot sedately, allowing each dog to show off his skills to the best, but on other days the same sheep will turn to face the dog and act as difficult as they can. This was one of those days and to make it worse the neighbouring farmer had fallen out with the trials chairman. Out of spite, he turned his cows out in the next field. Most of the dogs worked both cattle and sheep on their own farm, and the strawberry-roan cows were much easier to see than insignificant sheep huddled in a little group by the far hedge. The cows got a bit excited at being chased round the pasture field by strange dogs, so by the time the fourth dog went after them it all became a bit too much and they crashed through the fence onto the trial field. Of course, the dog continued to drive them and within a couple of minutes twenty-five cows were galloping amongst the spectators. Two or three other dogs managed to get loose in the melee and join in the fun. When the cows were finally driven into another field the trail of destruction included overturned tables and broken chairs in the refreshment tent and, to cap it all, one end of the beer tent lay collapsed on the floor.

No, it had not been a good morning, thought Joseph. At least when he went for his cup of tea the refreshment tent was back in business, allowing him to enjoy his snack in peace. On his way back he noticed Helen sitting on a rickety wooden chair, sketching. It was the first opportunity to have a word with her since being rained out of the hayfield. Looking over her shoulder, he saw the pie scene cartooned with a near-human grin on the dog's face. He laughed a compliment and turned the page back to see another grinning sheepdog milking a cow, with an irate farmer blowing furiously on a whistle and waving his crook. Before he could do more than chuckle, someone called, "Joseph, we need your help."

That was the last he saw of Helen for several weeks. Later and via Aunt Emily he learned that Helen was involved in recruiting staff for the new factory.

All the Bolton family missed Helen. Not least because by collecting a daily paper, which Anna had brought back to the farmhouse the next day, Helen had got them interested in the news. Joseph in particular now took an interest in both local and national events and, in her absence, made time to walk down to the village shop each Saturday for both a daily paper and the local Fletchfield News.

Leaning on the wall by the churchyard, he glanced at the local headlines. Just below them on the front page was always a small 'Late News' item. The heading this week was, 'Mill owner's wife seriously injured,' followed by a one-paragraph report of the accident, vaguely linking Helen. It was not clear how she was involved.

Desperate to find out more, Joseph rushed back to the farmhouse hoping that Anna would have returned from the Grange, but she hadn't. When his mother saw the article she said, "There's a strange car outside the Grange so why not go to the back door and ask Aunt Emily (everyone including Mainthorpe now called the housekeeper Aunt Emily) if she knows anything?"

When the housekeeper answered Joseph's knock and he had shown her the paper, she said, "Yes, it's true. Helen's here with a friend but she's very upset."

"What happened?"

"I don't really know, only that she was there and blames herself. I'll tell her you called and perhaps she'll come across and have a word with you later."

Joseph dallied in the Grange kitchen, making small talk with the cook but in reality hoping Helen would come. When for the tenth time he glanced at the inner kitchen door, his wish was granted. Standing hesitantly just inside, Helen said, "Joseph."

Dark smudges under each red-ringed eye erased whatever words were forming in his mind, frozen momentarily at the distress he saw. Within seconds Helen was in his arms. There were no words, just her arms clutching tightly round him and her face pressed against the base of his neck. It was the most incredible and confusing experience for Joseph. Having seen the pain on her face and feeling the tears soaking into his thin shirt, he was aware of her agony, of the cook discreetly leaving and another girl watching them for a moment or two through the open door. But the feel of her supple figure under his fingers and the firm breasts pressing against his chest was electrifying.

Chapter Twenty-Four

The doctor had said to just hold her hand and talk to her but Mainthorpe felt embarrassed. It seemed years since last they held hands. Then he had whispered endearments but not in recent years. Oh, he'd tried but Jessica no longer chose to listen. Convinced that she wasn't listening now, Mainthorpe held onto the motionless hand and drifted into memories. Jessica had a terrific figure and knew how to use it. He remembered their first meeting when she sprained her ankle just in front of his pony. Of course, he lifted her into the trap and drove her home but on the way a firm young breast brushed his elbow at each sway of the well-sprung trap. It had taken a couple of years for him to realise that the real well-sprung trap was the one he had fallen into.

Before that Mainthorpe had devoted his time and energy to business at the expense of social life. Freeing one of his garret houses by moving a young widow into a small cottage was simply business economics, until he called one night to see if she had settled. Over a cup of tea and a cream cake it became obvious there was more on offer and Mainthorpe recognised a need that up to then had been suppressed. And this was an experienced woman who knew how to satisfy that need. Although knowing it wasn't love, it helped him realise how much he needed a woman to share the whole of his life.

It was soon afterwards that Jessica conveniently feigned a sprained ankle and, for her age, Jessica had more than her share of feminine guile. With pretence of hot tantalising passion and a cool calculating brain she knew how to arouse and just when to say no. Mainthorpe was led through a very steamy courtship. Visiting that widow just twice each week fell far short of satisfying his physical needs and when, each time they kissed, Jessica tantalisingly pushed a shapely thigh between his it was soon marriage or else.

At first Mainthorpe had been so captivated by his responsive and attractive bride he dispensed with the services of his young widow. He chuckled now remembering how he had felt duty-bound to let her stay in the cottage, rent free of course, and to continue her allowance. That was a wise move because within months Jessica developed evening headaches and once she was pregnant it was separate bedrooms and had been ever since.

Even now, lying there as though just sleeping, Jessica was incredibly beautiful. Other than a bandaged forehead there was no other injury. Mainthorpe's thoughts were interrupted by the intrusion of a doctor who, after checking her pulse and lifting her eyelids, said, "It really does help if you talk to your wife, Mr Mainthorpe. It sometimes jogs the brain back into consciousness. But I think you should be prepared for the worst."

When the doctor left the room, Mainthorpe, taking hold of Jessica's hand again, said, "Well, you really did sprain your ankle this time. A witness has come forward who saw you come out of the mill and twist your ankle on the edge of a stone set. He reckoned that the car driver was well within the twenty mile an hour limit and that he hadn't a chance to avoid you. Anyway, you banged your head against the front wing so there's no scar other than on your head and your hair will soon cover those. But what did you say to Helen to get her so mad?"

Then Mainthorpe remembered what the doctor had said about being prepared for the worst. Where would that leave him with Helen? He released Jessica's hand and began to pace the floor. Up to now he had managed to pretend Helen was the daughter he would never have – but if Jessica dies? If she does die I'll be free – but free to do what? It came as a bombshell that the picture conjured up in his mind was not the Helen who sat across the dining table debating politics or throwing out ideas for the business. No, his mind conjured up a picture of long slim legs and a sensually lithe body.

It seemed a lifetime but in fact was little over a year since Helen first came to stay at the Grange and in that time she had never had a friend to stay. And now here was Jade, the most understanding friend anyone could wish to have. There was no artificial jollity or attempts at distraction, just quiet, supportive companionship and Helen loved her for it.

Jade finally lost her composure when the housekeeper left the dining room after serving the lunch main course. Jade giggled, "I'm sorry, I can't help it. Here we are sitting at table for a formal lunch but being waited on by your Aunt Emily who calls you Miss Helen. When the maid came in to light the fires this morning she just called you Helen. Are you all mad?"

Helen smiled for the first time that day. "It must seem it but Aunt Emily insists on being formal in front of other people. When I'm here on my own I always eat together at the kitchen table. It's the same when I'm with the Master; we always address each other formally in front of other people but when we're alone he's just Joshua."

"I'm beginning to wonder about your relationship with, er, Joshua, and who was that gorgeous man you were hugging in the kitchen this morning?"

Blushing a little at the memory, Helen said, "Oh, that was just the farm bailiff, Joseph. We go back a long way."

"The way you were clinging on to each other one could imagine that you might also go forward a long way."

Helen became quiet, realising that for the first time she had stood tight against a man. Not that she wasn't fairly close to Mark in that long grass, but this time it was so tight it made her blush, particularly because it felt good.

Lunch over, they changed into out-door clothes and walked hand-in-hand across the fields and up onto Quarry Moor. The curlews and plovers had finished breeding and left the moor to congregate in large flocks on the lower ground. The lambs were now large and looked woolly against their newly shorn mothers.

Out here was the peace that Helen had craved since the accident and, feeling that peace, Helen led Jade to her favourite rock.

Sensing that there were things in Helen's past that she never talked about, Jade asked her how she first came to meet Mainthorpe. Helen told her about that thunderstorm long ago and laughed at how thunder seemed to be around at vital times in her life. Finding release from talking, Helen told of her early relationship with Mainthorpe, of how she sat on this rock to decide her future and as a result went to live with Aunt Emily and Uncle Horace. Yes, for the first time Helen managed to talk about that attempted rape and how any man getting too close could trigger a frightening nightmare. "I'm naked with his arms round me, locking mine by my side and his coarse tweed trousers thrusting against me. It's terrifying."

"What happens then? Do you wake up screaming?"

"No, I didn't scream at the time and I don't scream in the nightmare. I just wake up sweating with fear."

They were wandering back down brook field when Joseph, in cord trousers and open necked shirt, walked out from Leckon Wood. They waited, watching him cross the field towards them. Without hat or coat, his sandy hair and lithe long strides seemed so full of vitality that Jade whispered to Helen, "If you don't want him, he's mine."

Joseph's blue eyes searched Helen's face. "How are you coping? Have you heard any more?"

Remembering the feel of his powerful arms and the strong masculine smells when her face pressed into the nape of his neck, Helen became unusually tongue-tied. Eventually she gained sufficient composure to reply. Joseph listened quietly and then fell in step alongside them. With a little prompting from Helen the conversation turned to the sheep-gather that was planned for the following week. Jade listened as they discussed weaning tups, wintering hogs, store sales and the Shepherds' Meet. Most of this was so incomprehensible that she asked, "What is the Shepherds' Meet?"

Joseph said, "There are two different farmers grazing Quarry Moor and three up on Leckon. With no fences between each flock we sometimes get a few mixed up."

"A few get mixed up? I would have thought they would all be mixed up."

Joseph smiled, "No, they're hefted. That is, they're bred to stay on their own part of the moor, but a few stray. It's the same right across these hills so we all make the gather on the same day and then the following week we have what we call a Shepherds' Meet at the Black Grouse. We put up a few pens and each drive any strays there."

Helen said, "It's a great day out. Some of the farmers bring their best tups and appoint someone to judge what looks to be the best. Most of the wives come for a good natter."

"And to drag their husbands home before they get too drunk," Joseph said with a grin.

Aunt Emily accepted an invitation out to tea when the two girls insisted they would prepare their own evening meal. As a result they had the Grange to themselves. Changing out of walking gear, Helen made a cup of tea while Jade walked through the house looking at different oil paintings. "Your Mr Mainthorpe, or Joshua, has a good eye for country pictures."

Placing the tea tray on the lounge table, Helen said, "He's not my Joshua, he's . . . he's, well, just like my uncle. But yes – sometimes when I'm here on my own I spend an hour just looking at them."

The telephone interrupted and Helen answered it. "Helen, I hoped you would be there; it's Simon. I've just heard the news. It must be awful for you."

Helen thanked him for thinking of her, gave brief details about the accident and rejected his offer to come over and be with her.

Helen was still trying to satisfy Jade's curiosity about Simon when the phone rang again. "Ah, Helen, I knew that's where you'd be."

"Joshua, how are you coping? How is Jessica?"

"Still unconscious. I'm waiting for the specialist to arrive from Manchester. In the meantime they keep telling me to hold her hand and talk to her. It's ironic isn't it? Much as I wanted to she's never let me, and now that I can talk all I want I find there's nothing to say. I've got lots I want to say to you, though."

"Joshua. Don't talk like that. Can't you see that I feel guilty enough without you adding to it."

"There's no need for you to feel guilty. Have you not heard? A witness came forward last night. He saw the whole thing. Jessica twisted her ankle. It was those ridiculous high heels she insists on wearing. Anyway, she fell sideways into the car. If it's anyone's fault it's Jessica's. She had no right to come there upsetting you. Grief, I wish I was there to reassure you. Helen, I've been thinking about us. I . . . ."

"You shouldn't be thinking about us. Just look after Jessica. Thank you for telling me about the witness; it takes a load off my mind. You look after your wife and I'll take care of the mill."

Putting down the receiver Helen turned to Jade. "What a relief! Someone's come forward that saw Jessica stumble in front of the car. That can't be my fault, can it?"

"I'm glad for your sake but I'm not sure about this uncle thing. That's not the sort of conversation I'd have with my uncle. Are you sure he's not developing a thing about you?"

"Of course he isn't. He has never made a wrong suggestion." Then Helen thought through the conversation and said, "But . . . but I have been aware of him looking a lot in the last few weeks."

Jade leaned forward in her chair. "Looking? How do you mean, looking? Where was he looking?"

"Well, he compliments me on my clothes much more than he used to, which is nice, but he is nice. Then sometimes I catch his eyes wandering to areas where I suppose no uncle should look."

With so many different events happening it was inevitable that Helen found sleep elusive. Why did she refuse Simon's offer? What did Joshua mean by saying that he been thinking "about us"? It seemed a strange thing to say when his wife lay unconscious. And as for Joseph holding her so comfortingly, he had always been there to console when she fell, grazing a knee or got into some other scrape as a girl – so it wasn't really a surprise. But then she remembered the strength of his arms, the feel of rippling muscles under her fingers and her tingling awareness of his masculinity. What did Jade mean by saying "If you don't want him, he's mine"? Joseph had always been a friend, someone she could turn to.

Sleep eventually came and this time there were no nightmares.

Staying at the Grange for most of the weekend failed to satisfy Jade's curiosity about the area. When Monday morning came, Helen suggested they took the long route into Fletchfield, through the village and along the valley. Although not prepared to admit it, for the first time since leaving college Helen was reluctant to go to work. Jade loved the quaintness of Gritstencrag with its seemingly haphazardly placed cottages and stonewalled gardens bisected by the rippling stream. The remote rugged farms along the valley equally enthralled her. As a result, there were a few stops to view the scenery.

Arriving at the mill midmorning, the girls were greeted by Ruth who had been hovering where she would see them arrive. After greetings and introductions, Ruth said, "The Master's been trying to get hold of you. He desperately wanted to tell you himself. I'm sorry, but it's bad news: Mrs Mainthorpe died early this morning."

Chapter Twenty-Five

There were more questions from the police inspector, really intimate, personal and intrusive questions. When Mainthorpe heard about it he made one of his rare visits into Helen's office, offering both sympathy and an explanation. "It's the insurance company. After our marriage I thought I ought to leave my new bride well provided for, in case something happened to me, and took out a life policy. Instead of being pleased, Jessica accused me of valuing my life more than hers. I couldn't make her understand and I didn't want to upset her so I insured hers as well, but they don't pay out on a suicide. Now the insurance company is trying to prove that's what she did."

"You mean if they can prove that we were having an affair then they might be able to say that your wife committed suicide?"

"That seems to be it."

The coroner lost no time and fixed the inquest for Friday. Although the police inspector seemed now to be satisfied that their relationship was just platonic, Mainthorpe warned Helen that because of the life policy there might still be awkward questions.

On the day, the inspector was quite adamant that he could find no cause for suicide. In response to the coroner's questions he said that, although the marriage was a little unusual, there was no evidence of anything improper taking place between Mainthorpe and Helen. He emphasised that by pointing out the fact that Helen's only known relative, her aunt, also lived at the Grange.

Even though he disliked his wife's mother intensely, Mainthorpe had pretended not to notice how his Jessica supported her financially. Aware that these handouts would now come to an end, when it came to her turn to give evidence Jessica's mother made much of how unhappy her daughter had been, and particularly about Helen's relationship with her son-in-law.

When Mainthorpe gave evidence, the coroner was still not satisfied and questioned him more about his domestic arrangements. Mainthorpe explained factually why Jessica no longer went to the Grange. Switching his questions to Mainthorpe's relationship with Helen, the coroner observed, "I find it remarkable that you should take a young girl out of Art College and give her both the run of your home and so much responsibility in your business."

Not used to having his actions questioned, Mainthorpe became irritated. "I've known that girl, as you crudely call her, since she was eleven and I didn't take her out of art college – I put her in there."

"But even so, for someone who had a male-only policy towards employing weavers, the way you have elevated a mere girl seems to me, to say the least, very unusual."

"Yes, but I employ men because hand-weaving is physically tiring. I do employ other women in senior positions. Anyway, I resent your implied suggestions and the way you sneeringly call her a mere girl – Miss Helen is a very talented and unusual woman."

"Then I had better question this very talented and unusual woman."

Prior to Jessica's death the demands of his extended milling business had distracted Mainthorpe from attending to matters on the farm. Although he managed to visit each weekend and have a brief talk with Joseph, there was no longer time to drive Joseph about the county. These were, of course, only occasional journeys and both men had benefited from that time together, whether it was to buy dairy cows or breeding tups. The conversation on the journey was of much greater benefit than any contribution Mainthorpe made to the buying decisions.

On one of his fleeting visits to the farm Mainthorpe rode across the field to where Joseph was working and, lifting his reins to indicate his horse, said, "Joseph, these things are just for pleasure. We're in the age of the motorcar, so go and buy yourself something that will be useful on the farm."

Joseph did just that. It was a second-hand Model T Ford Pickup with a bench seat in the front that could take three people at a crush and a platform area behind with sideboards on which to carry a few sacks of grain or a machine part.

The greatest benefit was to his family for there was no longer the tedious chore of harnessing the pony and hitching it to a trap. Market day in particular was much more civilised. If Joseph had a calf to take, he slid it bottom first into a sack, tied the sack round its neck and lifted it onto the back of the pickup. Other than making a loud verbal protest, the calf could do nothing but sit there until released at the other end. Then Mrs Bolton could ride in comfort and do the weekly shop while Joseph sold the calf and watched the dairy cow trade. The main business benefit was that Joseph no longer needed to rely on dealers but could watch for the right stock at the right price.

Excitement was building up in the Bolton household, as Joel's wedding loomed closer. That was to take place on the following Saturday but on this immediate Saturday it was the Shepherds' Meet. The sheep gather had gone well, the tup lambs were now weaned but the ewe lambs would go back onto the moor with their mothers for another month. Before that, while they were off the moor, John Smith could drive the twenty-one stray sheep across it to the Meet and afterwards drive any of their own strays back home. In previous years Joseph had walked with his shepherd but this year he was going to drive proudly in his new pickup.

Joseph knew the inquest had taken place that day and that the funeral was planned for the following Monday; because of that he had no expectations of seeing either Helen or the Master over the weekend. It came as some surprise to him, then, when walking across the yard at dusk on Friday night to shut in his mother's free-range hens, to see Helen in the Grange garden. After the usual greetings, Joseph asked, "What was the verdict?"

"They decided on accidental death but it was an awful experience."

"Why?"

"Because the coroner tried to find a reason that could have caused her to commit suicide. I had a real grilling when I gave evidence and Joshua didn't help by jumping to my defence. If it wasn't so serious it would have been funny, the coroner threatened to have him removed from the room if he interrupted again."

"How could he prove she committed suicide?"

"By trying to prove that we are having an affair."

"But . . . but you aren't having an affair . . . are you?"

"Oh, Joseph, how can you say such a thing? If it wasn't for Joshua I would have been in an orphanage, and look what he's done for me in recent years – not just college but my job and the chance to come here each weekend. It's like a dream and he's never asked anything from me in return."

Joseph wondered for a few moments about what, in fact, she did give back in return.

Helen had had a sleepless night, tossing and turning over the questions asked in court. Was her relationship with Joshua really innocent? He was a handsome and important man; even his gruff manner was appealing. Then, remembering how he covertly glanced at her legs or slid his eyes over her breasts, it always gave her a little tingle of excitement. Helen felt guilty. But guilty of what? Lots of men did the same but it didn't mean that she was falling in love with them or they with her. And then there was Joseph. In those early morning sleepless hours when the human mind is most vulnerable, Helen remembered Joseph doing the same and felt a shiver of excitement.

Over breakfast Helen told Aunt Emily about the horror of the inquest and what the coroner had insinuated and how the

Master had insisted she came to the Grange for a quiet weekend. Her Aunt was saved from having to give advice when Anna came in to take instructions and to light the lounge fire. As was usual, she joined them for a cup of tea and a brief gossip. Turning to Helen, she said, "Joseph's taking me to the Shepherds' Meet later this morning. How about coming with us?"

"Just what you need," Aunt Emily agreed. "It will give you something to think about instead of reliving the horrors of the last two weeks."

Anna held open the car door and said to Helen, "You're the smallest, jump in."

Although an older model, the interior was basically the same as Simon's car apart from the bench seat. Crushed in the middle, Helen found the seating embarrassingly intimate. No matter how she tried, her long legs seemed to be in Joseph's way as he fiddled with the controls. Each time he moved his left leg her skirt worked higher and, presumably because it was trapped under him, Helen couldn't tug it down.

It was an equally disturbing short journey for Joseph. Much as he tried not to, his elbow brushed intimate places and the feel of that firm thigh was electrifying against his. Relieved to get to the Black Grouse without having run off the road, Joseph jumped out and almost ran to help Tom Smith pen his sheep.

Anna knew most of the people there and introduced Helen to some of them. Among these country people Helen felt at home. The smell of sheep on their coarse tweed clothes was familiar and the soft hill-farming twang was quite different from the harsher Fletchfield accent. Having brought her sketchbook, Helen soon wandered away to perch on the side of a pen and capture the scene. The demands at work meant that she now had no more than an overseeing role in the design department. As a result, this sketchbook became her relaxation.

Turning her back to look out across the moor, in the distance she saw a lone man walking towards them. At first it was hard to tell what he was carrying then, as he came closer, it looked as though he was carrying a sheep across his shoulders. Anna joined her and together they watched this lone figure walk over the crest of a small hill only to vanish in a fold in the landscape. When he appeared again on the next crest they could see more clearly that there was indeed a sheep more or less held around his neck, its hind legs in one hand on one side and the front legs in the other. When Helen reached for her sketchbook, Anna said, "I thought it must be only a small sheep but it's not, and look at those shoulders, eh – he's quite a man."

Before Helen could speak, Anna walked out to meet him saying, "Can you just stand there for a moment? My friend's just sketching you."

His rugged face broke into a grin. "Well, don't be long. I've walked about three miles with this old ewe."

With Anna's help the stranger released the sheep into a pen and came over to look at Helen's sketch. "I'm Ben Hogan. I've come to farm with my Grandparents at Grabshaw farm."

"I'm Anna and this is Helen. We're from the Grange and it's our ear notch in that sheep you've been carrying."

"Is it? I'm afraid I don't know much about the different flock marks in the area. I'm not from these parts and anyway I'm just back from twelve years in the army."

"Oh, then let me introduce you to a few of your neighbours."

Helen was left to finish the sketch. When a steady drizzle set in, Anna returned and said, "Joseph and Ben have gone into the pub to have a pint and a meat pie so shall we go back to the car and have our snack?"

Out of the drizzle in the car, Anna reached for Helen's sketchbook and sat looking at that last picture. "Isn't he handsome? Look at those shoulders."

"You've got it bad, haven't you? He could be a married man."

"No, he isn't. That was the first thing I made sure of. Can I keep this picture?"

Chapter Twenty-Six

It was awful being in the Grange while Joshua was burying his wife. Although Mr Grimshaw and one of two other members of staff were attending the funeral, Mainthorpe had insisted that Helen didn't. Instead he suggested that she extended her weekend at the Grange.

She knew it was sensible to stay away but felt wretched knowing he would be standing by the grave alone. Although he was a busy man with a lot of business associates it had taken her a while to realise that he was also a very private man with few close friends. Perhaps it was a result of living in a town built around one industry where most of the businessmen were either in competition with Mainthorpe in some way or had at some time been outmanoeuvred by him.

Helen was learning fast the ruthlessness of business and believed that Jade's father and Mainthorpe were good friends because they lived far enough apart not to be competitors. Now her mentor would be standing by the grave of the woman who had in latter years rejected him, and without even the comfort of his mistress, a woman with whom he appeared to share nothing more than a twice-weekly physical release. Although Joseph would be there she knew that he would stand respectfully back from the grave.

Wandering restlessly through the Grange, Helen paused to take some comfort from some of the paintings before changing into walking clothes.

Isaac was helping the shepherd to move the sheep back onto the moor. Normally Helen would have walked across the field to them but this time felt no need of conversation. Then the sight of Isaac striding across the pasture with Joseph's faithful Rob made her pause to see if the dog would do his bidding. With the wind blowing from her to them it was like watching a silent film of running sheep, men gesticulating and dogs rushing about. Bob ran bold and upright whereas the shepherd's two smaller collies crouched with noses close to the ground. Between them, though, they got the job done and the sheep funnelled through the gateway before spreading out across the heather-clad moor.

Helen walked in the other direction towards Leckon Moor.

Leading the procession up the aisle the vicar intoned, "Accept thy daughter Jessica into thy house, O Father." Behind him the bearers shuffled in practised step. They ought to, Mainthorpe thought as he matched their pace; after all, I'm paying them enough. And as for that snivelling mother-in-law behind me, she's every reason to cry because she's not just lost a daughter, she's lost the goose that laid the golden egg. Through the corner of his eye he recognised town bigwigs and fellow businessmen standing solemnly in the pews on either side, but his face remained inscrutable.

Mainthorpe searched his heart for a feeling of loss but there was none, just regrets for the life he and Jessica could have had together. He particularly regretted the wasted years since she stopped caring. Now, instead of sadness he felt relief – relief it was all over, and particularly that he would no longer have to call that snivelling woman his mother-in-law.

It was finished. The hymns had been sung, prayers chanted and the vicar's intonations had at last droned to an end. Mainthorpe picked up a handful of soil and watched it scatter across the top of the coffin before turning his back on the grave and everything it represented. Without acknowledging anyone he walked, head bowed, through the surrounding people.

Joseph had got to know Mainthorpe more than most. Through their time together either on the farm or travelling about on farm business the two men had learned to understand each other. Joseph was well aware that the Master understood how he was hefted to this farm just as his sheep were hefted to their part of the moor and yet he never used it as a lever. On the other hand, he had long been aware that Jessica had no place in Mainthorpe's heart, his life revolving around his mill, the farm and Helen. Yes, there was no doubt in his mind that Mainthorpe was in love with Helen. It was in his voice when he spoke of her and it showed in the softening round his eyes when he looked at her. So while others believed they saw grief on that inscrutable face pushing through the throng of mourners, Joseph saw into the man's heart and was troubled.

The tragedy and the events that followed distracted both Mainthorpe and Helen from the business of the mill. Although Mainthorpe had a manager, his responsibility was mainly overseeing staff on the production side whereas the general management of the office, including buying and selling, was directly under Mainthorpe's control. Helen had taken some of that, which related to her side of the business, away from him but it was all still new to her staff. It followed that there was quite a backlog when they returned to work.

Matters were made worse when the autumn weather produced almost continuous rain throughout the week. The usually placid brook that meandered across the bottom of Fletchfield overflowed into the town, flooding some of the low-lying houses and disrupting traffic. As a result, many workers arrived very late or in some cases not at all. Even the trains didn't escape when a landslide closed the line for two days. The dependable Ruth, with no other means of travel, was absent for those two days and during them Helen came to realise just how important Ruth had become to the smooth running of the business. By Saturday morning the trains were running again and most of the workers, included Ruth, were at work. A full staff gave them the opportunity to complete some late orders.

By mid-Saturday afternoon, when the essential backlog had been cleared, Mainthorpe rang Helen. "I'm about done here and I still haven't eaten, how about you?"

"It's the same with me but we've more or less caught up."

"Good, then let's have something to eat and drive up to the Grange."

Although the rain had at last stopped, Ragil Brook was a raging torrent. In places it covered the road but was not so deep that Mainthorpe couldn't drive through. The Grange farmyard seemed empty; it took a few minutes to remember that all the staff had gone to Joel's wedding, including both Cook and Aunt Emily. Helen remembered how Joseph had teased her: "You'll do the milking on Saturday, won't you, Helen?" She had said yes knowing they had planned to return to do it later in the evening.

Surveying the empty yard, Mainthorpe said, "I'm going to saddle my horse and take to the hills before it rains again."

Leisurely changing into walking clothes and sauntering out into the yard, Helen was greeted by a clatter of hoofs as Bolesworth's tall hunter, blowing and lathered, came to a restless halt in front of her. She had never seen the estate agent so agitated, or for that matter had she seen his horse in the same state. It was making so much noise snorting and pawing the cobblestone that Bolesworth had to shout, "The dam's giving way. I've warned the villagers but your lambs are on the Bottoms field across the brook. If it breaks that field could flood."

When Mainthorpe looked out of the stable door Bolesworth shouted the same message to him and, without waiting for a reply, galloped out of the yard. Helen said, "I'll get Rob. I think he'll work for me."

She had never worked the dog but had watched Joseph often enough to know the signals and the big dog was always friendly towards her. It was so wet and treacherous that running down the steep bank towards the brook needed great care. Overtaking her on his surefooted cob, Mainthorpe looked back, shouting, "You go straight round them and I'll open the gates."

Trying to stay on her feet, Helen was watching where each foot went and as a result didn't see what happened with the horse but suddenly Mainthorpe was lying on the ground, writhing in agony. She tried to help but he said through gritted teeth, "Don't worry about me. Try and get them off on your own. Go on – I'll be all right until you get back."

With gates each side of the road bridge, the sheep would have to come out of one field, cross the bridge and turn into the next field gate on the other side. In a matter of minutes both gates were open and Rob was racing round the lambs. The Brook was already overflowing on to the low areas of the field; the dog sent up sprays of water when he splashed through the worst places but it didn't deter him. Just the sight of him running round the field made the lambs flock together and within a few minutes he was behind them, forcing the reluctant sheep to splash through the shallow pools towards the gate. Standing on the road below the bridge to make sure that as they came through the gate they would turn up over the bridge, Helen could only hope that they turned into the field gate on the other side. Sensing the urgency, Rob pushed them through the gate more quickly than he should and Helen didn't know the command for 'slow down'.

There was a bit of confusion when the lambs bunched onto the bridge and three managed to dodge past her. It took a few minutes for her and the dog to turn them in the right direction, by which time the others had run into the right field. The three lambs were galloping over the hump of the bridge followed by Rob with Helen a little way behind. Reaching the top of the bridge, Helen was horrified to see a wall of water some three or four feet deep racing down the narrow-sided valley towards her. It seemed to obliterate everything in its path. Two of the sheep managed to scramble onto higher ground but the third and Rob were swept away. The force of water slackened as it spread out each side the bridge and across the Bottoms field. To Helen's relief, in the slacker current Rob managed to swim to the opposite bank, but when she looked back Bottoms field was completely covered and she was left marooned on the bridge.

There was nothing to be done about it. Water raced both under the bridge and across each end of it, leaving her feeling very insecure on a small island between the two low parapets. Trunks of dead trees and other debris floated past and a cow, which must belong to a neighbour further up the valley, swam gamely towards her in the fast current. When it reached the slacker current it managed to scramble out and follow Rob on to the field where the sheep were now grazing. To her amusement, within a minute or two it too began to graze as though it was the normal way for a cow to go out to pasture.

Helen could see up the bank to where Mainthorpe lay flat on his back. Bored with waiting for Helen, Rob trotted up to him and licked his face. Mainthorpe pushed him away, eased up onto one elbow and, seeing Helen waving frantically, gave a feeble wave in return and flopped down again. Both relieved and worried, Helen paced the small island in frustration.

The water level began to fall almost immediately. Measuring its fall inch by inch on the stone parapets she heard a shout and looked up to see Joseph running down the field. He bent over the Master, who pointed towards Helen. Joseph spun round and within seconds was running dangerously fast down the steep slope towards her. As he skidded to a halt just across the water, Helen thought how comically funny he looked in his mud-splattered dark suit with its white rosebud buttonhole drooping. He shouted, "You all right?"

"Of course I am. How's Joshua?"

"He thinks he's broken his leg. I'll have to get the men to help carry him."

"The water's falling fast now. Within a few minutes I'll be able to get across. I'll run along the bank to the village and get the Doctor."

By the time Joseph reached the farm Helen was able to wade from the bridge to the higher ground on the field. Even though she skirted the debris left by the flood, it was so treacherous on the sloping bank side that running was out of the question. The body of the lamb lay among the deposited debris. Pausing to touch it with her foot but finding it lifeless she glanced back and saw not three but four men hurrying towards Mainthorpe. It was easy to recognise Joseph and his two men but who was the other? Who ever he was he seemed to tower above the other three.

In the village the flood had not reached the church or those houses close by it but there was a thick layer of slime on the low ground by the bridge and, when Helen crossed over, on the other side was chaos. Mud and debris covered both road and gardens; even the doctor's house had not escaped. The doctor, who was sloshing mud out of his kitchen, looked relieved when he heard about Mainthorpe and passed the brush to his less than happy wife.

It seemed a long walk back up the hill to the Grange, by which time the men were trying to make Mainthorpe comfortable on a bed in the lounge. Joseph said, "We couldn't get through with the car so there's little hope of getting the Master out tonight. Anyway, we brought a bed down. What do you think, Doctor?"

"I'll know better when I've had a proper look. Well, Mr Mainthorpe, where does it hurt the most?"

The others withdrew to the kitchen where Helen asked, "Who was the other man?"

"Oh, that was Ben Logan. I think he's come courting," Joseph chuckled. "Well, he's gone courting now because when I told him Anna and her mother was stuck the other side the flood he went striding off to rescue them."

The doctor was still working on Mainthorpe when Ben returned with the two women. Anna had become girlishly romantic after being carried in the arms of the handsome Ben and Mrs Bolton was equally flushed with the surprise that one man could carry her so easily across the muddy dam outlet.

Helen asked, "If you got in, can we not carry the Master out?"

"It would be very difficult; the road's impassable," Mrs Bolton explained. "It's covered in debris and I think there's a bridge washed away. I would never have got along those steep banks without Ben's help."

It was the middle of Sunday afternoon when the men finally cleared the lane. Even then it was very uneven. Where the torrent of water had gouged deep channels they could only do a temporary patch-up, carrying by hand large stones picked from the brook banks. Such was the force of the flood that the next bridge down, which was above where Helen was marooned, had been completely washed away. Taking a walk along the still-raging stream, Joseph could see bridge stones dotted along the banks for more than a hundred yards. Fortunately, it was below where Leckon Lane joined the one from Gritstencrag but the villagers would have to take the longer route round to Fletchfield until it could be rebuilt.

Fletchfield now boasted an ambulance service and one of them was waiting as they pushed the last debris off the road. Helen wondered whether she wasn't more relieved than Mainthorpe when it finally pulled up outside the Grange. It had been a harrowing night. The doctor had given him an injection but when it wore off Mainthorpe had been in dreadful pain. Distraught with a feeling of helplessness in that she could do nothing to ease his discomfort, she followed him into the ambulance. Even there she felt every jolt that made him groan or grimace.

A doctor was waiting at the hospital. After he had examined Mainthorpe and the nurses had settled him in a small private room, Helen went in to see him. Lying flat and looking pale but as inscrutable as ever, Mainthorpe said, "They tell me I'm going to have an operation tomorrow but before I do I want to see my lawyer. I want you waiting outside his office when he gets into work in the morning and bring him straight to me. Don't let him argue – just bring him here. Now go home and get some rest."

The Buxtons were out when Helen returned home so she made herself a light supper and went straight to bed. The last twenty-four hours had been so exhausting that she slept solidly until Mrs Buxton shook her shoulder. Breakfast and explanations to the Buxtons took but a short time and then Helen was quickly striding off to waylay the Master's lawyer on his office doorstep. He put up quite an argument about how he had an important appointment to keep. He was no match for Helen, though, and reluctantly got back into his car. Just to make sure, she jumped in the front seat alongside him, smiled into his scowling eyes whenever he looked her way, and only left his side when he reached Joshua's bedside.

Helen did a tour through the Old Mill telling the leading workers about the accident. Within minutes of reaching her own office, the scowling lawyer walked in unannounced, only he was no longer scowling. He slapped a piece of paper on her desk and tapped it with his finger. "That gives you complete authority to conduct the affairs of this business. Other than a limit to the amount you can pay on any one cheque, you have the right to reorganise the working of the business, order goods or cancel them, hire or fire staff, and when I've taken these other written instructions to the bank you'll be able to draw out whatever cash you need to cover the company's wages. Now, unless you have any questions I'd like to go and keep my appointment."

Chapter Twenty-Seven

Helen sat in her office for a good half hour looking at the 'To Whom it May Concern' note. Her mind was neither frozen nor in a whirl; it just raced round the options. Then she called in Ruth and Mr Buxton, showed them the note and said, "I hope you understand, Mr Buxton, but I'm putting Ruth in charge here." When he nodded agreement she continued, "Will you do it, Ruth? Good. Then you choose someone to take your place because I'll be working from the Master's office from now on."

It wasn't easy. David Brightwell, the Mill manager, became sulky and Mr Grimshaw looked as though he was going to have a heart attack. Helen left them to their mood for a day before calling each separately into her office to say, "You don't like it, I don't like it. But read this note carefully. Now, are you willing to cooperate?"

David Brightwell said, "Yes, Miss Helen."

When it came to Mr Grimshaw's turn, he said, "I've never taken orders from a woman in my life and I'm too old to start now."

Helen gave him until the weekend to think it over.

The chief wages clerk also answered directly to the Master. He was an unassuming, quiet man who in the past always had a pleasant word for Helen and now, at her request, he explained the usual working arrangements.

"As you know, Miss Helen, every one is paid a week behind. We do the piece rate workers' wages first because they take the longest to collate. The Master insists that I have their records on his desk first thing Thursday morning. He checks through them. He knows what every man should be doing and if there's anything that doesn't seem right he brings in David Brightwell. Meanwhile, we get on with the rest of the workers and by mid-afternoon the Master gets a list of who has had days off sick or arrived late."

"When do you draw the money out of the bank?"

"The Master draws a quarter of it on Thursday so that we can start on the wage envelopes; we put them in the safe overnight and do the others on Friday."

The next few days were, to say the least, hectic. Apart from overseeing the working of the business, Helen was called in by the bank manager, who then became difficult by trying to impose additional conditions about what she could or could not do. Helen tried to reason with him but in the end said firmly, "Here's the letter of instruction. If you don't agree with it then ring the Master's lawyer."

The bank manager huffed and puffed about giving all this responsibility to one so young, and a girl at that, but eventually, and still muttering it was very unusual, accepted Helen's authority.

That was on Tuesday. Mainthorpe had had his operation late Monday afternoon and even by Tuesday evening he was still too drowsy to hold a conversation. There was a problem over one of the customers' contracts that Helen didn't understand so she rang Jade for advice. Both Jade and her father were very concerned to hear of Mainthorpe's accident and asked her to pass on their best wishes for a speedy recovery. Jade not only gave advice but offered to come and help out in the office if Helen required it. She finished by saying, "Even if you don't need my help I'll drive my father out on Sunday afternoon. He can visit your Joshua while you and I have a cup of tea and a natter."

Mainthorpe was much brighter when Helen called in on Wednesday evening. There was a metal frame or calliper over his leg pushing tight against his groin at the top. This being longer than his leg, it clamped against the bottom bedstead with his foot tied to the bed to hold a continuous tension on the fracture. Mainthorpe said, "I've got to stay tied to this ruddy bed for a least seven weeks. Now tell me what's going on in the Mill?"

Helen consoled him at some length and passed on the messages of good wishes from several people, including Jade and her father. Mainthorpe said, "Good, now tell me what's going on in the ruddy Mill."

"It's not like you to use strong language," Helen laughed. "I can see you're going to be one very relaxed patient. I got your note of authorisation from the lawyer; the bank manager didn't like it but he came round. All the staff have accepted it other than Mr Grimshaw and he says," Helen imitated Grimshaw, " 'I've never taken orders from a woman in my life and I'm too old to start now'."

"Tell him to come and see me. If I can't change his mind then don't waste time arguing with him, just fire him."

Thursday proceeded as the wages clerk had said it would until late in the afternoon when he came to Helen with two wage envelopes and asked, "What shall I do with these?"

"Why? Who are they for?"

"Tom Brown and Primrose Night. They didn't have last week's either."

"Why not? Who are they anyway?"

"The Master usually deals with them himself."

Seeing a hint of a smile on the clerk's face, she smiled back and kept the envelopes.

After work Helen walked to the terraced house where, years before, she hid down the street waiting to see who visited. Now she knocked boldly on the door. Strangely, even though they lived in the next street to each other, Helen had never met the Master's mistress and was not sure what to expect. Would she be a painted tart like the ones hanging around pubs in town? Would she be elegantly slim, snobbish and wearing fancy clothes? The woman who answered the door was none of those things. Perhaps about thirty-five, she was wearing a discreet amount of makeup, an attractive, well-fitted dress enhancing her full but not tubby figure – and a look of complete surprise.

Helen didn't wait for her to speak. "Hello, I'm Helen Brindley."

"Yes, I know who you are; you'd better come in."

She followed her into a small, neat parlour that Helen observed was tastefully furnished. "Please sit down. Now tell me, how is Joshua?"

Helen explained about the fractured femur and that it might take two or three months to mend. This being his good leg, he would have to struggle to get going.

"Oh, I'm glad it's no worse. I suppose you'll be looking after the business."

"Why do you say that? Do you think I'm not capable?"

"Of course you are. Joshua often talks about you and how much he relies on you. He was a very lonely man before you came into the business. He would never talk business with me as he obviously does with you. He thinks the world of you."

Embarrassed, Helen quickly changed the subject. "I presume you are Primrose Night? And Tom Brown?"

"How did you guess? But I'm really Mary Bilstone. I know he shouldn't really pay me out of the business like this but it's how he's always done it. I must seem awful to you."

"I'm not here to moralise. How the Master runs his affairs is nothing to do with me but I'm sure he would want you to have these." Helen laid the pay packets on the table and rose to leave.

"Thank you." Mary Bilstone looked shy and embarrassed as she said again, "Thank you, and thank you for coming. I'm so glad to hear how Joshua's going on. I was really worried about him."

"Why don't you go and see him?"

"Oh, I couldn't do that; it wouldn't do, would it?"

"Of course it would. I'm going home to change and have a spot of tea so I'll call for you in about an hour and we will walk to the hospital together."

When she returned, Mary was still protesting that it wouldn't do and what would the Master say but Helen took no notice. She did notice several curtains twitching, however, as they walked side-by-side down the narrow street. It was understandable why people said how well Mainthorpe's mistress dressed, but it seemed to Helen that it wasn't that they were such expensive clothes; it was more that she knew both how to dress and how to carry herself with a touch of elegance.

Watching Mary walk into Mainthorpe's room, Helen was amused to see his initial embarrassment soon overtaken by the pleasure her visit obviously brought.

Discreetly leaving them to their privacy, Helen went to find the ward sister. Over a long conversation the sister explained about the healing process and that she was worried how his other leg would perform after so many weeks of inactivity.

When Helen returned to Joshua's bedside, Mary immediately gave Joshua's hand a squeeze, saying, "You've got a lot of business to discuss so I'll leave you both to it."

Mainthorpe said, "You will come again, Mary, won't you?"

Helen called after her, "I'll see you next week."

"How do you mean, you'll see her next week?" Mainthorpe asked.

"Primrose Knight, Tom Brown."

"Damn you, woman. I'd have a devil of a time if I was married to you. Still, it might be worth thinking about."

"If it's marriage you're thinking about then you ought to make an honest woman of your Mary Bilstone."

Embarrassed, Mainthorpe change the subject. "My car's still up at the Grange so when you go up there this weekend why not ask Joseph to teach you to drive?"

"I may not go this weekend. There's a lot to do, you know, and I've already told you that Jade is bringing her father to see you. She and I may spend an hour or two together."

"It would help you a lot if you could drive."

"What you really mean it is that it would help you a lot if I could drive you around when you come out of hospital."

Mainthorpe chuckled.

Chapter Twenty-Eight

Helen discovered a treasure. Of course she already knew Sarah, who did the Master's secretarial work, though Mainthorpe insisted he didn't have a personal secretary. According to him she was just someone who typed a few letters and kept his files in order. Through Helen's first week, Sarah, a timid spinster in her late fifties, was both unforthcoming and kept discreetly out of the way. It was only when, in exasperation, Helen said, "Look, I think you know more about this business than anyone and I need your help," that Sarah responded. And Sarah, after working for Mainthorpe for some thirty-five years, did know almost everything about the business.

There were a lot of things Helen couldn't understand, particularly why Mainthorpe had the telephone connected directly to his own desk. It seemed ridiculous for the Master to answer every call and, as a result, arrange all appointments himself. Perhaps that arrangement would have been all right in the early days, when first the telephone was laid on and the business was small, but now Helen found the constant interruption made it almost impossible to work. A visit from a telephone engineer resulted in the installation of the latest technology, allowing Sarah to act as a filter with both calls and appointments.

The following day, Sarah, with the confidence of a pay rise confirming her appointment as Helen's personal secretary, said, "That nice Mr Stoddard is due this afternoon for his usual monthly appointment. He and the Master go through his sales figures and anticipated orders so that the Master can tailor his production plans."

"I didn't know. I'm not prepared for it, I'll have to . . ."

Sarah cut in. "It's all right, Miss Helen; I reminded the manager yesterday, so everything's here for you to look at before he comes."

Expecting to meet the fanatical fisherman, Mr Stoddard senior, Helen was more than a little surprised when his son Edward walked in and hesitantly said, "Good afternoon, Miss Helen. I had no idea about Mr Mainthorpe's accident or that I would be meeting you. Your secretary just told me and I'm very sorry to hear about it – I mean his accident, not you being in charge. I hope . . ."

"Why are you here instead of your father?"

"I thought you knew. I've been coming for a few months. My father finds travelling too tiring. I hope that you'll forgive me for that . . . that . . . night, and that we can work together."

Helen remembered that night and the terrifying nightmare it inevitably triggered and not just on one night but for several. Edward interrupted her thoughts. "I'm staying in Fletchfield overnight and my father would expect me to visit Mr Mainthorpe. Perhaps you would have dinner with me afterwards?"

"Mr Stoddard I am prepared to do business with you, but only in this office. I'm sure the Master will be pleased to see you but, as for dinner, the answer is no. I have no wish to meet you outside this room."

Disappointed as she was to have to do business with Edward, his sales figures projected forward were extremely good. And because those products were fashioned in what had been Helen's part of the business, she knew without doing any calculations that Ruth and her team would be hard pushed to meet those orders.

It was Friday afternoon. Helen had finally got rid of Edward and was about to walk across to the New Mill to discuss how they would need to change the production schedules to fill the orders when Sarah knocked on her door. "There's a Mr Simon Beckerton to see you, Miss Helen. Shall I show him in?"

"Simon, it's nice to see you again; how are you keeping?"

"I thought I ought to congratulate you on the top job. Perhaps we can have a night out together to celebrate?"

"I'm sorry, Simon. Much as it is nice of you, I am terribly busy and I visit Joshua most evenings."

"Each time I've asked if we could meet you seem to make some excuse. Is it like that between us now?"

Lost for words, Helen made a hand gesture, which seemed to infuriate him because his smile was replaced by a sneer. "You think you're too good to talk to me now, do you? Well, you will have to talk to me because the rent on that New Mill is due for renegotiation, and now that I see what you're producing in there it's going to be a substantial rise."

Dumbfounded, Helen just stared at him. It wasn't just the implications of what he said but the way he said it that hurt. "You mean that you are our landlord?" Simon's smile was not pleasant. "You mean your father bought our mill because I indicated that Joshua was interested in the building, and all those times since, when we've been together, you've been quizzing me about his business – our business?"

When another sneering smile spread slowly across his face, Helen jumped to her feet. "You treacherous, deceitful man – you're no friend of mine. Get out! Get out!"

When Helen visited Mainthorpe later that night, the Sister waylaid her. "Miss Helen, can I have a word? I think you should know we are quite worried about Mr Mainthorpe. We are trying to keep him quiet and now that lawyer is with him again. It's the third time this week and the doctor thinks he should be resting, not being worried by business meetings."

"I didn't realise. I'll have a talk with him."

Helen walked purposefully towards Mainthorpe's small room, only to meet the lawyer coming out. "Ah, Miss Helen. We were just talking about you. Joshua is full of admiration for the way you are coping. Please remember, Miss Helen, if you have any problem don't be afraid to ask my advice."

Helen smiled her thanks and marvelled how on their first meeting he had treated her as an irritant, on their second with extreme curtness, and now he was smiling. Or was he, she wondered, just showing his teeth?

Leaving the question unanswered, Helen went in to the patient. "Joshua, you look tired. The Sister says that you should be resting more."

"Oh, blow the Sister. There are things that needed doing and I've got them done."

"Anything I need to know about?"

Mainthorpe grinned. "I've raised your salary equivalent to your responsibilities, for a start." Helen began to protest but he held up his hand: "The life insurance company have agreed to pay up, which will put a nice sum in my personal account. And, at Jessica's insistence, I also took out an accident policy, which is paying me another nice sum each month. So my late departed wife may have had her good points after all."

"You shouldn't speak of her alike that; it's wrong."

"Nonsense. Lying here I've had time to think and when I get out of this bed I'll tell you what I've been thinking."

"You are supposed to be resting."

"Nonsense. I've never felt more alive. Joseph's been to see me, by the way. He bought three strawberry-roan shorthorn cows in the market today. Anyway, he'll be waiting outside your office at twelve o'clock tomorrow. You are going to have a relaxing weekend – if learning to drive is relaxing."

Helen wanted to protest that he should try to organise her life to that extent but remembering what the sister had just said, decided not to argue. There was no way, though, that she could keep quiet about Simon's visit and his demand to renegotiate the rent. Recognising the implications immediately, Mainthorpe's voice rose. "You mean that pimply-faced youth who's been hanging around you for years is my landlord's son? So that's how he knew to jump in and buy it over my head – you must have told him."

"I didn't tell him, but perhaps I may have said enough for him to guess."

Mainthorpe was so furious he shouted, "Haven't I taught you anything? You should know that you don't talk business even to a friend."

Helen tried to placate him but the nurse came and ushered her out. "Mr Mainthorpe is not well. We've told you that he must rest, so please go."

The next morning Helen had only been in the office for about half an hour when the phone rang. Sarah took the message and came in to Helen. "The sister just rang to say that Mr Mainthorpe has suffered a mild stroke in the night."

Leaving everything and almost running down the narrow streets towards the hospital, Helen reached the gate only to stop there, almost rooted to the spot. Although she had visited the hospital almost every day during the past few weeks, its looks had never registered. Now they did, and they were hideous. The terraced cottages on either side of the gate, though covered with industrial grime, still revealed their Cheshire brick orange-red colour. Looking between them up the short drive, Helen saw the hospital's grey granite walls, covered with a few hundred years of the same industrial filth, looked more depressing than an undertaker's overcoat. Groaning inwardly, she wondered how anyone could come out of it alive.

The Sister must have been watching because Helen had only paused for a few seconds before she stepped outside. Believing Helen had paused through fear, perhaps dreading what she would find inside, she hurried forward to give reassurance. "It's not your fault; it could have happened at any time. We've been monitoring his pulse and heartbeat but no matter what we said to him he seemed unable to relax."

With a firm grip on her elbow, the sister continued to talk as she guided Helen in through the door. "It's only a mild stroke. Although it's affected his left side, he still has some movement in his left hand and can talk with difficulty. But you must not let him get excited in any way."

With those words, Helen was allowed to go into his room. He wasn't aware of her standing by his bed. Shocked by the haggard lines and grey pallor on the once handsome face, Helen reached down and touched his hand. Joshua's eyes opened. Neither of them spoke for a few seconds, and then he smiled lopsidedly. The bushy moustache that usually hid his expressions drooped to the left as he struggled to speak. Finally, on the third attempt, he managed to say, "I knew you'd come."

Squeezing his hand, Helen reassured him that of course she would come, but his eyes closed. After a while a nurse gently touched her arm. "He's gone to sleep now. I think he has been waiting for you."

As she sat by the bedside, Helen's mind was in a whirl. Her world revolved around this man; he wasn't just her employer, he had shaped her life. Their lives were so intricately involved with each other that Helen couldn't imagine living without him. Now, seeing him so ill, it terrified her that she might have to.

After some considerable time, the nurse came back. "I think he'll sleep for a while, so if there is anything you want to do why not see to it and come back later."

Without giving real thought as to the reasons why, Helen called to see Mary Bilstone on her walk back to the office. The news of Joshua's stroke was a complete shock to Mary. Helen took some time in trying to reassure her that it didn't seem to be too serious but, with Mary wringing her hands in consternation, Helen urged her to go straight to his bedside and see for herself.

Calling in to see Ruth in the new mill, Helen was presented with a problem. The colours in the last silk delivery were not vibrant. Ruth wanted to send it all back but Mr Buxton, worried about the work schedules, urged caution. Helen said, "If we are to produce quality then we have to demand quality from everyone, including our suppliers. It all goes back."

Helen rang the supplier and demanded it be replaced, sorting out the work schedules with Ruth. Then, satisfied that the staff had other work until the new supply came, Helen set off back to her own office.

Sarah was waiting with a list of problems. One of them was a dispute between the mill manager and one of the piecework weavers. Helen knew well the disappointments a worker felt when, his work not up to quality, he was both not paid and had to buy that piece of material. It could only be settled by her going up to the top floor and examining the material in front of both the weaver and her manager. The mill manager was right, the work was not up to quality. Helen soothed the weaver's ruffled feelings by reminding him that there was a shop in town that gave a good price for rejected silk. As to the quality of his work, she was uncompromising.

It was all part of everyday work but it had taken a considerable amount of time and then, to Helen's surprise, when she got back to her office, Joseph was waiting.

Through the last few weeks Joseph had watched newfound love shine out from his sister's face. He had watched, too, the anticipation on Ben Hogan's rugged features as he strode across the cobbled stone yard towards Anna, and this triggered the yearning in Joseph's own heart. He had felt a need for some considerable time. Helen's presence when the sheep were lambing and watching her stride across the fields in a lightweight summer dress disturbed him deeply, but it was much more than just a physical attraction. When, just a couple of weeks before, Helen had sought comfort in his arms, he realised that this was the one with whom he could share his thoughts, his dreams.

Anna had been aware of his feelings for some time for it was written on his face whenever Helen was near him. Now, having found her own happiness, Anna decided to take a hand in his.

Knowing just how sensitive Joseph was, though, she dare not just barge in. Instead, when they were sitting at the tea table, she casually said, "It's unusual the relationship between the Master and Helen. Considering they're not related, they get on so well together."

"I'm a bit suspicious," Ned said, injecting a fair amount of innuendo into his remark. "More than a bit about what really does go on between them."

"Not every one has affairs outside marriage," said Anna, matching the innuendo. "They just respect each other and get on together because there is no romance."

Her mother asked, "Are you sure?"

"Of course I am. With three of us in the house every day when they stay here, if there was any romance we couldn't help but know. Anyway, he's got a mistress in town."

"Anna, you shouldn't talk about such things," said Mrs Bolton disapprovingly.

Anna laughed. "Well, he does have one; and Aunt Emily told me Helen's found out that she has two wage packets made out to fictional names. Her name's Mary Bilstone and Helen said she's very nice."

Helen's relationship with the Master had troubled Joseph for a long time but now, listening to Anna, his mind was put at rest. The trouble was that, because of the events of recent weeks, he had had no opportunity to talk to her. So when the Master suggested driving lessons Joseph couldn't wait. But he was waiting now – in her office, being fussed over by someone called Sarah.

Helen dashed in and stopped dead on seeing Joseph. She apologised for forgetting that he was coming. Joseph expressed concern and sympathy about the Master and they each looked at the other wondering what to do next.

Helen said, "I should go back and see how he is."

"I'll take you there in the car," said Joseph, "because I'd like to have a look at him as well."

On the short journey Helen was preoccupied with so many different thoughts. Joseph had rehearsed what he wanted to say but, aware that now wasn't the time, he couldn't think of anything else to say, which meant that they arrived at the bedside without having spoken. They stood side by side looking down at the sleeping figure. Here was the man who had played such a part in both of their lives, yet neither of them spoke. Saliva drooled from Mainthorpe's slack lips. Watching Helen take a silk handkerchief from her sleeve and gently wipe it away, Joseph saw the tenderness on her face. Convinced that Anna was wrong, he quietly walked away.

Chapter Twenty-Nine

To be a farmer a man has to be a realist. When life and death confront a man every day he learns to take the quirks of nature in his stride. Joseph was such a man. He left Mainthorpe's bedside knowing that there would be no Helen this weekend and went back to the farm intent on farming.

There was a lot to do and the onset of really wet weather made it worse. The ground became so waterlogged that Joseph had to keep the dairy herd inside night and day, which made more work in the farmyard. It was time, too, to prepare the ewes in readiness for turning the tups into them. Both Joseph and Isaac helped Tom Smith work through the whole flock. It was dirty work for each man to catch a sheep and turn it over to sit against his knees while he trimmed each hoof and treated those that had footrot. When that was done each tail needed trimming, not just to prevent dung clinging to the growing wool but also to enable the tup to do his business. As Joseph's father had told him innumerable times, 'Many ewes fail to have lambs because a lazy farmer didn't clip their tails'.

The sheep kicked and struggled against Joseph's knees and his hands were covered in so much slimy muck that he had difficulty in holding his foot-paring knife. Straightening up, Isaac said, "Damn the rain! It's running down my neck, it's soaking through my coat, my knees are wet through and yet it never washes the muck off my hands."

Joseph said nothing but thought, 'No, but it's a good way to take your mind off other problems'. He had become a troubled man. He loved this valley and these hills; all he needed to make his life perfect was someone to share it with him. Now he believed he'd found the right one (although he blamed himself for being slow to realise it) she belonged to someone else. Not only to someone else but to the one person who owned this very place. Joseph wanted to leave; there was no way he could live here and watch Helen sharing this valley with someone else. It's better to just walk away, he thought, and start a new life elsewhere, but how could he? Not only did his family's home depend on his job but also he had taken a responsible position and no decent man would walk out on his boss when he lay seriously ill.

Joseph chose to stay away from town and his Master for a couple of weeks. During that time Helen didn't visit the Grange. News of the Master's progress came via Aunt Emily who not only kept in touch with Helen but also visited the hospital. Apparently the Master was doing remarkably well, but for Joseph it was the worst few weeks of his life.

On top of the usual problems on the farm, three cows had failed to come in calf. He would have to sell them as barrens in the cattle market and replace them with three newly calved ones. A cattle haulier was instructed to take the three cows to the next Friday market in Fletchfield.

In the little pickup Joseph was strangely quiet on the journey to Fletchfield. His mother and Anna, sharing the bench seat and not having been to town for a couple of weeks, chatted away but Joseph drove in silence.

Though the total price for the three barren cows just paid for one newly-calved cow, Joseph was relatively pleased with his day. Not only had he bought good stock, he had chatted to several neighbours and friends, which somehow, without discussing his problems, had help put life in prospective. At the close of the market he felt ready to visit the hospital without trepidation.

Walking down the short corridor to Mainthorpe's private ward, Joseph was surprised to hear banter and laughter and neither were voices he recognised. Mainthorpe's smile was genuine if a little lopsided. "Joseph, it's – good – to, er, see you."

It startled Joseph that one voice he hadn't recognised was that of the Master but he managed to hide his surprise by shaking hands. Mainthorpe's words were both throaty and hesitant; the authoritative, gruff man of the past now sounded unsure and vulnerable. "This is, er, Mary – er, Mrs Bilstone."

Joseph had heard rumours about a mistress long before Anna confirmed them, but the woman he shook hands with didn't fit the picture in his mind. Her pleasant smile and firm handshake scattered his thoughts as he said hello. Mary responded, "I shall leave you two men to talk business."

When Mainthorpe immediately objected, Joseph notice how his words came out more garbled and he only moved his right hand in protest. Mary said, "All right, I'll stay, if it's only to stop you from getting overexcited."

He lay back and relaxed. Then, in his hesitant way Mainthorpe said, "Mary's going to be my nurse when I go home next week." He struggled to clear his throat. "I've been out of bed today and my left leg isn't too bad. My arm is the worst but it's improving." He moved it slowly and flexed his fingers to prove the point.

Joseph said, "I thought you would have Helen to nurse you."

Mainthorpe's grin was more lopsided than ever. "Not at all. She's reorganising my business; I don't want her organising me as well. She's bossy enough just visiting me. I've been trying to persuade her to go to the Grange for the weekend. Why don't you take her?"

Joseph's heart skipped a beat. Had he misread that tenderness Helen had shown towards the Master on his last visit? Certainly that sentence seemed to confirm what Anna had said over the tea table. What a fool I've been, Joseph thought, and didn't wait to hear any more.

The efficient-looking Sarah recognised him and rose to tap on Helen's open door. "Mr Joseph to see you, Miss Helen."

Joseph strode in with a positive frame of mind. "I've come to whisk you off to a fairyland far away."

A smile slowly spread across Helen's face and, rising from behind her desk, she took both of Joseph's hands in each of hers and kissed him on the cheek. Then, still holding onto one hand she walked out through the door, saying to Sarah as she passed her desk, "I'll see you on Monday."

They were on the bench seat in the front of the pickup before Helen spoke. "Is your mother not with you today?"

"Grief, yes! I've forgotten about her. I'm supposed to meet her at the tea rooms in Queen Street."

Joseph was still explaining how Anna had come to town with them but had arranged to meet Ben when they drew up outside the tearooms. Inside Anna rushed to meet them, flashing a sparkling engagement ring. There were hugs and kisses between the girls and a more formal handshake between the men before Anna asked Helen, "Will you be my bridesmaid?"

Leaving the happy couple in the town to celebrate the occasion, Mrs Bolton squeezed onto the bench seat, squashing Helen tight against Joseph. It wasn't quite what he had in mind; being squashed against Helen was all right but not when his mother sat next to her prattling on about wedding dates and would he give the bride away. He stayed out of the conversation all the way home.

Dusk had long changed to darkness by the time Joseph parked outside the Grange. Mrs Bolton began to sense there was a strange atmosphere between them and quickly left. Joseph turned to Helen. "How about taking a walk?"

"Give me a moment to change into walking boots and a warmer coat."

Rain over the last couple of weeks had left the ground wet and squelchy underfoot but November did her best to set the scene with a watery three-quarter moon. Without hesitation Helen took his hand and they strode out towards Quarry Moor. Bullerstone Brook gurgled energetically under the bridge while leafless tree skeletons, black against the night sky, towered overhead. Both were aware of their surroundings yet neither thought of pausing but walked on up the hill in companionable silence.

When they reached the gate onto Quarry Moor they stopped and, without speaking, looked back at the scene. The moon revealed the jagged outline of distant hills but covered the contours in a fuzzy monochrome haze. In that feeble moonlight the Grange looked black and solid alongside the farm homestead. Lights twinkled feebly through the Grange downstairs curtains, while those in the farmyard went out as the men banged shut shippen doors and called goodnight to each other. Joseph would have taken her in his arms then but Helen stepped nimbly over the gate and ran gracefully across the heather-clad moor.

Taken aback, Joseph watched for a few moments before vaulting over the gate and giving chase; it was a few breathless minutes before he got near to her. When he did, Helen slowed, caught hold of his hand and pulled him down to sit by her side on a large boulder. Glancing about them, Joseph said, "You were heading for this all the time, weren't you?"

"Yes. It's my rock. Important things seem to happen when I'm sitting on this rock."

"And is something important going to happen now?"

"I hope so," Helen whispered.

Chests heaving from both exercise and emotion, their eyes searched each other's and, both seeing what they sought, they sealed its promise with a long, lingering kiss.

Chapter Thirty

A quiet hour in the office on a sunny March afternoon gave Helen time to reflect on the past few months. Anna's wedding had gone like a dream, even though on the day the temperature was below freezing with hard, rutted snow on the ground. Mrs Bolton had made fur-collared jackets to keep all three bridesmaids warm and, at Joshua's bidding, Mary searched through Jessica's still intact and substantial wardrobe to produce a beautiful ermine jacket for Anna. On the day, though, Helen's mind was in a dreamy world of her own, hardly aware of Anna's two small nieces following her up the aisle.

The dream for Helen was not the two pretty little bridesmaids behind or seeing Anna's radiant happiness. It was following Joseph, disturbingly handsome in his dark suit, walking ahead with Anna on his arm. When he guided Anna to Ben's side in front of the altar and then stepped back he was right beside Helen. The urge to grasp his arm and stand beside the happy couple was overpowering. The fact was they had talked about doing just that but Helen was determined to delay their marriage until she could be a proper wife to Joseph, and to be that she needed to be free of running the business.

That Joseph was the man for her was sealed on that unforgettable night sitting on her favourite rock. That feeble late November moon had not provided much light but there was enough to read each other's faces and what Helen saw had sent her heart racing. In the romances she had read, proposals were usually cool affairs where the girl was told to take her time and think about it, but on that rock it had been electric. That one tender kiss released emotions neither had experienced before. There was no need for a long courtship to get to know each other; they had known each other all their lives. Just discovering that each needed the other was enough to overcome any restraints that may have come from shyness. Perhaps the hard rock and too many clothes saved them, or maybe Joseph's whispering, "Will you marry me?" triggered an awe-inspiring moment of suspense. When it ended, the madness of the moment had been replaced by the wonder of a future lifetime.

Whatever the reason, they managed to restrain themselves then and were still doing so. What troubled Helen was Joshua's attitude to their engagement. When they stood hand-in-hand by his bedside to tell him the news he mumbled his congratulations and within a few minutes went to sleep. Or did he just pretend to go to sleep?

Joseph was marvellous. Not only did he give Joshua the benefit of the doubt but he also accepted the need to delay the marriage until Joshua recovered sufficiently to be able to run the business. She had never dared to tell him that on her next visit Joshua tried his best to talk or out of the marriage, saying, "He's only a farm bailiff; he owns no property. You can do better than that."

Helen remembered her anger. "It doesn't matter what he is – he is the man I'm going to marry. Anyway, what am I? I'm just . . ."

In his agitation Mainthorpe's words were slurred as he cut in. "You are . . . you're the most beautiful, most talented woman I've ever met. I can make you . . . make you . . ."

Too angry to wait for him to form his words, Helen said, "You can't make me do anything. I'll run your business until you're back on your feet, then I'm going to marry Joseph, and when I do I'll go wherever he goes."

"Partner . . . I meant partner . . . I could make you a Partner."

"Not at that price."

From then on Joshua never once discussed Joseph or her engagement.

Without any knowledge of that conversation, Joseph agreed with Helen that they could wait until May. By then Joshua should have recovered enough to at least decide how he could best manage the business without Helen.

Delaying their marriage was putting an awful strain on them both, testing their resolve to wait until their wedding night. Sitting in her office reflecting on all this Helen smiled, reliving the feelings that Joseph triggered, particularly on the previous Saturday night when they were relaxing in front of a roaring log fire. Aunt Emily had cooked the meal, shared it with them and then retired, leaving them to side away and wash up. She often marvelled how relaxed they were in each other's company. With Joseph taking an interest in her work and her sharing his love of the countryside there was always so much to talk about. But when Joseph's lips touched hers and his fingers caressed down her spine, the only word that mattered was 'No' and it was increasingly difficult to say.

May was approaching rapidly but Joshua's recovery was painfully slow. Still needing two walking sticks and tiring very quickly meant that he could only manage about three hours in the office each morning before being mentally and physically exhausted. To encourage him to come back behind his own desk Helen had converted a small storeroom into her office. While Joshua was behind his desk Sarah put incoming calls through to him but he didn't always act on them. He could discuss business and outline future strategy with Helen but if a crisis arose, perhaps because his brain would not work fast enough, problems were often left unsolved. Helen and Sarah developed a system that handed over those unresolved difficulties when Joshua had been driven back to his townhouse.

Incredibly, in spite of the uncertainty that this situation created, the business prospered. Helen had brought last year's accounts back from the accountant only the day before and had spent the morning going over them with Joshua and they were beyond his wildest expectations. It wasn't the profitability that was worrying Helen, it was Joshua. Not that he wasn't well looked after, for Helen had engaged a young man to drive the Master's car when he required it and in between do some maintenance work. Then there was Mary who, having moved in to nurse him when he came out of hospital, was still there to attend to his every need. That she did attend to his every need was obvious when Joshua spent a weekend at the Grange and Mary occupied what had been the mistress's bedroom. Aunt Emily whispered to Helen that the connecting door was left undone and her bed had not been slept in.

During that visit the struggle to get up and down stairs had been too much for Joshua, as a result of which he had not been back to the Grange since. Helen went most weekends but it was very different now. With the Master no longer staying there, the cook got bored and left and Anna had not been replaced, which left just Aunt Emily and Helen when she was there. If Joshua didn't need his car Helen drove there herself, but when he did Joseph would collect her and rush back for Saturday afternoon milking. After that, both the evening and the following day (barring the demands of the farm) were theirs to enjoy together, but those days were proving to hold too many dangerous hours to spend engrossed in each other.

There was some improvement in Joshua's health. Though still walking with two sticks, he was moving more freely and his left arm was getting stronger. Yet, since going back home after that weekend, he never once discussed the farm or Joseph or even her engagement. Hoping that it would help him to face up to reality, Helen had been trying for a few weeks to persuade him to go to the Grange for another weekend, and now at last he agreed.

The chance to slip away on a Friday night had long gone. With the mill throbbing at maximum output, each Saturday morning was very demanding and as a result it was mid-afternoon before Helen collected Joshua and Mary.

It was a strange journey. Although both passengers had been quite polite at the start of the journey, once they got on the way both were very quiet. Helen tried to initiate conversation but without success until they reached the high ground overlooking the valley. Stopping the car, she pointed. "Look how brown the hills are; there's no grass yet for the sheep. At least the tups haven't escaped so there are no early lambs this year."

Mainthorpe cleared his throat. "No. Joseph doesn't make the same mistake twice. There's a lesson for you there, Helen. If you're in business then you're going to make mistakes sometimes. It's not wrong; it's only wrong if you make the same mistake twice."

Surprised how good his diction had become and relieved that he was at last taking an interest in something, Helen said, "Every time I come I park here and look over the valley. Isn't it beautiful?"

Mainthorpe was quiet for a while and then said, "Suppose Joseph had to leave this valley, what would you do?"

"I would go with him. My life is with him regardless of where it takes me."

Helen was thinking about the implications of what he said when a thrush flew over the wall some twenty yards ahead and, as it reached the middle of the road, a sparrow hawk swooped. In a flurry of feathers the thrush was knocked down and the hawk stood balancing on the prone body. That the thrush was still alive was obvious from its wriggling head and pedalling foot but long, needle-sharp talons held it firmly down. Oblivious of the car, the fierce hawk stood upright surveying his surroundings; and, confident that there was no danger, he bent and began to pluck feathers from the breast. From the back seat Mary said, "Joshua, do something. It's cruel. You must stop it."

"It's too late for that. If we try to interfere it will only die from its injuries." As he spoke, Mainthorpe reached behind and gave her hand a squeeze. "Nature is cruel; only the fittest survive in the countryside."

The hawk again stood upright to survey his surroundings before bending to rip into the now naked breast. "I can't stand it," Mary said.

Mainthorpe patted her hand in comfort.

As the hawk resolved the problem by rising effortlessly on outspread wings to carry the now dead thrush over the wall and away, Helen pressed the starter and the car coughed and spluttered into life.

Chapter Thirty-One

Helen swung the car round opposite the door as Joseph strode across the cobbles to greet them. Mainthorpe's smile was still a bit lopsided but it looked genuine enough as he slid onto the cobbles and stepped forward to shake Joseph's hand. Helen couldn't see what happened next but it appeared that Joshua stumbled. Perhaps he was looking at Joseph rather than where he stepped on the uneven surface, but whatever the reason Joseph caught him just before he crashed to the floor. Mary rushed forward to help and between them Joshua regained his balance but was desperately embarrassed, apologising profusely.

Aunt Emily came out to greet him and with her and Mary clucking round like a pair of broody hens Mainthorpe walked slowly to an armchair in front of the fire. Before sitting down Mainthorpe turned and said to Joseph, who had paused in the porch to give Helen a kiss and a squeeze laced with a strong smell of cows, "I'd like you to join us for dinner tonight."

Joseph said, "Of course, Master. If you're all right now I'll get off back to the milking."

Helen was in the kitchen helping Aunt Emily put the final touches to the meal when Joseph returned. Even after a bath and a complete change of clothing the lingering smell of cows, for Helen both pleasant and nostalgic, remained.

That evening Aunt Emily chose to wait on rather than dine with them, but the fact that there were more people round the table than he had seen for a long time prompted Mainthorpe to raise his glass: "A toast to a full table."

Watching Aunt Emily carry in the steaming food Mainthorpe said, "I forgot. The greens are out of our own garden and the leg of lamb is from one of our own, so another toast – to Joseph and the gardener."

Not having seen his Master for a week or two Joseph turned the conversation to the farm. Mainthorpe asked a few questions prompting Joseph to go through the various enterprises, how the cows were milking, how well the sheep looked and would there be enough hay to last through until the cows could go out to graze in early May. The conversation jogged along in those general terms until the main course was over. Then Mainthorpe said, "Now I want to ask you two young people something; why have you chosen late May for your wedding?"

Joseph said, "It's a slack period on the farm. The lambing should be over by then and I shouldn't need to be back again before the haymaking at the end of June. Anyway, Helen's been working so hard in recent months I feel she needs a longer break."

"The haymaking could be over in about a month," Mainthorpe said. "Surely you could delay your wedding until, say, the end of July or early August? By then I'd feel that much stronger to manage without Helen."

Having anticipated what he was going to say Helen was ready with her answer. "No, Joshua. Had you not been ill we would have had a double wedding with Anna and Ben but now we are adamant – we are not going to delay longer. I've suggested several times that you need a general manager to take my place, and you stubbornly refuse even to discuss it. I know you hate the idea but I could have helped to train someone had you agreed."

"I want the staff reporting to me and not to some middleman who keeps me in the dark."

"Then I suggest that you let both Ruth and David take more responsibility. At the moment you insist they come to you with every little problem when they could resolve most of them themselves."

The conversation went a bit quiet until coffee had been served, then Mainthorpe brightened up and talked about other things. It was not long, though, before he declared he was tired. Joseph followed behind him up the stairs but there was really no need because he could now grip the banister with his left hand and with a walking stick in the right he managed quite well. Mary, of course, went with him leaving Joseph and Helen to sit sedately each side of the fire.

They didn't feel free to cuddle up together on the settee but with the doors closed they talked quietly. Helen said, "There's more to it than just delaying the wedding. He asked what would I do if you had to leave the valley. Does that mean he's thinking of selling the farm?"

"It could, I suppose, but what was your answer?"

"I said where you go I go. Oh, Joseph, you should know the answer. If you do lose your job it will make no difference to us."

Glancing around the room Joseph said, "Yes, but a farm worker's cottage might seem a bit of the come down after this."

That triggered a quick skip across the room to sit on his knee and give him a reassuring cuddle.

By the time Joseph finished his Sunday work looking after the livestock Helen was making a midmorning coffee. Over it, Joseph asked Joshua, "Would you like me to drive you round the valley, Master? You'd see most of the fields from the road."

"No, I don't think so, thank you. Mary will carry my coffee out into the garden; I'll sit and watch the vegetables grow for a while. But perhaps you and Helen would join us for lunch."

Though a little chilly the morning was pleasant enough to take a walk. The sound of the church bells ringing out across the fields was part of the valley's nostalgia but Helen had never been to Church since the vicar had more or less accused her of causing Jessica's death. He had suggested that her relationship with Mainthorpe had driven his wife to the depth of despair and, by implication, to suicide. Not having forgotten that it was the same vicar who had wanted to have her placed in an orphanage when Grandpa died, Helen had become angry and told him he was a pompous old fool, which didn't endear her to him.

On the Sunday evenings Joseph took her back to Fletchfield Helen went instead to the evening service at the Methodist Chapel.

The simple service and robust singing appealed to her, and it was there they planned to get married. Their discussion now ranged over that wedding day and inevitably to what would happen if Joseph lost his job. Helen was surprised, when suggesting that after they were married she might want to go out to work, by how readily Joseph agreed to the idea. The chilly wind didn't stop the curlews from calling, not just to each other but also to the core of Helen's consciousness. "Yes Joseph," she said, gripping his hand, "but wherever you take me let there be curlews to call to me each spring."

Lunch was a subdued affair. Joseph and Helen sat together in silent anticipation. As usual, Mary had little to say and Mainthorpe concentrated on his food. Though he now used his fork in his left hand, cutting up roast beef seemed difficult. Eventually he finished and, pushing his plate away, said, "It's obvious that I'm not going to enjoy this farm like I used to and Mary isn't too keen on the country life so we have talked it over." Under the table Joseph's grip on Helen's hand tightened. Still staring at his plate, Mainthorpe continued, "I don't want to sell and I no longer feel up to being the farmer so Mary suggests I need a tenant. Are you interested, Joseph?"

"Of course I'd be interested but I doubt if I can afford it. I've some savings but not enough to stock a farm this size, and I don't want to involve Mother. She needs her money to retire on."

Marvelling at how steely calm Joseph acted under pressure, Helen said, "I've got some savings, Joseph. Perhaps we can talk about it?"

Mainthorpe looked from one to the other for a while, and then said, "Helen's probably told you, we've had a fantastic year at the mill and it's all thanks to her. Because of that, for the payment of just £100 I'm prepared to turn over the farm lock, stock and barrel."

Joseph and Helen looked at each other in complete surprise. Mainthorpe watched them for a moment before continuing.

"There's a condition. I'll do it only if Helen becomes a director of my company."

Helen said, "But you are not a limited company; why do you need a director?"

"I've had my lawyer working on it. It's set up. It just needs my signature – and yours, of course."

Joseph asked, "What does being a director entail, Master?"

"Whatever we decide. In this case I want Helen in the office two or three days each week to take charge of design and development."

Surprised and speechless, Helen looked to Joseph who said, "We need time to talk about it. Now about the farm, Master – I appreciate that you're being very generous, in fact more than either of us deserves, but I'll only take it on if we have the security of a life tenancy."

Mainthorpe chuckled, "Oh, Joseph, you're a man after my own heart. You ask a lot, but I suppose both of you have given a lot. Yes, all right then, you can have a life tenancy – of the farm but not of the Grange. Though if I'm not going to be here and if you'd like to I'll agree for you to live in it for the immediate future."

Chapter Thirty-Two

A farm tenancy usually ran from Lady Day, which was on 25th March, but it was the first week of May before Joseph signed the agreement. Only then could they really celebrate by discussing plans for the future. The evidence of the slump in farm profits was all around. Many farm homesteads were looking neglected, with docks and thistles growing on once tidy fields. The year before, the government had introduced an Agricultural Credits Act with the idea of making loans easier for farmers but most farmers, being wary of borrowed money and banks, chose to struggle on.

Joseph was under no illusions. The Grange looked well because Mainthorpe's money had both paid for the improvements and enabled him to retain a decent labour force. Hardly a week went by without one or more men walking into the farmyard in search of a job, most of them saying, "Any job will do boss. If it's just a week or a day or even a few hours I'd be grateful."

From Helen he learned that it was much the same in town. Both Joseph and Helen took an interest in the events of the day. Neither of them could understand how on one hand the city institutes seemed buoyant and many who were in work were earning good money, while on the other there were hundreds of thousands of desperate people. Many had not worked since the General Strike of 1926.

There was no plan to make immediate changes on how the farm was run. With no borrowed money, under Mainthorpe's patronage it had paid the men's wages, including Joseph's, and left a small profit. Joseph had no intention of borrowing money until things improved. There was some cause for optimism though, because with the recent kind weather the lambing had gone well. By early May the once brown hills were greening over with new growth just when the ewes needed that growth to produce milk.

And after a long, dreary winter tied up in shippens, the dairy cows were at last able to enjoy the spring grass out in the fields. Perhaps the most important news was that the dairy where Mainthorpe had negotiated to sell his milk now agreed to take all that Joseph produced.

Joseph's one acquisition was a second-hand car. Helen needed a means to travel back and forward to the mill, and more immediately they had decided to tour Scotland for their honeymoon.

Joseph left Helen and Mainthorpe to decide what would happen to the furniture in the Grange. Mainthorpe wanted some of his pictures and a beautiful carved oak sideboard moved into town, replacing what he described as 'some of Jessica's modern junk.' Other than those, Joseph and Helen were free to keep everything else, and, at Joseph's suggestion, Helen promised Mainthorpe that his bedroom would be kept for him to use whenever he wanted a quiet few days in the country.

Not that Helen had much time to discuss the furnishing of the house. She explained carefully to both David Brightwell and Ruth Douglas just what decisions they had to take on their own. With Mainthorpe's agreement she designed a system whereby they could report to Sarah each important decision taken so that a record of it could be placed on the Master's desk each day. Ruth understood and responded immediately but David tried her patience by running to the Master over silly things.

The wedding was to be a quiet affair. Other than Aunt Emily, on Helen's side there were no relatives to invite and, as to Joseph's extended family, it was either invite just the close relatives or extend outwards into dozens and dozens. Jade agreed to be her bridesmaid and Joseph asked Isaac to be his best man. To her surprise, Joshua agreed to give her away. The Methodist minister took it all very seriously by insisting that they came to his home on two separate nights to discuss the implications of a Christian marriage. Even though he wasn't as pompous as the vicar, he went into such intimate detail that after each visit they giggled most of the way home.

The days flew so quickly that Helen was still trying to clear her desk at 5.30 on the Friday night before the wedding. On the drive home, the sun shining brightly from behind her out of the western sky highlighted every stone wall and craggy outcrop on the hills in front. Parking in her usual spot, Helen could see that the west side of the valley along the brook was already in the shadows, whereas the Grange and the moors behind it were magically illuminated. Enthralled, Helen whispered, "It is my valley now. No – Joseph, whatever you are doing, this is our valley."

Jade was waiting for her at the Grange and the two girls enjoyed an evening of laughter and, for Helen, tingling anticipation.

Had Helen been her own daughter Aunt Emily could not have been more excited; she had even persuaded them to hold the reception at the Grange. On the wedding morning several of her friends were busy in the kitchen while Aunt Emily fussed round Helen, re-combing her hair and fiddling with her veil until Helen said, "It will do. Where's Jade?"

"I'm here, Helen. How do I look?"

In a turquoise dress matching the colour of her eyes, Jade looked stunning and Helen told her so. "You don't look so bad yourself," Jade replied. "That dress shows every curve; your Joseph's a lucky man."

Helen trembled at the thought of Joseph's hands discovering how lucky he was.

Using just one walking stick and holding Helen's arm with his other hand, Mainthorpe struggled up the narrow aisle alongside Helen. When they reached the altar, not too quietly and to everyone's amusement, he whispered, "I'm the proudest man in the room."

Joseph took her hand and, to more laughter from behind, whispered in her other ear, "He's not, you know."

The Minister composed himself, cleared his throat and with a twinkle in his eyes reminded the small congregation that this was a solemn occasion.

Chapter Thirty-Three

After the grandeur of Scotland, the Pennines above
Fletchfield looked a bit tame when they first saw them in the
distance. Even so, as they drove nearer it was a great feeling to be
back. Soon the little car climbed above the town and reached the
spot where Helen often pulled up to overlook the valley. She
touched Joseph's arm. "Stop a moment. It might not be Scotland
but it's just as beautiful, isn't it? Isn't it amazing how our life
seems to be working out? We are going to be happy here, aren't
we Joseph?"

"After the last three weeks I think we could be happy
anywhere, but I suppose we'll make do here."

Helen gave him a playful dig in the ribs as he restarted the
car and drove towards the Grange. She would have rushed
excitedly inside had Joseph not caught hold of her and, lifting her
effortlessly off the ground, said, "Oh no you don't. This is one job
I have to do," and carried her through the threshold to the
amusement of Aunt Emily.

There was so much news to hear and tell. Aunt Emily
wanted to know, "Where have you been and what have you done?"
Then before Helen could answer, she continued, "I went to a large
house sale and bought an antique sideboard. Come and have a
look. It fills the gap where Master's used to stand."

"That's great, it's just perfect. It looks absolutely right in
this room. How much did it cost?" Helen enthused, stroking the
beautifully grained oak surface.

"It took a lot of polishing to get it looking like this but as to
the cost – there is none, it's my wedding present to you."

Joseph added his appreciation, slipped on his wellington
boots and set off round the farm. It was early Sunday afternoon
and there was no one about; not even his mother was in at the

farmhouse. Instinctively he checked each of the dairy cows as he walked through them to where Isaac had mown the first field for hay. With the sun shining on the newly cut grass its fragrance filled the air, which in turn triggered a feeling of immense satisfaction. "Yes, Helen, we will make do here."

There were greetings all round when Helen arrived at the mill on Tuesday morning, particularly from Mainthorpe who wasted no time before briefing her as to what had been going on in her absence. "You've just missed the excitement of the election," he said. "You'll no doubt know the result; Baldwin was a fool for resigning. Labour might have won a few more seats than the Conservatives but the Tories could have teamed up with the Liberals and stayed in a power. As it is we've got Ramsay MacDonald's expensive welfare plans and I don't like what's happening in America."

"What are you suggesting?"

"Sitting at home each afternoon gives me time to think. Perhaps too much time. We must have a directors' meeting as soon as possible. Can you be here tomorrow afternoon at about four o'clock?"

They promoted Sarah to act as company secretary with the added role of official tea maker. At four o'clock Mainthorpe stirred the sugar into his tea and without more ado proclaimed, "Right, your idea works. Both managers are making more decisions, which has taken a load off me. The trouble is that between the American boom and this Labour government I think we are in for a reckoning."

"How does that affect how the managers work?"

"They're being extra careful, buying in raw material too far ahead. It might be prudent but it puts a strain of our cash flow. If things carry on as they are we could manage it because . . . eh, you probably don't know, do you?"

"Know what?"

"This month we've actually paid off our overdraft. That's months ahead of our best forecasts."

"That's wonderful. I'm surprised because when I glanced through the books I noticed there is one or two accounts outstanding. The Stoddards in particular are getting further behind with their payments."

Mainthorpe looked surprised. "Right, Sarah, make a note to remind me to chase up every overdue account. This isn't the time to let things slip; there's too much uncertainty in the business world."

It was great to hear his voice nearly back to normal. Helen almost said so but, afraid that she might embarrass him, said instead, "I think you must have had too much time to sit and think. Other people don't share your pessimism."

They debated it back and to for a while. Eventually Helen said, "You realise that when this gets out people will think we're in money trouble."

"So be it; I've done a calculation. Here's the figure. I think we're better with that in the bank."

Although still not strong enough to do a full day in the office, Mainthorpe managed to stay until one o'clock each day. Helen did two fairly full days on Tuesday and Wednesday, also because Mainthorpe found that there was just too much to do, each Friday payday Helen drove into town midmorning. Aunt Emily usually came along to shop and spend the afternoon in town while Helen did her personal shopping before going to the office. A routine developed that she and Mainthorpe had a chat before he went for lunch and Helen finished the Friday business.

It was an incredibly happy time for Joseph. Not only was there the satisfaction of being completely his own boss but also there was the deep fulfilment that only a happy marriage can bring. During the hay harvest when Helen was not in town she often joined him in the hay field. His heart always skipped a beat when he looked up and saw her walking towards him. It might be at baggin time with a basket of food and a can of tea for all the men or it might just be with sleeves rolled up and a pitchfork in her hands. Whatever the occasion he always marvelled that this beautiful woman was coming to him.

The fact that Helen was going into town three days each week didn't upset him. The way his home was being run also gave him a lot of satisfaction; not only had Aunt Emily stayed but they had kept on Tom Smith's wife to do (or to skimp) the cleaning, whichever was her mood that day.

When Aunt Emily asked if she could stay on to help in the house Helen had said, "Yes, on one condition. That you have your meals with us because you are one of our family."

"Maybe so, but you young people don't want old folks round you all the time," Aunt Emily said, "So I'll share breakfast and lunch but not your evening meal. When you haven't seen each other all day you need time to talk."

And Joseph agreed, because they did talk. Helen always wanted to know what had been happening on the farm and Joseph was equally interested in Helen's day, particularly when Helen related Mainthorpe's pessimistic financial prophecy. Joseph reassured her that whatever happened in the city it would hardly affect him on the farm.

The hay barns were full; the first lambs made a good price at the autumn sheep sales. In fact, Joseph was more than content with his lot as he sat on a stone wall watching a cow calf while waiting for Helen to come home. Although it was already dark, Joseph marvelled how mild it was for the 18th of October and wondered what could have delayed Helen this Friday night to make her so late. The cow lay prone, straining, and at each instinctive push moaned with the effort. Judging by the size of the protruding feet, there was a large bull calf about to come into the world. With front feet forward it slowly emerged inch by inch until its ears flicked forward as its head came free; the cow rested for a few moments before giving an almighty push that freed the calf's muscular shoulders. It wasn't many minutes before the calf slipped completely out, snorting and snuffling in its efforts to free the membrane hanging round its nostrils. Joseph was stepping forward to help but the cow was up on her feet and beat him to it. With a feeling of satisfaction he watched the cow's rough tongue clean and invigorate as nature intended.

For once Aunt Emily had not gone to town with Helen so there was hot food spoiling in the oven. It smelled so delicious when Joseph went into the kitchen that he couldn't resist having a peep. A large simmering bowl of hotpot tempted him but worry about Helen's whereabouts took him back outside to stand in the yard. At last, car lights came up the lane and within minutes Helen pulled up near the door. "I was getting worried about you; where have you been?"

Up to then the summer had been beyond Helen's expectations. Joseph was fantastic both as a companion and as a lover. The nightmares of Uncle Horace were a thing of the past, but Joseph's muscular presence pleasantly disturbed many more nights than the nightmares had ever done.

Taking her responsibilities as a company director very seriously, Helen read different articles on company law. The working arrangement with Mainthorpe went well and as the summer progressed his brain functions improved to the point that Sarah had no need to pass unfinished business on to Helen. Even Mr Grimshaw now accepted her overall management, although Helen joked to Joshua that it was because she was only interfering with his department for two days each week.

On the days that she was at home Helen started to paint, laughing with Joseph that it was necessary to fill the empty spaces on the walls left by Joshua's removal of his favourite paintings. Not that Joseph argued. Repeatedly he would point out one or other of his favourite views. "Why not paint that? Wouldn't it look nice on such and such a wall?"

There were many such suggestions because when the weather was reasonable they began to walk further afield, enjoying the beautiful scenery across the boundaries of Cheshire,

Staffordshire and Derbyshire. Although Joseph had grown up among so much beauty he had taken it for granted. Now, with Helen to share the experience, it was almost as though he was seeing the hills for the first time. Often they followed the old salters' trails, or saltways as they were known locally, that crossed the Peak District from the Cheshire salt towns. These were packhorse trails that in places dipped down through valleys to ford streams and then climb up steep paths that were in places were no more than crude steps cut into solid rocks. Both of them became interested in the history of these hills, borrowing books to study in the evening so that they could use their imagination when following the rugged paths. Helen tried to picture in her mind the hardy men leading strings of tough little ponies carrying panniers laden with salt towards eastern towns, returning weeks later with trade goods to sell either during their journey or on their arrival.

It was a fairytale summer. The fascination they had with each other somehow gave them a greater awareness of the world around them. Helen said, "It's a fairytale that ends with the words 'And they all lived happily ever after'."

She remembered saying that and wondered if that fairytale had come to an end prematurely when Joseph asked, "I was worried about you; where have you been?" And she replied, "Have you not heard the news? The stock market's collapsed in America. Joshua came back to the office; we've been listening to the wireless together. I'm sorry, I tried to call you earlier on the phone but you must have been outside or something. Anyway, it sounds serious."

"It won't affect you too much, will it? You're a private company and apart from the few shares that he's given you the Master owns all the others, so why are you both so worried?"

"We're at the luxury end of the market. It depends on what happens next week, but if it runs on it could trigger a depression and we could be in trouble."

Chapter Thirty-Four

"I'm sorry, Joshua, but Joseph doesn't want me to drive home that late again on my own. There was a frost this morning and in places the road was icy. Anyway, he suggests I stay overnight each Tuesday so that I can leave earlier on a Wednesday afternoon."

"Are you going to do that this week?" When Helen nodded Mainthorpe said, "Well then, let's have our meeting tonight; we can talk over dinner. We could go out but it would be more private at my house, wouldn't it? Good, then I'll expect you straight after work."

"No, not straight away. Mr Buxton has finally bought his dream cottage. I've promised to walk round there after work to take a look at it. You don't eat until seven, do you? Then I'll be with you before then."

There was no feeling of gloom among the workforce. After all, shares had risen and fallen many times and, besides, most of the workers took no notice of city transactions. The day's work went smoothly and afterwards the Buxtons' cottage was just what they had dreamed about. Though it was in a rough condition, Mr Buxton explained that because of that he had managed to buy it for so little. Anyway, there was plenty of time and he was looking forward to tidying it up through the coming year. He even took Helen round the back to see how the garden would catch the afternoon sun, which should make his marrows grow. To Helen's amusement he enthused more about the possibilities of the garden than about the house.

Over dinner Mainthorpe said, "I've had a rent review notice today. They're suggesting a rise of 25%. Incidentally, I never asked how you managed to negotiate a nil rise last year with that spotty-faced friend of yours."

"I didn't negotiate with Simon. I've never spoken to him since that day in my office. I insisted I talked with his father and I had your lawyer with me. When he said he wanted a 25% rise and demanded that we sign up for five years, I said a no percent rise and to help him we were prepared to just sign up for one year. He settled for that."

Mainthorpe chuckled, "I have to admit my lawyer, as you call him, did tell me about it. He said you were brilliant. You tied the man in knots. And the fact that you settled for only one year could be of help now. I suggest you do the negotiating again this time but let's delay it until we see how the dust's settling in the city."

Helen said, "I've not lived long enough to know how the city works. How long will it take for the markets to settle down again?"

"There's all sorts of predictions. I don't think anyone really knows. Perhaps in a couple of weeks it will have bottomed out. In the meantime we have to guess how our sales will go and then decide how much raw material we buy."

Helen cut in, "We've got to decide that fairly quickly because we need to buy before the end of next week or we'll have to stop work."

"Then let's do just that!" Mainthorpe thumped the table in his agitation. "Yes, let's plan to lay the staff from Wednesday next week. If I'm being too pessimistic we can change our minds and arrange for an emergency delivery."

Mainthorpe wasn't being too pessimistic; in fact he could never have anticipated the events that unfolded. Just two days after that meeting, on the Thursday (later to become known as Black Thursday), panic hit Wall Street with nearly 13 million shares traded in a single day. On the following Tuesday – Black Tuesday, October 29 – some 60 million shares were traded, dropping share prices dramatically. Again Helen was having dinner at Mainthorpe's home. With the time lag between America and here they could listen to live radio reports, which didn't create the atmosphere for a relaxed meal. Mainthorpe pushed his half eaten dinner across the table muttering, "I should have sold! What a fool I've been – I should have sold last week."

Noticing that his voice was becoming more slurred in his agitation, Helen said, "What should you have sold last week, Joshua? I thought we'd done everything we could at the time."

"It's not you, it's not the company; it's me. I own a few shares. They're my reserve fund, or they were before this lot. Now we need them they'll be worth nothing."

Although the Wall Street crash seemed far away, Europe could not be isolated from it. Germany suffered more than most whereas in Britain the fall was not quite so great; even so, in some industries it was devastating. Particularly hard-hit were the old basic industries of iron, coal and shipbuilding. Though these were not basic Fletchfield industries, you didn't have to travel far before pithead-winding gear could be seen towering above the surrounding slag heaps and rows of depressed-looking terraced houses.

It was in these other basic industries that Mainthorpe had invested. Convinced that they would forever remain the cornerstone of Britain's industrial wealth, he believed them to be the most secure investments, but through the next couple of days it became obvious that those industries were being hit more than most.

During the weekend Mainthorpe became more depressed. When Monday came Helen went in early only to find that their own customers were adding to the despondency by cancelling orders. Mainthorpe said, "I expected that. They'll just as soon start ordering again, but in the meantime we've got no reserve funds."

It was late Monday morning before they told any of the staff about their decision to lay people off. Then it was only the wages department in strictest confidence, because of course they wanted the wages ready for Wednesday night. All the time, Helen kept hoping that it would not be necessary to close but events proved it was. Mainthorpe said, "We must explain to them personally. I'll never make it up to the top floors so if I start at the bottom and work up, will you go to the top and work down?"

Of course, a secret like that could not be kept quiet. The glum faces greeting her confirmed that they knew before Helen held up her arms to stop the handlooms chattering. They were not just mill workers; many were her friends. It was heartbreaking to confirm what they already feared and the best that she could promise them was that with luck the mill would be working again on Monday. As she worked her way down from floor to floor the same glum silence greeted her. Though they were angry at being laid-off, there was nothing they could do.

In the meantime Mainthorpe had only managed to climb one flight of stairs. Helen found him sitting grey faced and haggard, sipping a glass of water. Leaving David Brightwell to help him down again, she ran across the road to the factory where Ruth had already broken the news. Helen walked amongst the workers, answering questions and trying to give some reassurance.

Back in the office Helen was concerned to see how dejected Mainthorpe looked, sitting head bowed behind his desk. "Are you going to be all right, Joshua? Shall I get your driver to take you home?"

"The papers are calling yesterday Black Tuesday but this is our black day. This is the first time I've ever sent my workforce home. Yes, I'll be all right, and no, I'm not going home."

Looking up to see Helen hovering concernedly, he added, "You go. There's nothing more you can do here. Anyway, we may as well let the Mill close early."

Soon after that Helen looked in again only to see Mainthorpe still sitting with head bowed, seemly deep in depressed thought. She said to him, "There's nothing more I can do here so if you are all right I'll go home."

"Yes, go home. Can you come back midmorning Friday so we can make a decision about next week?"

If it was depressing inside, the weather outside was even worse. There was a damp, smoke-laden fog clinging to everything; not so dense that it was impossible to drive but it shrouded the town with the feeling of despair. The naked branches of most trees testified to the effects of the frost the week before. Only the oaks still clung on to their leaves and they looked a dirty brown in the damp, dull light, which didn't help to brighten her mood.

Stepping out of the car outside the Grange, Helen was aware of a dull knocking sound coming from the back kitchen. Thinking she recognised the rhythm, she hurried to investigate. "Hello, Helen; can you believe what I'm doing?" Aunt Emily said smiling.

"I can see what you're doing, but why?"

"The dairy sent Monday's milk back, they said it had gone off, but Joseph thinks it's just an excuse. Anyway, whatever the reason we're making butter again. Here, have a turn. It's just like old times only this is a much bigger churn."

Helen slipped upstairs to change into working clothes and join in the activity. When Joseph came in for tea she said, "If this was Monday's milk you already had it back last night, so why didn't you tell me when we talked on the phone?"

"I thought you had enough worries without hearing mine."

"Never think that – please, Joseph, never think like that."

Over dinner that night Helen explained what was happening at the Mill. "Although we sent them home we are still hoping that we can work again on Monday. We left the senior staff doing a full inventory of everything in stock. By Friday we should know what orders stand and what have been cancelled."

"It must be heartbreaking to stand down people you work with everyday," Joseph said with a shake of the head. "The trouble is, on the farm if my milk keeps coming back I can't send the cows home or the men that look after them."

"I suppose Aunt Emily's butter back in Flaxton was only worthwhile because she could sell it on her own milk round."

"Yes, and the butter that we'll make from just one day's milk could supply the whole village for a month. We aren't the only farm to have milk back, so if we all make butter the price will be on the floor anyway."

The office on Friday morning was not a pleasant place to be. Mainthorpe looked haggard as they sat listening to the two managers' reports. It appeared there was enough raw material in stock to work for a few days but orders were still uncertain. Helen spent a few hours on the telephone talking to different customers and at the end of it believed she had enough orders to justify working again on Monday.

Mainthorpe took some convincing but eventually agreed.

When Helen got back to the Grange, Friday's milk churns stood in a line outside the back kitchen. Coming out of the house to greet her, Joseph said, "I've talked to the dairy. They say that with so many people laid-off in town their milk sales have dropped alarmingly. They don't know what else to do but to send it back. Anyway, I've persuaded them to tell us when they don't want milk rather than us sending it in only to be returned."

"And how often will that be?"

"No one knows, but they are going to send each farm a postcard at the start of the week."

"I suppose it's not ready to churn yet," Helen said, lifting the lid to look and smell expertly inside. "No, it will take another day for it to go off and the cream rise enough to be skimmed."

Putting the lid back on again, Helen turned to Joseph, laughing, "Oh well, it will be a bit of arm exercise for Saturday afternoon."

On Saturday evening both Helen and Joseph were sitting, thoroughly exhausted, in front of the fire when the telephone rang. "Hello, Helen, is that you? This is Mary. I've got bad news – Joshua's had another stroke. He's in hospital."

Chapter Thirty-Five

They stood side by side looking down at the sleeping figure. The moustache looked more twisted now and saliva dribbled from the corner of his mouth. Helen reached for Joseph's hand. Mary, who had moved away from the bed when they came in, said, "He did wake up for a while but I could make nothing of him."

"How do you mean?" Helen asked without taking her eyes away from the prone figure.

"He didn't seem to be able to talk. He held my hand but he was just making funny noises. The nurse says he might never be able to talk."

The shock of seeing Mainthorpe so ill affected Helen deeply. They brought in chairs and sat by the bedside for some time in a sort of silent trance. Eventually they both admitted that it was pointless just sitting by the sleeping patient, particularly when Mary would stay there to keep a loving vigil.

Helen was deep in thought on the journey back to the Grange. At length, Joseph broke the silence. "I suppose this means that you could be in town all week?"

"I don't know what it means, Joseph; I just don't know what to do. How will I cope?"

"Well, you coped all right when he was ill the first-time, so why not this time?"

"It was exciting then, we'd made our plans. I knew just what we intended to do, it was just a matter of keeping it rolling. Now there are nearly two hundred people dependent on me and they are already reduced to halftime working. I can't think of any course of action to get them back to full-time; in fact, we may have to lay them off altogether."

Joseph drove on in silence for a while. Suddenly Helen let out a long moan. "Oh, God, no! It's not 'we' any more, there's just me. I have to decide what to do. And all those families dependent on me with Christmas just around the corner."

It was just as though a door had closed between them. Through supper and later in bed Helen was just lost in a thought world of her own, and Joseph couldn't reach into it.

He was already out with the cows when Helen woke the next morning. She exchanged a few functional remarks with her Aunt over breakfast before packing a case and going out to the car. Though the sun had yet to climb up over Leckon Moore, it had risen enough to break the day. Heavy clouds scuttled overhead and puddles lined the roads as she, huddled over the steering wheel, peered through the condensation on the windscreen.

The Mill was already buzzing with Monday activity when Helen arrived. As she stood at the bottom of the main staircase, the clatter and hum of machinery and the chatter of workers were like music but it could only go on for three days, and then what?

On the way she had called in at the hospital where Mary, already by Joshua's bedside, said that there was no change. Settling down behind her desk, Helen listened to a few messages from Sarah and then called the lawyer to tell him about Joshua. In desperation she said, "I'm at a loss to know what to do. I need help. Can you tell me what my options are?"

"You had a document empowering you to take charge of the business. If you still have it, then use it. In any case, Miss Helen, I suggest you come into my office this afternoon."

His was a dismal office with paint peeling off the door and files and folders stacked haphazardly across a threadbare carpet. Even the wallpaper was a faded, depressing brown. As an attractive young woman working in a man's world,

Helen had learned that the only way to do business with older men was to be direct, even blunt, in her dealings. Now, standing in the middle of this dreary room, she turned round twice to take it all in, and without thinking of the consequences said, "A coat of paint and a new carpet might brighten up your life and bring the occasional smile to your face."

Standing with mouth agape, the lawyer looked first at Helen, then at the walls, and the carpet, and finally back to Helen. Realising how tactless she must have sounded, she said, "I'm sorry, I just spoke without . . ."

The lawyer raised his hand. "No, my dear, don't apologise. You are right. Yes, of course you are right," he said, pulling out a chair for her. "Please sit down."

Taking a notebook out of her handbag, Helen accepted his invitation but before she could speak the lawyer passed over a large sealed envelope. "When Mr Mainthorpe was recovering from his first stroke the doctor told him that he believed it was caused by an aneurysm. You know what that is? Yes, well, he was warned that another could happen at any time. As a result, he instructed me to draw up a power of attorney, which would allow you to act on his behalf should he become incapacitated. I visited him this morning and am satisfied that he is . . ."

He carried on explaining what that meant but by then Helen had opened the envelope and, finding two papers inside, was no longer listening. One was the formal power of attorney empowering her to take complete charge of his private and business affairs. The other was a personal letter addressed *My Dearest Helen.*

If you are reading this then something terrible as happened. Please don't be too sad, because you've given me great happiness; in fact if events had worked out differently I might have proposed a more permanent relationship. But

*when Joseph stole your heart I realised with great
disappointment that I could only share part of you.*

*If I am dead then my estate is left completely in your
hands, if just incapacitated in some way I know you will act in
the interest of all concerned. Whichever is the case, my town
house is to go to Mary – but, please, she needs you to be kind
and look after her.*

*You must know that you have my deepest affection. May
God be with you.*

Joshua.

The lawyer discreetly looked out of the window,
waiting respectfully while Helen wiped her tears away. Only
when she had regained composure did he speak. "I know
what's in it because he dictated it to me when he was in
hospital, and I realise what a desperate situation not just yours
but every business is now facing. Have you read this
morning's papers?"

Still feeling a constriction in her throat, Helen shook her
head. When she didn't answer he went on. "Banks are
collapsing in America and businessmen are throwing
themselves out of upstairs windows. It may not yet be like
that here, but it's bad enough. I have a queue of desperate
clients wanting my counsel." Suddenly he chuckled, "With a
extra rush of business I might be able to afford a new carpet."

Helen stood up. "I need to go away and think about all
this and then I'm sure I'll have a list of questions. But there is
one thing I need to ask you now. Can I run the business alone
or do I have to appoint another director?"

"When you are a privately owned company then legally
you don't have to, but if you feel in need of someone to share
the burden then that's up to you. Give the matter some
thought; if you then feel that way I might be able to help you
with one or two names."

The afternoon was worse than any of her old nightmares. The enormity of the burden seemed too much to bear. The Buxtons' faces, the face of the young designer Peter's face glowing with the joy of a new baby, and even old Grimshaw's scowling countenance all flashed through her mind. What expression would they have if she failed to keep the business solvent?

At last Helen left the office and drove to the hospital. Though Mainthorpe was awake he seemed not to understand what she said and, when he tried to speak, it was no more than a repeated stutter that never reached a word. Helen wiped his cheek, held his hand and wept as she said, "I've read your letter, Joshua. I don't know if I can do what you believe I can but I promise that I will try."

With that she kissed him on the forehead and left the room. Mary followed and caught hold of her arm. "He knows what you're capable of. Just trust your own judgement."

At Mary's insistence, Helen returned with her to Joshua's home for both a meal and night's rest. She knew she had to economise wherever possible and, since Mainthorpe still maintained his domestic staff, she decided they might as well be put to use looking after her throughout the week. Even Mary didn't come out of the frugality drive unscathed. Helen looked at the Primrose Night and Tom Brown wage packets and decided to fire Tom Brown. Taking the news very well, Mary said, "Living in Joshua's home, everything is provided so I don't really need it."

For Joseph the week was long and miserable. Not only was his matrimonial bed empty but also there was a distance about Helen; it was as though she was living in another world when they talked on the telephone. Joseph understood the immensity of the task facing her but at the same time he did his calculations relating to the farm and came to the conclusion that, if the dairy continued to reject his milk two days each week, he would soon be in trouble. Although Aunt Emily and his Mother were very experienced at making good, sweet butter, they still had to sell it. For that the two women volunteered to stand at the Friday market with both butter and buttermilk on condition that Joseph would drive them there and bring them home later.

The week went better than Helen could have hoped. Enough firm orders came in, particularly from the Stoddards, to bring the staff in again for three days in the following week and possibly the week after.

Considering the uncertainty in the business world, it was a pleasant surprise that her suppliers accepted her orders for raw materials without demanding payment with order. If they would trust her, then in turn she had to trust her customers, but by Friday afternoon she was drained by the emotional strain of it all. Dealing with the business was bad enough but listening to Joshua's senseless gabbles each evening at the hospital was heartbreaking. In his letter he had declared his affections and she now realised just how deep her feelings were for him. She held his good hand, soothed his sweating brow and talked and talked, but in return there were only hints of comprehension in his eyes.

Sarah showed Aunt Emily into Helen's office. "I've stood with Mrs Bolton in that cold, draughty marketplace all day and we've only sold half the butter. Mind you, for what it's worth we've sold the buttermilk. Mrs Bolton's taken the empty cans back with Joseph. Now you'll have to take me back with this left-over butter."

Sarah interrupted. "Miss Helen, there are several workers here wanting to know if we're working on Monday. Can I put a notice on the door to save answering questions?"

"You can do better than that. Take this butter and give a packet to every family who comes to the door." Helen turned to Aunt Emily. "Tell me the best price you got at the market and I'll pay Joseph. Now let's go home and see if he is still speaking to me after neglecting him for a week."

Considering that Christmas was just round the corner, Joseph found the cattle market depressing; there were none of the usual hearty greetings. Farmers are basically in competition with each other so there is always a touch of secrecy about them. Now he noticed when they stood about in small groups that there was a near furtive manner about them, and there seemed to be little real business taking place. However, for Joseph the problem with butter making was a surplus of skimmed milk left unused, and there were two empty pigsties at the Grange.

Though he had never liked pigs, a few kept in those empty sties could convert that waste skim into money. Several litters of newly weaned pigs failed to reach the reserve price under the hammer, and one in particular caught his eye. Eventually, after thirty minutes of hard bargaining, the owner reluctantly accepted his offer and a little later, after another session of tough haggling, Joseph bought an ageing sow that was guaranteed and, to Joseph's inexperienced eye, looked to be heavily in pig.

Seeing how the trade in lambs had fallen dramatically in just a couple of weeks, it was a relief to know that all his lambs at the Grange had been sold earlier. As regards dairy cows, although there were a number of farmers standing round the sale ring there didn't seem to be any one buying. On sale as individuals, each cow came into the sale ring in turn to survey the surrounding uninterested farmers with matching bovine indifference. Undaunted, the auctioneer rattled away in an excited pretence of selling. The fact was that Joseph never saw a genuine bid. Finally, in frustration the auctioneer crashed his stick down on the rostrum muttering, "Sorry gentlemen, I can't quite go there."

One or two vendors, obviously desperate for money, revealed a disappointment near to despondency on their usually inscrutable faces when their cows walked out of the ring unsold. These were men no doubt dreading the prospect of going hungry or selling privately at a near giveaway price.

That it was heartbreaking for anyone in that position was brought home to Joseph by his new brother-in-law, Ben, who had brought two maiden heifers in to sell. Though just a couple of weeks earlier they would have made the price of a newly calved dairy cow between them, Ben had to watch disconsolately as they walked into the ring and, in spite of the auctioneer's exhortation, never had a bid.

Over a cup of tea in the canteen, Ben whispered in strictest confidence, "The trouble is that I've spent all my savings on the house. We divided it up so that my Grandparents could live in one end and I wanted Anna to have some comfort in the other half. I was relying on selling those two heifers to see us through to the New Year. Now I'm not sure what we'll do."

"Have you been to the bank?"

"Yes, but you must have heard? There are so many banks collapsing in America that ours have got the jitters and cancelled nearly every farmers' overdraft. No warning, just a letter in the post telling us to pay it off within seven days. That's why there's lots of farmers keen to sell something and almost no one buying today. Jack Ogden in the next village has done a moonlight flit – he's sold his few cows cheap for cash and vanished. Anyway, you can imagine the reception I got from the bank manager."

Over their evening meal that night Joseph had plenty to tell Helen, from his trip to the market, his pigs, and the trade in dairy cows to the fall in the price of butter. Helen said, "I know, Joseph, but my workers are only getting half a week's wage and many of them have young children. They are really desperate. I've bought your surplus butter today; what more can I do?"

"I don't want handouts, I want to sell my milk. Or at least get a reasonable price for my butter. Anyway, do you want to tell me how you've got on this last week?"

"I'm sorry, but I am just too tired to talk about it tonight."

Joseph never got round to telling her about the two heifers he bought from Ben.

Chapter Thirty-Six

Their first Christmas together was not a great success; in fact Joseph was relieved when the New Year came in. With the dairy cows inside both night and day they demanded much more of Joseph's time over the weekend. On top of that, the fact that Helen lived in Fletchfield through the week and often went back there to visit Mainthorpe on a Sunday left little time to relax together.

Even though the strains of life seemed now to put a dampener on their conversation, when they got to the bedroom Helen's beautiful body never failed to arouse Joseph. Though he tried to recapture the earlier excitement of lovemaking, Helen seemed too preoccupied to respond and, though not refusing him, was unable to match his youthful virility. The feel of Helen's placid submission aroused a need to try harder. He kissed and caressed and then, when he eventually took her, that lack of response triggered a roughness that afterwards left him feeling ashamed.

The first Monday in the New Year brought little change. Helen drove off to town leaving Joseph on the farm with Mrs Bolton and Aunt Emily churning the unsold milk into butter.

There was a cold east wind with a bit of snow in the air when Joseph drove the two women and the results of their labours into Fletchfield for the first market of the New Year. Mrs Bolton said, "I hope you appreciate what we're doing for you. Turning that heavy churn in that cold dairy is no fun at our age but now standing on these cold cobblestones all day is real punishment."

"It wouldn't be so bad if we could get a decent price," Aunt Emily said ruefully. "I used to get a better price for my own butter when I had a milk round. If you'd let me I'm sure I could sell some in the village."

"No, I've a good neighbour doing the village milk round and I'm not going to put him out of business now."

Later Joseph recalled a conversation when they were having a Boxing Day meal with his brother Joel. As usual, the talk round the table was of farming and milk prices in particular. Joel's wife said, "We can't make enough cheese – there still seems to be a good trade for quality farmhouse Cheshire cheese. Why don't you think of producing some yourself?"

"We'll bring you our surplus milk then," Joseph said, laughing.

"No, we've not got the facilities to cope with any more. We can only handle what our fifteen cows produce but I know a good cheesemaker if you want one."

Joel explained, "Her sister's looking for a job. Since she left school she's been living-in on a cheese-making farm across South Cheshire. Now she wants a head cheesemaker's job with a house, but you know these old farmers – they won't let anyone into a tied house unless they're married."

Joel's wife, Phoebe, interrupted. "Be fair, Joel, she has got a boyfriend. We're going to meet him soon."

The conversation moved on to other things but that Friday it kept coming back to Joseph as he walked round the cattle market. Casually mentioning using their own milk to perhaps manufacture cheese to four or five grumbling farmers, they all agreed it was time to do something different but none knew what.

There was just Ben who saw the potential. "Yes, it's a great idea. We're all being told to keep milk at home on different days. If we had one central farm with a large vat there could be a continuous supply."

The idea was in Joseph's mind as he drove the two women home, particularly when they showed him how little they had taken for their hard work. During dinner that night Helen seemed less tired than usual so Joseph outlined his thoughts about cheese. She said, "Over the last few years what I've learned about business is that it is absolutely ruthless. Your dairy may not take all your milk now, but if they get wind of what you're thinking they may take none at all."

"I wondered whether to get a group of farmers together to talk it over."

"Well, if you do," Helen warned, "then only get those you can trust and swear them to secrecy."

"It's just an idea that will go nowhere. Anyway, how was Joshua this week?"

"He's definitely improving but he still can't talk. So I talk to him, I tell him about the business, and how we are doing, and he seems to understand. Last night when I told him that the Stoddards have gone broke he looked really worried, until I said that they didn't owe us too much, and then he smiled in his lopsided way and raised his right thumb."

"I thought that they had a good business. What went wrong?"

"The banks are being ruthless on credit. It only needs two or three larger customers to renege on their bills and any of us could go down. Fortunately, much as I hate the man, Edward had the decency to let me know or we would have sent off a big order, and I suppose lost it all. Even so, I've still got to sell it one way or another, and I'll have to find another distributor."

There was a skittering of snow overnight, enough to make the countryside look white without interfering with the Sunday morning farm work. When Joseph went in for breakfast and found Helen up and enjoying a dish of porridge, he said, "When the sun climbs over the hill it should be a nice day. Let's go for a walk in the snow."

"I'm not sure – I wanted to look at some figures," Helen said hesitatingly. "I doubt whether we can work even three days next week."

Carrying his own dish of porridge to the table, Joseph said, "All right, you work. I'll take the dog for a walk."

"Joseph, don't be upset, I need to . . . No I don't; it will keep till later. Yes, let's go for a walk."

As the sun climbed above Leckon Moore it gleamed on the new snow and at the same time left long, dark shadows behind every outcrop of rock or stone wall. They trudged through a shaded hollow and the snow crunched under their boots but it was soft and melting when they climbed, hand-in-hand, into the full sun. There were great views. Highlighted by the snow, the rolling hills took on a different kind of beauty. The sound of the grouse's 'go-bec, go-bec' call ending with a throaty chuckle among the heather gave a hint of the spring to come, but for the two young lovers there seemed to be no magic in the morning. Though holding hands, each was lost in their own responsibilities. Helen kept wondering if it would be possible to keep her staff working even three days each week, and Joseph was aware that there needed to be a change in the returns he got from his dairy cows if he was to stay profitable. Without a change in farming returns, this valley and its beauty could be lost to him forever.

Since Mainthorpe's illness, there was one fat, lazy horse in the stable needing exercise so it seemed to Joseph a good idea to ride out on it occasionally. Although there had always been horses and ponies on the farm and as a boy he had often jumped on one's back for a bit of fun, Joseph never considered himself to be a riding man. Therefore, on the Tuesday morning when he saw a couple of inches of snow had fallen overnight, he saddled up the cob and rode out to visit some of his neighbouring farmers. And, on Helen's advice, he was only going to call on those he could trust.

After his third visit there was a clatter of hoofs on the lane behind him and Bolesworth, the estate agent, cantered up alongside. "Good morning, Joseph. It's not like you to be a riding round your neighbours. Is there something happening that I should know about?"

The truth was that, as a working farmer, Joseph was more than a little embarrassed to be caught riding out at all and, remembering Helen's warning about secrecy, he said, "I'm just wishing them all a happy New Year."

"No, Joseph. I'm wishing them a happy New Year – you are up to something. Seeing that you're calling on my tenants, I think you ought to tell me what it's about?"

When Joseph remained quiet, Bolesworth persisted. "Come on man, I can smell intrigue a mile off. So tell me about it."

Although Bolesworth was no longer directly involved with the Grange, Joseph had always held a lot of respect for the agent, and because of that decided to take a risk and explain his thinking. Bolesworth looked thoughtful. "A lot of my tenants were getting desperate before the stock market and just about every other market collapsed. Now, if you really are serious about making cheese then there's the old Mill empty in the village. I've pulled some of it down but there's one good block left that might do. The fact is that since the Mill closed the village is dying; your cheesemaker can have a choice of cottages."

Things happened very quickly after that. Joseph went to see Joel. To his surprise Grace, Joel's sister-in-law, and her fiancé David were there. Apparently cheese making was one job that had retained the traditional yearly contract and they had both ended theirs at the end of the year. It was then a matter of inspecting the building to see if it was suitable and of the young couple looking at the cottages.

The fact that the Grange was the largest house made it the obvious venue if a group of farmers were to meet together in private. Joseph arranged it for Friday night in expectation that Helen would be present to give some guidance, for he respected his wife's greater business experience.

By the time the Mill shut down on Wednesday evening Helen had failed to find anyone to take on the wholesale distribution even though Edward had, without the receiver's knowledge, posted a scribbled note listing some of his customers who took Helen's products.

Visiting Mainthorpe that evening, she explained her problem to him. "I've got the names of two or three who are willing to meet me, so I'm going to get in the car tomorrow and drive out see them. There are a couple of large customers in Manchester and a wholesaler in South Lancashire."

Looking agitated, Mainthorpe shook his head and reached for his notepad. Although his right hand didn't seem to be affected, he had only started to write over Christmas and even now, as Helen watched, the pencil seemed to move laboriously slowly. When he passed the pad across it said, "No, don't go. Your place is in the Mill. Make them come to you."

Helen said, "But I haven't enough work for even three days next week." Mainthorpe was already writing and this time it said, "Then you must fire some staff."

Helen was aghast. "I can't do that. Their jobs mean too much to them. I can't just sack half my workforce, at least not without trying."

By Friday afternoon Helen had shown her samples, receiving firm orders from two large stores, and had reached an understanding with a distributor. That, though, was subject to him visiting Fletchfield to have a look at the Mill. There was just one problem: it was snowing lightly and it would be a long drive home. Realising that Jade's family home was much closer, Helen made the snow an excuse and drove in that direction. It was not so much the snow as a group of farmers haggling about making cheese, and Joseph's rough lovemaking, that she really wanted to avoid. Anyway, Helen knew that Jade would be at home because they had talked on the phone earlier and Jade had suggested that a visit would be nice.

From the many conversations they had had through the recent troubled months, Helen knew that Jade's father had a government contract that, to Helen's envy, kept their factory going almost as normal. Therefore, it was no surprise that Jade was her usual happy, buoyant self. Greetings over, Jade said, "Mum and Dad are dining out tonight so there will be just you and me and Philip for dinner. Have you brought a dress?"

"Yes, but it's a bit low-cut at the back for a night like this."

When Helen rang to tell Joseph what had happened, he sounded both disappointed and surprised because there was no snow at the Grange. Later, when Philip came for dinner it was Helen's turn for a surprise when younger brother Mark, smiling confidently, followed Philip into the house.

Listening to the happy but frivolous conversation over dinner left Helen feeling like a staid old maid. These young people did so many exciting things whereas for many long months she seemed to have done nothing but work or take a walk in the hills. Even the gramophone, which was now beating out wild music, was new to her.

They danced and sipped wine, then swapped partners and danced again and sipped more wine. It was so exhilarating how her cares and troubles seemed to melt away. Before long Jade and Philip danced through an open door and, while Helen watched it close behind them, Mark's experienced fingers were gently caressing down the line of her spine.

Chapter Thirty-Seven

The chosen farmers sat quiet while Grace, the cheesemaker, told a little of the history of Cheshire cheese. How, way back in the seventeenth century, thousands of tons of cheese was carried by sea from the Chester and Wirral ports to London each year. The fact that sea haulage was only a quarter of the cost of hauling overland meant that the bulk of Cheshire cheese production developed in easy distance of those ports. Regardless of modern transport, it still remained on that side of the county.

Joseph could see how well Grace held their attention so he let her continue. "In those early days one cheese was made from the milk of about five cows and the ten or twelve gallons they produced each day would only make a cheese two to three inches deep, which is the sort you, or more likely your parents, made in this area before you sent your milk into Manchester. In fact, it's the sort my parents still make today. As the South Cheshire dairy herds got bigger, they developed a method for making a cheese six or even nine inches deep. It's more moist and mellow, it keeps much longer and sells for a higher price, and that's the sort I would propose you make here. We can probably buy a second-hand vat and the other equipment to go with it."

"Eh, it all sounds all right, Miss," interrupted one old farmer, "but I've only got ten cows and I'm short of money now, so how soon and how much would I be paid?"

"It depends whether you commit all your milk to making cheese or just that amount that the dairies don't want at the moment," Grace said. And she went on to tell them how much cheese they could expect to make from each cow, what price cheese was making at the moment and how long it would take that cheese to mature. Joseph was both fascinated and reassured by her knowledge and confidence, to the extent that he didn't take part in the questions and answers. Instead, he took a long look at Grace as she roved about in front of the farmers. With her black hair bouncing when she gesticulated and brown eyes, looking almost black in the shade, suddenly flashing with sparkling laughter, she was engaging. Not only were the farmers held spellbound, Joseph found it hard to concentrate on the words. Perhaps it was her shapely figure. Though not quite as tall as Helen – and lifting heavy cheeses had built up a few muscles – yet there were curves to compensate. Always getting a tingle at the sight of shapely legs, Joseph couldn't help but notice those curvy calves when Grace walked in front of him. His wayward thoughts were interrupted when one farmer said, "If we're serious about starting a small factory then we need someone to give us a lead. I reckon we need a chairman. How about it, Joseph?"

After the farmers had gone home, Joseph and Grace sat in front of the log fire reflecting on the evening. He said, "You were fantastic tonight. It's a pity your boyfriend couldn't be here to listen to you. By the way, where is he?"

"He's gone home to see his parents. We had a row. He said that if we take this on he'd be working for me, and he doesn't fancy that. Nor does he want to live in a village where there are too many of my relatives."

"But if that's the case you'll have to look for somewhere else," Joseph said. Then, seeing Grace smile, he added, "Or will you?"

"No. He's gone for good and I've had enough of living in a small attic bedroom. I had a taste of being the head cheesemaker when the boss sent me to help out when a relative's wife was ill. That's when I met David. I realise now that I wasn't really in love, it was just that to get the right job with a house I needed a husband. Mind you," she smiled provocatively, "I'm still ready for the right man."

Joseph quickly changed the subject back to cheese making. After talking over the possibilities for more than an hour, he said, "It's time I took you home."

When they looked outside and discovered that the snow that had kept Helen away had now reached the valley, Grace said, "You might not get your car back up this drive so I'll walk down the footpath through the village."

"I can't let you walk home on your own."

There was more mischief in Grace's eyes as she replied, "Are you going to ask me to stay the night?"

"I think we'll both be safer if I walk home with you."

Grace seemed surprisingly unsteady on the steep path down to the church so it was quite natural for Joseph to take her arm.

He reflected on the responsibility he had taken on over a lonely breakfast the next morning. The snow had fallen steadily overnight. There was no drifting but it lay too deep in the Gritstencrag lanes for the milk lorry to get up to the farm. As it was not a day to keep his milk at home, Joseph hitched two horses to his sledge ready to haul the cans of milk out to the main road and, to his surprise, Ned offered to help. "Is the building trade a bit slack, then?" Joseph asked. "I seem to see you around quite a bit this last week."

"What do you expect with this recession," Ned said. "We had a big job cancelled so if you need a bit of help with this cheese factory, I'm free. I even turned your butter churn for mother the other day."

"This recession's interfered with everything. I hardly see Helen now."

"Tell me about it. My woman's husband lost his job a couple of weeks ago and he's been hanging around home ever since. Anyway, it was getting time I looked for a honest woman."

They chatted away while waiting with some of the neighbours for Bob Fairclough's wagon.

When Helen rang later in the day to explain that she going to stay away another night, Joseph tried to talk to her about the Friday night meeting but she seemed distant and uninterested.

Saturday evening and Sunday were warm enough to melt much of the snow so it was something of a surprise when Helen rang just before lunch on Sunday. "I'm not leaving until after lunch, then I think I'll stay in Fletchfield overnight. I don't want to risk driving on those small lanes in the dark."

Aunt Emily had retired to bed with a heavy cold after breakfast, leaving Joseph to root around in the pantry for whatever scraps he could find for lunch. After dozing in front of the log fire, he was feeling more than a little lonely when Grace knocked on the door. Of course, he had to explain about Aunt Emily and that Helen had not returned home, which triggered Grace into womanly activity. Soon there was a hot cup of tea and a thick slab of fruitcake by his side, which he looked at with some surprise. "Where did you find that? I looked round the pantry and never saw any cake."

Grace grinned mischievously. "You men – I'll bet it was months since you were last in that pantry. Shall I stay and get your tea?"

"No, there is no need to do that. Anyway, I have to go out and do the milking before then."

"Then I'll come out and help you do the milking and then get your tea."

By Wednesday lunchtime Joseph was feeling really harassed. His mother had now retired to bed unwell, Aunt Emily was just sitting listlessly in front of the fire and there were 120 gallons of milk waiting to be churned into butter. His shepherd's wife's moaning disposition was beginning to grate as much as the half-cooked food she had served him the day before. Going into the house expecting more of the same, Joseph was surprised to smell delicious food cooking and see Grace bent over the stove. "Ha, Joseph; just on time. I brought the paper for you, so if you go and sit down I'll bring your meal through in a few minutes."

That evening, when he and Helen talked on the telephone, she asked, "How's Aunt Emily getting on?"

"She's not much better and now Mum's in bed as well."

Helen groaned, "Oh, no, there's all that milk to churn. I suppose I should come home in the morning and help you but I've got problems here."

"There's no need. Grace is going to look after it for me. Anyway, what are your problems?"

"Grace? Grace? Is she that cheesemaker you told me about? You've never told me what she's like. You asked about my problem – well, I can tell you only that I've had a dreadful day. I got the provisional three-months' figures back from the accountants and they don't look good. I took them for Joshua to see and, would you believe it and without even talking to me, he called in his lawyer. Now they've given me written instructions to the effect that if I don't increase the sales in the next week I have to reduce the workforce to match the output."

Hearing Helen's sniffling, Joseph said, "I'm glad he's taken the decision away from you, because you know it has to be done."

"How can you say that? You sound so heartless. These are good people who rely on me and I'm letting them down."

Joseph tried to console her but she rejected his comfort, telling him that he didn't live in the real world.

Chapter Thirty-Eight

That Friday evening the Grange was not the happy house it used to be. Aunt Emily was too listless to fuss over Helen, who in turn was disconsolately refusing Joseph's sympathy and her Aunt's half-hearted attempt to interest her in food.

Feeling rebuffed by his wife's frosty attitude, Joseph ate his tea in silence while she sat in front of the fire nibbling a piece of toast. The truth was that neither thought the other understood their problems enough to share them: Helen facing the enormity of having to make half her staff redundant and Joseph realising that, as chairman of what would be seen as a cheese co-operative, his present milk buyer might refuse to buy any of his milk before there was even a cheese made. Without his regular milk cheque and with no chance of a bank loan he would be in a desperate situation. Not being able to stand the atmosphere any longer, he said, "There's a cow going to calf; I'll go and take a look."

The cow was already calving; so Joseph stayed to supervise and ended up stripped to the waist, struggling to reach deep inside the cow for the calf's second front foot. Eventually, having pulled the foot up to face forward alongside the other, he sat on his bottom with his feet against the cow's rump and, with a firm grip on those two front feet, heaved each time the tiring cow strained. With considerable effort, the calf's head and in due course its lengthy body slid out so suddenly that it ended up across his legs.

The lounge was empty when Joseph ran through and upstairs for a much-needed bath. After the bath he slipped naked into the bedroom only to find an empty bed. Donning some clean clothes, he hurried downstairs thinking Helen would be back in the lounge, but the lounge was empty. He went into nearly every room in the Grange before he thought of the spare bedroom. There she lay, as beautiful as ever, sleeping peacefully. Or was it pretence? Joseph watched for a minute or two then reluctantly returned to the main bedroom.

Sunday morning was little better; Joseph felt rejected and Helen felt misunderstood to the extent that even over lunch the conversation was stilted. Afterwards Helen announced, "I'm going into town to visit Joshua and I'll stay overnight to be ready for an early start in the morning."

"Do you have to?"

"Yes, there's so much to do."

Joseph had little time to think about his personal problems on Monday. When Grace came to help in the house, she brought news of a farmer/cheesemaker who had just given up cheese production and was prepared to sell his equipment. Grace even had the price he was asking for the job lot, which prompted Joseph to call his five (two had dropped out) trusted farmers together and tell them, "Now's the time for commitment. I think we can buy this equipment for about a third of new price. We need to clean out the building in the village so that we can get it hauled over here and installed. Grace has worked out roughly what it will cost and divided it by the number of cows each of us own, so now we have to agree to invest that plus enough to cover other expenses, which includes a wage for Grace."

"How will that work out in the long run?" Ben asked. "Because you've got sixty cows and the rest of us have only got just over a hundred between us."

"Helen's lawyer will draw up legal documents allocating shares equal to your number of cows. It doesn't matter if some cows give more milk than others because we'll all be paid the going rate for what milk we supply. Eventually, if it works out, we'll divide the profits in proportion to the shares we each hold."

After a lengthy discussion, to Joseph's surprise all five agreed to commit their respective amounts. Joseph thanked them and said, "Right then, we need to start tomorrow and clean up our factory. Grace and I will be there at nine thirty and I hope as many of you as can will join us."

There were basically three rooms in the factory and Grace pointed out what each could be used for. "This small one with a fireplace will make a good office. The larger middle room is ideal," Grace said with enthusiasm. "It's large enough to hold a second vat, if you want to expand, as well as the cheese presses and other equipment. That leaves the end room for a cheese store."

"It's on the south end. Isn't it going to get too hot in summer?" One of the older farmers asked.

"Not with those tall beech trees towering over it. I don't see how you could have a better sunshade," Grace said.

The office was soon cleaned out and whitewashed. On the second day Joseph took some coal and a table. Several brought old chairs and Grace, knowing what encourages a man to work, brought a kettle and some beakers.

They were a happy few days but, inevitably, demands on the farm took first priority for the farmers, which left Joseph and Grace to do the bulk of the work. On the third day, Grace brought a saucepan of hotpot and placed it on the fire to gurgle away while they worked. She proved to be an incredible woman. Whether it was up a ladder sweeping down cobwebs with a long brush or shovelling out the debris, nothing seemed to daunt her. When it came to the hotpot there were only the two of them to enjoy it. During the meal Grace said, "I haven't told you before but where I worked last summer they made a blue Cheshire cheese. It was seasoned in a stone building like ours here."

"What are you saying?" Joseph asked. "That the cheese here might turn out to be blue?"

"No one can say until it's been in the store for some time, but the boss there believed it was caused by some sort of bacteria that lived in the stone walls. So who knows? We may just stand a chance here."

Pushing his empty dish away, Joseph said, "It would be a nice bonus but we can't be that lucky. Anyway, if your cheese comes out as good as this hotpot I'll be a happy man."

Laughing in appreciation, Grace said, "There's just two things a man needs to keep him happy – this is one and I suspect you're not getting much of the other."

When Joseph quickly left the table to go back to work, Grace called after him, "Don't forget, we're going off to look at that cheese vat next Tuesday."

After that disastrous weekend at the Grange things seemed to get worse for Helen. When the mill was closing down on the Wednesday evening, Ruth walked into her office and without preamble said, "This can't go on, can it? I've filled what orders we've got, though I suppose I can occupy my staff for a day or two making up scarves and ties for general sale."

Throwing up her hands in despair, Helen said, "I know and I can't offer you much hope. The market's dead."

"You've done all you can," Ruth said, reaching across to grip Helen's hand. "Now you've got to be ruthless. We're all aware how things stand and most of us expect you to do something drastic. If I have to go, don't feel guilty, just tell me."

"What I will tell you in confidence," Helen said, squeezing her hand, "is that at ten o'clock tomorrow morning I have to meet the Master and his lawyer in the hospital and I suspect they are going to instruct me as to what will happen. Please be here when I get back."

Mainthorpe's improvement was steady but slow. Although he could now manage to sit up and even wriggle onto the edge of the bed on his own, he still could not either dress himself or stand up without help. When Helen arrived on the dot of ten o'clock she was surprised to find him dressed in a dark suit and sitting behind a small table, spread out upon which were the accounts and other papers. Welcoming her with a handshake, Mainthorpe, now beginning to form a few words, said, "Want...help..." Then in frustration he wrote on his notepad and passed it to her. It read, 'You've had a terrible time; it's time I took some of the load. What I propose is...' It ended in mid-sentence. Obviously frustrated with the effort of writing, Mainthorpe reached towards the lawyer with his right hand saying, "You... tell ..."

The lawyer cleared his throat. "In the light of the continual fall in the stock market and the increasing numbers out of work, Mr Mainthorpe believes that the situation will get worse. The company is running out of capital and the bank is refusing credit; therefore my client believes that drastic action is necessary. In the light of an offer I have previously received for the old Mill, he has instructed me to negotiate with a view to selling, and at the same time to renegotiate a longer term lease on the new mill and factory."

Helen butted in. "You can't sell the old Mill; you're so proud of it. Anyway, who would want to buy it?"

Holding his notepad up towards Helen, Mainthorpe had written, 'Pride makes people bankrupt.'

The lawyer continued, "It's a printing company. They've been looking for larger premises for some time and, despite the recession; they're still doing well. I think it's printing all those bankruptcy notices and sale catalogues." There was a hint of a smile before the lawyer continued, "On the order of my client, I have prepared written instructions to the effect that you must stop all manufacture and dismiss all staff."

Feeling a knot tightening in her chest, Helen barely heard the words droning monotonously from the horrid man.

When he finally stopped she snatched the document out of his hand and rushed from the room.

Back in the office, both Ruth and Sarah were waiting to hear the outcome. Helen threw the document onto the desk and slumped dejectedly into her chair. Ruth began to read it while Sarah went to make a pot of tea. No one spoke until Helen finished drinking her first cup then Ruth said, "Right! It seems that we can come in Monday and Tuesday; complete any unfinished work and then you fire us all. Then after three clear weeks, if you have a suitable business plan, you can re-engage up to half your workforce. Do you want me to be part of that?"

"Of course I want you. I need both of you but I don't know what we're going to do."

Leaning across the table to grip her hand, Ruth said, "I've been fired three times; it's not so devastating. I suggest you go home and try not to think about it for the weekend. Leave Sarah and me to prepare the notices for Monday."

Wiping the tears from her eyes, Helen looked from one to the other, whispered, "Thank you," and walked out.

Home? Where was home? In town it's just a room in Mainthorpe's house and, convinced that he had just been using her, she wanted no part of him tonight. The Grange was Joseph's farm. All he could think about was that he might lose his family home – well, she didn't want to hear about butter or cheese or have Joseph watching her accusingly. Anyway, according to Aunt Emily he had been with another woman when she wanted to talk to him on Tuesday night and again on Wednesday morning. In the end she just got into the car and, without spare clothes or toiletries, drove away.

Never having driven beyond Nantwich before, Joseph became fascinated by the large farmhouses. Sparkling with excitement, Grace kept up a running commentary, explaining just how many workers were needed to run the big cheese farms, and that they were mostly young people who 'lived-in'.

"Have you heard why this farmer is going out of cheese production?" Joseph asked.

"Apparently he never believed anyone was good enough for his daughter, as a result of which she never married. I think she was in her mid-thirties and everyone thought she was resigned to her life as head cheesemaker. Well, she was more than that because, when her father's health deteriorated, it was the daughter who ran the whole business. They engaged a new worker and moved him into one of the farm's tied cottages with his wife and young family, and that was it."

"How do you mean 'that was it'?"

"Either he caught her eye or she caught his." Grace's flirtatious eyes twinkled at Joseph. "Anyway, when her father found out about it he tried to stop it, so she up and went regardless of the man's young family or her father's approval."

Carefully watching the road, Joseph said, "It sounds a sad story."

"If she thought it was her last chance, then why not?"

When they got to the farm and were taken through the dairy to inspect the equipment, Grace whispered, "It's in better order than I expected. Get it bought."

Joseph, though, conscious of his bank balance, pointed to a dent here and fault there before making a lower offer. In the end he and the farmer agreed to split the difference.

On the way home Grace said, "Well, it looks like we are in business but I don't think we should start off with a leaking roof. Do you know anyone who can fix it?"

"Yes, Ned's offered to help. I'll have a word with him tonight."

Though dusk was descending, the journey home was going nicely until they had passed through the town and were out in the country. Then the car began to splutter. Joseph climbed out and fiddled with the engine but when he started up it ran for barely a couple miles before spluttering to a stop again. The episode was repeated again with just one difference: when the car started to splutter there was a blacksmith's shop-cum-car garage by the roadside and they turned in there. An elderly man with grimy hands and a blackened face asked, "What do yer want?"

"We're in trouble," Joseph said, pointing to the car. "It keeps cutting out."

"Arr, well, it'll be petrol trouble. I've just closed up for' night but I can take a look at it in'morning if yer like?"

Joseph started to protest that it was still early but the old man cut him off, saying, "There's a pub about a half mile on. Yer'll get a bed there an I'll sort it out in'morning."

In the pub they met another equally taciturn character. "Broken down, have yer? Arr, well, yer don't need to worry. He'll fix it in' morning. He's good with engines is our Jack."

"You mean he's your brother?" Joseph chuckled.

"Arr, he sends me a few customers. Now about a room, I've got a double but yer'll have to give my Missus time to sort it out. Eh, are yer two married, because if yer not there's a wooden settle out back?"

Before Joseph could answer Grace said, "Of course we are. Now how about a meal?"

Chapter Thirty-Nine

It was lunchtime the next day before Joseph finally got back to the Grange. His explanation that the car had broken down got a knowing look from Aunt Emily, who added to it by saying, "Helen rang up last night asking after you. I told her that you'd gone off with that girl and I didn't know where you were and I told her the same when she rang again this morning."

When he rang her office, Sarah said, "Miss Helen is somewhere about the mill. I will get her to ring you back." But she never did.

He was busy outside on the farm until evening; then he rang Mainthorpe's house to be told that Miss Helen had gone to the hospital. "I'll get her to ring you back." But she never did.

The next day Joseph set off early with Bob Fairclough to collect the cheese equipment. Even with a couple of burly farm workers to help, it took some time to load up, which meant that it was well into the afternoon by the time they got back to the village.

After a long, tiring day, the sight of Grace waiting with the kettle boiling was very welcome. The sound of knocking on the roof told him that Ned was doing the repair. Ned came down to join them and was handed a large slice of fruit loaf by Grace. He took a couple of bites and said, "Did you make this?" When Grace gave a smiling nod he said, "By Jove, it's good. I love it with cherries in but there's an unusual flavour. What is it?"

"It's my own recipe; I use buttermilk to give it moisture and that's where that lovely tang comes from."

"Are all your cakes this good?" Ned looked at her speculatively. "I heard about your hotpot. What else are you good at?"

With eyes locked on his, Grace said, "I like a man who likes his food."

Just then Anna and Ben arrived offering to help, prompting Joseph to say, "I   f you two have finished admiring each other's taste in food, it's time we got to work."

There were enough helpers to unload the heavy equipment without damaging it but, even with Ben's great strength, it was still a struggle. When they finished, Anna, noticing Joseph holding his back, asked, "Have you hurt it?"

Before Joseph could answer, Grace said, "No, the silly man's been moaning about his back since he slept on that old wooden settle the other night."

As soon as Joseph got back to the Grange he telephoned Mainthorpe's house, only to be told by the housekeeper, "Miss Helen? We haven't seen her today. I presumed she went straight home from work."

Feeling completely defeated and unable to face either of the two men in her life, Helen started up the car intending to drive towards Jade's home. Thoughts clouded up her mind like a swirling fog. Why had Mainthorpe not allowed her more time? Why was Joseph not more supportive? Why would the bank not let her have just a small loan? She cried out in anguish, "Why, why will no one give me more time to save the mill?"

Driving almost automatically down what had become a familiar road, suddenly she remembered that there was not just Jade's home down this road, there could also be Mark's roving hands. She couldn't face having to fight him off again so she stopped the car at the next road junction. Confusion so clouded her mind that it seemed incapable of making a decision but she had to go somewhere. In the end, when she slipped the car into gear it turned towards the West as though it had a mind of its own. Losing track of both time and direction, Helen eventually stopped at a small garage to buy petrol. "Where does this road go to?" She asked the youth who was winding the petrol pump.

"It goes to Chester, Miss."

Suddenly there was an image of black and white houses through a break in that mental fog. "Then it's to Chester I'll go."

Though still numb, Helen's mind began to throw up a collection of facts learned at school. Roman fortress, later fortified by the Anglo-Saxons and still later fought over in the Civil War. Now, more recently, had she read something about Victorian restorations to Elizabethan timber-framed houses? Though they were all vague memories, they were substantive enough to create a tunnel of direction in the swirling fog.

The City of Chester hardly registered until Helen saw an immaculately uniformed commissionaire standing on the pavement outside an imposing looking Hotel. It looked expensive but Mainthorpe's weekly household wages and cash were still in her handbag as was her own money and two cheque books, so why not? "Can I take your luggage, ma'am?" The uniformed commissionaire asked.

"I'm afraid I haven't got any luggage."

"Then perhaps, ma'am, you would like to talk to the manager."

It sounded more like an order than a request, though when Helen saw her reflection in the mirror behind the reception desk she understood why. Dishevelled, mousy hair framing red-rimmed eyes above tearstained cheeks and a well-worn winter overcoat were not what the manager, from the way he raised one eyebrow, was used to seeing in his hotel. "Is there a problem, madam?"

"Madam has no luggage," the commissionaire said.

"Ah!" The eyebrow shot up a little higher. "We have an emergency vanity case holding everything a lady might need for such an occasion. I could add it to your account and – hmm – perhaps Madam would like to pay for the room in advance?"

Though physically relaxing, the hot bath did little for the turmoil in her mind, then having to walk through the hotel in the same well worn work dress made her cringe in embarrassment. It was the aroma of delicious food in the dining room that reminded her of just how long it had been since breakfast. As the evening progressed the tension eased a little but that tunnel through the fog that had brought her to Chester had now closed in, leaving her to thrash about, trying and failing to see either solution or direction, until well into the early hours.

When morning finally came, a dignified elderly waiter brought breakfast and the daily paper to her bedside. Perhaps because the emergency nightdress had the young and racy in mind rather than the old and frumpy, he discreetly averted his eyes while Helen sat up before placing the tray on the bed. Mixed stewed fruit, a boiled egg, toast and marmalade served in bed was a luxury to savour. She ate slowly, not just to prolong the experience but mainly because she had no idea why she was here or what to do next.

The dilemma remained unresolved until later when, down in the foyer, the hovering manager accosted her "Was everything all right, Madam? Will Madam be staying with us a little longer?"

"Why not?" Helen caught sight of another tunnel in that mental fog. "Yes, I think I will. Yes, I'll take the room for two more nights."

Her personal bank account had remained separate from Joseph's and, although she had reduced her drawings through the last few months, there was still a very hefty balance. She had intended to offer it to Joseph to help finance his cheese enterprise, but now he had spent the night with that girl Helen decided she would use some of it to do some much-needed shopping. And, as the luxury City in the county, Chester was designed to just that end.

That same Friday morning Joseph drove into Fletchfield to visit Mainthorpe. "I've lost Helen. Have you seen her? Have you any idea where she is?"

Mainthorpe wrote on his note pad, 'No. Ask Jade'.

Joseph said, "I have, and she declares that she hasn't seen her. Now I need the keys so that I can search the mill."

Mainthorpe wrote. 'No keys. Ruth's there. Go now.'

Surprised to find not only Ruth but also the mill manager and Sarah sitting round Helen's desk, Joseph said, "I thought the mill was closed. Why are you here?"

"We're working on a business plan to give to Helen when she comes in on Monday."

Realising from Joseph's face that something was wrong, Ruth asked, "How is she?"

When Joseph explained, Ruth immediately organised the other two to search the old mill while she went with Joseph to the factory. While they searched, Ruth said, "The pressure's been too much for Helen; she's worried about saving everyone's jobs. When you find her, tell her that the distributor has been here this morning. He likes what we produce so I took him to see Mr Mainthorpe. We're now working on a plan that will keep this factory going with about half the workforce."

The search proved fruitless. At Joseph's request Sarah found Jade's office number. Again Jade declared that Helen had not been in touch. When telephone calls to the police and local hospitals proved negative, he drove back to the Grange to check if there had been any message. Reluctantly, he allowed Aunt Emily to prepare him some food before going out to help with the milking.

Standing on what Helen presumed to be the main street, the hotel seemed surrounded by shops. Reading the uncertainty in her mind, the commissionaire pointed to his right. "Along The Rows, Madam, you'll find everything you need."

The Rows were strange four-storey buildings with display windows alongside the pavement and stone steps leading up to first floor shopping galleries above. A wall plaque claimed that not only were they unique to Chester but there were records of them going back to the thirteenth century. Seeing a display of ladies' clothes, Helen climbed stone steps up to the gallery above only to be entranced by the sight of motorcars and pony traps jostling each other along the noisy street below.

Since the collapse of the stock market there had been no time to think about personal shopping. Everything had taken second place to business, which meant that there were no really smart winter clothes in her wardrobe. It was debatable which was the colder, driving an unheated car or walking. Deciding that it made no difference because both demanded warm clothing, she turned from the scene in the street below to look in the shop – and there was the very overcoat. Calf-length pale grey and deeply trimmed with dark grey fur, it could have looked funereal and yet, as Helen slipped it on, the mirror reflected luxurious elegance, particularly when the shop assistant placed a matching fur hat on to her head. At the sight of a chequebook, the assistant called the manageress who was not satisfied until Helen produced business documents to prove her identity. Then there was the scurry of assistants bringing dresses for her to look at but, when they failed to excite, Helen wandered further along The Rows until a pair of fur-lined calf-length boots tempted her.

On impulse she walked straight through a teashop towards the cloakroom at the back only to have her path blocked by an obstructive waitress who looked her up and down and said, "Madam must use the conveniences further down the street."

"I'm going to have a cup of tea here, therefore I will use yours," Helen said as she pushed her aside and went into the back cloakroom. Carefully untying and re-tying her parcels, she exchanged old for new. When she stepped back into the teashop the waitress, now grovelling respectfully, escorted her to a prime window seat.

Choosing dresses, skirts and jumpers took up most of the afternoon. Eventually Helen returned to the hotel and collapsed exhausted on the bed.

Clothes do make a difference, Helen mused when, during the evening, several other guests engaged her in conversation. Her dowdy work clothes on the previous evening had obviously triggered a class barrier.

Chapter Forty

After a long, restless night Joseph helped with the milking and made sure his men knew what needed doing before driving back to Fletchfield. Again he went in to see Mainthorpe before going to the mill. To his surprise, even though it was Saturday morning, the three members of the management staff were in again. Ruth was equally worried about what could have happened to Helen and sympathetically agreed to search the mill again. But there was still no sign of Helen.

For Helen, sleep came quickly on that second night but with it came a weird nightmare in which she was walking the streets, out of work and penniless, when Uncle Horace dragged her into a dark doorway. This time it was different, perhaps coloured by the experience of Joseph's lovemaking. When Uncle Horace dropped his trousers there was no Aunt Emily to rescue her. After that, through the next restless hours Helen drifted in and out of sleep, moaning deliriously, "I've driven Joseph away and what will become of my workers – they'll be destitute. Joshua shouldn't have relied on me; it's all too much."

The waiter went through the pantomime of again averting his eyes and Helen once more enjoyed the luxury of breakfast in bed. An inside page of the Saturday morning paper reported in detail how businesses were collapsing in America and unemployment soaring. In the article the writer predicted that the Dow Jones index, which had reached 542 points only the year before, could easily fall to below the 100 mark, bringing the British stock market down in step. The resulting unemployment predictions for Britain made Helen realise that perhaps Mainthorpe was right.

Not wanting to think about it any longer, she threw back the bedclothes, dressed quickly and set out to explore Chester.

Collecting a booklet from a paper shop on the way, Helen climbed onto the city wall at the Watergate. It was hard to imagine that the Dee once flowed so close to the city that, where green meadows now lay close to the city wall, there had been a flourishing port in the Middle Ages.

Whether looking out across the river or down on the bustling Saturday shoppers in the city, there was so much to see in the winter sunshine. Silk and cheese were forgotten as Helen walked past the impressive Chester Castle and was rewarded with a beautiful view of the graceful Grosvenor Bridge spanning the river in one single arch. Her booklet gave her dates when the Castle had been rebuilt and told how Princess Victoria opened the bridge in 1832.

Lengths of the Wall were in disrepair and impassable, forcing her to descend to street level, but even then the distinctive variety of individual buildings held her enthralled. Quaint teashops tempted Helen to sit and linger, an experience she wasn't used to, and for that she blamed Mainthorpe. By the time she reached the cathedral the late afternoon sun was hidden behind dark clouds and inside it felt cold and a little depressing. Finding it hard to study the fine architecture, she eventually came to an old grandfather clock with an inscription that read:

' When as a child I laughed and wept, time crept.
When as a youth I dreamt and talked, time walked.
When I became a full-grown man, time ran.
And later as I older grew, time flew.
Soon I shall find while travelling on, time gone.
Will Christ have saved my soul by then? Amen. '

Reading those first three lines again, the fog suddenly cleared from Helen's mind and with it the realisation that she was full-grown and letting time run away, taking with it the things that mattered most.

Back at the hotel she waited impatiently while the telephonist repeated the Grange number twice before making a connection. Anna answered, "Helen, where are you? We've been out of our minds with worry."

"Why are you there? Where's Joseph?"

"I came to be with him. Now he's out looking for you. Couldn't you have let him know where you were?"

"I suppose I should have but he didn't let me know where he was when he spent the night with that girl."

"What girl?" Anna asked in amazement. "Oh, you mean Grace when they broke down? He didn't spend the night with her – he slept on an old wooden settle and has been complaining about a bad back ever since. Is that what this is all about? Because if it is you don't need to worry, I think our Ned's about to rebound into a cheese vat."

"No, it's a lot more than that. Anyway, if Joseph asks tell him I'm on my way home."

"What? You mean tonight?" Anna asked. But the line had gone dead.

When Joseph called at Mainthorpe's home the housekeeper declared she had not seen or heard from Helen, which left Joseph bewildered as to what he could do next. Having wandered through the town for most of an hour, the smell of cooking food coming from a restaurant reminded him that he had a healthy young man's appetite. When that was satisfied he drove back to the mill only to find it now locked up, which prompted him to go and revisit Mainthorpe.

Sitting by the bed, Mary said, "Joshua's so worried about Helen. You have no idea where she can be, have you Joshua?"

Trying to respond to the question, Mainthorpe said, "N . . . n . . . hmm, no."

"I've no idea where she can be either," Joseph said with a shake of the head. "She was under a lot of strain but something must have pushed her beyond her limit."

Mainthorpe reached for his notebook and wrote, 'My fault. I let my lawyer talk for me. It was awful for her.'

Between Mary's sympathetic questions and Mainthorpe's inarticulate words broken with laboriously written messages, Joseph stayed longer than he intended. Then, when he was about to leave, the nurse came in with three cups of tea. Finally, when he did get up to leave Mary persuaded him to call round at Mainthorpe's house in case his housekeeper had heard something.

The housekeeper said, "Anna has just been on the phone. She's trying to get in touch with you. Apparently Helen's rung the Grange to say that she's on her way back there."

"When? Where was she? Was she all right?" But to all his questions the housekeeper could only shake her head.

Helen settled up the hotel bill, rushed out to the car and drove towards home. Although clouds scuttled across the night sky, the cold northerly wind had kept the roads dry and clear. If only she had known the road, the drive would have been reasonably pleasant. Getting completely lost in Winsford, it needed directions from a policeman before she was back on the right route.

By the time she reached familiar roads the clear dry night had changed completely. Now it was heavy and black. As she turned in the direction of Gritstencrag, big wet snowflakes came so thickly that they almost obliterated her view. It wasn't the dry, dusty snow that would still be around in the morning; these large, wet flakes would be gone in an hour but in the meantime it was almost impossible to see.

Although Helen had walked along Gritstencrag Lane many times, the swirling snow overwhelmed the small windscreen wipers to the extent that she could barely see. In the end she was forced to stop and open the door to get her bearing. Recognising the trees between her and the stream, she drove on a little more confidently until, rounding a bend, she caught a glimpse of something just off the road and reversed back to look. It was the rear end of Joseph's little pickup, which stood at an alarming angle with its nose down in the brook. There were no lights or movement and to see into the cab Helen had to step into the brook. The icy cold water was already filling her new boots as she wrenched open the door, and there was Joseph slumped over the steering wheel. It was too dark to see any blood or injury but when she touched his hand it also was icy cold. Dragging herself onto the sloping running board, Helen reached up to his face and felt what she imagined to be wet blood running from his forehead. " Joseph, Joseph!" She called and, turning his face, to her immense relief she felt his breath on her cheek. The snow stopped and there was enough reflection from that which lay on the ground for her vaguely to see a crack and blood on the windscreen, but to her relief it wasn't shattered. Helen couldn't do the traditional petticoat tearing usually performed by heroines in films because she had to hold with one hand to keep her precarious balance. Instead, she drew a silk handkerchief out of her sleeve, crouched down and, soaking it in water, splashed it on his face. Remarkably, considering how cold he felt, this had an immediate effect, making him groan and open his eyes. "Oh, Joseph, I thought you were dead. Nothing else matters. No, don't move. Where does it hurt?"

Joseph flexed his arms and his fingers, then wriggled both legs before saying, "I'm okay. A bit of a headache but everything seems to work. What about you? Grief, I've been worried about you."

"I'm all right. I've come back to you." As she spoke Helen began to wipe the blood from his face. "Joseph, I'm sorry, I shouldn't have gone off like that without telling you anything. I love you. Can you forgive me?"

While she was speaking, Joseph wriggled to slide his arm around her waist. "It's me that needs forgiving. I demanded too much – in fact we all demanded too much from you." His lips found hers as he whispered, "I love you so much. Let's go home."